RED
VENGEANCE

RED VENGEANCE

A Novel of the Alien Resistance

Brendan DuBois

A Baen Books Original

Baen Publishing Enterprises
P.O. Box 1403
Riverdale, NY 10471
www.baen.com

ISBN: 978-1-4814-8249-3

Cover art by David Seeley

First printing, June 2017

Distributed by Simon & Schuster
1230 Avenue of the Americas
New York, NY 10020

10   9   8   7   6   5   4   3   2   1

Pages by Joy Freeman (www.pagesbyjoy.com)
Printed in the United States of America

This novel is dedicated to my older brother

Brian A. DuBois, former BM2 Surfman, U.S. Coast Guard

And with thanks as well to all those who have served,
and continue to serve.

Once again, I'd like to thank Toni Weisskopf and Tony Daniel of Baen Books, who are still making this teenage boy's dreams of being a science fiction author come true.

Thanks as well to my wife, Mona Pinette, for her editorial suggestions and advice, as well as my long-suffering first reader, my brother Michael DuBois.

And once again, I'd like to extend my deep thanks and gratitude to former U.S. Army Captain Vincent O'Neil, Company Commander, 1st Battalion (Airborne), 508th Infantry Regiment—a skilled author in his own right—who read the manuscript and offered key corrections and suggestions. Any military-related errors in the book are mine alone.

"Everyone's quick to blame the alien."

—Aeschylus, Greek playwright and soldier
(523 B.C.–456 B.C.)

RED
VENGEANCE

Chapter One

While serving in the New Hampshire National Guard and also studying as a junior at Fort St. Paul in Concord, one learns a lot about wars ending. You also see a lot of old black-and-white photos from the past: General Robert E. Lee outside on a farmer's porch at Appomattox Courthouse, German General Alfred Jodl signing the surrender papers at a schoolhouse in Reims, and American General Douglas MacArthur standing casually in front of a row of tophatted Japanese officials on the deck of the USS *Missouri*. All nice, clean and formal.

The funny thing now is that being present at what I hoped was the end of the war doesn't look so formal, staged or historic.

It looks like a muddy mess, it does.

I'm sitting in dirt, up against the front tire of an electric-powered Humvee, splattered with mud, exhausted. My best buddy Thor, a Belgian Malinois still wearing bandages along his side and a cast on one leg, rests his head on my lap as I idly scratch his ears. Up a ways is the dull gray-blue of a Base Dome for the invading Creepers. There's a large slit along one side, meaning the way is clear to get inside.

I shouldn't have lived long enough to see such a sight, but there are other crazy things to see as well, in this muddy field outside of Schenectady, New York, near the old Route 7. Beside the Dome are seven Creepers of the Battle mode, stretched out in submission, their weaponized arms lowered. For the past twenty

1

minutes or so, they haven't budged. Think of an exoskeleton about the size of a school bus, with a proportionally smaller tail and larger head than your standard scorpion, and lucky you, you're face to face with a Creeper.

I've never seen so many Creepers out in the open, either in my twelve years of civilian life or four years as a soldier. I don't think many folks have, since the war began, and so I want to focus on just scratching Thor and feeling his relaxing weight.

There are other people here as well. Specialist Serena Coulson, one year younger than me, who's with her brother, Robert "Buddy" Coulson. Serena and her brother are wearing forest camouflage BDUs, and she's holding a canteen cup in her hand, trying to get her brother to drink some water.

Water.

If I had my way, I'd beg, borrow or steal a rare, cold Coca-Cola and give it to the boy—he's twelve—for what he's done, for behind that quiet, studious and silent face of his is a brain that has learned some of the Creeper language. Enough of their chirps, whirls and clicks so they've surrendered to us.

About three meters away from the brother and sister is their father, Major Thomas Coulson, who is standing stiffly, shirtless, with bandages around his torso, wearing torn BDU trousers and muddy boots. A while ago a Creeper—now dead, killed by yours truly—had scorched him, and his daughter had expertly bandaged him up in the chaos afterwards. Despite his wound, he is talking with some enthusiasm to one Henry Knox, also wearing muddy and torn BDUs. Knox is wearing black-rimmed glasses and happens to be a colonel in Army Intelligence.

And my father.

I go back to scratching Thor's head. This poor guy has saved my life at least twice in the past week, having gotten burnt and stomped in the process, and he really should be at a K-9 veterinarian facility, but I like to believe he'll heal better with me at his side.

An illusion, probably, but what the hell, most of humanity is surviving on illusions nowadays.

There's a loud laugh, and Dad starts coming towards me, across the muddy and churned-up field. Thor gets off of my lap. Off to my left is a patch of woods, and in the frantic moments after I had burst through there, armed with an old-fashioned

M-4 rifle and a new-fashioned M-10—the only weapon capable of killing a Creeper—I had run through and over old trench lines surrounded by bones, uniform scraps, melted weaponry, shattered M1A tanks and 105 mm howitzers. This muddy field had been a battlefield once before, and now, any God listening up there permitting, it was a site of victory.

Dad looks down at me and says, "Thinking about where the statue is going to be placed?"

"What's that?"

"The statue," he says. "You know, the noble remembrance of what happened here. You with Buddy, yelling at the Creeper Dome, me and Major Coulson, standing there in the background. Even Serena and the ever-brave and noble Thor, doing his duty for us all."

The ever-brave and noble Thor is currently licking his butt. "I . . . I don't know, Dad," I say. "It's . . . I'm still having a hard time processing it."

"Aren't we all," Dad says. He turns to look at the Creepers and the open Dome and says, "If I wasn't so scared, Randy, I'd take Major Coulson and go for a walk. To see what's really inside a live Creeper Dome."

"I'd rather you didn't, Dad," I say. "Leave it to the experts."

"Son, we are the experts."

"And you're both dinged up pretty bad. Let me handle it."

I get up and go to the rear of the electric Humvee. Since the Creepers attacked ten years ago and dropped nuclear weapons into our upper atmosphere in a very planned and detailed pattern—thereby creating a world-wide EMP effect and frying every computer and bit of electronics—a lot of vehicles and other things have adjusted.

I rummage around the crowded rear of the Humvee and finally find what I'm looking for: a quick-release container of flares. With radios and most phones out, this man's Army—all right, this man and woman's Army—often has to fight with nineteenth-century technology. I take the wooden container out, open it up, and view the assortment of colored flares nestled inside. There are ones indicating a Creeper sighting, others seeking assistance, others marking an "all clear" and others designed for who knows what.

What the hell.

"Today isn't the Fourth of July, is it?" I ask Dad.

"You know it isn't. It's...hell, I know it's May. That's what I know."

I open up a bright orange flare gun, insert the first flare I can get my hand on. "Whatever day it is, maybe it'll be a new national holiday when this over."

Dad smiles. "Or a world holiday."

I lift up the flare gun, fire off a flare. I work quickly, snapping open the action, putting in another one, firing it off, repeating and repeating. I'm really tired now, muscles and bones aching, hungry and thirsty as well, and I need to have a vet check on Thor, and a medic check on my dad and Major Coulson, and most of all, I want to be done.

The flares all shoot up with showers of sparks and streamers, red, yellow, white, multi-colored, exploding a couple of hundred meters above us.

And like the universe is responding, there's a brighter flare of light, off to the west, as a chunk of space debris—a destroyed satellite, the remnants of our International Space Station, or even a broken chunk of the Creeper's orbital base, destroyed by the last of our Air Force last month—reenters Earth's atmosphere.

So what.

I drop the flare gun and wait for the cavalry to arrive.

Dad waits next to me. "What happens next?"

I fold my arms. Thor is curled over on his side, breathing easy. "First things first, we need to control whatever units show up. Whoever isn't helping out the refugees from Albany, they're going to get here and see an open Dome with seven Creepers outside. They're going to want to shoot first, and shoot second, third and fourth, and ask questions later."

"Good point. What then?"

"Above my pay grade, Dad," I say. "I just hope...well, I hope we're not wrong."

"Me, too."

"Yeah. Buddy over there, he said something to the Dome in the Creeper language. The Creepers emerged, surrendered. But is it just this base? The Creepers in New York State? The United States? The Western Hemisphere?"

Dad says, "That boy is key."

"We have to make sure he ends up with the right people. Your people. Major Coulson's people. Not..."

"Not the politicals."

"Yeah. You said you and Major Coulson, you were arrested for conducting unauthorized negotiations?"

Dad laughs for a second, takes off his black-rimmed Army-issued eyeglasses, rubs at his reddened and sooty eyes. "Yeah. Some negotiations. We were just trying to talk to them. Establish a dialogue...try to figure out...try to figure out their language. And for that, we were imprisoned. Everything has to go through channels, son, you understand how it goes."

He put his glasses back on. "Even if the channel is fuzzy and full of man-made static. Looks like the cavalry has arrived."

Sure enough, two men and a woman on horseback are gingerly emerging from the woods, and I go forward to meet them.

The woman is wearing Army BDUs, and her two male co-riders are wearing a mishmash of old fatigues, with a large S patch on their shoulders. Both men are bearded, and the woman—she has lieutenant's bars on her collars—has an M-4 slung over her back. Her male companions are making do with scoped hunting rifles.

I think of saluting her as I approach, but I'm not wearing a cover and she beats me to it by saluting Dad and Major Coulson. "Lieutenant Mitchell, liaison with the Schenectady County Militia...sweet Jesus, what the hell am I looking at?"

"Those Creepers have surrendered," I say. "Their Base Dome is also open."

A bearded guy says, "Bugs don't surrender. They've never surrendered."

"These have," I say.

Other bearded guy wipes at his eyes. Crying. "You know how many years those damn bugs have been in that Dome..."

Lieutenant Mitchell says, "Are you sure they've surrendered?"

"Pretty sure," Dad says. "We've managed to...well, we have a line of communications open to them. They were ordered to surrender. They did."

The lieutenant is in her early twenties and has a black wool cap over her head. The horse is nervous, whinnying, and she leans forward, rubs the side of his neck. There is suspicion and fear in her eyes, and I say, "Is there anyone else coming?"

"More of the militia, I'm sure," she says.

"When they get here, we'll need to set up a perimeter around this entire field. Once word gets out...every newspaper reporter and photographer within a day's march will be rolling in, not to mention curious civilians. You'll also need to dispatch a courier to the nearest Army unit. We're going to need the Army to take control of the situation, the prisoners, and whatever the hell is in that Dome."

The lieutenant looks to me, slight disgust on her face, and then to my dad the colonel, and to Major Coulson. Thor is sniffing the air. He doesn't like horses. Serena is still tending to her mostly mute brother.

"Excuse me for saying this," Lieutenant Mitchell says, sitting back up in her saddle, "but who in hell is in charge here?"

I see her point. She sees a sergeant, a colonel, and a major, who also happens to be a doctor. Plus one suspicious K-9 unit.

Major Coulson limps forward, with difficulty puts an arm around me.

"The sergeant is," he says. "The sergeant is in charge, and I suggest you listen to him."

Chapter Two

Within the hour, the regular Army does show up. It moves quietly and with stealth, and with seven Combat Creepers out in the open, I sure as hell am not going to give them a hard time for the response. There's some confusion at first and some raised voices—the first couple of squads wanted to start firing off M-10s, kill them all, and let the proverbial God sort it out—but Dad goes from one-time BU professor to full bird colonel and eventually gets everything straightened out.

I tend to Thor and then a sergeant comes to me and says, "You Sergeant Knox? The colonel and my company commander need to see you."

"Just a sec," I say, as I reattach a bandage to the side of Thor.

"Hey, pal, that was no request," says the sergeant, whose name is BRONSON. I'm pretty sure he's about my age—sixteen—and is olive-skinned, with bulky shoulders that mean he likes working out a lot in his down time. "That's an order."

"I've been following orders for four years, and I know what they mean," I say back, "and you're not my pal. Lead on. Thor, stay."

Thor is better at following orders than me, and he gratefully rolls back down on the ground, in the shade of the Humvee I had sort of stolen (or requisitioned) back in Troy. With M-10 in hand, I walk to a command Humvee that has a huddle of troops around it. Two of them are my dad and Serena's dad, and the other is an old, white-haired man wearing the stripes

of a company first sergeant, and all of them are paying attention to a slim captain who's gesturing to a topo map spread over
the hood of the Humvee. She has close-cropped bright red hair,
burn tissue along one cheek, and flashing, strong green eyes. Her
nametag says WALLACE. On one shoulder is the crossed bayonets
marking the 10th Mountain Division, one of the ghost divisions
from after the war started.

I catch her eye and she nods to me. "You're Sergeant Knox?"

"Yes, ma'am," I say.

"What unit?"

"Second Recon Rangers," I say. "First Battalion, New Hampshire
Army National Guard, attached to the 26th Division. Stationed
at Fort St. Paul in Concord. Ma'am."

From near me Sergeant Bronson snorts, and I know why.
Even though there's not much difference between regular Army
and National Guard, there's still a bit of rivalry, with the Army
thinking we Guardsmen are only good for putting down disturbances or escorting food convoys, while we think the Army is
always first, second, and third in line for the best in food, gear
and transport.

"New Hampshire?" she asks. "Far from home. Colonel Knox…
any relation?"

"My son," he says, with about two tons of pride in each word,
but Captain Wallace doesn't seem impressed.

"Good for you," she says. "Stationed?"

"Intelligence, Fort St. Paul as well."

"Hunh." She rubs at her chin and I note that two fingers of
her right hand have been mangled. "If I had my way, I'd make
sure relatives don't get assigned to the same units. Cuts down
on a lot of grief down the road. Major, if I may…"

"I'm assigned to Special Projects, up at Jackson Labs, in
Maine." He pointed out to the field. "That's my daughter, Serena,
a specialist, and my son, Buddy…who's on medical leave from
the Observation Corps."

"Christ on a crutch," the first sergeant comments with a harsh
whisper. His throat is a scarred mess. "What the hell is this, a
family freakin' reunion?"

Dad smiles thinly. "It sure does look that way, doesn't it? But
we could be a USO roadshow and what's out there remains the
same, Captain. Seven surrendered aliens, and an open alien base."

"And how in hell did you get those Creepers to surrender?"

Surprise of surprises, Serena's dad speaks up, and beneath that wounded, half-dressed scientist, exists a real live Army major. "Captain, we're wasting valuable time. You're to set up a perimeter-in-depth around this entire vicinity. Keep civilians and any members of the press outside. You're to also extend communications to the nearest Exploitation Unit and get them here soonest. Also notify...Wait, not the New England Command..."

"Upstate New York Command," she helpfully replies, though her voice is strong and even.

"That's right," Serena's dad says, nodding. "Upstate New York Command. We need to flood this area with resources. We've gained a tremendous advantage here, and we can't afford to lose it."

"I see," Wallace says, and she gently and carefully folds up her topo map, and right then and there, I'm so glad I'm an NCO and not in the view of those green eyes. She hands her map over to the old and scarred first sergeant.

"Special Projects, am I correct, Major?"

"That's right."

"I'm so impressed. Up in Maine, if I recall correctly?"

Major Coulson hesitates. "Yes, Captain, that's correct."

She turns her attention to my dad. "And you're stationed at Fort St. Paul, in New Hampshire."

"That's right, Captain."

"Glad to get that out of the way." She runs a hand through her short red hair, slowly puts her helmet back on, readjusts the chinstrap. "Let's get a couple of things clear. You're both out of your Area of Responsibility. You're not in my chain of command. Unless I'm convinced that my superiors are dead, captured, or otherwise engaged, I don't recognize your authority. Got it?"

Dad steps forward. "Captain, please, this is an important situation and—"

From the tree line I make out the sound of engines, and Wallace says, "What I have here is a situation I've never encountered. And I'm going to do it my way."

A crashing of trees and two shapes emerge, and if I was standing still earlier, I'm now frozen to the muddy ground. Two six-wheeled armored Stryker vehicles emerge from the woods, take up position on either side of the command Humvee. They're mud-splattered, worn, with black scorch marks along the side.

From poles at the rear, each is flying a tattered American flag, and the Stryker on the left is also flying a New York State flag while the other Stryker is displaying a blue flag with a white cross on it. The St. Andrew's Cross, the flag of Scotland.

Their engines slow down to a grumble and on each vehicle, in addition to a fifty-caliber machine gun, each Stryker also carries a an Mk-19 grenade launcher. I've heard that these grenade launchers have been converted to fire the same ammunition as the Colt M-10 I carry. M-10 rounds contain the binary gas canisters that are the only reliable weapon—besides nukes—that can kill Creepers.

Impressive enough, but what really impresses me is the front of each Stryker: the upper head segment of a main Creeper arthropod has been chained over the hull, like some ancient war trophy. I carry my own trophy around, a broken-off toe joint, but seeing the empty head segments strikes at me, hard and deep, and although I'm tired, achy, could use a hot shower and a good meal, I feel like I'd follow Captain Wallace and her crew anywhere.

But it's a brief feeling. I want to go back to Concord, back to my buds, back to where I belong.

She says, "My way starts with protecting my own. So yes, the perimeter's being set up, and first things first, it's going to aim at those Creepers, and if anything makes the hint of a threatening move, then my people are going to croak it dead."

"But—"

Wallace fastens her chinstrap even harder. "When I got word from the county militia about your situation here, I also sent couriers to my own commanders, as well as the nearest Exploitation Unit. The EU should be here before nightfall. Is that satisfactory, gentlemen?"

Dad and Major Coulson look slightly embarrassed, like they had been caught at playing soldier. My dad says, "Quite satisfactory, Captain."

She grins. "No worries, Colonel Knox, Major Coulson. It's been a long, rough day, and we were on our way to support relief efforts for Albany's suburbs when I was told to detour here. I thought it was the craziest damn story I've ever heard, but I still had to check it out."

Major Coulson nods and shivers for a moment. "Albany . . . have you heard if the President and the Cabinet escaped?"

She shakes her head. "Nope. No word on that, though I'd

imagine some senators and reps managed to get out. Some of those slugs always manage to survive. And the President, hell, it'd be a pity if he got smoked, wouldn't it? He's that close to serving out a full term. First Sergeant."

"Ma'am," he says, stepping forward, and I see his nametag says HESKETH.

She turns and looks over at the field. "I want to speak to the platoon leaders in fifteen minutes."

"Ma'am."

"In the meantime, if Doc isn't busy vaccinating the nearest cow, have her come over and check out the major. Also get some food and water for these . . . folks, as well as fresh clothing."

"Ma'am."

"If we hear back from any courier, I want to know soonest. And . . . one more thing."

Wallace looks closely at the ground around us. I look too, seeing the churned up soil, the old collapsed trench lines, the broken and melted weapons, and the bones. Lots and lots of bones.

"Tom, if we have a spare courier—"

"I don't think we do, ma'am."

"All right, send out a volunteer runner to the nearest Graves Registration unit. Might be one hanging around in Schenectady. I want a detail to come back here and . . . make things right."

First Sergeant Hesketh takes a glance at the field. "I'm sure it's on their site list, Captain."

"Then pass them along a cheery note from this unit, saying this field gets up to the top of the list, or I'm gonna come up there personally and pluck out their eyeballs with my nail clippers."

He nods, says, "Yes, ma'am," and slips away.

At one of the old 6x6 trucks, a quartermaster corporal gets me some fresh clothes, though I'm careful to transfer my unit insignia and name patch to the new stuff. The corporal's a skinny girl, maybe sixteen or seventeen, and her own clothes seem two sizes too large. Her nametag says CELLUCCI. As I slip on my patches, I see Serena's dad being escorted into an electric van that's been painted in Army colors and has the Red Cross on its side. A short, plump woman wearing a white lab coat is leading Major Coulson in, accompanied by Serena and Buddy.

"Hey, Corporal?"

"What's up, Sergeant?" Cellucci replies, checking off something on a clipboard. She's sitting on the tail of the truck, legs dangling, cardboard boxes full of gear behind her.

"Earlier, your captain, she said something about your unit's doc not being busy vaccinating a cow or something. What did she mean about that?"

"Oh, that means Doc Pulaski, before she joined up, she was trained as a vet."

"For real?"

"Yeah, for real," she says, looking up. "She's a good doc, knows a lot. Besides, it's tougher being a vet. You gotta figure out what's wrong with your patient without being able to talk to them."

"Maybe she'll be asked to treat the Creepers."

"Yeah, sure," she says. "Treat them each with an M-10 round or a Stryker burst."

"But they've surrendered."

She looks up at me, and even with her slight build and skinny frame, there's something hard and solid behind her look. "They're bugs; they're aliens. What, you don't think they're smart enough to pretend to surrender? We scrubbed their orbital base last month, and a few days ago, they scorched Albany and thousands of civvies. Doesn't sound like an outfit ready to surrender."

I don't know what to say, so I ask where the field mess is, and Cellucci says, "Follow your nose," which is what I do, but not before grabbing Thor and bringing him along.

I get a dented and scratched white plastic tray, and under a canopy tent about twenty meters into the wood line, I grab some chow. It's black bread with rehydrated potatoes and some stew with gravy that tastes like it's real beef, and with a metal cup of water, I find a wide pine tree trunk to sit against while I eat. Guys and gals about my age—with a few younger and a few older—slide in and out of the mess tent, and it's nice to be hanging around with a unit that looks tight. The past couple of weeks I've been mostly on my own, and I don't like it. I've felt alone, exposed and right out there at the point of the damn spear, and I'm tired of it all. I want to go home and let the rest of the Army take care of the Creepers.

I slip some bits of stew to Thor, and he gently takes it from my fingertips and licks my fingers clean.

"Hey." I look over and it's Sergeant Bronson, standing over me, looking down.

"Hey yourself," I say.

"You look pretty comfy. Who said you could get our BDUs, eat our chow?"

I spoon up the potatoes. Rehydrated but I have to give the company's cook credit, for he or she had spiced it up some so it's damn right tasty.

"Your company commander," I say. "The lady with the red hair, big helmet, captain's flashes on her uniform. Ask around, I'm sure you'll find her."

He says, "Your mutt. He shouldn't be eating food from the mess tent."

"He's not," I say, giving him another piece of meat. "He's eating from my tray. Look, what's your problem, Bronson?"

"Who says I have a problem, Knox?"

"Me," I say. "I'm a good judge of character. You've been one pissy bastard since you folks showed up."

His face tightens, and I don't think he likes being talked to like that, which causes me maybe a nanosecond of concern, and he says, "I don't like being pulled away from a mission to come to the rescue of . . . a gang like you."

"Them's the breaks," I say. "Sometimes a unit's in trouble, you have to help out."

A slight laugh, his fists on his hips. "Unit? I don't see any unit. I see a couple of old guys that managed to keep their heads down during the past ten years, a pretty girl and her younger, dumber, brother, and a mutt."

A pause. "And the mutt has a dog with him."

When I finish with my tray, I hold it out to Thor. He cleans the tray with four big laps, looks at me with that look of sweet accusation—"Is that all you've got?"—and then he lays back down.

I'm at a disadvantage, being on the ground, Bronson looking down at me, and with several of his guys within easy sprinting distance.

Which is why I smile up at him, slowly get to my feet, and then snap up the hard plastic tray so it goes between his legs and hits something he's terribly fond of.

He drops back, hands dropping to his crotch, and says, "You son of a bitch!"

I stand at ready, tray in hand, and say, "You're repeating yourself."

"What?"

"You called me a mutt earlier, and now you're calling me an SOB. Both dog-related. You're repeating yourself."

His face reddens, fists clench, and I know he's a second or two from coming right at me, but Thor notices this too, and he's on alert, staring, a low, grumbling growl that you can feel in your chest, the fur along his back bristling.

Bronson takes a breath. "Call your dog off."

"Off from what?" I ask. "He's just standing there, clearing his throat."

"You know what I mean," he says. "This isn't fair. You and your dog."

I toss the tray aside. "You want fair? I'll tell him to freeze, and while we're dancing, he won't even move."

"Good."

A runner scrambles to us, breathing hard. He looks like a new recruit, maybe twelve or so. "Sergeant Knox?"

"That's me."

"The captain wants you to join her," he says, panting between each phrase. "The Exploitation Unit is approaching."

I squat down, pick up the tray, head back over to the mess tent. "I'll be right there."

Bronson calls out. "I'll be waiting for you, Knox."

"Don't wait too long," I call back.

Back at the command Humvee—which now has a canopy tent erected nearby—Captain Wallace is sitting on a folding stool, with my dad and Major Coulson, around a table covered again with a topo map. Wallace has her helmet off and my dad and Coulson look much better in their new uniforms, though Coulson's arm is in a sling. Something else I notice straight off is my dad's black-rimmed Army-issue eyeglasses. One stem's always been fixed to the frame with white tape, but no longer. Seems like in Captain Wallace's unit, even a set of eyeglasses can be repaired.

Regular Army. I'm impressed.

I slide in under the tent, and there's another low growl of vehicles approaching. Wallace looks over and says, "My, summer camp sure is getting crowded."

Two up-armored Humvees come through the tree line, followed by—of all things—a diesel-powered Winnebago RV that's been painted Army green—and behind that, a heavy truck that has a refrigeration unit hanging over the front cab. An Exploitation Unit, used to respond any time there's the possibility of a captured Creeper, or a damaged Dome that can be examined. Scary, complex work. The Humvees stop, and heavily armed soldiers, bearded and wearing bandanas around their heads, bail out and take position.

"Special Forces," Major Coulson says.

"The same," Wallace says. "Guys who've got the guts, or the craziness, to go into Creeper Domes."

I say, "They look pretty sharp."

Dad says, "They're all orphans, Randy."

I turn to Dad and he continues. "Orphans. Their immediate families . . . all have to have been killed by Creepers. That way, they have the . . . tenacity to get the job done. And they sign up, knowing that for the most part, it's a posting that doesn't have much of a shelf life."

The RV comes to a halt and two more soldiers exit, followed by two older men. One is in BDUs, with a single star on his rank strip—a brigadier general—and the other is a short, plump man in a black jumpsuit, zippered up the front, with a holstered pistol strapped across his chest. They both start walking with determination to the tent and we all stand up. Wallace says, "Young man."

"Ma'am?"

"You ever meet a spook before?"

I'm not sure what she means, and my dad helps me out. "From the CIA, Randy. Central Intelligence Agency."

"Not that I know."

Wallace says, "The short guy to the right. He's CIA. Hoyt Cranston. And . . . that's General Brad Scopes, next to him. They're in charge of exploitation and intelligence in this part of the Empire State. Colonel Knox, do you know General Scopes?"

"No, not really," and then the men come in, and there's a flurry of introductions. General Scopes is in his forties, tired-looking— come to think of it, every adult I know is tired-looking—with thick gray hair, parted to one side. His companion, Mr. Cranston from the CIA, is about a foot shorter, with a wide smile, twinkling eyes, and thin, unruly white hair that springs up like it's constantly receiving an electrical current.

One other odd thing about Mr. Cranston. During the introductions, he said, "Hoyt Cranston, Langley," which didn't make a lot of sense to me, since the CIA headquarters there in Virginia has been a series of water-filled pits for ten years. Later Dad explained to me that the surviving CIA officers, intelligence analysts and interpreters considered themselves to be like monks, in service to their nation, and that Langley was their long lost temple or shrine.

It sounded like a lot of adult hooey to me, but since nobody asked me for my opinion, I kept it to myself.

Mr. Cranston then goes to the edge of the canopy tent, slowly shakes his head as he scans the open Dome in the distance and the surrendered seven Creepers, right there in a row. The Special Forces soldiers that have just arrived are gingerly approaching the silent and unmoving line of aliens. Cranston puts his hands on his hips and turns his head. His voice is thick, like the emotions racing inside of him are threatening to silence him.

"This . . . this is unbelievable," he says, looking back at us. "I . . . I never thought I'd live long enough to see this. Seven battle Creepers, lined up like this, like they're ready for review or something."

He turns back. The wind shifts and the strong scent of cinnamon returns. His shoulders move, and then Serena walks in, holding Buddy's hand. Cranston raises a hand to his face, and I realize he's weeping.

Cranston coughs, turns back again. "Who did this? Who's the soldier who did this?"

I start to say that Buddy Coulson had done it, all with his translation abilities, but Major Coulson shoves me forward. "This one did it. Sergeant Knox."

The man from Langley comes to me, opens his arms, grabs me in a bear hug, and starts sobbing.

Chapter Three

The interior of the Winnebago is clean, warm and spacious, and Cranston takes me to a center where there's a round table, comfortable padded chairs, filing cabinets, and a civilian woman sitting behind a manual typewriter at a typing stand. There's an area forward that has two large padded seats, like something from the inside of those luxury airliners that used to fly around the globe when I was a six-year-old boy. Beyond the center space is a narrow hallway, a kitchen, and closed doors that probably lead to bedrooms or something.

Cranston sits me down and the civvie woman gets up, returning shortly from the kitchen with two mugs of coffee and something black on two plates. I look at the plates and see that it's cake. Cake! The last time I had cake was on my thirteenth birthday, and it looks delicious. My mouth waters.

Silverware, a small metal container with milk, and another with sugar, appear on the table. Cranston gestures to the luxurious spread. "A little snack while we debrief, is that all right?"

"That . . . that'd be fine," I say, staring at the thick slice of chocolate cake. "But really, it was Buddy Coulson, the private. He's the one that did it all. He's the one that knows the Creeper language. I was just there."

He laughs and works on his coffee mug, brings it up to his lips. "Right. Just there. That's not what I heard. I heard that you dragged the boy to the Creeper Dome, threatened to kill him unless the Creepers came out and surrendered...and when they did come out, you killed one of the Creepers for not moving fast enough. True?"

By now the woman—in her mid-fifties, wearing a black jumpsuit like Cranston—is typing fast along, and now I know that everything I say here is being transcribed. It's a feeling both creepy and prideful: creepy that my words are being captured, and prideful that someday, historians might read these words.

"Fairly true," I say. I pick up a fork, take a small piece of the cake, and bring it to my mouth. The chocolate taste barrels right through my mouth with a burst of joy, and memories roar in as well, not only from my thirteenth birthday, but earlier...much earlier. I remember running through a large house, chasing my older sister Melissa, laughing because I have a piece of cake in my hand and I'm going to rub it in her hair, and Mom is there, sitting with a laptop in her hand, raising her hand, laughing, saying, "Oh, you two..."

I swallow the cake. I try to hold onto the taste, hold onto the memory. Mom and Melissa, dead right after the war began.

I take another piece of cake, not wanting to speak right away, wanting to gather my thoughts, my emotions. I sip from the too hot but very tasty coffee and say, "I was looking for my dad, and Specialist Coulson's dad. We were able to track them to this Dome...and I was able to free them both before they were taken into the Dome."

"Then what?"

"Then I found out about Dad and Major Coulson's research into the Creepers...their motives...and why they were here on Earth."

"I see," Cranston says. "And what did they tell you?"

I open my mouth, hesitate for the briefest moment, and say, "It was pretty confusing. Something about the Creepers coming here for some sort of religious reason. Or a belief system. I don't understand. But Buddy...supposedly he was good at learning the Creeper language. He was..."

A prophet, that's what Dad said. A prophet.

But what would the man from Langley think about that?

"He was something to the Creepers. Because he could speak their lingo. So I dragged him out to the field, and told the Creepers that unless they surrendered right now, stopped the war, that I'd kill him."

"Why?"

"Why what?"

"You brought that young boy out there, thinking the Creepers would value him so much that they would stop fighting. What made you think that?"

"Because...he was valuable. He could speak the language. It was...a gamble, I guess."

His face widened in a grin, his white hair still sticking up, and he says, "A gamble all right. A gamble that really paid off."

"Mr. Cranston..."

"Yes?"

"Does this mean...the war? Is it really over?"

The woman typing away stops. Cranston takes another healthy sip from his coffee. "Let's go back to what happened when you first arrived in the field."

The questioning goes on and on, and I do my best to keep up, but I'm also growing wary of Cranston. He's friendly enough, very courteous, but I get the feeling what would make him happy would be to trip me up on some aspect of what I had done earlier today. So I keep my answers simple and to the point, hoping he comes away from our conversation thinking that all that happened here today was due to the luck and thickness of a sixteen-year-old National Guard sergeant from New Hampshire.

Boy, I wish my dad was with me.

Or Thor.

Then he looks down at his handwritten notes and says, "Well, Sergeant Knox, I guess we're through here. I have to commend you on your courage and quick thinking."

"Thank you, sir."

He finishes off his coffee—I had done the same much earlier, along with the cake, and I did my best to ignore the urge to pick up the plate and lick it clean—and says, "You were awarded the Silver Star a few days ago, weren't you? From the President."

"I was."

"And for what?"

"I'm sure you know," I say.

He laughs. "I do. I know many, many things...which sometimes makes it hard to sleep at night. All those secrets I keep, from my first days with the Company, dealing with countries that barely exist anymore, like Iran, Iraq, Nigeria, Afghanistan...and for the past decade, this...this challenge."

I'm not sure what to make of that, because his voice gets more meditative. "I've made arrangements for you, your father, Major Coulson and his children to stay at a lodging facility about a half hour away, which we use sometimes for the Company's guests."

"Thank you," I say, and I mean it. From what I had done in Albany and Troy the previous days, from stealing a civilian car and a Marine unit's Humvee and weapons, I was fairly sure I'd be going to the closest stockade.

Cranston's arrangements sound so much better.

He gets up and says, "Is there anything else I can do for you, Sergeant?"

I look to the hallway and say, "May I use your latrine, Mr. Cranston?"

He smiles, waves an arm. "Go right ahead."

I get up and go past him, and sure enough, past the kitchen area, there's a closed door that opens into a small bathroom. I use the facilities—steal a small wrapped piece of soap—and then go out. I spot Cranston chatting with his typist, going over some sheets of paper, and I also spot a round dish with more cake on it.

Why not? I slice off a chunk, wrap it in a piece of paper, and slide it into my other pocket, making sure it doesn't share space with the stolen soap.

I ask around and find Dad back in the woods. The two Strykers have moved around and are now hull-down, facing the surrendered Creepers and the open Dome. Camouflaged netting covers them both, keeping them from being easily spotted by our constant eyes-in-the-skies, the Creepers' killer stealth satellites. They can fire lasers or metal rods to destroy anything using electronics, anything flying, or anything else that gets their attention.

The Special Forces soldiers are gathered in front of the Creepers, and I briefly think of the aliens contained within. What must they be thinking, pondering, considering, as they stay frozen in one place, while their human enemies move around in front of them?

I recall a piece of history, when Cornwallis surrendered to Washington at Yorktown. The British band played "The World Turned Upside Down," and if the Creepers played music, or enjoyed music, I'm sure they'd be tuning up the Creeper equivalent right about now.

Dad is in a large tent, with canvas on the floor, chairs and tables set up, and he's eating a meal with Captain Wallace. The two of them are laughing at something.

I don't like the view.

But Thor sees me and trots over, tail wagging, limping slightly, and I rub the top of Thor's head. Dad turns and says, "Randy, how goes it?"

"Goes fine," I say, and I duck my way into the tent. Wallace smiles up at me and says, "I hear the President made it out of Albany, and that he awarded you the Silver Star a few days ago."

"He sure did."

Before them are two white plates, empty of whatever meal they've just had. From my coat pocket, I take out the wrapped piece of chocolate cake. Dad loves chocolate, and lots of times over the years, I've secretly given him my chocolate ration, even though he's never really noticed it.

His eyes widen as he sees the crushed cake. "Where did you get this?"

"From Mr. Cranston," I say. "He gave me a piece. I thought you'd like one, too."

He gingerly picks up the cake, tastes a crumb, and he looks like he's never tasted anything so fine. I feel pretty good, and a second later, I feel like crap.

Dad slides the cake and the smeared paper napkin over to Wallace. "Kara, I'm stuffed to the gills. Would you like this?"

Wallace grins, picks up a fork. "Would I ever... Thanks, Henry."

Kara's a captain, and Dad's a colonel. And now they're on a first-name basis.

She gives up a slight moan of delight and I turn, and Thor follows right along, and Dad says, "Where you off to, Randy?"

"Wherever Langley wants me," I say.

It takes some digging around, but I locate my M-4 and my Colt M-10 and battlepack, and with Thor at my side, I feel pretty set. Most of the soldiers have pulled away from the perimeter and are in the woods, and there's an odd tension in the air. Having the Creepers staying still like this is too much for most of them to handle, I guess, so they're keeping busy cleaning weapons, grabbing something to eat, and trying to goof off without their platoon sergeants noticing.

I try to overlook the thought of Dad giving up that piece of chocolate cake, and I hear a friendly voice. "Randy!"

It's Serena Coulson, alone this time, and she comes over and tears come to her eyes. She's still the most beautiful woman I've ever met, and the past couple of days on the run haven't changed my view. Her smooth face is streaked some with soot, her fine blonde hair is pulled back in a ponytail, and she's wearing plain BDUs, but she still catches my eye.

"Hey, Serena," I say, and I sit down on the chunks of an old stone wall while Thor gives a friendly bark and goes over to greet her.

"You okay?"

I lie and say, "No complaints. Hey, where's your brother?"

"Buddy's with my dad, and both of them are with Hoyt Cranston, being debriefed." She plays a bit with her ponytail and says, "You'll be joining us later, right? At the place . . . the lodging facility Cranston's set up for us."

Thor flops down at my feet, bandages still in place. He's breathing easy, and his tail thumps twice. "I don't think so."

Serena sits down next to me. "Why not? It sounds lovely. Soft bed, hot water, free meals."

"It sure does, but I think I'll sack out with these guys," I say. "Just find a place to curl up with Thor, get up tomorrow morning, and try to find transportation back east."

"But . . . you can't do that," she says. "You're famous."

"No, your brother Buddy is famous," I reply. "He's the one that knows some of the Creeper language. He's the one the Creepers see as . . . hell, I don't know, prophet, ambassador, representative of mankind. All I do know is that he got those battle Creepers to surrender, and to keep their Dome open."

"You were there with him."

"Yeah, I was there all right," I say, "threatening to blow his head off, convince the Creepers to listen to him. And if I remember right, you didn't like that approach. You damn near busted my jaw."

She smiles, leans into me. Even in her BDUs, it's a nice feeling. "What do you expect? That was my brother. I just saw my dad get scorched. That was hard to handle, after just getting out of Albany before it got blasted."

I keep quiet. I like the idea of bivouacking with this company, going back to the world where I grew up and where I belong.

Something warm is on top of my hand, my dirty, scarred hand, with its broken and blackened fingernails.

Serena's hand, with nice red nail polish. She slides her hand into mine, gently entangles my fingers, and says, "Please. Will you do it for me? No offense, if you stay back, it'll be me, Buddy, and our two dads. I'll be bored out of my mind."

Well. I squeeze her fingers. Out there a sergeant is yelling something about setting up a KP detail, and the wind brings the familiar stench of cinnamon, of Creepers.

"I suppose I could stick around for a bit."

That earns me another lean of her body into mine. Thor looks up, gazes at me with those firm dark brown eyes, and then flops back down.

The lodging the man from Langley has set up for us is a quiet-looking yellow house, built in the nineteenth-century Victorian style, with a front porch and turrets and black shutters. We are driven over in a 1960s Lincoln four-door sedan by a Special Forces soldier who has a patch over one eye and two hook prosthetics at the end of his forearms.

Smoke rises up from two chimneys, and there are two young men in gray work slacks, white aprons and white cook blouses, sharing a cigarette and eyeing us as we exit the Lincoln. Both have sidearms at their waists. A slim woman steps out of the front door and says, "Welcome to the Drake House." She's dressed in clean yellow slacks, a white turtleneck sweater, and has thick, well-trimmed black hair. Looking at our motley crew, she manages to keep a wide smile as her two kitchen workers go back inside.

And motley it is, consisting of me, Thor, my dad, Major Coulson, Buddy and Serena. We're all in BDUs, including the silent Buddy, and our luggage consists of battlepacks, reused plastic bags, and one knapsack. Thor is off leash. He sniffs at a juniper bush, raises his right leg, and lets loose a stream of urine.

The woman steps down, still smiling. "I'm Lucianne Drake, your hostess. I've been told to treat you very special, because you've all done something quite heroic."

Serena's dad says, "We're ending this day alive, which is pretty heroic, I guess."

Thor sniffs at her feet and she says, "What a beautiful dog. We have a shed out back that'll be just perfect for him."

I say, "Is there a cot and mattress back there?"

Lucianne clasps her hands together, sounds confused. "I... no. But there are some old blankets and hay. I'm sure that'll be comfortable enough."

I pick up my battlepack with my two weapons—the M-4 and the M-10—attached by straps, and I say, "I'm sure it will be, because where my dog goes, that's where I go."

Lucianne's smile seems like it's drifting to a grimace, and she nods. "That won't be necessary. Won't you all step in?"

Serena winks at me and loops an arm through mine, and the three of us—me, she, and Thor—go up the front stairs as one.

We get a room on the second floor with a real bed, a bureau, AM radio, private bath, and a window overlooking the rear yard, which—incredibly—looks like it's mowed and maintained. Outstanding. In the bureau are two spare wool blankets, which I carefully fold up and lay out on the hardwood floor. Thor sniffs the blankets and then jumps up on the bed, rotates three times, and settles down. He wiggles some, lowers his head, and lets out a heavy sigh.

"Yeah, bud," I say. "Rough life."

I enter the bathroom, see there's no shower but one of those real old bathtubs with claw feet. I run the water and it comes out pretty hot. I slide in and clean up the best I can, washing with the lodging house's soap, not using the one I stole from Cranston, the man from Langley. I'm saving that for later.

That makes me think of Dad again, and the cake, and Captain Wallace, and I scrub some more while listening to my dog snore.

Dinner is at six p.m. and I'm stunned to hear we have two meal choices: lake trout or chicken. We all go for the chicken, except for Major Coulson, who goes with the fish. Our dads get a table and I share a table with Serena and Buddy, while Thor patiently sets up a begging station underneath. We have the dining area to ourselves, and I marvel at the white tablecloths and the cheerfully burning fireplace.

We even have a choice of drinks—water, locally made root beer, or cola—and I decide to splurge and go for the root beer. Buddy eats in silence and Serena, while still wearing her BDUs, is freshly washed and looks good. When our chicken, fresh-cut fried potatoes and salads are finished off, Serena says, "Why are you in such a hurry to get back to New Hampshire?"

"That's where I belong."

"To do what?"

"Serve out my term."

"Answer the question, Randy," she says. "To do what? What happened yesterday...the war's over. My brother has the ability to talk to the Creepers, to command them, to tell them to surrender. Their orbital base was destroyed last month. Your job in the Army...it's to kill Creepers. With no more killing to be done, what are you going to do? What's your real talent?"

"Not sure, but I'm sure I know what your talent is, Serena, and that's to irritate the hell out of me," I say, slipping the rest of my chicken to Thor, who gently licks it from my fingers. "Congratulations, you're an expert at it."

She laughs and a little while later, Lucianne comes back, clears our dishes, and offers us dessert, which is homemade vanilla ice cream with blueberries scattered on top. When she comes back and distributes the little bowls, I say to her, "What kind of place is this, ma'am?"

"It's a bed and breakfast," she says, expertly holding a tray in one hand.

"I know that, but...there's no sign on the road. Or outside the building. And except for us, the place is pretty empty. How do you make do?"

"We have clients in the area," she says.

"Like the government?"

Her smiling eyes don't reveal a thing.

"We have clients in the area."

It's getting dark, and our respective fathers go upstairs. I take Thor out to do his business, and Serena volunteers to keep me company. Out front there are two gas lanterns flickering their light, and Thor stays at my side. I walk around the side and to the rear of the house, and Serena slips her arm into mine.

We're at the rear of the building, with the mowed lawn and

the woods before us. It's darker out here, with some flames visible from inside, where the kitchen must be. I lift my head, look up at the familiar and distressing night sky. Ten years ago, when the Creepers first came, it seemed like they were a constellation of comets, unexpectedly coming to give us one hell of a nighttime show. Well, that was pretty much true, for when the Creepers revealed themselves, their first assignment was to destroy every satellite in Earth's orbit, including the unfortunate crewmembers of the International Space Station, the first official victims of the war.

Now, even a decade later, the night sky isn't truly night. There are streaks of light, burning tails of flame, bright and unexpected explosions, as the debris from those hundreds and hundreds of satellites finally come home. And to add to the mix, last month, the last remnants of our Air Force launched a surprise strike against the Creepers' orbital base, destroying it. So that means a lot of the debris we see burning now are the chunks from that orbital base, including no doubt several thousand Creepers, the remains of the missiles the Air Force used, and the six pilots who flew them, each one of them knowing they were going on a suicide mission.

My hand finds Serena's and I squeeze it tight. Thor does his night business and trots back to us. Up above us the sky is lit up with the burning reentry of objects both man-made and alien-made, and I pull at Serena, wanting to bring her back into the house. I realize that save for Thor, I'm unarmed out there, and I don't like it.

But Serena doesn't move. "Some nights," she whispers. "Some nights it's almost beautiful up there, don't you think?"

"Maybe," I say, but now I really want to get moving. My arms are tingling and I feel Thor move, and I know he's on alert. I move around and then, Serena is in my arms, and damn, I'm kissing her, and everything gets fuzzy and mixed up and quite warm, and at first, all I can realize is her sweet taste and sensation.

And then we're lit up by something that turns the backyard into day.

Chapter Four

A voice—human, thank God—says, "Freeze!" and I say, "Shut the damn light off, now."

The light remains on, but at least it's lowered. I blink hard a few times and Thor growls, and I say, "Easy, boy, easy."

The voice comes from the rear of the bed and breakfast, and then the light moves, as a young man comes into view. It's one of the kitchen staff we saw earlier, and he says, "Sorry about that. We keep a tight perimeter around here, for thieves or Coasties." He has a Remington pump-action 12-gauge shotgun on a sling over his shoulder.

My arm is around Serena's slim waist. "That's all right," I say. "Understandable."

He says, "No offense, but it's pretty late now, at least for us. You should probably head back in."

"No offense taken," I say, and Serena nudges me with her hip, says with a lowered voice, "Speak for yourself, soldier boy," and we follow the kitchen guy back into the building.

My room is toasty warm and I get things ready for bed. My M-4 and M-10 are unstrapped and put up against the wall, and I check my 9 mm Beretta and put it on the nightstand. Thor watches me with interest as I get my gear together, and I'm thinking of what this fine place might make for breakfast. I'm already hungry thinking about it.

I wash up and brush my teeth, and I'm tempted to take another hot bath—never waste an opportunity to eat or wash up, one of the many lessons I learned in Basic when I was twelve—but that bed looks damn inviting. There are two lights burning in my room, both gas lanterns, and I shut them off and see there's a big lump in my bed.

"Thor," I say. "Really?"

He doesn't answer, of course, but he graciously moves to the side and gives me room. The sheets are crisp and clean and smell of soap. Once upon a time nearly everyone here in this country slept on similar sheets and didn't worry about dinner, or breakfast.

Yeah, once upon a time.

I stretch out, rest my head against my hands, and stare up at the ceiling, thinking of how in hell I had ended up here, in upstate New York, lots of miles away from my home station of Fort St. Paul. It had all started with a simple courier job, escorting a representative of the governor to Albany, along with Serena and her younger brother. Yeah, simple, no such thing as a simple order. I had gotten them to Albany—after an apparent Creeper ambush that destroyed our train and killed the governor's man—only to learn later that getting Buddy to Albany had been my real mission. Quiet Buddy, who had once worked in the Observation Corps, tracking the Creepers' killer stealth satellites via telescopes, binoculars, and eyeballs, and who also had a talent for memorizing and learning the Creeper language.

Quiet Buddy, who had convinced the Creepers back there to open their Dome and to surrender, and to end this damn war.

Quiet, dangerous Buddy.

I can't get comfortable and I don't feel sleepy, so I switch on the AM radio and find two stations: Armed Forces Radio and Voice of America. The VOA station's playing old rock music from the 1980s, and the other station is doing a news program. Both stations fade in and out as their signals bounce from one transmitter to another, to avoid being targeted by a Creeper satellite. Every now and then a civilian station comes back on air, and it usually lasts a week or two before getting smeared.

I skip the news station for now and work through the tuning knob, hearing crackles and bursts of static. Sometimes if there's a skip or something going on with the ionosphere, you can hear broadcasts from overseas. I've picked up stations from someplace in Eastern Europe more than once, but I couldn't understand a word they were saying. One time I heard a show in Japanese that went on for a while, the male broadcaster almost shouting in a way that sounded damn spooky.

For me the best ones are from the BBC, with news about battles along the English Channel and the Highlands of Scotland.

But no skips tonight. Just noise.

I turn the station back to Armed Forces Radio, and it must be the top of the hour, for they're broadcasting a round-up of the latest news from the United States and from bits of the world that can still be reached. The lead story, of course, is the recent attack on the capitol by the Creepers, and the escape of the President, most of Congress and the Joint Chiefs of Staff. Most military units in Vermont and New York are responding to the area for R&R—back in the day, known as rest and recreation, but nowadays known as relief and recovery.

Then some more headlines, about relief convoys trucking into Denver after its years-long siege had been lifted, optimistic reports about wheat output coming from Kansas, Montana and the two Dakotas, and increased oil production in Texas and Louisiana. From around the world, rumors of a Creeper offensive nearing Beijing, reports of Argentina increasing its beef exports, and the latest on the medical condition of the young King of Great Britain, wounded a couple of weeks ago while leading troops against a Creeper offensive line south of Manchester.

More news drones on and I finally switch off the radio, settle in. Thor moves and lets loose a heavy sigh, like he's finally happy that I've turned off the other voices out there in the ether, yapping and talking and keeping him awake. I roll over, pull up the blankets, and something is bothering me, something is nibbling at the back of my mind, and I finally realize it.

Not once during the news hour that I had been listening to, not once was there any mention of the Creeper and Dome surrender, something that should have been at least story number two.

I move the pillow around. Then again, what the hell do I know?

Like I keep on insisting to Serena, I'm just a soldier.

My morning starts with a thumping at the door. I roll out, toss on a pair of BDU pants, and in bare feet go to the door, pistol in hand. Hell of a breakfast service this place had planned.

I open the door and surprise of all surprises, Sergeant Bronson is standing there, in full battle rattle, Colt M-10 hanging off his shoulder, helmet on, gear hanging from his harness, muddy boots on the nice rug outside of my door, stairway behind him.

"Morning, Sunshine," he says. "Time to roll."

"Sorry?"

He looks at the pistol in my hand. "What, you expecting a baby Creeper to come up those stairs and piss on your bare feet? Saddle up. We're moving out."

"What the hell do you mean, moving out?"

His face creases into a knowing smile. "Get the hell dressed, grab your gear, and get the hell out. Captain Wallace is waiting on your skinny ass, and you never want to keep the Captain waiting. Move, Knox, move."

Bronson turns around, clomps his way down the stairs, and I whisper a few obscenities and go back in to do as I'm told.

A few minutes later I'm out in the cold morning air, and there's an old 6x6 truck at ease, belching smoke and steam, the command Humvee, and one of the Stryker vehicles I had seen yesterday, its two flags hanging limply from the rear staffs, the American one and the Scottish one. Captain Wallace is talking to my dad, looking down at a topo map spread out on the hood of the Humvee. I come down off the porch, yawning, with Thor by my side.

Dad spots me and says, "Morning, sport."

"Hey, Dad, what's up?"

Captain Wallace says, "What's up is that we need to get you moving."

I'm not so tired anymore. "I'm sorry . . . ma'am. It was my understanding from Mr. Cranston yesterday that I was going to be sent home, back to Concord."

"Really?" Captain Wallace asks. "Well, it's a new day, and a new reality. You and the colonel are accompanying me up the road to Amsterdam. There's a Creeper Dome waiting for us."

"Dad?"

He says, "Cranston and his folks, they debriefed Buddy, and they've recorded his messages. We have a PsyOps Humvee attached to Captain Wallace's unit. We're going there to broadcast the message, get those Creepers to surrender. When it works, that same message is going to be duplicated and sent throughout the Army. That's what we're doing."

"Buddy and Serena," I say, looking to Drake House. "Where are they?"

"They and their father are with Cranston and General Scopes, going for additional meetings and briefings."

"They're already gone?"

"Yes, Randy."

I look back again at the quiet building. Not even a chance to say goodbye, not even a chance to see how she was doing, no chances at all.

"Dad, it isn't fair," I say, knowing my voice sounds weak and pathetic.

Captain Wallace seems amused by our little spat. I say, "It's been a long time since we were both back in Concord. We should go back."

"Things change."

"Dad, you know it isn't fair!"

My dad's eyes tighten and he picks up a new helmet, used to keep one edge of the map stretched out, puts it on his head. "Sergeant," he says, voice cold. "You and I have been officially detached to Captain Wallace's company. You have your orders."

I take a breath and since his head's covered, I salute him.

"Yes, sir," I say, and I turn and head to the vehicles, their engines grumbling.

Chapter Five

At the vehicles I head to the Stryker, and Bronson can't wait to set me straight. "Up to the M35, Nat Guard boy. And make sure your mutt doesn't piss and poop."

My ears—including the scarred one—burn with embarrassment and I go to the old truck, powered by wood and steam, and go to the open tailgate. Bronson looks me over and says, "You Nat Guard guys always run around overarmed?"

"Not sure what the hell you're talking about, Bronson."

He laughs. "Look at you. Pistol at the side, M-4 and M-10 over your shoulders. Big bad doggy running alongside. What? The Creepers peek into your dorm room back at Fort St. Paul and make you wet yourself, you gotta carry so many weapons?"

The soldiers up on the truck are pretending not to see or hear what's going on. I say, "So what's your beef?"

"The beef is," he says sharply, "is you're humping too much. All that stuff hanging off of you, it'd be easy to fire off an M-4 round and take off the top of one of my troopers, or to send an M-10 round up in the air and waste it, when it could be used on a kill. You know how much those rounds cost?"

"Ten new dollars each," I say. "Anything else you want to know?"

He steps forward. "Yeah. The M-4 or the M-10. Take your pick. You can't carry both."

I pause for a moment, wondering how in hell I had gotten on Bronson's bad side, and decide it's a waste of time trying to figure it out. So I take my M-10 off, lean it up against the rear of the 6x6. I take the M-4 off, clear the chamber, remove the magazine, reinsert the 5.56 mm cartridge, and with two spare magazines in a cloth pouch, I hold the whole kit out to Bronson.

"Here it is," I say.

"Hell, no, don't bother me with that," he says. "Hump it back to the ordnance officer."

I say, "I don't know who or where the ordnance officer is, so if you want my M-4, Bronson, come and take it."

"Don't mess with me, Knox."

I say, "Not messing with anything...Sergeant. Thing is, I was content to carry the M-4. You got all pissy about it. You want it, here it is. Otherwise, leave me the hell alone."

He glares at me but steps forward, jerking it out of my hand, examines it and shakes his head. "Damn thing is a piece of crap. Is this what they're issuing from your Nat Guard unit nowadays, Knox?"

"No," I say, walking past him. "I got it off a Coastie in Massachusetts."

Bronson barks out a laugh. "How? You strip it off him after he was dead?"

"In a manner of speaking," I say. "I stripped it off him after I killed him."

Bronson leaves and host of unfriendly faces look down at me, and a voice from the past, an old drill instructor when I was just twelve years old, says, *suck it up, Knox*, and that's what I do.

"Give me room, fellas, all right?" I ask, and there's some grumbling, and first I lift up my injured Thor and bring him to the truck. One of the soldiers rubs his head and I'm proud of my boy, the way he accepts unwanted attention. I swing up my pack and weapons, and I grab a dangling chain and work my way in. There's more grumbling, but there's a tiny space on a wooden bench, and I squeeze myself in.

"Thanks," I say, and the corporal next to me, with a black eyepatch and a nametag stating DE LOS SANTOS says, "Whatever."

Thor lies down on the wooden floor, avoiding the booted feet, and Bronson comes by, looks up and says, "Hey, Knox, riding in style, ain't ya. I hear most Nat Guard units still use horses and wagons. Welcome to the Army of interstellar warfare."

Other guys in the truck laugh and he lifts up the tailgate with a grunt, fastens it with a couple of chains, and walks around the side. A few shouts and the truck jolts, burps, and grumbles, and we're on the move.

Out on the road we join up with the rest of Captain Wallace's company, with four other up-armored Humvees—one with a trailer marked with the Red Cross—two more troop-carrying 6x6 trucks, two support trucks, and the other Stryker, plus a Humvee with loudspeakers mounted on the roof. PsyOps, I guess. Prewar an Army company consisted of three platoons and a heavy weapon platoon, and the same is true today, save most of the Army operates at about half-size, with platoons taking on jobs usually left for companies. Too much fighting and dying, and not enough replacements. The constant history of this damn war.

I look around at my fellow soldiers, most of them around my age, a mix of male and female, except for one older guy sitting up near the cab. Next to me is a girl with PFC chevrons and a BALATNIC name patch, wearing a helmet that looks ridiculously large on top of her small head.

"So who are you guys?"

She says, "First Platoon, K Company, First Battalion, 14th Army Regiment."

"Hell of a mouthful," I say. "Is your ell-tee on another truck?"

"No, man," a voice says. "This is the First Platoon, all of it. And our ell-tee got her head scorched off two weeks ago."

I count the faces. There are nine here. Nine. Usually a platoon is minimally staffed at eighteen.

"Who's in charge then?" I ask.

Balatnic says, "Sergeant Bronson, for now."

"I'd think he'd be up forward, instead of one of the Humvees," I say.

Somebody laughs, there's a muttered obscenity, and Balatnic changes the subject. "Where are you from, Sarge?"

"Fort St. Paul in New Hampshire," I say.

Another voice: "What unit?"

"New Hampshire National Guard," I say. "Second Recon Rangers, First Battalion, attached to the 26th Yankee Division."

A voice further back says, "Oooh. Nat Guard. Guess we've won the war after all and can go home."

I keep my mouth shut, not wanting to engage in the years-old feud between National Guard and regular Army. Truth is, there isn't much difference now, but some governors—like ours in the Granite State—pretend they have overall control of the National Guard units, and as a matter of pride, keep their unit names.

Again I note the crossed bayonets of their division patch and say, "Where's the 10th hanging their hats nowadays?"

De Los Santos says, "We tend to roam around a lot, Sarge. Home base used to be Fort Drum before the war. But we tend to hang out in Rome and then change operational bases every few months. Don't like to be a sitting target."

"The rest of your regiment back there?"

Oh my, silence, such that I can even hear somebody talking in the front cab. I have the horrible feeling I've just trespassed onto something forbidden, something taboo, and De Los Santos spits on the truck's floorboards. "No," he says. "Rest of the regiment is in Kabul."

Afghanistan. When the war began the military went from a time when the White House could talk to a squad leader in a desert in Iraq, to a time when every form of electronic communication was destroyed overnight. That meant hundreds of thousands of soldiers, marines, sailors and airmen were instantly cut off from their homeland. Only now, with the reintroduction of steamships and telegraph systems, have very basic communications been reestablished.

But what happened to these abandoned units—collapsing into armed brigands, turning into mercenary forces for local governments, or staying on with their traditions and laws of a nearly forgotten land—still isn't very well known.

I just say, "Sorry," and De Los Santos shrugs and says, "You run into many Creepers there in the Nat Guard, Sarge?"

"Enough."

He laughs. "Shit, Sarge, you're gonna learn a lot hanging with us. We eat Creepers for breakfast, lunch and dinner. You ever kill one?"

"Yeah," I say.

"How many?"

I don't think they'll believe anything I say, so I reply again with, "Enough."

We're on State Highway 5, heading west, consisting of two

lanes in each direction. The roadway is cracked and bumpy, and abandoned cars have been pushed or dragged to the side, making for a relatively straightforward ride, although after years of no landscaping work, trees and brush are crowding us in.

A young woman leans into the middle of the group and says to me, "What the hell was going on back there, at the Dome? Never seen nothing like that, ever. Seven Creepers out in the open...not even moving! Were they all dead?"

"No," I say. "They surrendered."

That quiets them down, and for about a quarter mile nobody says anything, and then someone says, "The hell you say. Surrender? You sure they weren't killed?"

"They surrendered."

De Los Santos says, "How come you're so sure, Sarge?"

"I was there."

Another bit of quiet, except there's one hell of rattle as we go over a patch of Highway 5 that's turned into gravel and crushed asphalt. A soft voice. "That's what I heard, you know. That they had surrendered. How did that happen?"

I adjust myself in the wooden seat, take in the surrounding landscape, mostly flat farmland and trees. The sky is overcast and there are some flickers of light out to the west as another chunk of space debris comes back to Earth.

"I'm still not sure," I say. "There's...a young soldier. Private. He has...special abilities. He learned some of the Creeper language. He convinced them to open their Dome and surrender."

Balatnic is excited. "Does that mean the war's over?"

And another voice says, "Your ass is in an Army truck, heading to a Creeper Dome. Does that look like the war's over?"

She blushes and I feel bad for her, and she looks down at her feet. I rummage in my coat pockets, find a bit of dried venison, and I pass it over to her. "Want to give this to my dog?"

Balatnic brightens up, takes the meat from my hand. "Sure! What's his name?"

"Thor," I say.

She says, "Hey, Thor, hey."

Thor lifts his head up and takes the meat from her fingers, and licks her fingers. She smiles. "What kind of dog is he? He looks like a German shepherd."

"He does, doesn't he," I say. "He's a Belgian Malinois."

Thor lowers his head, rests it between his paws. Balatnic says, "Does he bite?"

I smile at her. "Only if you've been very, very bad."

We thump along the bumpy road for another hour, and then the convoy approaches a turn-off to the right and slows down. There are a series of horn blasts—sending out signals to the drivers I'm sure—and one Stryker comes to a halt, while the rest of us move ahead and spread out. There's a shout of, "Take a break, stretch those legs," and we all tumble out.

But there's something wrong.

I stand with Thor next to me, considerably lightened up by not carrying the M-4, and I stroll over the cracked asphalt with the grass and weeds growing knee-high. All of a sudden I wish I was carrying my M-4, which are designed for shooting humans, not aliens, for humans are the trouble right now.

The exit is blocked by three junked cars, pushed together, and there's a wooden fence and a large sign, professionally painted, which surprises me. The sign is black letters on white background, and states: SANCTUARY ZONE: NO MILITARY ALLOWED. Two men in jeans and black coats are standing before the sign, carrying scoped hunting rifles, and there's an older woman there as well, talking quickly to Captain Wallace, hands moving around. The woman is well dressed in clean jeans and a light brown corduroy jacket, and her white hair is pulled back in a bun.

"What the hell?" I ask. Balatnic is next to me, her helmet still ridiculously large, and she says in a soft voice, "No go zone."

"No go zone for who?"

"Us," she says. "Military, militia. People who've set up no go zones, they think if they leave the aliens alone, the aliens will leave them alone. That means not letting military units travel through their territory."

"You're kidding me."

She says, "That look like kidding to you? Don't you have peacers back in New Hampshire?"

"A few," I say, remembering the odd protest out in front of Fort St. Paul. "Our base . . . the National Guard seized it from a prep school after the war started, moved in and took over their quarters. We get protests every now and then from former teachers and faculty members looking to kick us out and get their school back."

"What does your base commander do?"

That would be my uncle, Colonel Malcolm Hunter. His sister married my dad, an event that he's never forgiven Dad for, because my Uncle Malcolm believes Dad caused her death, and the death of my sister.

Not that Dad has ever said anything to me about it.

I say, "He ignores them, tells the rest of us to ignore them, and then when they leave, he sends them some leftovers from our mess. Hearts and minds, that sort of thing."

A sergeant from another platoon stomps by, murmuring something, and with my bum ear I can't make it out, but Balatnic says, "Shit, so that's the problem. They're blocking the quickest way to the Dome. If they don't let us through, that's another half-day travel."

"Well," I say.

"Yeah," she says. "You wanna talk about hearts and minds? If Sergeant Cooper has his way"—the sergeant that just went past us—"those peacers are gonna have their hearts and minds splattered all over that pretty sign."

Since we're just standing around not doing anything, I walk with Thor up to the barricade. Captain Wallace is there, with her grizzled first sergeant, a lieutenant—a skinny blonde woman who looks to be over two meters tall—and Dad. Wallace has her helmet held in the crook of her arm and her voice is low and firm. "Ma'am," she says, "I promise, we don't plan to stay in your township. We just need to pass through."

The woman's voice isn't as calm, slightly high pitched, but she's not giving an inch. "The hell you are," she says. "Ever since I was a child, the military has lied and lied. It lied in the Gulf of Tonkin, in Vietnam, in the Middle East, in Nigeria, and now, here. Well, it ends here. We citizens voted in a regular, fully legal town meeting to exclude all armed forces from trespassing here."

"Ma'am," Wallace says. "With all due respect, we're the armed forces of your nation. How can we be trespassing?"

Her chin juts out in defiance. "Because we don't want you. Because this is a sanctuary township. No armed forces, nothing to provoke the aliens. We leave them alone and, God willing, they'll leave us alone."

"Do you think they even recognize or appreciate what you've done?"

"I don't know," she says. "Do you think they recognize or appreciate how many of them you've killed since they arrived here?"

Both the lieutenant and the sergeant start to talk, mostly about who started what upon their arrival, but Wallace remains calm, lifting up a hand. "I see. But wouldn't you agree that their aggression upon arrival, by establishing the orbital base, setting off the high-altitude nuclear weapons, and dropping asteroids to cause the tsunamis...don't you think they realized they would get a military response?"

Some of the troopers mutter about how we're wasting time, how we need to get going, that these crazy folk are just holding us up, and the woman says, "Who knows? For ten years we've been killing them. Perhaps if we tried something else, accommodating them and being open for discussion, to air our mutual grievances, perhaps that would end with a positive result for the both of us. Those aliens...perhaps they're just refugees, fleeing a dying world or dying star. Is what they did to us any different from what our European settlers did to the First Peoples here?"

Captain Wallace looks like she's going to grind her teeth down to dust, keeping calm, and then she puts her helmet back on, tightens the strap, and says, "First Sergeant."

"Ma'am."

I think all of us are just not moving at all, wanting to hear Wallace's orders, wanting to know what all of us are going to have to do to get either around, through, or above the barricade.

She says, "Move the convoy out. We'll take the alternate route."

Some more mutters and the first sergeant says, "Yes, ma'am," and we move out, leaving the people of peace and their town behind us in just a very few minutes.

We drive along, sitting in silence, and I look to the rear at the rest of the convoy, still rattling along on this potholed and cracked highway. I spot the rear Stryker, with its Creeper skull on the front, and the two flags flying at the rear.

I turn and say to Balatnic, "What's up with the other flag back there, the Scottish one."

"Give it a guess," De Los Santos says.

It then comes to me, about our abandoned troops stuck halfway around the world when we all went back to the late nineteenth century. Why wouldn't it happen for other forces?

I ask, "Does that mean there's Scottish troops mixed in here? Or British troops?"

More laughs. A soldier up in the middle says, "Man, didn't you ever see the movie *Braveheart*? The one with that crazy Aussie actor?"

Too many times, I think, and I say, "Sure, I've seen it."

"Captain Wallace," the soldier says. "She's a direct descendant of William Wallace, that Scottish rebel."

Balatnic chimes in. "Plus she's also related to General William Scott Wallace, the guy who ran V Corps during the Second Gulf War. His crew attacked Iraq back in '03, drove more than five hundred miles in less than two weeks through enemy territory. Hell, Sully up there, he was in on that run, right?"

Sullivan offers a slim smile. "I was. Better class of people back then, too."

More laughs, and I guess this is an old joke among the First Platoon. The first soldier adds, "Captain Wallace...she takes her history seriously, as well as her job."

Balatnic nudges me, "But God, don't start in about bagpipes."

"Sweet Jesus, no," De Los Santos says, and I get comfortable in my seat, get comfortable where I am.

Chapter Six

The road eventually narrows, with trees crowding in so much that branches and leaves are slapping at us as we move down one lane, and then the road opens up, and there's a crossroads, and a roadhouse, and the convoy rattles to a halt. Captain Wallace trots from her command Humvee, followed by the first sergeant, and they enter the roadhouse. There are four horses tied up to a hitching post, another horse and wagon, and three pre–computer era pickup trucks, rusted and being held together with rope and hammered pieces of lumber. The place is called Vihan's Cross-roads to the World.

"What's that about?" I ask. "Captain getting coffee for her outfit?"

"That would be something," Balatnic says. "But that roadhouse, it's got a working phone hooked up to the county network. She can call into base from there, beats sending out a courier. Plus there's a storage unit and fuel tank that they let us use."

"Who's Vihan?"

Balatnic says, "Vee? Nice Indian guy. Immigrant. He and his extended family run the joint. Good people...but poor guy still thinks one of these days, he's gonna get back to India and collect the rest of his family."

The door opens up and four kids run out, two boys and two girls, dark-skinned, the girls wearing gold jewelry around their wrists and on their ears. They're carrying large pots with spouts, and a bucket full of glasses. They scatter around the convoy and

I reach down, with the others, and drink a small glass of hot, sweet tea.

The kids laugh and chatter in Hindi, I guess, and when they collect the empties and head back, Wallace is at the door, beside an Indian gentleman with a thick black moustache and black-rimmed glasses. Wallace shakes his hand, as does the first sergeant, and they go back to the convoy, rapidly talking to each other.

"Hell of a way to run a war," I say.

"An interstellar war, Sarge, don't forget that."

The convoy gets going and races ahead, making a left turn, and then a right turn, and then we slow down. The road has widened and I wonder who's trimmed back the trees and the brush, and I see cold ashes and charcoal from burnt trees and recognize Creeper sign.

There's another sign as well, spray painted in bright orange letters on a slab of plywood, sagging from age despite being held up by wooden fence posts.

CREEPER DOME UP THE ROAD STAY AWAY

Below that, someone with a dark sense of humor has scrawled:

Abandon All Hope Ye Who Enter Here

Balatnic says, "What the hell does that mean?"

"It's from an old Italian poem," I say. "That's what it says at the entrance of Hell."

De Los Santos grunts. "Considering what we've seen and what we've done, there must be a lot of damn entrances scattered around this part of the state."

The convoy moves ahead, and there's a change in the attitude among the troopers in the rear of the truck. M-4s and M-10s are checked. The young girl soldier next to me, Balatnic, is carrying an M-4 almost as long as she is, and she notes my M-10. "Next year," she says, "the captain says I'll be trained on the M-10."

"It's a good weapon," I say.

"I know," she says, smiling ruefully. "But it gives one hell of a kick, don't it. Last spring, I fired a test round, and the recoil blew me back on my ass."

The vehicles slow down, stop, and there are whistles and the tailgate comes down with a big clatter. I get off and help Thor, and with battlepack in hand, I stand with the rest of the First Platoon as a dry Sergeant Bronson comes up. "All right, kids, real deal coming up. Let's strip and get ready for action. You too, Knox. About time you learn something about the regular Army."

I don't rise to his bait and then see something that makes my hands and feet cold.

Damn.

All of the platoon members are removing Firebiter protective vests from their battlepacks. The Kevlar vests from a long time ago were designed to protect humans from fellow humans. These vests are made of layers of an Insulfex cloth in a camouflage pattern, then some sort of protective membrane and then aluminum foil bonded to woven silica cloth to reflect the cutting lasers and flame weapons the Creepers use. They weigh fourteen pounds, and sure as hell aren't perfect, but as one sergeant back at Basic—a bald, grumpy guy named Lamontagne—once said, "It's better than nothing."

And I don't have one.

Check, I do have one, and right now, it's safely back at Fort St. Paul. I go through the line of the other soldiers gearing up and checking each other out, and I find Sergeant Bronson.

"Hey," I say, getting his attention. "I don't have a Firebiter."

His is on and he offers me a smirk. "Sounds like a personal problem. You always go out in the field underequipped like this?"

"No, today's a special day," I say.

"Quartermaster truck, near the end of the line," he says. "Go see if she has anything for you."

I trot back with Thor following right at my side, now feeling the energy from the other soldiers gearing up, cracking jokes, getting ready to put their asses out there. If all goes well, this won't be combat. The PsyOps Humvee will go out and do its job, and things will be cool, without a single shot being fired in anger, or disappointment, or whatever.

But since when did anything go well in wartime?

The quartermaster corporal, the nice young lady who helped gear me out the other day at the Dome site, sees me approach the rear of her truck and says, "Make it quick, Sergeant. Things are about to get interesting."

"Firebiter vest," I say. "I don't have one."

"Shit. Well, let's see." She climbs up and into the rear of the truck, small flashlight in hand, moves around and kicks things through, and there's a triumphant sound. She comes back and tosses it at me. It's a Firebiter all right, but...well, there are dark brown stains around the collar, and tears here and there. It's old and has been well-used and smells of someone else's body.

"Best you can do?" I ask.

"Only thing I can do," she says. "Those things are pricy and whenever a shipment gets sent out, sticky-fingered rear echelon assholes—who've only seen Creepers on newsreels or in *Stars & Stripes*—pick 'em out."

I hold up the vest. "It's been used."

"Yeah, by a nice guy named Flanders. Last month, he got caught up in a raid we were making on a Creeper gathering point. He didn't make it, but at least his vest did. Don't worry, the vest wasn't hit."

I start putting it back on. "What was hit, then?"

"Everything above the shoulders."

I clench my teeth, buckle up the vest. It feels sodden and moist, like Flanders's blood, tears and sweat are now part of the fabric.

Back I go and Bronson is talking it up with his platoon, but I see Dad, Captain Wallace, two lieutenants and the first sergeant loudly discussing something at her command Humvee. I think I hear Bronson call out my name as I slide by, and I ignore him. With my medically certified twenty percent hearing loss in my left ear, I tend to ignore a lot...which sometimes gets me into trouble.

Like I care.

Up at the Humvee Captain Wallace is shaking her head. "Damn it, the only thing I know is that there's a Creeper Dome somewhere over there, to the north, just above a stream. And that's not enough."

The tall blonde lieutenant says, "I can take a couple of squads out on a skirmish line, work through the woods and—"

Wallace looks up at the gray sky. "Because of those damn peacers, the sun will be coming down soon. I want this mission wrapped up now."

It's like I'm no longer under my own power, and I step forward, elbowing aside a lieutenant I haven't met yet—a black guy older than me, nametagged JACKSON—and I say, "Captain Wallace?"

She says, "What is it, Sergeant?"

"Ma'am...my MOS...well, I'm a Recon Ranger."

Jackson says, "So?"

"So I've got my K-9 unit with me. We've got experience

sniffing out Creepers and their Base Domes. You give us the word, ma'am, we'll set out right now and be back, as soon as we can, with their position located and mapped out."

Dad is quiet but looks proud. Wallace says, "You run this by Bronson yet?"

"No, ma'am."

"Why?"

"Because it made sense for me to contact you, ma'am."

"But you're assigned to his platoon."

I rub Thor's head. "Sorry, ma'am, that wasn't made clear to me. I just thought I was with Sergeant Bronson's platoon because there was an extra space on his truck."

Dad covers a smile with his hand, and Wallace hands me a folded-over topo map with grid coordinates overlaid on it.

"Get out there and get back," she says. "Quick as you can."

I salute her. "Yes, ma'am."

I'm getting a canteen filled and checking my gear one more time when Bronson approaches me. "What, you forget something you learned in Basic?"

"What's that, Bronson?" I say, fastening the canteen to my side.

"Never volunteer, ever," he says.

My M-10 is leaning against the side of the truck I was riding in, and I pick it up. It's heavy, tubular and bulky as hell, and it and its brothers have saved my skinny butt more times than I care to remember.

I sling it over, check the bandolier. Three 50 mm rounds safe and secure. If I'm very, very lucky, I'll be walking back later to this truck with Thor, with all rounds unexpended.

"Guess we skipped that part," I say, "when we learned all the different ways to sneak up on a Creeper. Later, Bronson. Keep yourself safe and dry."

He stares at me but I've stared back at nastier things before, walking on six legs, and I say, "Thor, come," and off we go.

I don't want to make a big deal of it and just want to get away, so I take a quick compass fix, figure out where north is, and into the woods Thor and I go. With each step I guess I should have been getting scared of what my boy and I were getting into, but truth is, I was glad to get away from that mob. Oh, they seemed cool enough, once they figured out you knew which end of the boot to pour piss out of, but I missed my own crew, and as Ranger Recon I'm used to working alone, save for canine companionship.

Thor is happily trotting next to me, sniffing, tongue hanging out, bandages secure around his middle. I stop and he stops and I squat down on one knee, rub his head. He licks my wrist.

"Let's take it easy today, boy, all right? Just a hunting mission, that's all."

His brown eyes take me in, and he licks my wrist one more time. I get up and check the compass reading. North was over by that big pine tree. We'd head there, find another landmark, and do our best. I carefully look around, checking the scenery, just low brush, mix of pine trees and a couple of birches.

I pat Thor on the head. "Thor!"

He snaps to.

"Hunt!"

And off he goes.

I keep eyes on him as best I can, as he races side to side, stopping to sniff the air, doubling back to make sure he doesn't miss anything. One sure sign of Creepers are the smell of cinnamon— which our white coats still can't explain—but with his sniffing skills, Thor can track and detect better than any human...better than most K-9 units I've come across.

I take my time, looking for any disturbances that mark Creepers—burnt homes, trees, broken trunks, excavated cemeteries— and also look for running water. For some reason, the alien bastards tend to move around flowing fresh water.

Why?

See cinnamon, scent of, mentioned before.

Thor is a blur of black fur out there in the distance. I note a clearing up ahead and slow down.

An old campsite, it looks like. Underbrush and saplings have been cleared away. There are two depressions where tents have been set up. There's a firepit. I stick my hand in the firepit. Cold, dead ashes. Long time ago. By the base of a tree there's some broken brown glass. Beer bottles. Broken ale bottle with a familiar but faded label, showing a red human hand crushing a miniature black Creeper. RED VENGEANCE. Yeah, we'll see about that.

So. Outpost? Coastie encampment? A couple of local guys wanting to have some fun before going into Basic?

Who knows.

I stand up, and Thor barks.

I start moving.

He barks again, and I can tell he's standing still.

Good boy!

I move quickly and surely through the woods and the bushes, making sure nothing gets caught on my gear. Years before, when I was younger, dumber, and considerably more excitable, I would race like a goat with its ass on fire, trying to get to Thor as quick as possible, and usually falling on my ass when I ran into a low-slung branch or spun around like a drunken top when a length of brush grabbed onto my MOLLE vest.

It looks like the woods are thinning. I'm checking my compass reading. Still heading north. A good sign.

There's Thor, sitting, panting contentedly, head turning to me as I approach. He lets off another bark, and I come up, rub his head. "Good boy, Thor...real good boy."

I check my pockets, find no treats. Just a piece of soap. Damn. "Later, boy, okay? Later."

Thor's excited look is tinged with disappointment. He whines, moves in a circle, and barks once more. "Promise," I say. "Promise."

I move slowly and say, "Stay," and he does just that.

I go through the thinning tree line, and—

Nothing.

The trees are gone.

Just a black ribbon of ash.

I kneel down, hide as best as I can behind some pine saplings. Not much cover but it'll have to do.

Out there is a large farm with rolling pasturelands, fences, siloes, and several barns and outbuildings. A beautiful sight it must have been, years ago, but now the pastureland is burnt and reburnt crusty dirt and grass, and most of the fences have either been scorched or smashed. The buildings are in lousy shape as well, with broken windows, shattered walls, and sunken roofs. One of the three siloes has been split from top to bottom. I note heaps of bones scattered across the blasted land, some in a heap, like they were trying to escape. Horses, probably, or maybe cows.

And who's responsible?

Creepers, of course, maybe the same ones living in that Dome right in the middle of the fields.

Or the second Dome, built so that part of it crushed an outbuilding.

"Well, that's interesting," I whisper, because Kara's Killers were only supposed to approach one Dome, and here we were, with two, same shape, same size, same color.

So when did that happen?

Unfortunately for me, there's no signs or plaques denoting when these blue-gray Domes were constructed, or how. Still a mystery after all these years is how the damn things get built. They literally appear out of nowhere, or at least, in a very few seconds. The best idea I've heard is that at night, when one sees the hard line of light marking an attack from an overhead killer stealth satellite, that the beam of light is somehow transmitting a Dome-in-waiting, which unfolds and sets itself up.

Not a bad theory as theories go, but above my pay grade. Thor is at my side, trembling, and I rub his head and back. "Good boy," I murmur. "Good boy."

I look out at the farm again, take out the topo map with the plastic overlay. I match up some landmarks, see a stream crossing over there on my left, and with an attached wax pen, I mark up on the map where the Creepers are located.

Now what?

Now to get back to Captain Wallace. I turn and think, well, it would be relatively easy to backtrack and report to the captain where and how I located them, along with the intelligence that there are two Domes waiting for us, not one.

But that would only be a partial mission success. Captain Wallace needs to get to this spot with that PsyOps Humvee, and so far, she doesn't have a way to do it.

Which means it's time to get going.

I check on that stream, see it moves parallel . . . to an access road. Or dirt driveway, or however you want to call it.

"Come along," I whisper to my buddy. I move back into the tree line, and then head off to the access road. I travel slow, knowing that the two Creeper Domes are close enough for me to be seen and heard, and Thor moves with quiet care, right along me.

Then we come across the access road, which cuts to the left. I check the topo map.

There.

The road is crumbling and washed out in several places, but

it seems to lead right back to the state road where the convoy had parked. After slowly thrashing through some brush, we make it to cracked and bumpy asphalt.

The state road.

Thor comes to me. I rub his head again. "Recon Rangers come through again."

We walk for about five minutes when a voice calls out, "Halt."

I do just that, but my hand rests on my holstered 9 mm Beretta. Two soldiers emerge from the woods on the right side of the road, and one—who's desperately trying to grow a moustache—says, "You're Knox, right?"

"Yep."

"We're from the Third Platoon. Part of a picket line up and down this road. Orders are, we come across you, we get the map and send it down the line."

"I can do that."

A third soldier emerges, pushing a battered mountain bike. "Combat courier. Think you or your dog can outrun me?"

"Probably not," I say. I hand over the precious map and say, "I've marked it here, but make sure Captain Wallace knows this: there are two Creeper Domes at this location, not one."

The combat courier is a young guy wearing non-issue black bicycle shorts, but I know if a courier is fast, that bit of uniform play is always overlooked. His legs are thick, muscular, and scarred here and there with shrapnel wounds or burns.

He takes my map, tucks it into his jacket. "Imagine that," he says. "An intelligence failure. Later, guys."

He bikes off and I have a sweet memory of my Abby, back home at Fort St. Paul, one of the best combat couriers I know, and someone I was dating before I got entangled with Serena and her quiet, deadly brother.

I wonder what she's doing right now.

The thought troubles me, and I take Thor over to a cleared spot at the side of the road, settle down against a couple of exposed rocks.

Wait, I think. Just wait.

The two other soldiers share a forbidden cigarette. I hear an engine noise that quickly rises in volume, and then something on two wheels roars by in a blur. I get up and say, "Hey, that looks like a motorcycle."

"Good eyes," the moustache kid says. "You been in the Army long?"

"Too long," I say. "Combat courier?"

"Yeah, for long distance communications."

I shake my head. "We're still using just bicycles, back in New Hampshire."

Another grinding of engines, and the lead eight-wheeled Stryker vehicle rolls in. I spot the rest of the convoy stretched out behind it, including Captain Wallace's command Humvee. I walked around the scarred and battered Stryker—this one bearing a flapping American flag and a New York State flag.

And something else I hadn't noticed before: two adhesive signs on the rear (called bumperstickers, I believe), each saying the same thing: I HEART NY.

Nice to see somebody remembering.

Captain Wallace emerges from her Humvee and says, "Well done, Sergeant."

"Thank you, ma'am."

She looks up and down her convoy, her company, and says, "Let's get this war won, shall we?"

I just nod in agreement.

An Excerpt From the Journal of Randall Knox

Among the many rules and regulations in my world—including not keeping a diary, which rule I'm obviously breaking—is one about compiling or inquiring about civilian causalities. Oh, information's passed along when units are attacked or do the attacking, and the Red Cross does its best to notify next-of-kin when someone is injured or killed in action, and sometimes there are little notices in local papers or bigger notices in Stars & Stripes *if a general or colonel gets charred, but that's not what I'm talking about.*

What I'm talking about are the detailed reports of what happened during the first few days of the war, after the Creepers took up station in orbit, dropped the NUDETs to smoke our electronics, and then shoved asteroids into Earth's atmosphere to land in the seven seas and cause tsunamis to drown most of Earth's coastal cities. That was the curse, I guess, of how humankind developed, how so many of its most populous cities were built along the coastline. Think of it: New York, Rio, Mumbai, Tokyo, London, Shanghai . . . so many millions at risk, so many millions drowned, and yet, no official word of just how many died during those first few weeks.

Why?

Morale, I guess. The surviving governments or armies-in-charge don't want the population to feel like the war is already lost, with cities drowned or abandoned because of lack of power, with millions of corpses littering the countryside or stuck inside skyscrapers.

Me, I think there are more folks alive than whatever authority is out there gives credit. When the war began, most governments told their people to shelter in place, or stay at home. But I think that most folks did what was reasonable at the time: packed up and got the hell out of a target area.

Good for them, they survived. Yet their survival led to another problem, that of coastal refugees—known as Coasties—who live as gangs up and down the coastlines, refusing to go into resettlement camps or adjustment centers, who dream of the day the waters will recede and their home cities are revealed, dried out, and have the power restored.

Nice fantasy, I guess. Another fantasy is that of survivors out there, wandering the landscape, working years later to come home. I remember a few years after the war started—I was probably ten or thereabouts—seeing flyers, placards and signs at Red Cross centers and crossroads, listing photos, names and last known addresses of friends and relatives. I asked Dad a couple of times if I could make a flyer listing Mom and my sister Melissa, and he always agreed to help, though his face would look heavy and his speech would slow, watching my handiwork.

This led later to an argument I had a couple of times with him: what happened to Mom and Melissa when the war started? All I know is that we got separated from them, and that we lived and they didn't. At the time we lived in Marblehead, Massachusetts. The last time I said something was probably four or five years ago, when I asked Dad once more, and he sat in his favorite old chair in our shared quarters back at Fort St. Paul. With tears in his eyes, and a shaking voice, he said, "Randy...I will give you this house, I will cheat to help you advance in the Army, and I will steal to keep you fed, but please, please, please...never ask me again."

So I haven't.

Probably like thousands of others out there.

Which I don't think does much for morale, at least mine.

Chapter Seven

A skirmish line has been set up at the end of the access road—or long driveway—that leads from the paved road to the destroyed farm and the two Creeper Domes. The lead Stryker has taken cover at a smaller barn off to the left, and there's a depression in the ground that allows a dozen soldiers to sight their weapons toward the two Domes.

The Humvees maneuver around and so do the trucks, and we move out. Captain Wallace goes from platoon to platoon, squad to squad, and says to me, "How do you like your new position, Sergeant?"

Bronson and the others look at me, and I say, "I'm loving it, Captain Wallace."

She laughs. "Glad to see you're fitting in."

When she leaves Bronson points to me and says, "Knox, over there by that birch tree. You and your mutt stay still and don't do anything without an order."

"You got it," and I wander over, M-10 in hand, Thor moving right next to me. Bronson and I are at the same rank, but he's also in temporary command of the First Platoon, which means he's above me...barely. But I don't want to make too much of a fuss. I find the birch tree and start scraping away a trench, using a small entrenching tool.

The young Balatnic joins me, M-4 in her hands, and says, "Did Bronson tell you to dig in?"

"Nope."

"Then why are you doing it?" she asks.

I pause. "Over there are two Creeper Domes. Not one. I don't like it. Each Dome has scores, if not more, of Creepers. I just like to keep my head down. It's not particularly good-looking, but I'd like to keep it on my shoulders."

Balatnic looks past me, at the scorched pasturelands and broken buildings, and two quiet Domes. "Can I borrow your shovel when you're done?"

"No," I say.

"Sarge..."

I playfully toss a shovelful of dirt into her lap. "I'll dig a slit trench big enough for us both."

She smiles at me and helps, moving the piles of dirt with her hands.

In the slit trench Balatnic is near me, holding her M-4 and Thor is between us. Other platoon members have seen what we've done, and there's a nice line of shallow foxholes around me, the deepest one having been dug by the old vet, Sullivan.

A slow whine and the Humvee with the mounted loudspeakers comes up. Captain Wallace, Dad and the first sergeant go over and talk to the driver. Wallace looks around, like she's evaluating the situation, and she says something to the first sergeant. He runs off and a few minutes later, four soldiers come back to the Humvee. Even at this distance I can see they're limping, injured and old. Two of them have prosthetic arms, and Wallace talks briefly to each of them, slapping them on the back when she's done.

Then a whistle is blown, and Bronson says, "First Platoon, listen up! They're getting ready to move out!"

Balatnic squirms deeper into the dirt. She says, "Wish I had the M-10."

"Yeah, but your M-4 puts out more firepower."

"Not enough to kill a Creeper. Only way I'll kill a Creeper with this"—and she lifts it up for a second—"is with a golden BB, getting through their armor."

"Well, you'll make some noises and scare them. That's a good thing."

"Hah."

I undo my M-10, take out a round from the bandolier. The thick cartridge is set on safe, and there's a dial on the bottom that can be twisted so it'll explode at ten meters, twenty-five meters, or fifty meters. The cartridge contains a binary chemical warhead that will kill a Creeper if it explodes close enough. What's in the cartridge is one of the most closely guarded secrets of the war, one that I'm not tempted to learn. So long as it works, it can contain honey and rosewater for all I care.

I spin the base so it's primed, and set it for fifty meters. Bronson sees what I'm doing and says, "Knox, anybody give you orders to arm your weapon?"

"Nope," I say, opening the breech of the M-10, sliding in the cartridge, sliding the bolt shut.

"Then why the hell are you doing it?"

"Just showing initiative, that's all."

A couple of laughs and somebody says, "There it goes!"

I look past the birch tree and the Humvee with the loud-speakers maneuvers out onto the field. The team of four soldiers moves in a straggling line behind it, all of them carrying M-10s, though from where I am, they look old and desperately tired.

The little unit rolls and walks towards the two Domes, and there's something noble and tragic and hopeful in what they're doing, four men, the Humvee driver and Humvee, going up against the Creepers in the two Domes.

Balatnic burrows herself deeper and I say, "How old are you?"

"Fourteen, Sarge."

"You doing okay over there?"

"Not really," she says, wiping at one eye, and then another.

"What's going on, then?"

She lets out a heavy breath. "I . . . I've never been this close to a Creeper Dome, never mind two. I'm usually in a support role, you know? Oh, I've seen Creepers and I've been in skirmishes and raids . . . but damn. This is something else."

"Well, you know what they say."

"What's that?"

"Those bugs are more afraid of us than we are of them."

I think she smiles. I'm not sure. The Humvee and the squad move slowly along the blackened pastureland. I say, "What's your first name, Balatnic?"

"Loretta."

"Loretta, you stick with me, and everything's going to be fine. Okay?"

She wipes at her eyes again. "Okay, Sarge."

But in a few seconds, it doesn't stay fine at all.

From the Humvee's speakers, there's a burst of static, and then a squeal of feedback. Some nervous laughter from my fellow soldiers. "Guess we're gonna burst their eardrums, if those damn bugs have eardrums," someone says.

One Dome dilates open, and then the other. Despite all that brave talk from a few moments ago, my chest and stomach clench hard at seeing Creepers emerge. There are three types, as designated by our whitecoats: Battle, Transport, and Research.

The ones coming out are all Battle.

A strong smell of cinnamon sweeps over us, and we all hear the familiar *click-click* sounds of Creepers on the move.

"Jesus," De Los Santos murmurs. "Play the tape. Play the damn tape."

We wait.

I look down the line, at the overgrown driveway, at the slight hollow where Captain Wallace, Dad, and a few others are waiting. All have binoculars, all are watching what's going on . . . or not going on. Something square and familiar-looking is on the hood of Wallace's Humvee, but I can't place it. It looks like a very small suitcase.

Another burst of static. A soldier about two meters away on the left is murmuring a prayer in Arabic, and I hope his God sure is listening because with each passing second, more Creepers are emerging and—

A loud voice comes out of the speakers. It's a collection of clicking, sputtering, and whirring sounds, just like what Buddy yelled out yesterday, just like—

No.

It's wrong.

It's all wrong.

The Creepers maneuver into two lines. Another prayer is lifted up to Whoever might be listening, and I slap Balatnic on the helmet, say, "Whatever happens, keep your head down!"

I grab my M-10 and battlepack and break out of my slit trench, start running, hunched over, feeling terribly exposed. Thor is at my side, whining, because he knows what's out there, a couple of hundred meters away, and he doesn't like it either.

"Knox!" Bronson yells at me. "Get back in line, damn you!"

I ignore him. Keep on running, still hunched over, gear rattling. The alien sounds from the loudspeakers seem to repeat themselves, starting again from the beginning, and I breathe heavy, trying to get to the command Humvee, suddenly feeling like I'm in that dream where everything goes wrong, your legs can't move fast enough, your boots are stuck in mud or some sticky substance.

I hope I'm close enough. I scream, "Captain Wallace! Captain Wallace!"

She turns to me.

"Something's wrong! That's not Buddy on those tapes! Those aren't the same phrases from yesterday! They're not going to surrender!"

Captain Wallace whirls to her first sergeant, yells out, "Recall, now!"

Hesketh holds up some sort of hand-held siren, triggers it, and the sound cuts through the air and almost overwhelms the alien sounds coming from the Humvee.

I keep on running towards Captain Wallace.

I look over to the Humvee and four exposed soldiers.

The Creepers rise up.

It's too late.

The Battle Creepers fire from their large claws, a mix of flashing laser beams and lengths of flame. The Humvee is caught first, instantly blows up in a fireball. More flickers and flames dance around the exposed soldiers. The one on the right manages to live just for a few seconds, still walking in a straight line, still following orders, ablaze from head to foot.

"Fire, fire, fire," comes the order from a bullhorn. The Stryker starts firing off its M-10 rounds. I skid to a halt, aim at what I think is the closest Creeper, and press the trigger.

BLAM!

The recoil knocks me back, as it always does, and the battlefield quickly becomes a confusing mess of Creepers charging, lasers and flame weapons firing, gas clouds popping, and Captain Wallace yells, "First Sergeant, number four, four, four!"

Flares suddenly rise up into the air, colored red and yellow, and I'm scrambling to eject my spent shell, insert another round, and Dad appears, grabbing my elbow.

"Randy, get the hell out of here!" he yells. "We're falling back!"

I grab a round from my bandolier. "I haven't heard an order!"

"It's coming!" he yells. "We can't hold here! Get a move on!"

I break free from Dad's grasp, remove a round from my bandolier, rotate the base to fifty meters—probably too short but I don't care—and as I move the M-10 up to my shoulder, another sergeant I don't know races by, yelling, "Back to the roadway! Back to the roadway! Now!"

Up where I had been before, the birch trees are on fire. There looks to be a couple of blackened lumps up there as well. We all start breaking away, me running, the command Humvee bouncing its way down the old driveway, the trucks gasping and stuttering as they try to join them, the Stryker bringing up the rear, laying down M-10 fire as best as it can.

I don't jump on any moving vehicle, for I'm not going to leave Thor behind, and they're not going to slow down to let me put him on board. I glance back at the advancing line of Creepers, emerging now from the smoke and gas clouds—it only looks like two have been killed—and I keep running, because I don't think any of these vehicles are going to survive another minute.

I move along to a ditch, staying low, joining other soldiers, splash through a stream, Thor still at my side, the good boy, and from overhead, comes a thundering, booming sound, like scores of sheets a mile long are being torn in half.

Explosions thunder in the field, lots of them, lifting up fountains of dirt and smoke.

"Yeah!" someone yells. "Get some!"

Now I know what those flares were: signaling flares Captain Wallace had cleared with a field artillery unit out there somewhere, providing them with the coordinates I had given. And if things had gone badly—quite the understatement—Wallace would have a way of providing covering fire for a retreat.

No, not retreat. That word's been forbidden for as long as I can remember. High command would call this a tactical redeployment.

Some of the advancing Creepers are on their sides, or on their backs. Their body armor is impervious to most everything save a nuclear blast, but we've learned—after a lot of bloodshed and heartache—that artillery rounds, chewing up the dirt and landscape, can slow them down.

Not kill them. Just slow them down.

Good enough.

I keep on trotting along, head low, Thor right by me. We go into a thin wood line and then I move to the left, to higher ground, and somebody says, "The hell are you doing, Sarge? Safer this way."

"Quicker this way," I say. "Driveway should be right over there."

I scamper through and sure enough, break free from the thin trees and brush. My chest hurts and I know it's from the heavy breathing. Five soldiers—three girls and two boys—join me. We kneel in a circle, take stock of the situation. Three of the soldiers are carrying the M-10. The other two—the boys—are carrying the M-4.

"What platoon?"

A brunette named Stoll—a corporal—says, "We're from Second."

"Anybody see what happened to First? They were up on the ridgeline, by the birch trees."

One of the two boys says, "I saw some of them hauling ass, heading down the slope when the firing broke out. But it looks like most of them got scorched."

"Yeah," the other boy says. "Barbecue bait for sure."

I don't want to think what I'm thinking.

Corporal Stoll says, "Sarge, c'mon, let's get a move on."

"Hold on," I say.

The well-made dirt driveway has narrowed here, and there's muddy, swampy land to each side. Off down at the other end, toward the road and out of view, there are distant shouts, the grumbling of vehicles.

A private with an M-10 nervously looks back. "Hell with this, I'm outta here."

"Hold," I say.

Thor starts whining. He knows what's coming. "Corporal, what's it like out there, on the roadway, just as you come in?"

"Nothing much," she says. "Fields. Pastures."

"Yeah," I say. "Way out in the open. Even if the company starts trucking, they're going to be exposed when the Creepers get there."

"Sure are, and so are we," she says. "So let's hump our way back into the woods and—"

"No," I say. "We're gonna stay here, just for a bit. Slow down the Creepers, give the company a chance to get the hell out."

"No!" a private says.

"Yes," I say.

Another private says, "Corporal, he's not our sergeant, we don't have to listen to him, do we?"

"The name is Sergeant Knox," I say, "and yes, Private, you've all got to listen to me. Right now."

Corporal Stoll gives me the evil eye but she nods and says, "Sergeant?"

I say, "Any of you guys have some Detcord?"

Quick looks all around. Stoll says, "Picard. Give it up."

Private Picard says something nasty for a girl so cute, takes off her battlepack, dives into a pocket and comes out with a coiled length of Detcord, green and waxy looking, like thick string.

Two pine trees are nearby, on either side of the driveway, both leaning in. "Set those two trees to blow, Private, to block this road."

Picard has another private help her, and they work quick and efficiently, wrapping the Detcord around the trunk of each pine, about a foot off the ground. She and the other private—Hopi—attach mechanical matches to the end, yell out, "Fire in the hole!" and pull the trips for each match. They run away from the trees and we join them, going down the driveway, and there's a quick *blam-blam*, and sighing and crunching noises, as the trees separately fall across the driveway.

"Corporal!"

"Sergeant!"

"Whoever paces best from your squad, I want fifty-five meters paced out from the blown trees."

"Not fifty?"

"Fifty-five, and get on it," I say. "Corporal, you and the other M-10 shooters, you're with me."

Luckily for us this is a pretty straightforward stretch of gravel and dirt. Hopi turns, fear on his face, and says, "Clicking! I hear them clicking! They're coming!"

I don't hear a damn thing—understandable because of my bum ear—but I'm sure the private is right.

Another private, walking slowly and deliberately, stops and turns, sliding her booted foot across the dirt. "Fifty-five meters, right here."

"Great."

I take in the situation. Some boulders on either side of the road. Good. "Stoll . . . you and one other M-10 shooter, you're across over there. Ah, Juarez, you're with me."

Stoll starts to the boulders. "What about Hopi and Beverly?"

The two boys with the M-4s stand together, like they're brothers, though one is an American Indian and the other is African-American, but as far as I'm concerned, they're both just Army green.

I waste a few seconds. Current Army doctrine is that even troops armed with M-4s—which could kill a Creeper about the time I'm chosen Army Chief of Staff—should lay down distracting fire, on the off chance that it may indeed wound or kill a Creeper. Plus, it's thought that being close in battle would give M-4 armed soldiers experience of facing the buggy aliens.

Maybe so. I see two kids about twelve or so, in baggy uniforms, huge helmets, and M-4s being held in too-small hands.

"You guys scram," I say. "Hook up with Captain Wallace if you can. We'll . . . we'll be right along presently."

The two young soldiers turn and start running down the dirt and gravel, helmets bouncing on their heads, carrying the M-4s in their grateful hands.

Birds start flying in the same direction. Thor growls. I go across to the other boulder. Juarez has pretty brown eyes, thick black hair, and two simple gold stud earrings. Her fingers are scarred and ridged with burn tissue.

"How's it going, Private?" I ask.

She lifts up her M-10, aims it down at the tree trunk tangle. "Outstanding, Sergeant Knox."

"Glad to hear it." I yell across the lane. "Corporal Stoll! The first Creeper will crawl over that barrier . . . it's ours. You and Picard take the second one as it tries to get over its mate!"

"Got it, Sarge!"

Click-click.

Click-click.

Thor growls even louder. I bring up my loaded M-10, take a breath, quickly lower my left hand, rub his head and back.

"Stay," I say. "Stay."

From surrendering Creepers the day before, to attacking Creepers today.

One hell of a way to run a war, interstellar or otherwise.

"Here they come," Stoll announces, at about the same time the whiff of cinnamon comes our way.

"Yeah."

The lead Creeper is moving quickly on its six mechanized legs, two weaponized claws up in the air, the center arthropod—where the alien is centered—raised upright as well. The exoskeleton is the same blue-gray color as the Dome, and there are two Creepers riding herd right behind her. All three are Battle Creepers, and I don't think they're in the mood for surrendering.

"Ready up," I call out.

The Creeper column is approaching the downed trees. I have a brief, random thought of what this horse farm must have looked like, ten years ago, nice and peaceful and prosperous, plenty of water, power and food, the horses running around safe and free and—

Stop it.

Here we go.

Almost there.

Waiting for the lead Creeper to crawl over the tree trunks, and when it's on the ground—exactly fifty meters away—me and Private Juarez will nail it, just as Stoll and Picard fire at the second Creeper crawling up.

My finger on the trigger.

To Juarez, "When I call it."

"Sergeant."

Right at the tree trunks.

The heavy M-10 is rock-solid in my hands and against my shoulder. Juarez is right next to me, unmoving as well. Thor pants and whines.

There.

And the first Creeper doesn't hesitate, flying over the tree trunks—not crawling, not slowing down—coming right at us.

Chapter Eight

"Fire, fire, fire!" and I pull the trigger, knowing our targeting is off, but we don't have to time to change out the rounds.

BLAM!

BLAM!

Juarez and I eject the spent shells, and I yell, "Fire at will, choose your own range!"

I take another round, spin the base and arm it and see the second Creeper is faltering on the near side of the tree trunks, partially engulfed in a gas cloud from the outgoing rounds. The first Creeper is on the ground. I eyeball where it'll be approaching, and set the round to twenty-five meters—letting Juarez, Stoll and Picard choose their own ranges and targets—and there's another series of loud *BLAMS!* as we all fire once more.

Shouts, yells, and the flickering flashes of laser beams pulse out from the tangle of Creepers in front of us. Juarez and I duck down behind the boulders. I spin the next round to ten meters—after that, we're cooked—and I pop up see the lead Creeper faltering, and I fire off, and so does Juarez, and I duck down, mouth dry, panting, and Juarez looks at my way and says, "Well?"

"Wait," I say. "Let me eyeball."

I peer around the boulders. Two dead Creepers are tangled up by the tree trunks, exoskeleton legs quivering and shaking. Classic dying Creeper moves. It makes me very happy to see that.

But I don't see the third Creeper.

Now I'm not happy.

Did it run back down the driveway? Did it blast its way into the woods, and is it now outflanking us?

I know who can find out.

"Thor! Close hunt! Go!"

Thor blasts out from the boulders, starts going down the driveway, dodging the dying Creepers. On the other side of the gravel and dirt road, I spot Stoll, hunched over. "Private, let's go."

Juarez joins me and I move a few meters and catch a whiff of burnt meat. I bite my lower lip, keep on moving.

Corporal Stoll looks up, eyes wet. Private Picard, the cute girl who reluctantly gave up her private stock of Detcord, is on the ground next to Stoll, not moving. I get off the road and Stoll has Picard's booted feet in her lap. Stoll's hands are shaking.

"I need to get her dog tags," she says. "One set's in her boot laces. I can't find the other set."

I walk around Stoll and my chest feels so heavy it's like it's sagging down my entire torso. Picard is there on the ground, all right, but everything above her upper torso is gone, lasered off. Not much blood because of the instant cauterization, but lots of exposed and burnt bone, muscles and tendons. There are scorched chunks spread about a meter or so from where her body rests, including her helmeted head.

"Give me a sec, Corporal," I say, breathing through my mouth. Juarez is behind me, kneeling down next to her comrade. I walk gingerly, not wanting to touch . . . anything I shouldn't, and I note a small, oblong object. I pick it up and there's a length of chain on it. The surface is scorched but I'm sure it's her ID.

I go back to Stoll, who's still tugging at the tight laces on Picard's right booted foot. "Corporal," I say. "Here's her dog tags. Come on, we've got to get moving."

Her fingers are still tugging at the laces, and Juarez covers one of Stoll's hands with her own scarred fingers. "Corporal, we gotta get outta here. We gotta."

Stoll lowers her head for a second, and I wonder what in hell I'm going to do, when she quickly moves the dead soldier's feet out of her lap and says, "Got it, Sergeant."

She stands up, wipes at her eyes, and says, "Where did the third bug go?"

"Not sure," I say. "My K-9 is out there now, hunting. Let's . . . salvage what we can and get moving."

Stoll says, "Okay, I—"

I say, "No. You and Juarez, you start off. I'll catch up. Do it."

"Her body—"

"I'll take care of it. Get a move on. Now."

Stoll stands still but Juarez picks up her corporal's M-10 and battlepack and starts pulling at her arm. They get moving and I take a glance back at the two dead Creepers and the downed tree trunks. No movement, and no barking, either. A good sign. Thor knows that a "close hunt" means working in a hundred meter circle, and unless the Creeper is close or on the move toward him, he keeps quiet.

The stench of burnt flesh seems to get stronger. What to do?

I could call Thor back, get a move on, and no one would know that I had left the body uncovered, except for Graves Registration, but I'm not too sure when or if they would ever get here. They're one busy outfit.

The empty driveway leading to the roadway, where the company was gathering, looks so damn inviting. It's getting dark. Overhead, some sparks sputter as another chunk of space debris roars through our upper atmosphere. Picard's battlepack is a burnt mess, the only thing surviving a half-burnt Book of Mormon and some socks. Her M-10 is a fused mess. But there are two M-10 rounds that I salvage from her bandolier and slide into mine.

Light's fading fast. The paved road is so very, very close.

So close.

I load up my M-10 with a round aimed for fifty meters, and rest it against a near boulder. There's a dirt depression at the boulder's base, and I kneel down, and start digging and digging. At some point I get up, go over to Picard's boots, pick them up, and drag her over to the hole. She doesn't fit—and I haven't even picked up her head yet—so I go back to digging.

When I finally finish and start back down the driveway, I hear a slight noise and turn and see Thor trotting back, tongue out, looking pretty pleased with himself. I stop, rub his head, and say, "Good boy, good boy," and with no treats or rewards in my coat, I say, "Later, pal, okay? I promise."

I like to think he knows what I'm saying, but his moist brown eyes still look disappointed.

I move at a quick pace down the driveway, over another

little bridge, and then it widens. There are two old stone pillars on either side of the road, and a broken wooden gate I hadn't noticed before. A sign rests against the base of one of the pillars, and in the dimming light, there are some letters saying RING FOR ACCESS and I'm thinking, yeah, I'm sure the goddamn Creepers really rang your bell when they arrived.

Then I step out onto the paved road, and there are Stoll and Juarez, waiting for me, on the other side. The two young boys—Hopi and Beverly—are gone.

And so is everyone else.

I go across and say, "You guys okay?"

Juarez says, "Hanging in there, Sarge. You find that third Creeper?"

"Nope," I say, "and that's fine by me. I think it skittered back to its Dome."

Juarez stands up and so does Stoll, and I look up and down the empty road. By where we're standing there's a mess of discarded bandages, burn ointment packages, some bloody clothing, and a few other pieces of trash. "Corporal, any idea where Captain Wallace would have gone?"

She says, "A number of places. I'd imagine right now she's going to a telegraph office to report what's happened, and to see where Battalion wants her to go."

The road is still empty. "Big view, that makes sense. Small view...where in hell should we go? Up or down?"

Stoll says, "Either one, Sarge."

"I see."

I walk back out to the center of the road, right across from the entrance to the long-ago horse farm. Something catches my eye, a couple of meters up. I walk over and call back to Stoll.

"Your captain...she seems pretty smart."

"Smartest officer I know."

I point down to the cracked asphalt. There's a large arrow, spray-painted in orange, and beneath that, two letters: KK.

Kara's Killers.

"That's where we're going. Saddle up."

We move in a long line along the side of the paved road, with Thor and me on point. Juarez and Corporal Stoll follow behind.

The sky is darkening and around us are nothing but fields, pastures and woods. An empty farmhouse, garage or cottage would have been perfect, but it seems like perfect left a long time ago.

Over in the east there's a long stream of sparks and flares, as more things come back to earth. When we cross over a stone bridge that spans a stream, I say, "All right, this is a good place to hole up for the night."

Juarez and Stoll follow Thor and me into woods that thankfully thin out. There's a slight bowl-like depression that will hide us some from sight, and I say, "This is it."

My two companions don't say much and I'm sure I know what's going on: the usual comedown after a battle, the pain of losing a friend, the jumpiness that comes from knowing you're separated from your unit. I push them so we have a fair site built up, with a small fire hidden in the center, after cleaning out pine needles, pine cones and other flammable materials.

Our meal is bread with meat spread, a soft sloppy quarter-piece of a Hershey's Bar that I've been saving for a special occasion, and water. I give half of my ration to Thor and Juarez rolls herself up in a blanket and instantly falls asleep. I envy her. Stoll stays awake, blanket around her shoulders, staring into the fire.

"What's up, Corporal?"

"Thinking," she says. "Doris, she was a good soldier."

"Doris?"

"Picard," she says. "The one that got barbecued at your little ambush."

"Sorry."

"Yeah, I bet you are."

I reach over, rub Thor's belly. "Something on your mind, Corporal?"

"Just wanted to make sure you knew something about Doris," she says. "Her family was from Utah, here as refugees once the war started. One of five girls, the oldest one. Was pretty religious, which I always ragged her on, considering how God's been otherwise occupied these past ten years. Lately she's been looking for a transfer, provide security and support to the Red Cross. Now . . . well, what's left of her is dumped in an unmarked grave, and for what?"

"To give the rest of the company time to bail out."

"So says you."

I rub Thor's belly even more. "Sorry it happened, Corporal, but that's the way of the world. We blocked the Creepers long enough for the company to get away. Hard facts, but a simple equation."

Thor starts to snore. She folds her arms. "Thing that bugs me ... is who's gonna remember her, besides her family? Who's going to remember her service, what she did for this country, how she died on some crappy driveway from a burnt-out horse farm?"

"We will," I say.

"And what happens if we get scorched tomorrow?"

I say, "I don't plan on dying. And neither should you."

Later she says she'll take first watch, which is fine, and I say I'll take the second watch, in two hours. I curl up with Thor at my back, trying my best to doze off, with the heat of the flames before me. I don't have a blanket in my battlepack, and I do my best with a spare jacket, which I toss over myself. I also keep on my Firebiter upper body armor, as pre-used as it is, for it'll help keep me warm. As my eyes grow heavy, Stoll is still there, awake, staring and staring into the fire.

A nudge. I wake up. My turn for watch, then.

But Stoll and Juarez are both sleeping, both snoring.

What the hell?

Another nudge, and it's Thor, pushing his nose against the back of my neck.

I wake up, tossing off my spare jacket, and check my watch, a wind-up Timex Retro Dad got for me when I was promoted to sergeant. More than three hours have passed. Stoll should have woken me up an hour ago. Damn.

I wonder how much of a fuss I should make when there's another nudge from Thor, and I turn to him, barely visible in the glowing embers, and from his chest is a low, rumbling growl.

"Got it," I whisper.

I gather up my M-10, spare rounds, and make sure my 9 mm Beretta is holstered at my side. I slide away from the fire and say to my K-9 friend, "Thor, lead."

He moves past me but doesn't run. Thor slips through the woods and I do my best to follow, not wanting to trip over a root or to have a branch snap at my face.

We don't go far, ending up at the road, and I make out lights and I think, hey, the company's doubled back, let's run out and get picked up.

But Thor freezes.

And so do I.

I step back, quietly open up my M-10, and by practiced feel, I remove a cartridge, spin it off safe, and set it for ten meters, the closest point allowable for detonation. The snapping back of the bolt seems quite loud in the woods, almost loud enough to drown out what I hear.

Click-click.

Click-click.

I walk slowly to the edge of the woods and brush line, peer through, and then I kneel down, for my legs start shaking.

There are three Creepers out there on the road, close enough for me to toss a rock at them.

Deep breath.

Focus.

One of the Creepers is illuminating the roadway with ... some sort of lighting device at the end of one if its claws, and I recognize this Creeper is a model we've come to call Research. Over the years, this particular model has been seen examining human artifacts, buildings, bridges, doing live vivisection of human prisoners, and other delightful tasks. This one is lighting up part of the roadway.

Two other Creepers—regular Battle—are standing on each side.

Click-click.

Click-click.

I smell cinnamon, nice and thick.

What the hell is going on here?

The Research Creeper's other arm—the one not holding the light—is up in the air, moving around in circles, around and around, like it's looking for something. The two Battle Creepers rotate as well, moving on either side of the Research one.

I nearly scream when something brushes against my arm, and then I calm down.

Only Thor.

He whimpers.

I stroke his head and muzzle, hoping he can't sense the depth of fear coursing through me, for in my years in war and combat, I've never seen anything like this.

And what the hell is that Creeper lighting up anyway?

I shift, get in a better position, and it looks like a discarded bandage.

That's all.

A bandage probably tossed aside or fallen off as the company raced up along this road, driving way from the ambush site.

So what's the interest?

Then the Research Creeper stops, moves around, and the light—

Lights us up like a goddamn bonfire!

I don't dare move.

Don't even dare breath.

Thor is well-trained, and sits still as well.

Click-click.

Click-click.

The damn bugs . . . it's like they're looking for something.

The other arm is still up in the air, moving around.

Or . . . smelling something.

Smelling a trail, then?

The light suddenly moves away from us, and I blink my eyes. I want to reassure Thor, but I don't dare move.

Click-click.

The Research Creeper lowers the moving arm, and then it sprints up the road, followed by the two Battle Creepers.

Following the trail of the company.

Damn.

Back at our little bivouac, I sit and think and brood, and Juarez bestirs herself and says, "Sergeant?"

"Yeah?"

Beside her Corporal Stoll is still sleeping. Juarez says, "Isn't it time for me to take watch?"

"No," I say. "Go back to sleep."

She yawns, rubs at her eyes. "You sure?"

"Oh, yeah," I say. "You know how it is. Burden of command and all that."

Juarez murmurs something and rolls back to sleep. Thor is sleeping as well.

I stay awake.

In the morning breakfast is bread and water and, after policing our bivouac area, we start off with the breaking dawn. We get out to the paved road and I recall last night, seeing that squad of Creepers, checking out the roadway. I had never, ever seen anything like that, and I don't share what I've seen with the two other soldiers. Why give them something else to worry about?

As we step out Corporal Stoll says, "This is one screwed-up war."

"Yeah," I say.

"I mean, last month, we were told the war was over, that the Air Force destroyed the Creepers' orbital base. That was their main base, their headquarters, their ... everything. And with the base destroyed, it was just mopping up."

"Yeah, we got told the same thing. War was over."

"Then ... shit, Albany got hit. What the hell was that, then, if the war was over?"

Juarez speaks up. "Two to make peace, only one to make war. I'd say the surviving aliens didn't think the war was over."

I say, "That sounds about right. At least that one Dome surrendered."

Stoll says, "Yeah, and we were supposed to do it again, back at that farm. The Humvee with the loudspeakers ... it was broadcasting something in Creeper, right? But they came out, pissed and ready to fight. So what happened?"

"There was something wrong with the Humvee's recordings."

Juarez spits on the ground. "Damn understatement there, Sarge."

"You know how it is," I say. "Mistakes were made."

Stoll says, "That could be the name for this war once it ends. The Mistake War."

"Sounds good to me."

We move along and I keep an eye out for a farmhouse, or crossroads or anything that will allow us to scrounge for some food, or to find a landline or telegraph station, but this is one deserted patch of New York landscape. That's easy to understand, with the two Domes just down the street.

Juarez says, "Sarge?"

"Yeah?"

"You smell that?"

I unsling my M-10, bring it around to my front. "Cinnamon?"

"No, diesel."

"Got it."

I hold up my hand, check it out. Up ahead, to the left, some crushed brush and grass. Tire tracks. We move across the road,

I sling my M-10 over my shoulders, and pull out my Beretta. Creepers don't use diesel.

Pulled in is a battered Humvee, and on the side, spray-painted in black stencil lettering, is K A R A ' S   K I L L E R S.

Creepers ain't named Kara.

I peer in the near window. A private is sprawled out in the front seat. His chest is slowly rising up and down. I pound my fist on the hood of the Humvee and he sputters awake, grabbing an M-4, swearing, and I say, "Hey, pal, we seem to have lost K Company. You know where they might be?"

The specialist looks out and says, "Shit, yeah. Up the road a bit."

Stoll looks in as well. "Murphy, what the hell are you doing here?"

"I'm supposed to be rounding up any stragglers from that ambush," he says sheepishly.

I go to the rear, open up the door, help Thor get inside.

"Outstanding, Specialist," I say. "A job well done. Let's get going, all right?"

Chapter Nine

We travel a few more klicks away from that old horse farm. I keep my M-10 at ready access, and a close watch on Thor. But he's content to squeeze in between me and Juarez, and he droops his head over my lap. She rubs the back of his neck, just above his bandages, and he seems to enjoy the attention.

But I still can't get the thought of that Creeper squad last night out of my mind. The way they were moving, the way they were somehow communicating with each other. I've seen Creepers out in the open singly, and operating as a combat line, but I've never seen a trio at work like that, with two Battle Creepers escorting a Research Creeper.

And one other thing I've never seen before is the way that first Creeper had leaped over the log barrier back at the driveway. Creepers can crawl, run, and move at various speeds. But jump like that?

Two unseen things in one day. I didn't like that.

Murphy knows where he's going, and we go down one unmarked road, take a right at another unmarked road. There are a few farmhouses now, with early morning wood smoke rising up into the gray sky. Nice to see some life, even if it is hidden away. The land thins out and for a minute or two, we travel parallel to a set of railroad tracks. Right near the tracks is a long line of overturned Amtrak passenger train cars, and the sides of the train are scorched and lasered-open, windows shattered, metal rusting. It looks like the train had been attacked right after the war started. Based on what I know, it was probably one of the last of the refugee trains, desperately getting out of the Hudson Valley to some mythical place of safety.

I turn away.

The Humvee turns as well, down a dirt road. Our driver comes to a complete halt.

Waits.

Waves an arm out of the open side window.

Waits.

Ahead I think I see a flicker of light, like a flashlight or lantern being used, and then, after the hidden sentries clear us, we start going down the dirt road again. We head to the left and find Company K.

"Nice driving," I say from the back.

He says, "Don't get paid to get lost in this woman's Army, that's for damn sure."

The vehicles from the convoy are scattered around a wooded area that has plenty of open, flat spaces for parking. The near vehicle is one of the Strykers, its grenade launcher pointed down the road. Camouflaged netting is overhead, and small fires are lit. Our driver says, "Let me get you to Second Platoon," and I say, "I need to see Captain Wallace first."

"But she told me that I was gonna bring any stragglers back to their platoons."

"I'm not a straggler," I say. "I was fighting a rear-guard action, and I need to see Captain Wallace."

He shrugs, turns us down a lane. "Whatever. You get to face her, not me. She's in a mood, for damn sure."

I say so long to Stoll and Juarez, and Thor stays by my side and I notice his bandages are dirty. Time to get them changed. Up ahead is the command Humvee, with a tarp and camouflaged netting stretched overhead. At a table covered with maps and dirty mess dishes I find Captain Wallace and my dad, along with two platoon lieutenants—Morneau and Jackson—along with Sergeant Bronson and First Sergeant Hesketh. Dad sees me and calls out, "Randy!"

"Good morning, Colonel," I say, conscious of him being around this unit's command structure.

He gets up and comes around the table, shakes my hand,

slaps me on the shoulder, and then squats down, rubbing Thor's ears. "How about a treat, buddy?"

My stomach is grumbling but I say, "That'd be great, Colonel. He's overdue."

Dad picks through his plate, picks up a couple of bacon rinds, and walks over to Thor, as Bronson says, "Where the hell have you been, Knox?"

"Nice to see you, too, Sergeant Bronson," I say.

Bronson says, "I asked you a question, Sergeant Knox."

"I was unavoidably detained," I say.

Captain Wallace's face is scarlet, and her eyes are reddened. "Knox, stop it right now. Answer Sergeant Bronson's question."

I say, "With the . . . redeployment from the two Domes, I encountered five troopers from the Second Platoon. I believe we were among the last to leave the area. We were proceeding along the dirt driveway, following K Company's vehicles."

"But you didn't get there in time," she says. "Why?"

"Ma'am, we came across a narrow spot in the driveway that seemed to be a good place to set up a counter-ambush, to slow down Creepers in pursuit."

"What did you do?"

"With the assistance of two troopers from the First Platoon, we dropped tree trunks across the road," I say. "Three Battle Creepers came at the barrier approximately five minutes later."

Dad says, "That's . . . unusual. Creepers usually return to their Dome after an attack."

"That's what happened," I say. "We engaged the Creepers, killed two. One retreated."

"Any casualties?" Wallace asks.

"Specialist . . ." God, don't let me forget her name, and thankfully, it comes up. "Picard. Doris Picard. Killed instantly. Corporal Stoll secured one set of her dog tags."

Bronson doesn't look too happy and Wallace rubs at her eyes. "Damn . . . that makes four KIA and seven wounded from that screwed-up mission. We're already thinned out . . . we can't be effective with these casualties . . . especially unnecessary ones."

Wallace seems to snap into focus and her green eyes bore right into me. "You. You're the one who warned me that something was wrong, that the voice from those speakers wasn't right. Explain yourself, Sergeant."

Dad catches my eye and I'm not sure what he wants, so I decide to tell the truth. "Two days ago, when we got the Dome opened and the seven Creepers surrendered, it was due to Buddy Coulson and his knowledge of their language. He told them to surrender, and they did."

She says, "That was the son of that major from Special Projects... Coulson."

"Correct, ma'am."

"How did he learn the Creeper language?"

Dad is really staring at me, even though Thor is licking his fingers. I say, "I'm not sure. All I know is that he learned the language, and I... encouraged him to talk to the Creepers and have them surrender, ma'am."

Her eyes slightly widen. "You're telling me that a boy that's not even old enough to shave got those Creepers to surrender? After ten years of war?"

"Yes, ma'am."

"And did he come up with this idea all on his own? Just decided to stroll up to that Creeper Dome and start talking to them?"

I pause. "No. I encouraged him, ma'am."

"I see. And what brought you to this realization?"

"It seemed... there was an opportunity at the time. With Buddy and his language skills. With a Creeper Dome nearby. And... the Creepers, they had captured my dad and Major Coulson and were bringing them both to the Dome. There was a skirmish. I killed a Creeper... and I was determined to exploit the situation."

Everyone in the tent is staring at me. I'm sure Wallace was briefed on what happened but I don't think she's heard all of the details. Wallace says, "You said you encouraged young Buddy Coulson to speak to the Creepers. I understand he has difficulty... talking to people. How did you encourage him?"

I say, "I put my Beretta against the back of his neck and threatened to blow his head off." A pause. "Ma'am."

Wallace returns to the map and says, "We're going back to Battalion, back to S-2, to give them a full debrief of this fiasco. And then I'm going to track down that Langley man, Cranston Hoyt, and..."

She doesn't have to finish what she's saying. While I enjoyed the comfort and food of Hoyt's Winnebago, I sure as hell don't envy what's approaching him. Wallace scribbles something down, Dad returns to his spot by the table, and I say, "Ma'am?"

She doesn't look up. "Yes, what is it, Sergeant?"

"I . . . saw two curious events yesterday, ma'am, that I think you should know about."

Bronson steps in. "Save it for later, Knox. We're going back to the First Platoon."

She looks up. "No, go on. What did you see?"

"At the ambush site on the farm's driveway," I say. "A Battle Creeper approached the trees that had been dropped across the road. The Creeper didn't crawl over it. It flew."

I feel everyone's look is right on me. Wallace says, "It . . . flew?"

One of the platoon lieutenants, the black guy Jackson, says, "Creepers don't fly."

"Or jumped," I say. "The barricade didn't slow it down. It went right over it."

Bronson seems to be trying to hide a smile. So does Lieutenant Cooper. Wallace says, "I see. That was the first incident. What was the second?"

"Last night, with the two troopers with me, we bivouacked at the side of the road. I had the watch. My dog Thor responded to Creeper sign. The two of us went out to the edge of the woods, by the road, and observed three Creepers."

Wallace says, "Where were they heading?"

"At that point, ma'am, they weren't heading anywhere. They . . . were stopped. One was a Research Creeper. It was examining a piece of clothing . . . from a wounded trooper, I'm sure. It . . . it was studying it. The other two Creepers, they were Battle Creepers. It was like they were escorting the Research Creeper."

"How long did they examine the piece of clothing?"

"About five minutes or so."

Bronson says, "Why didn't you attack?"

Good question. I say, "Sergeant, we were exhausted. Corporal Stoll and Private Juarez were fast asleep. I decided the best approach was to leave them be."

Wallace says, "What happened after the clothing examination?"

I hesitate for the briefest of seconds. There was that moment last night when I felt like the Research Creeper was staring right at me, even past my hiding place, and didn't do a thing, and moved on. But how could I say that without them thinking I've gone nuts?

I say, "They kept the piece of clothing. They moved on up the road."

Dad looks to Wallace and says, "This report should get up to S-2 Battalion, as soon as possible, Captain. With the failed ambush at those two Domes, and this unusual Creeper behavior, something is going on."

"Agreed," Wallace says. "Sergeant . . . write up your report, present it to me, and then get something to eat. We're going to be on the move in an hour . . ." and for a brief moment, she smiles. It's a wonderful sight. "We'd hate to leave you behind for a second time."

The meeting breaks up and although I don't want to, I sidle up to Bronson and say, "The Captain wants a report from yesterday and last night."

"Yeah, I was there," he says. "A report about dreaming shit, that's what she's gonna get. Flying Creepers. Creepers sniffing clothes."

I gently place my hand on his upper arm and say, "Bronson, what did I ever do to you? Huh? Give it a break. I need to file a report. Where can I get some paper around this joint?"

He shakes off my touch. "You're so smart, I'm sure you'll figure it out."

Bronson stalks away from me and Thor is by my side, and I look to him. "I've said it once if I've said it a million times. The more I spend time with you, bud, the better I like dogs than humans."

Thor doesn't look up. His nose is twitching, and I think he's trying to find some more bacon.

I say, "If you're going to sniff something out, how about some paper?"

I start walking.

I don't think I'm that smart, but after a few questions I hook up with the quartermaster's truck, the one that had supplied me with a spare uniform and the soiled Firebiter protective vest that I still have on. I tell Corporal Cellucci what I need and she goes back into the truck and comes back with a white legal pad of paper. "How's your handwriting?"

"Passable."

She eyes me from her perch up on the rear of the truck. "A report for the captain."

"That's right."

"Can you type?"

"Sure," I say. "At Fort St. Paul, we take classes when we're not on duty. One of my best ones was typing."

"Here," she says. "Take this."

I take the pad. She goes back into the truck and comes out with something that looks like a small, metallic suitcase. She jumps down, puts the suitcase on the truck floor, unsnaps and opens it up. It's a small, portable typewriter. I whistle in appreciation.

"You promise not to pound the crap out of it, and if you can write your report on a single page, do it here," she says.

I gently tear a sheet of paper off the pad. "Thanks a lot, Corporal."

"No problem," she says. "Besides, I hear Bronson's been riding your skinny ass since you hooked up with us. You deserve a break, I guess. Sergeant."

I take the precious sheet of paper, roll it into the typewriter. "He sure is. Any idea why? He doesn't like New Hampshire or something?"

"No, he hates you," she says.

I stop rolling the sheet of paper. "C'mon. I've never met him before. Why in hell would he hate me?"

Corporal Cellucci hoists herself up back into the truck. "Because he blames you for his family. You see, his mom, dad, and younger sister, they lived outside of Albany. This company was ordered right to that neighborhood, to help with relief and recovery. Then we got detoured to meet up with you folks."

I go back to working the piece of paper into the typewriter. "Not my fault."

"Yeah, I know, but that's logical. And when does logic have anything to do with the Army?"

I type slowly and deliberately, not wanting to make any mistakes or strikeovers, and I pause a lot between sentences, knowing I only have a single sheet of paper to do my report. I carefully gauge the sentence length in my head, and then, just when I'm finished, I pause, fingers over the keyboard.

Corporal Cellucci sees that I've paused. "What's up, Knox?"

"I'm trying to decide how to sign it."

"If you can't write your name, make an X and I'll witness it," she says.

"Hah hah," I reply. "No ... I'm wondering if I should sign this under my name and unit, or my name and your unit."

"Sorry, don't understand the issue."

I say, "Yesterday Captain Wallace said I was assigned to Company K, First Platoon."

"She say that official?"

"Yeah."

She picks up a clipboard and pencil. "Then best you sign it like you've been with us since you were twelve, or Captain Wallace will be one pissed-off c.o. And you might end up in armory support, cleaning weapons. That sound like fun?"

"No, it doesn't," I say.

I type in SGT. R. KNOX, FIRST PLATOON, K COMPANY, 14TH RGT. I gently roll the sheet of paper out, and feeling like I'm an imposter, I scrawl my signature above it.

I fold the sheet in thirds, the quartermaster corporal staples it together, and I say, "Do you know where Captain Wallace is?"

She smiles. "Sorry, not my day to watch her. Wander around, you'll find her. That's what she likes to do ... wander around, sticking her big nose in things, keeping us on our toes."

"Thanks."

With Thor by my side, off we go.

I do ask around the encampment, and no one's too sure where the Captain has ended up. I pass Bronson and decide to keep on passing him, so he can keep his bitter mood all to himself. I also pass by the mess tent—just a huge tarp with some portable stoves being watched over by two cooks—and Thor whines, and I know he's telling me how hungry he is.

"Lighten up, big guy," I say. "At least you got something to munch on from Dad."

But there's no line at the serving counter, and I'm so tempted to stop and grab some late breakfast. Yet I recall what Captain Wallace earlier told me to do: write the report, present it to her, and then get something to eat.

Near the other Stryker, there's a call of, "Sergeant Knox!" and coming around the corner with rags and a wrench in her hand is

Private Balatnic. Seeing her smiling and slim face under her huge helmet just makes me feel warm and comfortable for a moment. The last time I saw her had been up at by the birch tree back at the horse farm, before everything went south with a vengeance.

"Hey, Private, good to see you," I say.

Still holding the wrench, she wipes at her hands and says, "Good to see you, too. Last time we were together . . . thanks for helping me out back there."

"Glad to do it," I say. "Hey, think you could help me out?"

"Sure."

"I'm trying to track down Captain Wallace. So far, no joy."

Balatnic points with her wrench. "I saw her go over there, just five minutes ago."

I look to "over there." Just an open spot between two pine trunks. "Where does that go to? A latrine or something?"

"Beats the hell out of me," Balatnic says.

An older soldier by the front of the Stryker yells out, "Hey, Private Balatnic, we still got work over here if you can tear yourself away!"

"Coming, Sergeant!" she yells back, and with another smile, she goes back to work, and I go into the woods.

There's not much of a path but I can see where someone has been, by the disturbed pine needles on the forest floor, a couple of small, broken or bent branches. I feel silly walking through, carrying an officially typed report in hand, but orders were orders: Captain Wallace wanted my report, and I wasn't about to give it to her first sergeant or anyone else.

Thor pokes around and then stops. I stop as well.

There's nothing unusual that I can tell is going on, no smell of cinnamon, no *click-click* noises.

But he's stopped.

"Stay," I say, and I push ahead.

I now hear a stream, and the woods open up and I see some large boulders on either side of the flowing water. I push forward and there's a small tumble of rocks before me, then a larger boulder, right by the boulder, and sitting there, all by herself, is Captain Wallace.

I start to open my mouth and just as quickly close it.

Wallace has her helmet off, as well as her protective gear and

MOLLE vest and everything else. Her torso is just clad in an olive-drab T-shirt, torn and repaired here and there, and she's hugging herself tight, rocking back and forth, back and forth, and she's sobbing.

I'm frozen in place.

Wallace's face is bright red and tears are wetting her cheeks, and I recall the last time I saw her, back under the tarp by her command Humvee, and her eyes were swollen there as well.

The sobbing continues, and I feel like I'm intruding and violating something very private, something that no one in the company should see or know about, and I step back.

And knock over a rock.

Wallace lowers her arms, picks up a 9 mm pistol, whirls and aims at me.

I freeze again.

She stares at me, cheeks wet, eyes red and swollen.

I don't know what to say.

So I don't.

I hold up my carefully written and typed report, lower it down on top of a near boulder, put a smaller rock on top of it.

Hands up again, I slowly turn and walk back into the woods, and Thor is there, waiting patiently for me.

"Come," I say, and we go back to the encampment.

Chapter Ten

I do get something to eat, though being one of the last ones through the line, it's cold coffee—with grounds floating around the bottom—and equally cold oatmeal and strips of bacon. But since they were about to clean up, I managed to get double rations for Thor and me.

He sits by my feet and I hand him cold lumps of oatmeal, which he nuzzles and leaves alone, and I give him greasy strips of bacon, which he eagerly takes. I rub his head and see the gray and black of his bandages, and when I bring my dishes back, I ask one of the cooks, "Where's the medical tent?"

"Over yonder," he says, "and best you hurry up. We're heading out in about ten."

I go over to where I think yonder is, and there's a Humvee with a Red Cross trailer. A plump female captain wearing eyeglasses and a white coat with captain's bars on the collar is at the rear of the open trailer, carefully putting cardboard boxes in place.

"Captain Pulaski?"

"The same," she says.

"May I see you for a moment?"

Back still turned, she says, "Sick call was at eight a.m. That was nearly two hours ago. Unless you're gonna die in front of me, I suggest you wait until sick call this evening."

"But it's not for me, Captain."

She starts to say, "Well, who's it for then—" but she turns

and halts, and she smiles widely. "Well, look at you, you good-looking boy."

I know she's not talking to me, and I'm okay with that. She comes down and kneels in front of Thor, rubs his ears, scratches his chin, gently pats the side where he's bandaged, and checks the cast on one of his legs.

"What's this brave fellow's name?"

"Thor."

"How long has he been with you?"

"Two years."

"Handsome, handsome lad."

Thor is open to meeting new people, and can either be reserved or fall all over himself to show affection. For Dr. Pulaski, he goes around in a circle a couple of times, and then gently flops over, paws drooping, tongue oozing from his mouth, bandaged belly exposed.

Dr. Pulaski laughs and gently strokes his belly, and I say, "Don't let appearances fool you. He can be a stone-cold killer when he wants to be."

"Mmm, I'm sure," she says. "What does he need?"

"His bandages are getting pretty dirty. I was hoping they could get changed out."

"Excellent idea. Hold on for a second."

The veterinarian-turned-people-doctor gets up and goes back into the trailer, moves a few things here and there, and then comes out. She kneels down and says, "Okay, Thor, let's see what's what. Will you stand for me?"

Thor does just that and she starts cutting away the bandages with a small pair of scissors. Thor stands there stoically, letting her work. She gently unrolls the bandages, exposing burnt-off fur, burnt and sutured skin. Tears come to my eyes, but Dr. Pulaski talks to Thor in a soothing voice, checks his skin, and slathers on some ointment.

"Somebody did nice work here. The cast is in pretty good shape, too. Who was it?"

"Hero Kennels, outside of Albany."

She nods. "Know it well. They do good work."

"Do...do you know if they survived the attack on the capitol?"

"Beats me, Sergeant," she says, unrolling a fresh bandage spool. "If there was any mercy in this world—which I now sincerely doubt—dogs and cats would never, ever be hurt again. Okay, pal, let's put on a fresh bandage."

She gently works on my boy, and I'm happy to see the snow-white fresh bandage being wrapped around him. "Those sutures are looking good. They can probably come out next week. Where did he get these injuries?"

"Creeper attack."

"He with you at the time?"

"Yeah."

"Battle Creeper?"

"No," I say, recalling that desperate one-man and one-dog stand we did together, on our journey last week to Albany. "Transport Creeper...it was moving on a refugee camp, Brooklyn North."

She fastens the bandage and rubs Thor's head. "I thought I recognized you. There was a little story in *Stars & Stripes*, with a photo. You're the sergeant who killed that Creeper by knifing the crawling bastard. Yeah...hell, you got the Silver Star for that, didn't you? From the President himself, at the Red House."

I stand up. "Thanks for taking care of Thor."

She gets up, too. "My pleasure. It's nice to go back to my roots. At least dogs, cats and horses...they may whine, but they sure as hell don't complain all the time."

Pulaski gathers up the bandage scraps and says, "Hold on for a second, will you?"

"Yes, ma'am."

Back into the trailer again, and there's a thumping noise, and she swears, and then she emerges. "Here. Thought I had some left."

She's holding a clear plastic bag, tied at the top. There's a colored cardboard box inside. She opens the bag, revealing... an old box indeed. Dog biscuits. The lettering is faded but still readable: MILK BONE.

Thor whines some, wags his tail. Even I can smell the dog biscuits. Pulaski reaches into the faded box. "I can't tell you how long I've kept these, or how many times I've been tempted to empty it. When we've been traveling hard, not stopping for meals. Or the times we were on short rations. Or the times civilians have come by, begging for food, for scraps, for anything edible."

She took the biscuit out, broke it in three pieces. "But our dogs...most of the time they're starved or roaming without a home. If I can, I give those dogs I find a little something special."

Thor lifts up his head, gingerly takes the offered dog treat from her hand, and licks her fingers. "There's nothing wrong in that, is it? I mean...if there's anything I hate about the Creepers is the way they've killed, and keep on killing, the innocents. Humans...we're all guilty of something. But dogs...cats... horses...why should they die?"

Another dog biscuit is offered and gently consumed. "Maybe I'm more guilty than others. Maybe these dog biscuits should have gone to a starving old woman, or a hungry child...But I don't think I did anything wrong."

She looks to me and I say, "I think you're right."

A smile. "I think you might be lying, but that's okay. I made my peace years ago." To Thor she says, "One last bite, friend," and the broken biscuit is gone. But she takes out one more, hands it to me, and says, "For later."

"Thanks," I say, as I slide the precious treat into my coat pocket.

"There," she says, wrapping the plastic tight again with the Milk Bone box inside. "Enough left for a while. In the meantime, word I hear is that we're heading back to Battalion after fueling up at Vihan's Crossroads. Better food, bunks and showers. Get yourself squared away, sonny."

It's been a long time since I've allowed an adult to call me sonny, but considering what she did for my best bud, I let it slide and leave to get squared away.

Back with First Platoon, I help Thor up in the truck, and climb up, seeing Balatnic and De Los Santos. There's slightly more room than yesterday, and I know better than to ask: I'm sure the extra space here is due to yesterday's casualties. The truck starts up and other engines grumble as well, and I take a quick look around. I'm stunned at what I see, or what I don't see. The place looks like no one had been here, everything's gone, no scraps of trash or debris left behind.

I say to Balatnic, "Your captain runs a tight outfit."

"None tighter," she says, and a few of the other soldiers snort or make rude noises. I check out who's on the truck and with a trace of innocence in my voice—just a trace, mind you—ask, "Where's Sergeant Bronson?"

De Los Santos adjusts his eye patch. "I hear he has a blister on a foot."

Another soldier says, "Maybe his butt."

"Or his head," someone adds.

De Los Santos says, "There's a difference?"

Laughter, as the First Platoon leaves the bivouac, and goes out to join the other vehicles. The wind feels good against my face and for once, I have a relatively full belly after my late breakfast. Two soldiers are up forward, leaning over the truck cab, one with an M-4, the other with an M-10, just in case we run into enemies, either foreign or domestic. The rest of us, me included, stretch out, try to get some rack, because one of the oldest rules in any army—past, present and future—is that you sleep and eat whenever you can.

So we travel, and run right into the other army rule, that things can go to shit in seconds.

Up ahead there's a roar of horns blaring, in a staccato pattern, and First Platoon is up as one, ready to go, weapons in hand. I don't know what the hell is going on but I'm on my feet, too, as the truck brakes to a halt at the side of the road. Balatnic and another soldier drop the tailgate, and out there the two lieutenants and Sergeant Bronson are screaming, "Go! Go! Go! Perimeter B, set up Perimeter B!"

I don't know what that means, so I stick with Balatnic as she races to the side of the road and flops down. The truck starts up and backs away, the rear gears whining, and the other trucks move away as well.

We're now on foot.

I smell smoke.

I look down the road, at the roadhouse, and there's just a billowing cloud of smoke. Thor is with me, whining, and I tell him to settle down, which he does, reluctantly.

"Shit," De Los Santos says. "Vee's place got torched."

More obscenities, but we keep our position, aiming our weapons up the road where the trucks have disappeared. Their departure makes sense but still leaves a bitter taste in my mouth, for it clearly signals that the trucks are precious, to be saved, and us grunts aren't.

A Stryker grinds its way past us, goes over a crumbling stone wall, takes up position overlooking a pasture.

The smoke drifts to us, along with something else.

The smell of cinnamon.

I check Thor. He's panting but looking around, definitely on alert. A runner comes up the road, says, "First Platoon? First Platoon?"

"Here," Bronson answers.

The runner—a girl maybe twelve or so, not even bothering to wear a helmet—says, "Sergeant Knox. The captain needs to see Sergeant Knox."

Before Bronson can answer for me, I'm up with my M-10 and Thor, and we follow the runner down the road.

I guess the sight of the burning building is heartbreaking, and I'm sure it is, but I don't have time to process that. The roadhouse has collapsed upon itself, burning along, and there's a prewar pickup truck and automobile that's been scorched. The trees around the dirt parking lot have been burnt too, and the smell of cinnamon is stronger. There are laser burns along the surviving parts of the walls, and Captain Wallace is there, with First Sergeant Hesketh and Dad. A young Indian boy is standing there, one of the kids from the day before who had served tea. His cheeks are moist with tears and his legs are shaking.

Wallace says, "Sergeant Knox."

"Ma'am."

"Three Creepers attacked this location an hour ago," she says. "You said you had an encounter earlier this morning with three Creepers. True?"

"Yes, ma'am."

She says, "Mohammed, Vee's son here, he says they were three Battle Creepers. But you say otherwise."

"Yes, ma'am," I say. "There were two Battle Creepers and one Research Creeper."

Dad softly says, "The boy might be wrong."

"He might," Wallace says. "He just might."

She squats down before him, wets her thumb, wipes some soot away from his cheeks. The poor kid looks like he's a thousand klicks away. "Okay, fella, let's say you come with us for a while, okay?"

He nods, snorts some snot from his nose. First Sergeant Hesketh puts a large hand behind the boy's head, moves him to a parked Humvee on the other side of the parking lot. The fires are continuing, and when Hesketh returns from placing the kid inside the Humvee, Wallace says, "First Sergeant, get a couple of details together. See what we can salvage, but make it quick. I want to get on the road and to Battalion as quick as we can."

She looks around, sniffs the air, and then looks to me. "Your dog. He sensing anything?"

"Only that the Creepers were here," I say. "They're not here now."

"Yeah, thanks for that news flash," she says, and she looks at me oddly, like she's trying to see if I'm going to say anything about our brief encounter this morning, but she's not going to get anything from me at the moment.

Dad says, "Without the resupply, will we make it to Battalion?"

Wallace sighs. "Yeah. But not with the margin of safety I'd like. Damn it."

"If I can make a suggestion, there's an Air Force station within driving distance."

"Griffis? Nothing there but white coats and jet jockeys crying over their dead Eagles and Falcons."

"But there's resources there and—"

Wallace says, "With all due respect, Colonel Knox, no. We're heading to Battalion. That's it."

Dad just nods and I say, "Captain... where's the rest of the boy's family?"

She rubs at her eyes. "Over there," she says, and "over there" is the still burning rubble of the roadhouse.

In ten minutes we're on the road once more, and there's no more sleeping or goofing around in the rear of the truck. Everybody is up with their weapons at the ready, either M-4s or M-10s, and De Los Santos calls out, "Hey, Sully! This bring back any fond memories, you doing the Thunder Run back at Baghdad?"

Thunder Run, one of the ballsiest moves an armored unit ever did: back in 2003 when a task force with the Third Infantry Division roared right up a highway into the center of Baghdad, in a probing move to see how deep and organized the Iraqi defenses were. Long story short, they weren't deep or organized, but those armored forces racing in didn't know that.

Sully looks around, white hair visible underneath his helmet. His eyes are dark and unblinking. "Didn't like it back then. Used to have nightmares about it. Now it seems like a goddamn summer vacation."

Nobody says anything to that, and the convoy moves along. A couple of horns blare, and the convoy starts moving at different speeds, braking, swerving, slowing down and speeding up. De Los Santos sees my expression and says, "If we don't got time to hide out from the killer stealth satellites, we keep hauling ass and swerve around, try to screw up their targeting."

"It works, then?"

"We're still here, ain't we?" A couple of soldiers near De Los Santos laugh, but not Sully. His hands are tight on his M-4.

The road narrows and there's so much overgrowth and trees growing overhead that I can't tell where we're going, or what's behind the tree line. Could be a bunch of farms or small towns or whatever, but the green stuff grows fast when there's no more landscaping or highway departments around to trim it back.

A honk of horns from up ahead. We pass a faded yellow sign, with black letters faded to gray. BRIDGE AHEAD. A bolt has come loose and the sign hangs at an angle, which is okay, I guess, for it's no longer accurate.

There's no more bridge ahead.

It's been freshly dropped into a deep river valley, and there's only one explanation:

Creepers.

Chapter Eleven

I get out and walk over to the command Humvee, where a map has been spread out, and Captain Wallace, Dad, and First Sergeant Hesketh are talking.

While looking at her map, the captain shakes her head and says, "Well, we've just lost the best route back to Rome and Battalion." Wallace folds up the map and looks at the dropped bridge. "Between them destroying Vee's place, and knocking this bridge down, those buggy bastards are beginning to get on my nerves. First Sergeant."

"Ma'am," he says in his raspy voice.

"Get the platoon leaders over there. We need to get this convoy turned around and headed . . . well, headed up to the next main intersection, where Route 113 crosses over. We might run out of fuel before we get to Battalion, but we'll be close enough to hump it in if we have to."

"Captain," Dad says.

"Colonel," she briskly replies, folding up her map.

"With this latest development, I strongly recommend that you deploy your unit to Griffis," he says. "Check your map, the location of battalion HQ and the Air Force base are nearly the same distance apart."

"True, Colonel, but at least I know when I'm running out of fuel and provisions outside of Battalion, I'll have friendly faces waiting for me when I walk in. I can't guarantee the same for Griffis."

"Ma'am, I believe the right decision is—"

"—not going to Griffis," she says, handing over her map to First Sergeant Hesketh. "We roll in there, we might get a smile or two and a dry corner in an empty warehouse to sack out, but as far as fuel and other supplies… paperwork will have to be filled out, requisitions processed, and maybe some command-level bickering and decision-making. And a week or two later, then we'll be able to move. Ain't gonna happen."

"Captain—"

"Colonel, this convoy is moving out. If you don't want to walk or borrow a courier bicycle, I suggest you climb into the nearest Humvee."

The command Humvee is the closest, but Dad's eyes are flashing behind his brand-new Army-issued eyeglasses, and he says, "Captain, I believe there's an opening in the lead Stryker for a passenger. You'll find me there."

"Very well," she says, and Wallace sees I'm still standing there, and I quickly get the hell out.

There's a quick mess of maneuvering and backing up and making turns, but K Company, "Kara's Killers," are back on the road, reversing course away from the destroyed bridge. De Los Santos settles in with a grunt and says, "Quick reaction force my ass, all we're doing is going around in circles."

In the back, the old soldier—Sully—laughs and says, "When my uncle joined up, last century, the Army promised him he could see the world. Guess he never expected that one of these days, another world would come to see us."

Big laughs at that. Up overhead more sparkles and flares of light as space debris reenters the Earth's atmosphere, burning up.

The convoy picks up speed. Clouds move in. All about us are abandoned homes and farms. Lots of survivors picked up and moved in closer to villages and towns, for better defense at night, when the Coasties came out, or when hungry neighbors decided to raid not-so-hungry neighbors.

We dodge some old wreckage. A Greyhound bus, pulled over to the side, rusting bullet holes in the side, tires long ago flattened, all the windows gone. I'm pretty sure it's apparent what happened there, years back. A bus full of refugees, not stopping when told to, and then a firefight.

Nobody on the truck says anything as we go by.

Rain starts, gentle at first, and then comes down pretty steady. Some groans as we all retrieve our rain gear, and Thor stands up all fours, standing still.

He starts to whine.

Balatnic says, "Your pup doesn't like rain?"

"No, it's not that," I say.

Thor is tense, trembling. His whining increases. I take in our surroundings. Low rock walls, some brush, and empty fields on either side that look like they might be mowed occasionally for hay.

Barking now.

I get up. "Creeper sign. We got Creepers nearby."

The soldiers look up at me, and they go for their weapons, and somebody up forward shouts to the driver.

"Creepers!"

"Hey, we got Creeper sign!"

"Pull the truck over, pull it over!"

The truck is rattling and shaking, and I push my way to the cab, holding onto the side so I don't fall on my ass. Thor is behind me, barking frantically, and I hang over the side and yell in at the driver, "We got Creeper sign! Pull it over!"

A young soldier, thirteen or so, the steering wheel enormous against his skinny chest. "No! I got orders! Keep up with the Humvee in front of me!"

"Pull it over!"

"No!"

It takes some maneuvering and I almost drop the damn thing over the side, but I get my Beretta out and shove it against the driver's ear.

"Now or I take your head off!" I yell. "And signal the convoy we got Creeper sign!"

For such a young soldier he has an impressive collection of obscenities, and he brakes hard, jogging us over to the side of the wet road. He pounds the horn and the tail gate rattles down, and the First Platoon jumps down, and they look to me and I say, "First Squad, take position across the road, behind the stone wall. Second Squad, this side of the road is all yours."

I rush forward, slap the side of the driver's door and say, "Move it! Get this truck out of here!"

In front of us and behind us, other vehicles of the convoys

have stopped. The rear Stryker has halted, other soldiers are start-ing to deploy and, following the First Platoon's lead, are setting up skirmish lines behind the stone walls. Sergeant Bronson runs up to me and screams, "Who the hell told you to pull your truck over? And who the hell told you to take command?"

I push by him, heading to the command Humvee. "Question one, my dog Thor. Question two, check in with me later."

He grabs my shoulder and I spin by him, and Thor is now barking hard, and I say, "Hunt, Thor, hunt!"

He races by me, and even with bandages and a cast on one leg, he scales the stone wall, heads out into the field. Bronson yells at me, "Your damn dog's gone crazy! There's nothing out there!"

I race ahead, getting to the command Humvee, and Captain Wallace is out, binoculars in hand, and sees me approaching and it looks like she's conflicted about a lot of things, but she just says, "Report."

"My K-9 unit detects Creeper sign."

"Close?"

"Very close," I say. "He's out in that field right now."

Thor is racing across the field, going parallel to the road. Nothing else is in sight. The tall blonde woman lieutenant—MORNEAU—says, "Looks like a false sign. There's nothing over there."

I say, "Thor doesn't react to false signs."

The lieutenant gives me a smug look. She's probably all of eighteen. "Always a first time."

"Not with Thor," I say.

First Sergeant Hesketh says, "Ma'am?"

She really gives me a hard look and says, "Skirmish lines, up and down the road. Evacuate all vehicles except the Strykers. Make it standard, First Sergeant."

"Yes, ma'am," he replies, and the older lieutenant shakes her head at me and heads to her platoon, and in a few minutes, the trucks and Humvees have scampered back down the road, leav-ing the company and two Strykers.

Rain is coming down heavier.

Thor is still out there, running back and forth, back and forth.

Wallace says quietly, "Eager dog you've got there, Sergeant Knox."

"Yes, ma'am."

"I hear you're the one that stopped us here, and you even deployed First Platoon, and not Sergeant Bronson. True?"

"Yes, ma'am."

She says, "Seems like you and your dog share an eagerness quotient. Get the hell back to First Platoon."

"Yes, ma'am," I say, and I spot Dad, standing by himself, a pistol in his hand, looking pretty damn lost. I run back to the First Platoon and Sergeant Bronson comes up to me and whispers harshly, "Just wait 'til the end of the day, Knox."

"You and I are still walking and breathing around then, Bronson, you got it."

I join the other soldiers in a shallow ditch, up against a stone wall, overgrown with grass and moss. The rain is coming down heavier. They look scared, wet, hungry and...scared. No brave thin red line here. And speaking of brave, their platoon leader is with the Second Squad, on the other side of the road, opposite the field where Thor is running back and forth, making a ruckus.

Up the line there's movement as Second Platoon prepares and I say, "Balatnic, how far off is my dog?"

She raises her head a bit. "About twenty-five meters, Sergeant."

"First Squad, those with M-10s, cycle in for twenty-five meters, load up. Those with M-4s, make sure you're locked and loaded."

I remove a cartridge, spin the base to twenty-five meters, load up, and wait, the barrel of my M-10 on top of the stone wall.

Thor is barking hysterically, sitting at one point. Somebody whispers, "Somebody shut that dog up."

I whisper back, "You shut up. That dog is saving your life."

I hear "Prove—" and I'm sure the second word was going to be "it," but it doesn't get that far as Thor leaps back and the ground opens up. An enormous flap of dirt and grass is propelled back into the air, like the lid of a giant buried cardboard box, and a damn Battle Creeper emerges, firing bursts of flame from one weaponized arm, and green laser pulses from the other.

I yell, "First Squad, hold your fire!" and by God, these well-trained troopers do just that, while up the line, there's a roar of heavy thuds as M-10 rounds are fired, along with a fast burst of M-4 fire, and gas envelops the Creeper, which gets off a few more bursts before it collapses to the ground, giving enough room for a second Battle Creeper hidden behind it, which explodes out of the hole, damn near flying, and I yell, "First Squad, fire, fire, fire!"

While the other squads and platoons are desperately reloading, we manage to get off a ragged volley that doesn't nail the Creeper right away, but does cripple it as it lands on the ground, some of its legs collapsing underneath it. An articulated arm rotates, firing off brief bursts of laser fire, and then it, too, dies, shaking and quivering and tumbling into a mess.

A yell from up the line. "There's another one!"

And like before, another dirt and grass flap lid flies away, and this Creeper is the Research bug, and doesn't attack, fight or do anything threatening. It just scampers across the field, at a damn fine rate of speed, and then leaps over a far stone wall, and then is gone.

The rain is still heavy, thinning out the gas clouds that had killed the two Battle Creepers.

De Los Santos moves near me. "That was an ambush."

"Sure was."

"Never knew Creepers could bury themselves like that."

"Me neither."

Thor has stopped barking, and prances around the field, giving off pleased little yelps, happy his dopey human friends finally understood what he was trying to tell us. I stand up and look across the field, at the two dead Creepers. Up at the other end of the line, something is burning, for there's thick black smoke billowing up.

"Thor, come!" I call out, and he trots back to us, limping some because of his cast-enclosed leg, and he tries to get over the stone wall, doesn't quite make it, and before I can move over, two soldiers—Sully and a young woman named Price—scramble over the stone wall and help him out. His head is rubbed and so is the unbandaged part of his back, and a runner approaches and says, "Captain Wallace's compliments, Sergeant Knox, but she wants to see you, straight away."

"You got it."

When I get up the line, I see where the smoke's coming from: the lead Stryker looks like it took a burst of flame and two of its tires are burned and damaged. There's a group of soldiers around it, arguing, probably trying to figure out what to do next. Captain Wallace is walking across the field, accompanied by Dad and First Sergeant Hesketh, and I scramble to catch up, with a heavy breathing Thor right behind me. She hears the *slop-slop-slop* of my boot falls in the wet field and turns and says, "That's some dog you have."

"That's right, ma'am."

"None of us heard any clicking sound, or smelled cinnamon. But your dog knew there was an ambush waiting for us."

"Yes, ma'am."

"Good thing you listened to him, and nobody else."

I don't know how to answer that, so I don't. We move across the field, and I take a moment to reload the M-10, dialing down the cartridge to the lowest setting. It's been a strange couple of days, with Creepers digging and Creepers flying, and it wouldn't surprise me too much if these little bastards were just faking it.

"Well," Wallace says. "Colonel, you being in Intelligence and all, mind telling us what the hell just happened here?"

"We dodged an ambush," he said.

"Very good, Colonel, a stunning grasp of the obvious."

A sweet little insult, but Dad either didn't hear that, or doesn't care. He's too busy. He's examining the joints and legs of the second Creeper, getting too close for my comfort, and I whisper, "Dad, not so damn close, okay?"

But he's doing a pretty good job of ignoring me as well. He scrambles up for a second, the rain streaking his hair and fogging up his glasses, and then he jumps back down and instantly falls on his ass. First Sergeant Hesketh laughs and then tries to hide it. Wallace helps up Dad and he says, "Captain, do you have a camera with your unit?"

"No."

"All right then, a sketch artist? Anyone who can draw pictures?"

Hesketh says, "Jones from Third Platoon is pretty handy with a pad and pencil."

"Excellent," Dad says. He points to the joints and bottom pads of the Creeper's legs. "These legs . . . are different. They've been strengthened, improved, so that this type of Creeper can leap now. We need to get that information recorded and out as soon as we can. A lot of our installations are defended by dry moats. They're now vulnerable."

Hesketh yells back to the line, and I step closer to the edge of the rectangular pit where the first Creepers had come from. Dad and Wallace step next to me. It's well made, with room for two Creepers, one behind the other. Good ambush maneuver, the first one coming out shooting, and to take any incoming fire, while the second one leaps up and over, avoiding the initial response.

Wallace's voice is quiet. "You ever hear of this type of ambush?"

Dad removes his glasses, does his best to clear them with part of his sodden jacket. "No. And that's something else to be passed on."

"I don't like any of this," Wallace says.

"Me either," Dad says. "Randy?"

I toe one of the joints of the Creeper's legs, note a difference in its shape and external support from what I've seen before. Now there's a familiar stench in the area, as the two dead Creepers inside their armored arthropods start decaying. A real challenge in this war is trying to capture them and interrogate them, to find why in hell they're here and what they're trying to achieve.

I hold up my M-10. "We've designed new weapons, developed new strategies to deal with these bastards since they invaded. Makes sense for them to do the same."

Wallace says, "Agreed." She walks up to the main arthropod, holding a hand to her nose from the stench of dying Creeper. She's looking up at the abdomen, where there are overlapping plates, allowing the center arthropod to move, and where there's also a permeable membrane that lets Creepers breathe our atmosphere.

Wallace backs away, her face flushed, looking sour, like she had bitten into a rotten apple. "Thank God everything looks the same up there. If they've changed their membranes or hardened their breathing apparatus, then we're dead."

True enough. Except for nuclear weapons, the only way to successfully kill the Creepers are with the binary cartridges used in the M-10s and other grenade launching systems. Oh, in the early days of the war, one other way to kill the Creepers was to use a sniper's rifle with a heavy cartridge—like NATO 7.62 with a depleted uranium round—that when aimed very, very carefully, could slip through the armor plating and kill the Creeper inside.

And a few days ago, I learned another way, of holding onto a Creeper while it tries to kill you, by using a Ka-Bar knife to stab at it through the cracks, though I don't recommend it.

Wallace takes a flashlight off her MOLLE vest and goes to the edge of the pit. Flicks on the light, and we all lean over and check it out. My M-10 is up, just in case... Well, just in case.

Nothing to be seen. It's a rectangular bunker, the dirt and

floor having been fused into something like cement, it looks like. I kneel down, touch the surface. Rough but firm. Creeper technology of some sort, sprayed over the dirt, freezing it into place.

"Interesting," Wallace says.

"Quite," Dad says.

They get up, Wallace turns her flashlight off, puts it back on her vest. There's the second pit but we leave it alone. The two dead Creepers haven't moved, which makes me very happy indeed. Dad walks back and stares up at the frozen legs.

Dad says, "These exoskeletons need to be examined by an Exploitation Unit, soonest."

"Agreed, Colonel," Wallace says, voice tired. "But we've got more immediate problems to face. Let's head back."

I turn and start back to First Platoon, and Wallace says, "Where you going, Sergeant Knox?"

"Ma'am?"

She crooks a finger at me. "I still want you with me. Come along."

I know better than to ask anything, so I walk with Dad, Wallace and Thor, as the four of us trudge across the sodden field, the heavy rain still falling, and about the only good thing about the walk is that it gets us away from the stench of the two dead Creepers.

Then we encounter another smell, of burnt rubber and burnt something else.

We climb over the wall and Wallace starts to slip, and Dad catches her upper arm, stopping her from falling into the mud. She smiles at Dad. I think it's the first real smile I've seen the captain give since I hooked up with her unit. The two of them get over and Thor stops, looks at me.

"Really?" I ask. "Not even going to make the effort?"

His eyes just look at me mournfully, and I grab him and hoist him over, and he trots off after Dad and Wallace. The two of them are headed to the damaged Stryker. There are fresh scorch marks on the port side, and two of the three tires on that side have been hit. The lead tire is a melted, charred mess, and the second tire is flat, looking like it was cut open by a laser beam from one of the attacking Creepers.

But Wallace ignores all that and walks to the front. An injured soldier is leaning up against the front starboard tire, grimacing.

Dr. Pulaski is working on his right arm, which is gone from the elbow down. His helmet is off and the sleeve on his jacket has been cut away.

He says, "Damn it, Doc, can't you do something for the damn pain?"

"Once we get you stabilized, Hernandez, we'll do that."

He sobs. "Damn it to hell... How am I gonna work the farm with only one damn arm?"

Pulaski sprays something on the stump, which has instantly been cauterized by the Creeper's laser. She waits, and then sprays something else, as the other soldier works on the wounded man's remaining arm—also cut free from its jacket—sliding in an IV needle attached to a plastic tube and old fashioned IV bottle. The bottle is hung from a chain that's holding up the Creeper's arthropod head.

"Shit," Hernandez whispers. "Oh shit..."

Pulaski says, soothingly, "Hernandez, you just relax, okay? You still got your elbow left. That'll mean a lot when the VA fits you out for a prosthetic."

"But the farm..."

"Screw the farm," Pulaski says. "Worry about getting better. Besides, there's government programs that help out injured vets. You know how it is. You won't be alone."

Hernandez opens his mouth, his eyes waver, and he passes out, the tire holding him up pretty well. Wallace says, "Doc?"

Pulaski is working on a bandage. "We got to him pretty quick. The bugs clipped him off, sealed the wound. Right now shock and infection are his worse enemies. We're pumping him up with fluids. He should pull through, but we need to get him to a hospital or MASH unit, soon as we can."

Wallace says, "Yeah, well, that's a problem right now, Doc."

She goes around to the damaged side of the Stryker, where a sergeant with a wrench in one hand and oil stained rags in the other is kneeling down, examining the large tires. Two soldiers are behind him with open tool kits.

"Sergeant Merlino," Wallace asks. "What's the situation?"

"Cap," he says, without getting up. "Situation is, this here Stryker is going to be blocking traffic for a number of hours. That is, if there was any traffic."

"Go on."

He taps the first melted tire with the wrench. "The book says it takes about two hours to change out a damaged or destroyed tire. But the book was written before those buggy bastards landed here. This tire's been melted right onto the rim, burnt right into the frame. It's gonna take a half day at least to get it off and get it cleaned up to take the spare."

"I see."

"But that there's the problem, Cap," he goes on. "We got this tire here, split by a laser. No problem, if we had a second spare. But we ain't got one. Tommy's Stryker used his spare a week ago."

Wallace squats down next to the sergeant. "Can it be repaired?"

The sergeant slowly gets up, Wallace joining him. "Yeah, it can be repaired, Cap. I can't guarantee how long it'll last, the roads being in the shitty condition they are. But that's another couple of hours."

Wallace takes in the surroundings. Two dead Creepers, the rest of the company, the tail-end Stryker, and now the grumbling of engines, as the Humvees and trucks make their way to join up.

"We'll need to disperse, Sergeant Merlino," Wallace says. "But before we do, we'll set up some netting."

Merlino shakes his head, wipes his hands again. His face is leathery, with white bristles. "Ma'am, with all due respect, that don't make no sense. It's gonna take time to get the netting out, the support poles, and the ropes . . . and that's time better spent for the rest of the company to get dispersed, and for me and my boys to get this job done."

"Sergeant Merlino . . ."

"Ma'am, please, time . . . okay? Let me and the boys get the tires changed out, you and the rest of the company, go where you can stay out of view of the killer stealth sats, all right? You know it makes sense. Ma'am."

Wallace stares at him, chews her lower lip, and I recall that phrase, again and again taught to me back at school: the burden of command.

Merlino's right, as much as Wallace doesn't like to admit it.

"First Sergeant Hesketh."

"Ma'am," he says, stepping forward.

"Have the platoon leaders get their people squared away. About a half klick up this road, if I recall right, there's a wooded area where we can hole up for the day. Get a move on."

Hesketh salutes, says, "Yes, ma'am," and he starts yelling, motioning. I make to move and Wallace says, "Sergeant, still with me."

"Yes, ma'am."

Merlino says, "Don't you worry none, ma'am. We'll be along. Those bugs won't bother with a small target like us."

Wallace says, "Make it quick."

"We'll make it quick and right." Merlino adjusts the wrench in his hand, and notices Thor for the first time. "Damn, that's one fine-looking dog. That's the one that told us about the Creepers 'fore the ambush, gave us time to set up, right?"

"That's right."

He squats down, holds out a hand, lets Thor sniff it. "Mind if I pat 'em?"

"Go right ahead," I say, as soldiers start gathering up the gear and making their way to the trucks and Humvees.

He rubs Thor's head and says, "German Shepherd?"

"Belgian Malinois."

"Yeah, they do look alike, don't they," he says, voice soft. Two soldiers come out of the rear of the Stryker, carrying tools, and Merlino says, "Had a cute German Shepherd when I was younger, back in college. Guy's name was Frankie. Good dog. When our family bailed out of Chicago when it got hit, Mom insisted Frankie stay with us . . . and he did . . . for two years until . . . until . . . well, I don't want to think about it."

A corporal comes forward, with a schematic map. "Sergeant?"

Merlino gets up, wipes at his eyes. "Too many memories that won't get forgotten. Thanks for letting me pet your boy."

"Glad to do it," I say, and I'm also glad to leave.

Chapter Twelve

In a couple of hours we're set up in what was once an apple orchard, and the trees are high enough to provide overhead shelter. The remaining Stryker covers a dirt road leading to the orchard, and there are dried apples on the ground that a squad is detailed to pick up to supplement our rations. The rain is now a steady drizzle.

I stay with Wallace, although I don't know why until she has a tarpaulin set up near her command Humvee. Dad is with an older woman who's a corporal, with thick fingers and equally thick black hair, and she's sketching something as Dad talks to her, describing the enhanced arthropod joints that we've encountered.

Under the tarpaulin there's a table and three folding chairs. Wallace and First Sergeant Hesketh take two chairs and gesture for me to sit down. I do, helmet in my lap, M-10 leaning against the front of the Humvee. Thor lies down and flops on his side, pants with contentment.

"Sergeant Knox," Wallace says.

"Ma'am."

"That was a good move back there, stopping the convoy. Allowed us to put ourselves in a good defensive position when the Creepers attacked. Otherwise . . . they would have T-boned us as we went by."

"Yes, ma'am," I say.

Her eyes glower. "But to do that, you had to threaten a fellow soldier with shooting him in the head, am I correct?"

"Sort of, ma'am."

"What do you mean, sort of?"

"Well, I didn't exactly mean that I would do it," I say. "I just wanted to get his attention, make him aware of the tactical situation. After he had stopped, I meant to apologize to him."

Hesketh has a hand in front of his face. Wallace's eyes, though, are still glowering. "Did you apologize to him?"

"No, ma'am."

"Why?"

"Didn't have the time. Ma'am."

"I see," she says. She looks to First Sergeant Hesketh and back to me, and says, "There's going to be a slight change, and you're going to be part of it."

"Very good, ma'am," I say, and then I freeze at her next words.

"You're taking command of First Platoon."

Lots of thoughts go stampeding through my mind. I'm not trained for commanding a platoon. I'm just a sergeant; most platoons are led by lieutenants. I'm a Recon Ranger, used to working at the squad level or by myself. I've been with Company K for just a couple of days. I don't know the other platoon leaders, or the dynamics of the organization. And the biggest thought of all is that I'm a stranger, an outsider, someone from away. How will these soldiers react to somebody outside of their company stepping in to take command?

I clear my throat. "Yes, ma'am."

"Good," she says. "First Sergeant will take care of anything you need."

"Yes, ma'am."

"Now, what about Sergeant Bronson? He's not going to like being demoted. I can put him somewhere else in the company."

Another quick thought and I say, "That's fine, ma'am. He can stay in First. I'm sure we'll get along just fine."

A sliver of a smile. "I'm sure. Now, one more thing before you leave. Second Platoon took a hit at the skirmish back at the old horse farm, and Third Platoon is our Stryker force and heavy weapons platoon, such as it is. They're going to be tapped out when night falls. So First Platoon will have picket duty tonight. Understood?"

"Yes, ma'am."

"Very well," she says. "Get to work."

✧   ✧   ✧

I trudge back to where First Platoon is set up, and I see Sergeant Bronson, leaning against a Humvee fender, drinking something from a cracked red plastic cup that's probably been washed and rewashed since the war started. Other members are sprawled out, cleaning weapons, doing a bit of kit work, or just curled up, sleeping. He says, "Well, about time our golden child got back."

"Stow it, Sergeant Bronson," I say. "You and I need to talk. Let's find someplace quiet."

"Nah," he says. "I like it here."

I say, "Not going to happen."

He finishes off his drink, crumples up the precious plastic cup. "You're going to make me, is that it?"

I sense other members of the platoon are now keying in to what's going on, and I say, "Fine, have it your way. There's been a reassignment. Captain Wallace has put me in command of the First. You're my platoon sergeant."

He tosses the plastic trash to the ground. "The hell you say."

"No, I'm just passing news along."

"The hell with you," he says.

I step closer to him, and closer, and get inches away from his face. "Sergeant, I understand you're upset, you're confused, and you don't like what's going on. Fair enough. I'm giving you a bit of leeway in that, but that bit is done, consumed and gone. I'm in charge here, and I won't tolerate any more lip. Do I have your full and complete understanding?"

Now all of the other platoon members are on their feet, watching this little drama take place. Bronson stares at me and I give it right back to him. "Sergeant Bronson, I asked you a question. Do I have your complete and full understanding?"

He licks his lip. "Yes, you do."

"Yes you do, what?"

He blinks slowly. "Yes, you do, Sergeant Knox."

"Very good," I say. "I want a quick look-see over our supply situation, and then there's a platoon meeting in fifteen minutes. Got it?"

"Yes . . . Sergeant Knox."

The supply inspection is pretty quick, for all we have are a few spare bits of uniform, iron rations, first aid kits, ammunition for the M-4, and some spare rounds for the M-10, under lock and key in a red-painted footlocker. Pretty pathetic, actually, and all bundled in the back of one Humvee.

I ask, "What's with the M-10 round box? Why is it locked?"

Bronson says, "You know how much stolen M-10 rounds can get out there in civvie land?"

"I can imagine. Who has the key?"

"I do."

"Hand it over."

He reaches with two hands around his neck, pulls out a thin chain with a key dangling from the other end. I unlock the box, slip the lock off, lift up the cover. There's foam padding inside, with twenty-four M-10 rounds nestled within. I snap the lock shut, toss the key and the lock inside the box, and close the lid.

"We're in the middle of a firefight," I say. "I'm not going to waste time trying to get that damn box undone."

Bronson says, "Very well, Sergeant Knox. It's your responsibility."

"Thanks, but I don't need a refresher course in responsibility."

I make the platoon meeting quick. There are just twelve of us, pretty understrength for a platoon, but that's been the case since I was six years old, so why make a fuss over it. I know some of them already—Sully, De Los Santos, Balatnic—and I know I'll have to learn everyone's name and rank within the hour.

I make my talk quick. I say I'm from another unit, temporarily assigned here, but I've seen them in action and they're as good as any I've served with. Sergeant Bronson is my deputy, but if there's a problem or concern, feel free to take it to me. Any questions?

None.

I say, "Later on tonight, we've drawn picket duty."

A couple of groans. "Second Platoon is still pretty thin after that farmhouse attack, and Third Platoon has its hands full getting that first Stryker back in the line. Sergeant Bronson."

"Sergeant Knox," he says, with a touch of sullen in his voice.

"Work up a schedule," I say. "We're taking turns tonight, First Squad and then Second Squad. Plan the perimeter accordingly, and then get back to me."

Bronson says, "Which squad goes first?"

"Flip a coin," I say. "If you can't find a coin, a rock or a stick will work. Use your best judgment."

✧   ✧   ✧

Later I introduce myself to Second Platoon Lieutenant Morneau, the tall blonde woman, and she's all brisk and professional, and says, "You got a good platoon over there, Sergeant, but they can be sloppy. If we set up a line, sometimes we don't have contact on the flank with your guys. That leaves a big damn hole. Fix that, will you?"

I say, "I'll be on it. Do you know where Lieutenant Jackson is?"

"He's with the disabled Stryker, helping out."

"I see."

"Yeah," she says, looking over my shoulder to the area where the road is, and then lifting her head up to look at the overcast sky. "Hell of a thing, to be working out in the open like that. Knowing any second a killer stealth satellite can nail you with a laser shot, particle beam, or kinetic rod."

"Hell of a thing," I agree, and I check out the perimeter myself, seeing what's what, and note we're in an orchard that butts up against a wood line that slopes down to a river at its western end. Up on the northern end of the orchard is a flattened farmhouse. I can't tell if it's been that way for ten years or twenty, and decide it doesn't make any difference.

A mess tent has been set up and as I go there with Thor, there's an ear-splitting *crackBOOM!* and an accompanying flash of light from the direction of the road that makes everybody drop and kiss the ground. The sound of the explosion echoes and reechoes, and we all slowly get up. A killer stealth satellite shot, no doubt about it. Nearby are two soldiers from Second Platoon and one says to the other, "Shit, we just lost the Stryker."

"Damn," the other soldier says, brushing mud off his knees. "Perez is over there. Guy still owes me a buck from last week's poker game."

"Sucks to be you," and then they start slowly heading to the mess tent, and there's a yell, "Hey, look at that!"

I move around a parked truck and coming up the dirt road to our encampment, safely under cover from trees, is the disabled Stryker, moving slowly but surely. Hoots, hollers and applause break out from K Company, and nearly as one, we move up to the vehicle as it turns and growls to a halt. The rear ramp grinds down and Lieutenant Jackson steps out, along with Sergeant Merlino and other soldiers. They're filthy, covered with dirt, grease and there's still the smell of scorched rubber, and Merlino nearly shouts out, "Those bugs are getting clumsy, those sons-of-bitches. They missed us by almost a meter!"

More laughs, which is good to see in an Army unit, at any time, any place.

Dinner is a bowl of beef broth and a chunk of white bread covered with cheese paste, and a glass of fruit juice. Dad is in line in front of me, with Captain Wallace, and he says, "Care to join us, Randy?"

"No, sir," I say. "I've got things to cover with the platoon."

He nods in agreement. I sense some hurt in his eyes, behind those black-rimmed glasses, but he should know better. I've got a hell of a job ahead of me, and I can't be seen spending valuable time with superior officers.

There's a pause in the chow line as a fresh container of beef broth comes out, and Dad and Wallace take a small folding table by themselves. Wallace laughs loud at something Dad says, and briefly reaches out to touch his hand.

The gesture makes me feel queasy.

Dusk approaches and a small fire is built in the center of the company's parked vehicles, carefully shielded. I walk the perimeter again and check on the positioning of First Squad, which has first watch tonight. It's a thin crew and they're set up in a triangular position, covering the site, but it's the best I can do, and I say to Bronson, "Where's their trenches?"

"Their what?"

"Foxholes, slit trenches, holes in the ground," I say. "I want everyone in a hole."

"Knox, that—"

"Sergeant."

"Sergeant Knox, that's gonna take a while, and Christ, we're just spending the night here. This isn't a permanent setup."

"If our guys are out in the open and a Creeper races up from that river bank, this orchard will be permanent indeed," I say. "Slit trenches big enough to hold four, two from each squad, in case we're attacked during the night and Second Squad comes out to reinforce."

He grimaces. "Yes, Sergeant. But we've only got five soldiers in First Squad. That means one hole is going to be at half-strength."

"No, it won't," I say.

"Why?"

"Because I'll be in that hole, covering as well."

"Oh," Bronson says. "And what happens when Second replaces First?"

"I won't have far to travel, because I'll still be there."

It takes another hour to get things sorted out, and I arrange First Squad so each hole has a soldier with an M-4 to take care of trespassing Earth-based life forms, and a soldier with an M-10 to handle everything else. I quietly ask Bronson to give me the youngest soldier, and I'm hooked up with a twelve-year-old boy named Tanner.

We settle in just before the sunlight fades away, and I point out to him some landmarks—the rusted tractor, the solitary boulder, the cracked apple tree—so we have good battlefield awareness. It doesn't help to be screaming, "Shoot there, shoot there!" if you don't have a handle on what "there" means.

His skin is pale and he's wide-eyed, and his hands are holding his M-4 so tight I can practically see his knuckles glow in the dark. Thor jumps in with us and turns around a few times, lying down on a poncho that's protecting us from the wet soil, and I say, "How long have you been with K Company, Private?"

He says, "About five months."

"Seen lots of action, I'm sure."

He softly laughs, a high-pitched sound. "More than I thought I would. This company... Captain Wallace, she loves to get in the thick of things. I got out of Basic and got assigned here, and we hit two Creepers on my first week. First dead Creepers I've ever seen... and first dead soldiers I ever saw, too. One in each attack, drilled with a laser shot to their heads. Didn't even know their names."

Another little brittle laugh. "And last month... boy, it sounded like the war was over, when the Creepers' orbital base got destroyed. How come we're still fightin'?"

That would take a good chunk of the night to discuss, so I rearrange my imaginary platoon leader hat and say, "That's beyond our pay grade, Tanner, sorry to say. You comfortable?"

"Doing okay, Sergeant."

"Good."

He says, "You've done this before, right? Platoon Leader?"

I sense what he's asking, which isn't a straight-up answer. Tanner wants to make sure that the FNG—freakin' new guy—has experience and isn't going to get him and his mates killed.

I say, "Sure. Plenty of times."

"Okay."

Overhead the clouds are breaking away, which reveals the night sky and enough ambient light from the stars and burning trails of old satellite wreckage to light up the perimeter better, which eases some of my strain. Back in the good old days of bloody war fighting, even fresh privates like the one next to me had the latest in night-vision technology that would illuminate everything around them. Ah, yes, back in the days of electronics. I had a few memories of smart phones, tablet computers, and huge television screens, and I knew Tanner next to me would have none of those memories. Made you wonder who was the most disadvantaged.

From behind us there comes a screeching noise that nearly lifts me straight out of the foxhole, and even makes Thor sit up and take notice. Tanner laughs. "No worries, Sarge, that's just MacRae. Not much of a soldier but man, can he play those bagpipes."

And the screeching noise rises up to a bagpipe tune, a haunting, slow melody that goes right through me, and I can barely make out the shape of the piper, standing near one of the parked trucks. The tune goes on and on, and then slowly dribbles out. A couple of hoots and some applause, and that's that.

"What was the tune?"

"What amounts to *Taps* for the Scots," Tanner says. "Called *Sleep Dearie, Sleep* or something like that."

"After all that screeching, I'm so wound up I don't think I'll be able to sleep for a while."

Tanner says, "That's probably the point."

The night settles down and I keep watch out there, just scanning, looking out the corner of my eyes, which are better at seeing things in the dark. It feels pretty calm. Other soldiers to the rear of us are quieting down as they prepare to go to sleep, though there was the soft murmur of voices from where the hidden campfire was located.

After about ninety minutes I check my watch and retrieve my M-10 and Tanner instantly snaps to. "What's wrong? What's wrong?"

"Nothing wrong's, Tanner," I say. "I'm just going to slip out and check on the other positions. I'll be back in a bit."

His voice is shaky. "Can...can I come with you, Sergeant?"

I take a breath. According to the Department of Defense, the Department of the Army, the Congress and the President— wherever he is nowadays—this guy next to me is a Specialist in the Army of the United States, one in a long line going back all the way to 1775.

But he's also a scared, twelve-year-old kid out in the dark, facing real-life monsters.

I say, "Tell you what. I'll leave Thor here with you. How's that?"

I can't see his smile but I sense it. "Hey, that would be great. Thanks a lot!"

"Not a problem," I say. "But keep your eyes open, keep it tight. If you see something...do what you have to do. But word of advice. See if Thor responds, okay? He's pretty good at gauging any possible threats."

"Okay, Sergeant."

I say, "Thor, stay. Thor, guard." My boy sits up and looks out into the fields, and then I get up, roll over the top of the hole, and slip away.

The inspection goes fine checking the other two holes, and then I'm back with Thor and Tanner, and nothing happens, and we stay there and stay there, the only interesting thing seeing a huge piece of space debris burn up and split into four trails, and hearing muffled *booms!* as they strike somewhere. When four hours have passed, Second Squad comes out to replace First Squad, and Private Tanner says, "Have a quiet night, Sarge."

"You too, Tanner," I say, and he's replaced by an older guy, maybe fourteen or so, with the name of Ramirez, and after a few exchanges and such, he settles down to business and so do I. I take a couple of catnaps and then I'm out again, leaving Thor behind, going from hole to hole, and at the second hole, I find Balatnic and another specialist, Gould, and I find them fast asleep and curled up in opposite ends of their slit trench, their weapons uselessly standing against the dirt.

Damn.

A choice is presented to me, and according to doctrine, I make the wrong one. I loudly cough and Balatnic stirs, and I slide into their hole. She and Gould scramble to the lip of their hole, eyeing the dirt road and clumsily picking up their weapons.

I say, "See anything?"

Murmurs of "No Sergeant" from both.

I put some edge into my voice. "Hard to see anything through your eyelids, am I right?"

Both are quiet. "Who's senior here?"

"I am," Balatnic says.

"Gould."

"Yes, Sergeant."

"Get out to where the fire is. See if there's coffee or tea brewing. Grab some for yourself and Balatnic, get back here as quick as you can."

"Yes, Sergeant," and there's eagerness in his voice as he slips out, his shouldered M-10 bouncing as he scurries away into the darkness.

Balatnic says, "Sergeant, I know—"

"Stow it," I say.

I keep quiet for a bit, wanting her to think of what might be awaiting her. I say, "How long you been in the Army, Balatnic?"

"Two years."

"So I don't need to explain the importance of being alert on guard duty."

"No."

"And if I come around on picket duty in the future, while I'm commanding this platoon, I can count on you being awake and alert."

"Yes, Sergeant."

"Good."

A voice from behind us. "Private Gould, coming in."

He scurries back into the trench, carefully carrying two mugs of hot liquid. I wish I had been smart enough to ask him to bring back one for me, but I let it be.

"Gould?"

"Yes, Sergeant?"

"Stay alert, all right?"

"You can count on us."

"I better," I say, and as I slip out, Balatnic says, "Are you going to report this to Captain Wallace?"

I say, "Report what?"

Then I'm out and back to my trench, and Thor checks me out and Ramirez says, "Welcome back, Sergeant Knox."

"Good to be back. Anything go on?"

"Quiet as the grave," Ramirez says, and I say, "Next time, find a better metaphor, okay?"

"Meta what?" he asks, and I leave that be.

When dawn comes I get up, stretch and Thor leaps out, trots out to the field, and does his business, and I hear the rest of the Company getting up and stirring about. The light is dim but good enough to let me walk around, and as I head to the command Humvee, to see if Captain Wallace is up and about, Bronson finds me and says, "We got movement, out on the dirt road coming this way."

"Humans?"

"Yeah."

"All right, show me."

I follow him as we go past the parked vehicles to where the repaired Stryker is covering the approach and sure enough, there are about a half-dozen civilians, two of them hauling small wooden wagons with wire-rimmed wheels.

Bronson says, "Sergeant?"

I say, "I'll go out and see what's what. In the meantime, see if the mess is ready to handle these civvies."

Bronson says, "Christ, we keep on feeding everyone we run across, we'll be eating our boots by the time we get back to Battalion."

I go down the damp road, Thor at my side, and I make out an older male and female, accompanied by two boys, and bringing up the rear, mostly hidden, a young female and a young boy.

The male is dressed well in a black suit, white shirt and boots. His face is bearded, gaunt, and he smiles. "Looks like we're lost."

"How can I help you?"

"We . . . we were evacuated from outside of Albany, heading to a Red Cross camp. Our bus got a flat tire, we started walking . . . got separated from the main group. Been wandering around for a couple of days, and then we got word the Army was here. Can you help us?"

I say, "I'm sure. In the meantime, how about a sit down and something to eat?"

The woman says, "Oh, God, that'd be great."

"Then head up over there, and someone will help you."

The older man and woman walk by, the small wagons with battered suitcases and plastic bags creaking some, and then the two boys, about eight or so, faces dirty, holding hands, and then, bringing up the rear, dressed in tattered civilian clothes, are Serena Coulson and her younger brother Buddy.

Chapter Thirteen

She looks at me, face haggard, blonde hair dirty and tangled, and Buddy is his usual quiet and morose self. Thor whines and I whisper, "Stay," and I mean to say something to Serena, when Bronson comes up to me and says, "What do we have, Sergeant Knox?"

Good question. When I saw them last, back at the surrendered Creeper Dome, they were both in uniform, getting ready to head out with their dad, the man from Langley—Hoyt Cranston—and General Brad Scopes from Intelligence, for additional debriefing and meetings.

But now they are here, quiet, and definitely out of uniform.

Meaning...

Deserters?

Or something else?

I say loudly, "What you see is what we got. Civilians, looking for a Red Cross refugee camp. Get them to the chow tent, all right?"

"Yes, Sergeant."

Serena glances at me as she passes by, and I'm hoping for a look of thanks, or appreciation, but I get neither, just a look of desperation.

I find Dad curled up in a sleeping bag, underneath an up-armored Humvee. Thor goes in front of me and licks his face, and Dad sits up, bangs his head, says, "Shit, Randy, what the hell is this?"

"Dad, we got a situation."

He rubs at his head, fumbles around inside his sleeping bag, retrieves his glasses and puts them on. "What's going on?"

"Serena Coulson and her brother Buddy. They've just shown up, in civvies, part of a refugee party."

Dad struggles to get out of his sleeping bag, and I reach over, grab the zipper, pull it free. He gets out and says, "Serena? Buddy? Here?"

"That's right."

He stands up, coughs. He's wearing faded green gym shorts and a Boston University T-shirt, and his skinny legs are white and covered with old scars. I get this disquieting feeling, seeing my father like this, old and tired, barely awake. I don't like it. He rubs at his face and says, "Is Dr. Coulson with them?"

"No."

"Damn," he says. "Does Captain Wallace know they're here?"

"No," I say. "Nobody's recognized them except me. Right now, they're just a couple of refugees."

He reaches into a knapsack, pulls out his BDUs, starts getting dressed. "All right. I guess we should tell Captain Wallace and go on from there."

"Dad..."

"What?" he says, pants still around his ankles.

"The civilian clothes."

Dad doesn't say a word. I go on. "They might be deserters."

He nods, reaches down, pulls up his pants, almost falls down. "Okay. Look, there's a wooden lean-to by the lead Stryker. I'll be there. Bring Serena and Buddy over, we'll see if we can figure out what the hell is going on."

"On it."

I head back to the temporary mess, and Serena and Buddy are sitting underneath a pine tree, eating quickly from plastic bowls. Thor runs up to Buddy, tail wagging, and Buddy quietly puts his bowl down and rubs Thor's head and ears. Thor licks Buddy's face and there's the briefest of smiles.

Serena scrapes the last of the oatmeal from her bowl. I say, "You done there?"

"I could probably go through the line at least two more times," she says, "but I don't think they'll let me."

"My dad wants to see you both."

"Good."

She picks up Buddy's bowl, puts it on top of hers, and hands them to me. "Do you mind bringing them back? I'm afraid... some of the soldiers here might recognize me or Buddy. I don't want that."

Desertion, I thought. Definitely desertion. And here, just a few hours ago, I was worried about two soldiers dozing on guard duty.

"Fair enough. Stay here and I'll fetch you."

I walk quietly and quickly to the end of the serving line, where dishes are being piled up for later washing, and then I head over to the tree when First Sergeant Hesketh shows up.

"Sergeant Knox, the Captain wants all platoon leaders at her Humvee in five minutes."

"Got it, First Sergeant."

I try to walk around him and a strong hand grasps my upper arm, and his raspy voice says, "Knox, you're heading in the wrong direction."

"You said five minutes, I'll be there in five minutes. In the meantime"—I tug my arm free—"go worry about something else, First Sergeant."

I catch the attention of Serena and Buddy, and they follow me as I head to the lead Stryker. There's still a stench of burnt rubber as I go around the Stryker, and Sergeant Merlino is examining the repaired tire, tapping on it with a small hammer and whispering obscenities. Other members of his platoon are still sacked out, and Lieutenant Jackson calls out, "Hey, Knox! Come on, we're meeting up with the Captain."

"I'll be right there!" I call back, and give a glance to the rear, where Serena is following about three meters back, holding onto Buddy's hand.

I move to the left, dodging the picket hole that had been dug here last night at my command. I slog through some thick grass and reach the lean-to Dad had described. He pokes his head out. I say, "They're right behind me."

"Good." Dad looks up and says, "Heavy weather coming in."

True enough. The clouds are dark, full, threatening. There's a rumble of thunder out there, and a flash of lightning in the clouds that reminds me of debris from LEO coming in and burning up. A rusted-out lawn mower is in the middle of the lean-to, along with a jumble of broken tools. A small workbench has fallen over, and nailed up on the wall, faded and soiled, is a calendar from an outfit called Irving Oil. The calendar is ten years old and is set to that year's October. The very faded photo shows an attractive young blonde woman driving a red convertible.

More thunder.

Serena walks in, almost out of breath, still holding Buddy's hand. Both of their clothes are patched, dirty, held up by lengths of string. Only the footwear is the same from when I last saw them.

Dad says, "What happened?"

Serena's face is dirty, eyes puffy. Buddy moves to pull his hand away but she won't let go.

"The Langley guy...Cranston."

Dad nods. "Hoyt Cranston. Go on."

"We drove for a number of hours, got to this old base...up in the hills. Decommissioned except for a couple of buildings. Run by the Navy. Never even got to know its name. We got first class treatment, private rooms, showers, food like you wouldn't believe. Separate rooms for me, my dad, and Buddy."

"What went wrong?" I ask.

Serena takes a deep, shuddering breath. "A day later, the mood changed. Cranston demanded that Buddy tell him about his language training, where he learned the Creeper lingo, how much of the language did he know, why did he come up with the exact phrasing that made those Creepers surrender. Buddy just...sat still, smiled."

Dad says, "Thomas...I mean, Major Coulson, was he there? What did he do?"

"Dad didn't know what was going on," Serena says. "He had gone off with General Scopes after the first day, and I couldn't find him. Nobody would help me. The Langley guy...he cut off my food. Hot water. Put me on a cot in a dirty room the size of my closet. Told me I had to cooperate, tell Buddy to talk to him, or things would get worse."

She wipes at her eyes with a free hand. "Finally I told Cranston that Buddy wasn't going to cooperate unless Dad came back, and Cranston said, fine, we'll set up a special room for your brother, and we'll go on from there."

Another lightning flash and a few seconds later, a deep rumble of thunder. Serena says, "The few Navy guys at this base...I played dumb. Like a little lost girl, confused about what was going on. I was taken to a bathroom and I asked my escort—a Navy gal younger than me—could I please see the room where Buddy and I were going to be in tomorrow? This girl...couldn't have been more than eleven or twelve, but she was an ensign, she took me to the room, and I think she knew it was a mistake, the moment the door was open."

Dad stays silent but I say, "What was in the room?"

Serena's eyes swell up and tears start rolling down her cheeks. "A padded table. With restraints on both ends. Folded cloths. Buckets. A sink."

I look at Buddy's plain, smart yet scary face. My stomach feels like it wants to slide out of my mouth. "They were going to waterboard him."

"That's right."

"And that's why you ran off."

"Right again."

Dad moves closer and then there's a very bright flash of lightning, and one chest-thumping boom of thunder, and the rains start. I don't know what to say but that's okay, because somebody else steps in.

Captain Kara Wallace, looking very pissed-off, followed by an equally pissed-off-looking First Sergeant Hesketh.

She says, "Is this a private party, or can anybody pop in and take part?"

Dad says, "Kara, look—"

She snaps, "Colonel, it's Captain Wallace. I'd ask you to remember that."

"Captain," I start out, but she won't have anything to do with me. She steps closer and says to Serena, "I recognize you. You're the specialist from back at the Dome surrender...and your younger brother, the linguist." She gives them both a good, piercing stare. "You two were assigned to General Scopes and the man from Langley. What the hell are you doing here? And why are you out of uniform?"

The tears from Serena are really rolling along her dirty cheeks, and her lips are trembling, and I say, "There was an event."

Wallace cocks an eye. "An event? Pretty slippery word there,

Knox. That can mean anything from a surprise birthday party to a hundred Creepers marching up the Hudson River Valley."

"Serena and her brother were taken to a Navy base. Buddy was interrogated by Hoyt Cranston, the man from Langley. When Buddy wouldn't cooperate, Cranston was getting ready to torture him."

"Torture him how?"

"Waterboarding," Serena whispers.

"I see," Wallace says. "And what would be the point of the waterboarding?"

Dad speaks up. "Kar—" and I wince, wondering if Wallace is going to snap at him, but no, she lets him be. "Cranston was looking for information on how Buddy learned the Creeper language, what phrases he knew, how did he know to speak the right way to make those Creepers surrender."

Wallace crisply nods. "Very well. You say your brother was going to receive enhanced interrogation to pass along information that would help Mr. Hoyt of the CIA tell his superiors about the best way to get the Creepers to surrender? Am I correct?"

"Hey," I say, and Dad speaks as well, and Wallace holds up her hand. "Enough." The contempt in her look is something that chills me right down to my ankles. "To get this war ended . . . by interrogating this boy . . . I . . . what I would do . . ."

She turns to Hesketh. "First Sergeant, escort this . . . group back to my tent." To us she says, "I don't have the capabilities, or arrangements, or anything else to put you under arrest. But I'll make sure that if any one of you leaves my side or sight, you'll be shot."

Wallace heads out into the rain, and we follow. Serena comes past me and I take her free hand, and I'm pleased she doesn't pull away. So we walk, me holding Serena's hand, she holding the hand of her brother.

As we get to her tent there's a burbling grumble and a mud-splattered motorcycle rolls up nearby, and an equally mud-splattered courier gets off, wearing BDU pants, a leather jacket with the 10th Mountain Infantry Division on the back, black wool cap and goggles. He passes over a dispatch case to Wallace and I hear her say, "Go take a break. I'll be with you shortly."

Hesketh points us to a rotten pine log and we all sit down,

and I'm still holding hands with Serena, not a gesture—I realize now—of affection, but of reassurance. Dad is Dad, looking
up through his glasses, and I wonder why he doesn't just take
command, as a colonel. But he's a colonel in Intelligence, not the
infantry, and I can't see Kara's Killers following his lead because
of his rank.

Wallace drops the dispatch case on a wooden table, opens it up,
reads the message. She sits down, stretches out her legs, reads the
message again. When she stops reading I say, "Captain Wallace."

She doesn't say anything back. Just tilts her head up and
looks at the dark green canvas overhead, which is dripping water.
Hesketh stands to the rear, hands clasped behind him, like some
sort of guardian angel or android, ready to do whatever his
princess requires.

"Please," I say. "Captain Wallace."

Now she pays attention to me. "What is it, Knox?"

"The recorded Creeper message, the one that was broadcast
back at the farm, that was supposed to be Buddy's voice. It wasn't."

"So you've made clear."

I say, "Maybe Buddy knows what message was really recorded,
what was really sent out with that PsyOps Humvee."

She crosses one muddy boot over the other. "Seems to be
quite the stretch."

"Perhaps," I say. "Maybe so. But with all due respect, ma'am,
I think it would be a better approach than threatening to take a
twelve-year-old soldier, out on disability, and turn him over to
the CIA to be tortured."

Hesketh scowls but Wallace doesn't move. Serena squeezes
my hand. Dad stays still.

She says, "One hell of a nasty shot there, Sergeant."

"No offense meant, ma'am. Just wanted to point out another
approach."

Wallace lowers her feet to the ground, looks again at the
dispatch notice. Water has dripped on a corner. "Specialist . . .
am I right? Specialist Coulson. You seem to be your brother's
keeper, your brother's defender and translator. Is that possible?"

"Yes," she says, her voice so faint.

"So do it."

Serena says, "I can't."

"Why?"

"Because I was at Buddy's side all the time before we left with the general and Cranston. We didn't hear about any recording. Not at all."

Wallace nods. She swivels in her chair, crooks a finger at Hesketh, and he comes over, bends down. Some whispers are exchanged. Hesketh shakes his head a few times, until Wallace says, "That's an order, First Sergeant."

Hesketh looks like he's going to explode, lips tight and white, but in his raspy voice he says, "Yes, ma'am. I'm on it."

"Thank you, First Sergeant."

Hesketh goes out into the rain, which has settled down to a steady downpour. For some reason Wallace seems relaxed after leading us out from that lean-to, and I can't quite figure out why. Back there she seemed ready to shoot us. Now, it seems she's content to wait.

Something to do with the dispatch she just got?

"Captain?" I ask.

"Sergeant," she says.

"Permission to ask a question."

A very tiny smile. "Aren't you the questioning one this morning. Go ahead."

"Back at the horse farm, just before the two Creeper Domes were approached with the PsyOps Humvee, I saw you talk with the squad that was going out there in the field."

"Go on," she says, voice even.

"There were four of them," I say.

"I know. I was there."

"Well, begging the Captain's pardon, ma'am, those four... they seemed old. Wounded. All of them had prosthetics. Not the type of soldiers you'd expect to be lead on approaching a Creeper Dome, not to mention two, anticipating that Creepers are going to come out and surrender. Ma'am."

Wallace nods. "You seem to want to make a point, Sergeant."

Dad leans forward from his perch on the pine tree log and gives me a warning look, which I instantly ignore. "It seems you were preparing for something... to go wrong. Perhaps a trap. Perhaps a misunderstanding. Perhaps the Creepers coming out in full force like they did and opening fire."

Wallace's voice is now bleak. "How long have you been in command of First Platoon?"

I know she knows but I answer anyway. "Not even a full day, ma'am."

"Then welcome to the joys of command. Sometimes...you have to prepare to make sacrifices."

Hesketh comes back out of the rain, bearing a dull metal suitcase, not too large, maybe big enough to hold a few changes of clothes. He puts it down on the table and steps back, and he looks fidgety, like something is wrong, something is bothering him.

I don't like it.

Anything that might disturb this first sergeant is something I don't want to see.

Wallace says, "Thank you, First Sergeant." She looks around the encampment, and says, "Now might be a good time to... move a few of the personnel."

"Ma'am," he says.

"And you may join them, if you wish."

"No, ma'am," he says, and he steps out in the rain, bellows a few orders, and around us, soldiers are gathering up their gear, moving away.

My throat is suddenly dry.

By the suitcase handle there's something that looks like a built-in combination lock, and Wallace quickly flips through the numbers. "Let's see if we can get this started before the first sergeant comes back," she says. "I'd let the rest of you join him, but unfortunately, circumstances don't allow that."

The lock snaps open and the lid comes out, and from within the padded interior, she pulls out a rectangular, metal and plastic object. It looks so very familiar, and then the top flips open, she presses a round switch above a small keyboard, and there's a *ping!* noise and it comes alive.

A functioning laptop computer.

Serena screams and I force myself to stay put, though I so desperately want to run away.

An Excerpt From the Journal of Randall Knox

My memories of the first years of the war—which began when I was six—are fuzzy and incomplete, and probably for a very good reason. Dad didn't share much and as a real young kid, I don't have that many memories of what happened after the war started. The memories before the war...I don't like to think about them that much. After the war began...it's a jumble, of moving around a lot, sleeping under itchy wool blankets in a smelly canvas tent, or doing lots of walking, or being carried on Dad's strong shoulders.

I remember being hungry a lot, and crying when I couldn't get anything to eat, but then it got a bit straightened out. Our family grew up in Marblehead, Massachusetts, right on the coastline of Massachusetts, and Dad was a history professor at Boston University, and Mom drew pictures for children's books. We lost our home due to the tsunami strike, and in the confusion later, we slipped over the border into New Hampshire. Dad could claim New Hampshire citizenship because of a cabin we had on Bow Lake, during the time when it wasn't clear if there was anything left of the Federal government, and most states sealed their borders with their own National Guard and state police units.

Eventually, though, things settled down—and I don't mean anything went back to normal, no, not that—and we moved around some, as Dad reupped in the Army, having been in the Reserves. When I turned eight, I joined the local Cub Scouts, and with the rations assigned both to the military and outfits like the Scouts, we managed all right, although food was pretty thin, especially during the famine years. But there was a Federal government, damn weak, but a government, and we were fighting back against the Creepers, in desperate battles that saw the deaths of thousands at a time as we began to learn their weapons and tactics.

Dad worked lots of long hours, days and weekends, when the armed forces were trying to keep up the fight and try to adjust to the new reality, and in the Cub Scouts, we were doing a lot more than its original mission of learning citizenship, knot-tying, and the like. We worked with the Boy Scouts—older boys—who in turn were under the command of local National Guard units, and we were doing survey work.

Sounds pretty fancy, but we would go into some abandoned suburban neighborhoods in New Hampshire or in Massachusetts border towns, checking out the homes. If they were locked we'd mark the mailbox at the end of the driveway, letting follow-up crews know that this was a house that needed a more secure follow-up, to break in and remove clothing, bedding, canned food, bottled water, stuff like that. Anything unlocked or having signs of being broken in were left alone, the thought being that the places had already been robbed.

We worked in our little Cub Scout dens, associated with our Cub Scout Pack, and usually led by an old and out-of-shape National Guard soldier who was armed with a rifle, or shotgun, or something in case we ran into looters or other gangs. We had two rules while working: don't break into locked homes, and do not, on any occasion, retrieve or try to start up any electronic device.

Steam the Creepers left alone. Coal they left alone. Diesel—if it wasn't used in a military application—was usually left alone. But anything electronic, from computers to cellphones to power plants to . . . well, almost anything and everything, would be spotted from LEO and destroyed by their killer stealth satellites, controlled by their orbital base.

Anything electronic.

Anything.

So we were told to leave electronics alone, for they were like waving a big bullseye target, begging to be struck.

One summer day, we were in a suburban area north of Boston—I don't remember the name now—just trudging along, going from house to house. It was a hot day and our water bottles were getting low. There were five of us, plus Bobby, a retired mechanic who was in the New Hampshire National Guard and who carried a shotgun and wore a camo jacket—the only real sign he was in the military—and a Boy Scout named Keith, who was tagging along and seeing what we were doing.

The homes were nice big ones, with three-car garages and wide lawns and stone walls. Three years into the war, the lawns were overgrown, most of the driveways had fancy cars that would no longer run and were resting on flattened tires, and the occasional dog would trot by, probably still wondering what had happened to his or her family.

We had passed by three houses that were locked and secure, and Bobby had tied yellow bits of cloth on the tilting mailboxes, and he called for a rest break, and we plopped ourselves down underneath an oak tree that gave us lots of shade.

After a while Bobby sat up and said, "Hey, anybody see Keith?"

We all looked around. The five of us were in ragged clothes, sneakers or shoes kept together with gray duct tape or black electrical tape, the only real sign that we were Cub Scouts being the kerchiefs around our necks.

"No," I said. "I don't know where he went."

And nor had anybody else.

Bobby said, "Shit," and got up, holding his shotgun out, and he said, "You guys stay put, all right? Any trouble, run into the woods, try to get back to the church hall."

"What kind of trouble?" one of the Scouts asked, but we others kept our mouths shut. We had seen lots of trouble over the years, and would know it when we'd find it.

Then trouble came to find us.

Keith came down the empty street, the asphalt cracked and worn, laughing, holding up something in his hand. He was dressed just like us, except his kerchief was a different color, meaning he was in the Boy Scouts.

"Guys, look what I found! Just like one I used to play with!"

We stood still as he approached and Bobby said, "Keith, what the hell do you got there?"

Keith held up his prizes in his hands. "A Nintendo 3DS XL game system, with a spare battery pack! Can you believe that? A spare battery pack!"

Bobby said, "Put that stuff down, Keith."

Keith would have none of it. "C'mon, Bobby, let's take a break. Let's have some fun..."

Bobby said, "You boys, get moving. Get moving... now."

We started moving, just like we were told, and Bobby held up his shotgun. "You stop right there, Keith. I mean it. You stop right there and you put that crap down on the street."

The five of us were moving as we were told, but we kept on looking back at Bobby and Keith, who was still walking towards him. Bobby said, "I'm ordering you, Keith. You put that stuff down, now!"

Keith stopped and put the battery pack down, but kept the game system in his hands. Tears were now in his eyes but his face was full of excitement. "Are you kidding? Are you crazy? Do you know how long it's been since I've played a real game... not one with cards or on a board? I mean... a real game! This is just like the one I used to have!"

Bobby yelled, "Put it on the ground!"

"No! This is mine! You can't have it... and I'm not giving it up!"

Bobby started walking backward, shotgun in his hands, wavering, and now his voice was shaking. "Keith, you put that down."

Keith started examining it.

"Boy, don't you dare start that thing. Don't you dare!"

Keith pushed a switch and Bobby swore, and started running toward us. "Go! Go! Don't look back!"

Keith sat down on the road, the Nintendo in his lap, his face so alive and happy. Then he laughed and held up the console.

"Look! It still works! Look! Everything's okay! Everything's okay!"

I wasn't looking so I wasn't temporarily blinded when Keith was struck, but two of my Cub Scout buds screamed when they couldn't see for a while, and while I'm sure their eyes hurt, at least they were spared the view of seeing the black and smoking chunks of Keith strewn across the road.

On the long walk back to the church hall where the Cub Scout pack and Boy Scout troop were quartered, Bobby kept on shaking his head and said, "I warned the boy. I warned the boy. Jesus, I warned the boy."

Chapter Fourteen

I swallow hard and squeeze Serena's hand tight, and Wallace says, "I'll be quick."

She taps a few keys and now I know why Wallace told her first sergeant to move the troops, and I remember having seen this square object before, sitting on the hood of the Humvee, back at the farm with the two Domes. Serena's squeezing my hand so tight it feels like the blood is being cut off, and I look to Buddy, who seems fascinated by the flickering images on the screen, and Dad looks on too, looking...mournful? Sad? Worried?

Me? Seeing a live laptop computer screen brings back a flood of memories I didn't even know I had, most with Mom. So many games. Cartoons. Doing something called—Skip?—when I could see Mom or Dad when they were on a trip, and I could talk to them, and they could talk to me, and I gulp a sob, knowing that so much of what was the Internet was recorded, and maybe, buried in some vault or salt mine would be moving pictures of Mom talking and laughing with me, and maybe someday when the war was really over, I could find out where those ten-year-old recordings are kept...

I turn my head, not wanting anyone to see the tears in my eyes, and I wipe at them and look back, and Wallace is tapping at the keys and says, "Specialist Coulson?"

"Yeah?"

"Your brother...he knows some of the Creeper language, right?"

"That's right, ma'am."

"Could he translate something right now, or does he need . . . oh, I don't know. Warning? To be prepared? A cup of coffee?"

Dad says, "I . . . I think I know how, Kara."

Wallace says, "Then hurry the hell up, will you? Or we're going to get a rod from God in our laps if I don't quickly shut this down."

"Buddy," Dad says. "Buddy . . . look over here, son."

Buddy slowly turns and I don't see his face, but I see the concern on Dad's face when he says, "Buddy. Authorization Papa Tango Papa. Understand? Papa Tango Papa."

Dad stares and Buddy turns his head, and he just . . . nods. That's all. He just nods.

"Go," Dad says. "Whatever you've got planned, do it, Captain Wallace."

Wallace presses a key, and from the laptop's speakers, the whirling, clicking, sputtering noise, and I suddenly realize what I'm listening to: it's a copy of the recording that was broadcasted back at the horse farm. The same tones, the same level of sound, the same damn voice.

Which wasn't Buddy's voice.

Yet Wallace had the presence of mind back then to record it.

Then the sound stops, and Wallace moves quickly, shutting down the laptop—Mom's laugh, her sweet voice, seeing her on that screen, a memory now back and sweet and making me nearly cry—the laptop lid slamming down. She then closes down the lid of the small metal suitcase and pushes it away, like it's suddenly radioactive or a bomb that's ready to explode.

Wallace takes a deep breath. "Well."

First Sergeant Hesketh comes back under the tent and says, "Captain?"

She slides the suitcase over to him. "Put this under cover, lock and key, as before."

Hesketh gingerly picks it up. "Yes, ma'am."

He leaves and I look up at the wet canvas, imagining I'm up in low Earth orbit, among all the shattered and broken satellites, and there's a Creeper killer stealth satellite in its orbit—whether automatic or operated by a Creeper inside, still not known—and maybe it detects a computer being turned on, in an area of North America, and . . . Now it's off. Does the satellite do anything? Does it fire off a laser? Drop a metal rod? Or does it just slide on, not bothering?

Or maybe there's no satellite overhead at all.

I look back at this little group of humans, feel a quick sensation of pride, here we are, battered, dirty, hungry and wet, and yet we fight on.

"Colonel Knox?"

"Yes, ma'am."

She lifts a hand in Buddy's direction. "Let's hear it."

"Buddy," Dad says. "Please. Authorization Papa Tango Papa. Understand? Papa Tango Papa."

Buddy quickly nods. Serena stares at him. Wallace leans over the wet and dirty wooden table. Dad shifts his position on the log.

Here it comes.

Buddy stands up. All of us stare at him, like he's a prophet, and I recall the briefing I got from Dad days ago, that Buddy is one of the first to learn most of the Creeper language, that they've talked to him in an attempt to convert him to their religion, belief system, whatever, and that he's precious to the Creepers, for his knowledge, for how he can speak their language.

Buddy licks his lips.

Here it comes.

His voice is so much stronger than the average twelve-year-old, and it's easy to make out every crisp word.

"Eat shit and die," Buddy says.

Dad looks shocked, Serena looks stunned, and Wallace ... I can't really explain what I see on her face.

I say, "That's it? Eat shit and die? Serena ... Dad. What the hell is going on here? Is this some sort of joke?"

Buddy smiles. "Eat shit and die."

I say, "What the hell?"

"Eat shit and die."

Dad gets up, gingerly touches Buddy's shoulders, says, "That's all right, Buddy. That's enough. Good job."

He smiles and looks to his sister, and then sits back down on the log. The rain lightens up some. Soldiers start trickling back to their positions.

"Dad," I say. "Is this a joke?"

"No joke," he says. "That's what Buddy heard. That's what he translated."

I shake my head. "Eat shit and die. Really? That's what got

them off like that? Hell, most of us got told that when we were eight or ten years old. What's the big deal?"

With a gentle voice, Dad says, "You don't understand, Randy."

For some reason, I get ticked off at Dad. Most of the time we get along okay but it's when he puts his Intelligence Officer hat on, along with his I-know-more-than-you-do voice, it really pisses me off.

Which is why I say, "Maybe I don't, Colonel, but please explain if you can, sir."

Dad doesn't seem to hear me, and says, "What little we know of the Creepers and their home planet...and how they evolved, the Creepers' ancestors...they developed underground, in burrows. Keeping the burrows clean and healthy was an important, almost holy responsibility for their race. We believe that when Creepers reached a certain age, they were tasked to do their part to keep their burrows, their environments, their cities clean. To tell someone to 'eat shit and die,' it's a terrible, almost religious insult. It says you refuse to be part of the tribe, clan or family. You refuse to help your race, your people. You tell others that they should eat the refuse, rather than have you take part in doing your duty. It's a terrible, terrible insult."

Wallace's face is like stone. I say, "So instead of having that PsyOps unit go out and ask the Creepers to surrender, they insulted them in the worse way possible."

"That's right," Dad says.

"That message came from Hoyt Cranston," I say. "He set us up. He sent us out there with that message, knowing we would get torched and slaughtered."

It becomes quiet and I say, "Damn him. Damn him."

Dad says, "Captain?"

His voice seems to jerk her awake. "Yes, Colonel?"

Dad doesn't say anything, and Wallace looks to Hesketh and says, "First Sergeant."

"Ma'am."

"Are we ready to move?"

"Ready as we'll ever be," he says.

"How's Private Hernandez?"

"I checked with Doc Pulaski about thirty minutes ago, ma'am," he says. "He made it all right through the night but he needs to get to a medical facility or MASH unit sometime today."

"We'll make it happen," she says. "All right, we break camp soonest and head out, back to Battalion. There, we'll refuel, load up with food and supplies, and regroup."

Dad says, "Then what?"

Wallace smiles with a look that seems to freeze my blood. "Then we're going to find Hoyt Cranston and I'm going to put his head on a pike."

We get up and I take Serena's hand, and say, "It's good to see you."

"Same here."

"What happened, with that recording?" she asks. "I don't understand."

Trucks are starting up and the tarpaulin next to Captain Wallace's Humvee is being dismantled. I say, "Two days ago, we approached two Creeper Domes about ten klicks away. We had a PsyOps Humvee with loudspeakers attached, and it supposedly carried a recording of Buddy's voice, with Buddy telling the Creepers to surrender, like he had done at the first Dome."

Serena says, "But the recording that Captain Wallace played, that's the one that was broadcasted?"

"Yes."

"But it wasn't the surrender message, was it."

"No," I say. "You heard Buddy's translation. 'Eat shit and die.' The wrong message was given to us."

"God," Serena says. "What happened?"

"The Creepers boiled out of the two Domes and set up a skirmish line, and attacked. The Company lost a half-dozen men and women, plus the PsyOps Humvee. Then the Company hauled ass and got the hell out."

"God," she says.

"Yeah, and there was a three-Creeper ambush on the state road the next day. It's been pretty goddamn busy."

Engines are starting up. Wallace is going into her Humvee and looks to me, makes a gesture. Serena says, "Now what?"

"You heard Captain Wallace. The Company's going back to Battalion for a refuel and re-equip, and then she means to get Hoyt Cranston's head on a stick. The wrong recording was given to us by mistake, or on purpose, but either way, Wallace is one unhappy company commander."

A horn honks. I take Serena's hand. "Let's go. The Captain wants you and Buddy to ride with her, and she's not one that likes to be kept waiting."

I walk with Serena's hand in mine, and she's holding Buddy's hand, and good ol' Thor sticks close to his new best friend. When we get to the Humvee Wallace says, "You two, get in. About time we get the rest of the company saddled up."

The overhead camouflage netting and tarpaulins have been dismantled, and there's the fresh stink of diesel, and I spot the truck that's carrying my platoon—my platoon!—and I know that's where I belong, but I still have a few seconds left with Serena and I intend to use them.

I briefly stroke her cheek. "You still look pretty good there, Specialist."

"No, I don't."

"I'm a sergeant," I say. "Don't contradict your higher up."

Buddy climbs into the Humvee, and Thor jumps up with his two front paws, tail wagging, and Buddy rubs his head. "I guess it's time."

Serena pulls away, gets into the crowded rear of the Humvee, and Wallace is striding back, and I suddenly think of something and lean down. "Serena?"

"Yes?"

"Your dad? Do you know where he is? Did you get to see him before you and Buddy slipped out?"

She stares straight ahead, Buddy's hand in hers, both hands in her lap. "Yes. We saw him just before we left, because he helped us escape. He was right there as we got out of the compound, slipped into the woods."

Serena turns to me, her face red, scrunched up, and she says through tears, "He said he would be right along with us. But he stayed behind. He was shot. They killed him, Randy. They killed my daddy."

Chapter Fifteen

I feel numb and out-of-sorts as I lead Thor to the truck carrying my platoon. I had known Major Thomas Coulson for only a couple of hours, and I had been charmed with his intelligence and his obvious love for his daughter and son. A very, very smart man who had worked with Dad to figure out some of the Creeper language, to contact the Creepers, and find out a) what the hell they were doing here and b) how we could end this war.

As far as I knew from Dad and Serena's dad—and through Buddy's knowledge and experience with the Creeper language—we knew part of a)—the Creepers were here as part of some sort of religious or belief mission, to convert the humans to their way of thinking, and some of the Creepers had seen Buddy as a human prophet, or at least their first true convert. That change in Buddy had allowed us to get the Creepers to originally surrender.

Now things were really fouled up, because Buddy's knowledge wasn't used during the confrontation with the two Creeper Domes, and Company K, "Kara's Killers," had been chewed up and nearly wiped out.

Oh, and by the by, we still didn't have any clue of b), how to end this war, this decade-long war that had blasted humanity back into the nineteenth century.

A voice: "Hey, Sergeant Knox."

I snap to. I'm at the rear of the truck. Specialist De Los

Santos, the kid with the eyepatch, is looking down at me. He says, "You looking to trot behind us with your K-9, Sergeant?"

A couple of grins from the soldiers back there, but not Bronson. He's sitting still, face blank, like he still cannot believe I've taken over his platoon. "No," I say. "Besides, he's a better trotter than me. Help me with him, will you?"

I grab Thor by his midsection and I must have done a clumsy job, because he gives off a little yelp that cuts right through me, almost as bad as any wound I've ever received in combat, but he stands up okay and Balatnic says, "I saved a piece of bacon for him. Can I give it to him?"

"Sure," I say, and then I get my gear, my M-10 and my butt up into the rear of the truck, and to my surprise everyone—including Bronson this time—reaches into their pockets or pouches, and come out with little bits of bacon for my boy. His tail wags as he works his way up between the sitting troops, and De Los Santos says to me, "Your boy did good yesterday, Sergeant. Saved our asses from being scorched."

Thor comes back and flops down, as the diesel engine starts up and we start leaving our bivouac area. I give him a good scratch behind his ears. "That's what he does."

"Yeah," a soldier up forward says. "But he did it damn fine."

In the late morning we get back on the state highway, start heading northwest, back to Battalion headquarters. Wallace promised us rest, relaxation and refit, and I'm looking forward to three things: a filling hot meal, a nice hot shower, and dumping this used Firebiter vest so I can get a new one that doesn't stink of someone else's sweat and blood.

Then we're supposed to go back out in the field and find Hoyt Cranston and put his head on a stick. I'm fine with that, except I remember when I first met the man from Langley, he had a squad of Special Forces soldiers with him, along with General Brad Scopes from Intelligence. That might make Wallace's goal a bit difficult to achieve, but knowing what I've seen so far from the captain, I'm sure she has a plan bouncing around in her head.

Speaking of bouncing, this part of the highway is cracked and very bumpy, and there's a long stretch of abandoned cars and trucks, having been pushed to the side after the upper atmosphere NUDETs struck during the first days of the war. There are a few farmhouses as well, and families out working the fields, and most of them ignore us as we roar by, save for one young boy with a tall scythe in his hands, who waves at us. A couple of my guys wave back.

I feel better as we move, the klicks passing by, the road rising some in elevation, and then there's a honking of horns up ahead, and we pull over to both sides of the road, engines grumbling. I lean over, M-10 in hand, and Thor is panting with contentment, so I'm not concerned.

First Sergeant Hesketh is striding down the road, talking to each vehicle as he passes, and when he gets to us, he says, "Just got a dispatch rider from Battalion," he says. "The Captain's reviewing the information, so everybody gets a fifteen minute break."

Sounds good to me, and the tailgate is lowered with a nice loud *bang!*, and I get out, helping Thor down, and I stretch my legs. Thor goes to the near truck tire and lifts a leg, and I say, "Keep that up, bud, and I'll get you for damaging government property."

Balatnic laughs and we move about, and a couple of the guys slip into the woods to let loose, and so does one of the woman soldiers, Chang, who's been a quiet sort since I took command.

The minutes pass.

I get a drink of water.

The couple guys come back.

I walk up to the front of the truck, look down the road. Small groups of soldiers are huddled together, sharing a smoke or a water bottle.

Behind us the rear Stryker has maneuvered so it's covering the road we've just passed, and Balatnic and two other soldiers are sitting on the broken asphalt, each taking turns rubbing Thor's belly.

I don't feel right.

The sky is partially overcast, and there's a nice chunk of blue sky visible, which doesn't happen that often. Usually that's one heck of a cheery sight, but not today.

Something is off.

Bronson comes by, and it comes to me. "Bronson."

He glares at me. "Sergeant?"

"Specialist Chang. Have you seen her?"

He makes a point of glancing around. "Nope, I haven't."

I say, "Get a detail, couple of guys heading up and down the convoy line. She's not around."

"All right," he says, and then I remember when I had seen her, walking into the woods, and I go in, and start moving quickly, it becoming dark with all of the crowded trees overhead, and I unsnap my holster, take out my 9 mm Beretta, and maybe I should have gone back and grabbed an M-4 and another soldier or two, but I want to move, and I want to move quick.

I don't have far to go. I move, stop, move again, looking for colored objects, or things that have straight lines, things that don't belong in nature. I go through the woods as quietly as I can, wishing I had Thor with me, and now I'm pretty pissed at myself, for moving too fast and not thinking things through. Some goddamn platoon leader I'm turning out to be.

I see a flash of blue off to the left. I slow down my movements, get closer, I hear a murmur, and then silence.

I pause, take my time moving forward, Beretta frozen rock solid in my hands, and I slide past a thick pine tree trunk, and the woods open just a bit. I can now make out BDUs, a young woman wearing a helmet. The blue I had seen earlier belonged to a pair of jeans, stretched out on the ground, being worn by someone that looked...

That looked pretty dead.

"Chang," I whisper.

She whirls around, knife in her hand. There's blood on the knife and her hand. I step forward, looking around. She's down on one knee. There's an open plastic bottle of water at her side. She takes the water bottle and washes her hands, and then the knife. The man next to her isn't moving at all, probably helped along by the severe gash in his throat. He's bearded, maybe in his twenties or thirties, and his eyes are staring wide open in surprise.

"You okay?"

In a whispery voice she says, "I am now. I came out to the woods to tinkle, and I was jumped by this man and his friend."

With a dirty rag, she's polishing the blade. I ask, "Where's his friend?"

She nods in a direction deeper into the woods. "Out there

somewhere. I think I got him pretty good before he ran off." She finishes wiping the blade and slips it back into a hidden scabbard in her right boot. "Sorry, Sergeant," she says. "Should have been more situationally aware. Those two shouldn't have been able to surprise me like that."

I slowly take in a 360-degree sweep of the area. There are broken twigs and a bent branch where it looks like someone had made a hasty retreat. "I think they got the worse of the surprise. You sure you're okay, Chang?"

A quick nod. "Ready to roll, Sergeant."

"Okay," I say. "Head back to the convoy. I'll be right along."

She looks troubled. "Can I take a minute?"

"What for?"

She nods at the dead man on the ground. "I still haven't peed yet."

I move ahead slowly, making sure I take everything in, and on a couple of branches, there's fresh blood, so Chang had in fact paid back her second attacker. Good for her. I just want to follow the blood trail for a couple of minutes, see where it leads, see if these two have any friends or companions out there, companions with weapons who might start heading to the convoy to exact revenge.

But I'm surprised at how quick it all concludes. The woods end at a hayfield, and up at the top of a rise is a nice house that was probably worth a hell of a lot when it was first built, more than a decade ago. Two full stories, exposed brick and stone, nice windows, nice shingles, two big stone chimneys and either end of the house. There's also a big attached garage, and in the rear yard, an empty swimming pool, some playground equipment, and what looks to be a big powerboat on a trailer, covered with a torn tarp, the wheels of the trailer flattened into the ground. A couple of outbuildings have been built—post-war, of course—and there's a fenced-in area where some chickens are rooting around.

Oh, and at the end of the woods, another bearded man, sitting still, hands over his chest, breathing ragged, blood seeping through his fingers.

I squat down in front of him. Behind his thick beard his skin is graying out. He notices me and says, "I'm hurt bad."

"I can tell."

"Will...will you help me? You're Army. You've got medics and shit."

"Tell me what happened back there, and I'll see what I can do."

He coughs. Frothy blood is coating his lips. "I'm...I'm hurt..."

"You're repeating yourself, and we don't have much time. What happened back there?"

He closes his eyes and I think he's about to pass out, but he rallies and says, "My brother Rick. He comes runnin' in. Says a convoy stopped by. Says we should check it out...We get there... See this cute Chink chick...all by herself...all by herself..."

Another ragged cough. "It's been so long...you know? The two of us...our parents were in Europe when the bugs attacked... just the two of us...and...it's been a long time..."

"So you thought you'd have a little fun with the young girl?"

He closes his eyes, grimaces. "C'mon...you're a guy...it's been...it's been a real long time..."

I stand up, holster my pistol. His eyes are wide open. I say, "You got neighbors that'll check in on your farm if they don't see you or your brother walking around?"

"Yeah...at some point...Shit, man, I hurt...will you help me?"

I reach over, pat the top of his head. "I'm right on it," I say, and I walk away.

At the convoy there's still not much going on, but Specialist Chang is there, and so is First Sergeant Hesketh, and he says to me, "Captain's compliments, Sergeant Knox, but you and the other two platoon leaders are wanted by the captain." He points up to the end of the convoy line and says, "About ten meters from the lead Stryker, head to the left. Overgrown driveway, leads to a barn. Inside you'll find the captain."

"Thanks, First Sergeant."

He sees Chang's face and mine, and says, "Anything going on I should know about?"

Chang looks a bit concerned, and I say, "Strictly routine, First Sergeant. Strictly routine."

I grab my M-10 and head out.

I walk up the cracked roadway and Thor decides to break away from having his belly scratched some more, and we pass by the troops and parked Humvees and trucks, and Thor looks pretty damn pleased with himself as a few more bacon pieces are tossed his way, and he manages to catch every single one of them in the air.

"Show off," I mutter, and he gives me a look as if to say, hey bud, I'm getting treated like the hero I am, what's your problem?

As Hesketh said, there's an overgrown driveway, the paved asphalt torn up and cracked, chunks missing, grass and bush growing through. The driveway ends in a gravel lot, and there's a huge barn before me, paint peeling, main door open. Captain Wallace's Humvee is there, and besides the barn, that's about it, just fields of hay rolling around on either side and to the rear. Her driver is standing by the driver's side mirror, scraping his face—or pretending to shave, I can't really tell—and I ask, "Where's Captain Wallace?"

He shrugs. "In the barn."

"And where's Specialist Coulson? And her brother?"

"Sorry, Sarge, they went for a walk with Corporal Miller."

I walk past the grooming soldier, check out the gloom of the barn's interior. "Where there? I don't see anybody."

"Go a little deeper, Sergeant," he murmurs, scraping some soap off his left cheek. "You'll find a ladder to the left. Start climbing. You'll trip right over her, I promise."

Inside the barn there's a smell of old hay and fuel. There are two John Deere tractors, back to back, their green and yellow paint scheme still pretty bright under dust and bird poop, but the tires are gone and it looks like some nests have been built in the exposed engines. Thor is behind me but when he spots the ladder and sees me start climbing, M-10 over my shoulder, he whimpers and lies down on the hay-strewn wooden floor.

"Oh, so now you're not so brave," I say. "Fair enough, take a nap. You probably need one after eating all that damn bacon."

He doesn't disagree and I start up the wooden ladder. It's worn, shaky, and the wooden rungs creak as I go up, and my heart just ups its beat a bit, because I've never really liked heights that much. I feel pretty good when the ladder ends at a loft, and I can get off.

And I do that, and there's no one around.

Damn.

A ways down is another ladder, and now I hear voices. I walk over, wood creaking even more, and I go up the ladder, and thank God it's shorter, but Wallace's driver is right, I practically trip over Wallace as I get to the end of the ladder.

We're all in tight quarters, with me, Wallace, Dad, and Lieutenants Jackson and Morneau. It looks like we're in a steeple—cupola, maybe?—of this barn, and the slats here have been punched out. The wooden floor is practically white and gray from all the bird droppings, and Wallace takes notice of me and says, "We have a situation here, Sergeant Knox. Care to take a look?"

"Certainly, ma'am," I say, and I elbow my way in and look out the opening. Damn, we're high. I swallow and take a good look of the countryside. I can barely make out the state highway we're on, and then the landscape drops away, a whole bunch of trees and green, and a few roofs nearby. In the distance—and it's hard to judge, maybe ten or so klicks to the northeast—there are two billowing clouds of black and gray smoke.

Wildfire.

Or Creeper sign.

Or probably both.

Wallace says, "What do you think, Sergeant Knox?"

"Can I see a map, Captain?"

"Absolutely."

She passes over an old U.S. Geological Survey map of the area, and it's been folded over and clipped to a metal clipboard. I take a couple of moments to puzzle it out, to see the state highway we're on, compare it to the small hill to the left, and the taller peak to the right, and further to the west, there seems to be a river. I say, "The smoke's coming from this state highway and Morristown Road."

"Very good," Wallace says. "Go on."

I look to the map again, see where the roads converge, where they departed from, and I say, "Creepers are attacking on both of these roads, and it looks like they're headed this way. They're cutting off our approach to Battalion headquarters."

"Good again," she says. "More?"

More? What more could I say? I was just a sergeant, a newly minted platoon leader, and I'm not used to being the center of attention with two lieutenants, a captain, and a colonel, even if the colonel happens to be my dad.

"Sergeant," she says, voice sharp. "Time's wasting. We're here, the Creepers are out there. What do we do? Attack? Retreat? Hide?"

Hide? That's not what the Army does. Attack? Two Creepers—at least—moving in a pincer position, ready to assist the other and force us to split our already thinned-out ranks.

Retreat?

No.

"Regroup," I say, handing over the topo map to the captain. "My . . . Colonel Knox has indicated there's an Air Force installation nearby, hopefully within driving distance. We go there, regroup, rearm and take some down time."

There's silence in the tiny quarters, and Lieutenant Jackson grinds his jaw, takes a pair of binoculars, looks at the plumes of smoke. I think I know what he's thinking. *Kara's Killers don't run.*

Wallace gives me a funny look, and then catches Dad's attention. "Some smart boy, you got there," she says, handing the topo map and clipboard to Morneau. "Because that's exactly what we're going to do."

I half-expect Dad to look happy or triumphant, but he looks scared, which in turn scares me. He's usually one cool and calm guy, under all circumstances, but something else seems to be going on.

"Lieutenant Jackson, your binoculars, if you please," she says.

"Ma'am."

He hands them over and she brings them up to her eyes, focuses just a bit. "There you are . . . two Creepers, maybe two columns, on a move, heading this way. Colonel?"

"Captain?"

"Creepers have attacked large units in the field before, taking aggressive maneuvers if they feel threatened, like when we've moved division strength units close to their Domes. Or they'll attack targets of opportunity when they're out in the field, doing whatever it is that's so damn important to them. But this . . ."

She turns her head away from the binoculars. "It looks like they're responding to us, to my company. Ever since that horse farm disaster, they've either been chasing us, blocking us by dropping that bridge, or prepping for an ambush. You're in intelligence. Am I making sense?"

Dad speaks carefully. "It certainly seems that way, Captain."

"Hunh." She turns back to the outside, binoculars to her eyes again, and she starts murmuring. "Why are you damn bugs so pissed off at me? Did I insult your queen? Kill a member of the royal family? Or are you still pissed at that 'eat shit and die' comment? Hey, that wasn't my fault...but still, I bet you don't care. Damn."

A pause, and she speaks again in the same murmur. "Why are you after me and my troops?"

Then she lowers the binoculars and her voice is crisp and louder. "All right. Everybody down to the ground. Colonel Knox, give my driver and the other lead drivers directions to this Air Force installation. Platoon leaders, make sure everyone's ready to head out. Time for us to ask the Air Force for help, as much as it pains me."

So we head down the ladders, and Wallace being the good officer that she is, climbs down last.

Chapter Sixteen

We're moving again, and I'm hoping that this Air Force place has hot showers, food, and at least a cot to sleep in, because my butt is seriously dragging.

I make sure my platoon is in the transport truck, all squared away, and I help Thor up into the rear, and remember I need to do something. I walk around and go forward to the cab, grab a side-view mirror stanchion and haul myself up.

"Hey," I say to the driver. "Sorry about the other day, when I pulled my pistol on you."

The young soldier just looks at the dials and then over the steering wheel, which he can barely do. "Sergeant?"

"Yes?"

"Get the hell back where you belong, okay?"

"Okay," I say, for what else is there to say?

I go around and I haul myself up in the rear of the truck. K Company reverses course and the lead Stryker—with its Creeper main arthropod head out forward—goes off, followed by an up-armored Humvee, and then Wallace's Humvee, and I strain to look and I think I see Serena sitting in the back, but I'm not sure. With a belch and a bellow, our platoon truck makes a three-point turn and heads along, and Bronson—sitting two up from me—shakes his head and says, "Kara's Killers, running. Never thought I'd see that."

Bronson looks right at me, like he's daring me to say something, but I don't rise the occasion.

"Running," Bronson says, swaying back and forth as our truck hits a bump. "Ever since we met you, Sergeant Knox, and the rest of those oddballs—including your daddy dearest—we've been screwed from the get-go. Ambushed twice, lost some good people, running around in circles, and now we can't even get back to Battalion."

De Los Santos says, "Lighten up, Bronson. It's just a retrograde motion, just like in the book. We're not running."

Bronson glares at him. "Call it what you like. I call it running."

I sense the rest of the diminished platoon is paying very strict attention to this little playlet, so I decide I have to step in and take my part in the action.

"Sergeant Bronson?"

"Yeah?" he sneers.

"If you like, I can get you off this truck, maybe get you as a driver in one of the Humvees," I say, slow and steady. "That way, you can drive and set your own path, and if you don't like where Captain Wallace is sending the company, if you think in all of your experience and knowledge you can do a better job, well, you could drive ahead and do just that."

Most of the other soldiers are smiling. I press on. "Plus, if you're driving, if you're scared of where we're going, why, you can just drive away. Would you like that Sergeant Bronson? Something I could arrange?"

He turns away and I speaker louder. "Sergeant Bronson, I asked you a straight question. What's your answer?"

Bronson turns back to me, face red. "No, Sergeant Knox. I'm fine where I am."

"I can't tell you how relieved that makes me," I say, and there are a few laughs, and even Thor looks up at me, like he senses I've done something right for a change.

We travel west along the Troy Road, also known as State Highway 7, which is an old, rough and crumbling three-lane road, with the center lane designed for the time when there were plenty of vehicles looking for a turning lane. The surroundings are mostly single-family homes, some farmstands, and a number of farms. The closer we get to a city called Schenectady, we join other vehicle traffic as well, including a few diesel trucks, some precomputer cars with A or B gasoline ration stickers on the windshield, and a fair number of horses and horse-drawn wagons.

Some of the underbrush and trees have been cut away, and I'm impressed to see that abandoned vehicles from ten years before have either been dragged away or pulled to the side of the road.

That demonstrates organization, a government, and considering what few bits of news comes from overseas about tribal and ethnic slaughters in former nation-states, it's a good thing to see. Some kids on bicycles even stop and wave at us as we go by. Another good thing to see.

I say to no one in particular, "What's the deal with Schenectady? They seem to be hanging in there."

A soldier named Buell with wispy-thin black eyebrows says, "Last century they were known for General Electric and also for making train locomotives. GE still has a presence—doing a lot of government stuff—and they've gone back to making trains and shit like that."

"Good for them," I say, noting a couple of smokestacks spewing gray and black smoke up into the cloudy sky. The convoy slows down, makes a few more turns, and we're on Erie Boulevard, with the Mohawk River on our left. Buell says, "Got an uncle there, at GE. Rumor has it, they're working on making shielding material so the bugs up in orbit won't zap computers or anything electronic in nature."

"That's bullshit," Bronson says.

I'm pleased to contradict him. "No, it's not. I was in a V.A. hospital in Albany last week. Most of the floors have power. I even rode in an elevator. And I stayed a night at a hotel that even had television."

"The hell you say," Buell says, awed. "Then how come it's not widely used? Shit."

"Supposedly it's very expensive, hard to produce, and is only used here and there. What does your uncle say?"

Buell smirks. "He says he could tell me, but then he'd have to kill me."

"Might be a fair choice," comes a voice from the other side of the truck, and there're some laughs as the convoy starts to slow down and haul over to the side of the road. There're a couple of horn signals and our truck finds a spot underneath a big spread of maples.

We wait, engine gurgling.

We continue to wait.

I say, "Hang tight, I'm going to see what's going on. Thor, stay."

With my M-10 over my back, I swing off the tailgate and jump to the ground, wincing at the pain in my left knee, which had been dinged up a couple of years ago back in Nashua, and which had earned me my second Purple Heart. I walk up the road, noting how the rest of the convoy has dispersed, and the ground falls some down to the Mohawk River, and I see why we've stopped.

There's not much of a bridge there, leading to the other bank, and to where the Air National Guard base is located. There are some cables, pontoons, grating, but no sure way across.

For the moment, we're stuck.

By the edge of the road are two dull yellow New York Department of Transportation dump trucks, along with a road grader and two other large Army trucks, with trailers attached to the rear. It looks like the crew here—a mix of Army Corps of Engineers, City of Schenectady workers and workers from the DOT—are building a pontoon bridge at this crossing. Wallace is talking to heavyset woman wearing captain's bars as well, and as I get closer I hear her end of the conversation.

"...should have it up and ready for you in a few hours."

Wallace looks over at the floating pontoons, the slabs of metal grating being lowered in, and she says, "Can't you move it along? We've got to be someplace and soon."

The Corps of Engineers captain says, "Going as fast as we can, but we want to do it right. About six months from now, a permanent bridge is gonna be installed here, Lord Jesus and the State of New York willing, and we want to be able to take 'er out as quick as we can when the time comes."

There's a DOT worker and a city worker standing behind the captain, and I say, "How did the original bridge go? Creepers?"

"Hell no," the state worker says. "Ice buildup this past winter."

Wallace looks to her map. First Sergeant Hesketh is standing behind her. "Says here there's a bridge on...Route 5, spanning the river, just south of here," she points out.

This time it's the city worker's turn to speak. "Nope, that bridge is down, too."

"Winter ice again?" I ask.

Nobody answers my question, and I have a pretty good idea why. In the first frantic months of the war, when columns and waves of refugees swept across the Interstates and state roads, looking for any kind of safety or shelter, some cities and towns destroyed bridges in a last-ditch attempt to prevent themselves from being overwhelmed.

It happened, but still, nobody likes to talk about it much.

Wallace steps back and says to Hesketh, "Get the company dispersed as best as possible. Tell Second Platoon they have picket duty. Everybody else can stand easy until we can get moving again."

She spots me. "Sergeant Knox?"

"Ma'am?"

"What are you doing here?"

"I wanted to see what was going on."

Wallace says, "Not your problem. Meanwhile, your platoon needs you. Get back to them."

I salute her and trot back, still not used to the expression "your platoon."

We find shelter in an old service station that used to hold a convenience store, and pretty much everything's been stripped or stolen over the years. I grab a blanket from my battle pack, find a corner that's not being used, and roll up in it to get some sleep. I'm almost snoozing when something thumps into my side, and I open my eyes and see its Thor, cuddling up next to me.

"All right," I say, patting his hindquarters. "Just let me sleep, all right?"

He doesn't sigh, pass gas or move, so maybe he is paying attention, and despite the hard floor and my pillow made from my pack, I quickly fall asleep.

Then the nightmares come. No need to describe them, except I always know when I have them, when I start panting heavily. Dad has heard me before, and my fellow soldiers, and I'm told it's like I've just run a marathon and can't catch my breath, and with every deep breath, there's a moan to go along with it.

"Knox!"

I can't move, I can't really see much, but all I know is that I'm being chased, and I had an M-10 round in my hand, and it's fallen into the snow, and—

"Knox!"

Something's coming something bad something's coming—

"Knox, wake up!"

I start to, and look up at the face of Wallace, peering down at me, a concerned look on her face, and I'm instantly embarrassed. I sit up and rub my face and say, "Sorry, Captain. I was having a bad dream."

"I can tell," she says, "and so can half the county."

I make to get up but there's something in her face that keeps me still, and she shakes her head. Her helmet is off and her red hair seems freshly washed, and she says, "How old are you, Sergeant?"

"Sixteen, ma'am."

"How long have you been in the Army?"

"Four years, ma'am, when I joined the National Guard."

"Your parents both allowed you in?"

I shake my head. "My mom and sister died in the first week. My dad was the one that let me join."

She nods, an odd expression on her face. "Your dad . . . has he always been in the Army?"

"No, ma'am," I say. "He was in the Reserves, and was also a history professor at Boston University."

"A smart man," she says.

"He is."

"But pretty secretive."

I say, "Well, he is in Intelligence."

She smiles at me, and right then I realize that she's probably the age my mom was, when the war began. Old enough to be my mother, and something warm and squirrelly slides around in my chest, and she says, "All right, get your platoon together. The bridge is ready and we're heading out."

"Yes, ma'am," I say, getting up, rolling up my blanket and getting the rest of my gear, and we start off to the truck, where our old soldier Sully is talking to Balatnic. Apparently he found an old magazine back at the service station—something called *TV Guide*—and he's showing it to a skeptical Balatnic.

"Look," he says, "Right there. It's listed. Do you see what I mean?"

She says, "You're telling me that there was a television program, I mean, a real television program, where people volunteered to get dumped in a jungle or on an island with no clothes, and no food."

"That's right."

"Sully, you mean people actually volunteered to sleep outdoors? With no clothes? And to starve to death? In front of cameras?"

"Look, it's right on this page," he says, pointing to a soggy page. "It's listed right here."

"And the people who volunteered, they'd starve? How come the folks there taking the pictures—"

"Recording the video."

"Whatever," Balatnic says as they approach the truck. "Didn't they feed the people when they started getting hungry?"

"No, they didn't."

"You mean they stood there and watched them starve?"

"Yeah."

"Didn't they have enough food to share?"

"Yeah, but that was the point, you see—"

Balatnic shakes her head, tosses her battle pack into the rear of the truck. "Sully, give it a rest. I can't believe any people would be that stupid."

Sully throws the old magazine onto the ground. "Trust me, we were."

He gets up on the truck—puffing and panting—and when I'm sure everybody's aboard I help Thor up. I'm about to join my platoon when I hear, "Excuse me," and I turn around, spotting a woman in her thirties or thereabout, with a knapsack on her back, but dressed in civvie clothes—but good civvie clothes—heavy boots, dark khaki slacks and camo jacket with a hood at the rear. Still, she's got a leather belt around her waist with a knife and holstered pistol. Her face is engaging but worn, like she's been outdoors a lot, and she has a wool Navy watch cap on her head.

"Yes?"

"Sorry to bother you," she says, and I see she has a pencil and notebook in her hand, "but I'm working on a book. My name is Pam Lockwood...I'm on leave from my job at *USA Today*."

"A book?" I ask, intrigued. "What's it about?"

"Ten years later, that's what," Lockwood says. "And I'm traveling around the country, talking to people, finding out how they're going on after the war started."

"Okay," I say.

"And I was hoping maybe I could talk to you and—"

The truck grumbles into life and there's a honk of horns up

forward. "Sorry," I say. "I gotta join my platoon. Good luck on the book."

She turns and steps back, watches as I get up on the rear of the truck, Thor looking happy I'm with him. Another blare of horns and we go back out onto the road to join up with the rest of the company, and as it's true most days in the Army, it's hurry-up-and-wait time. I'm not sure what's going on up ahead, only that there's a traffic jam of horse-drawn wagons and some civvie vehicles, mixed in with our lead Stryker and Wallace's Humvee. I stand up, looking for the woman who's writing a book about what things are like ten years after the start of the war— still sucks, would have been my contribution—but I can't see her.

I sit back down, and wonder how Serena and Buddy are doing, and I'm also wondering about their dad.

Dead.

Dead while trying to help them escape from the compound where they were being held.

By the man from Langley, who also seemed ready to torture Buddy in the CIA's approved method.

Earlier Wallace said she wanted to put Hoyt Cranston's head on a pike, and I was ready to help hold the base secure.

A couple of enterprising young folks are going up and down the convoy line, holding up things for sale, from sandwiches to fruit to...

One young girl, wearing overalls and in bare feet, topped off by a New York Mets T-shirt, holds up a plastic bucket filled with ice. And in the ice, all by itself, is a twelve-ounce bottle of Coca-Cola.

Wow.

She gets to our truck and holds up the bucket, and I say, "How much?"

"Fifty cents," she says. "And I get the bottle back."

I look to my platoon and no one says a word, and I start digging through my pockets, and two side pockets of my battlepack, and I scrape together a quarter, two dimes and five pennies.

I lower my hand, and thinking better of it, I say, "Take the bottle out, will you? We'll make the trade at the same time."

She says, "Show me your money."

I count out the coin from one hand to the other, and she puts the bucket on the ground. Up comes the Coke bottle and down goes the change, and the bottle feels nice and cold in my hand. I twist the top and give it a smell.

The real thing, it smells like.

I can sense everyone looking at me. I turn, hand the bottle to Balatnic. "Have a sip. Pass it around. Everybody gets a sip, okay?"

She nods, smiling, and smacks her lips when she's done. Up the bottle goes to the rear of the truck, and down it comes, every soldier getting a good little swig, until it reaches Bronson. He takes the precious bottle, which has just barely enough Coke to cover the bottom. Bronson lifts the bottle to his lip, swigs, and lowers it.

I'm surprised. It looks like he barely took a sip.

"Finish it off, Sergeant Knox."

"Thanks, I will," I say, and the Coke is still cold, frosty, and all too soon, gone.

I return the bottle to the young girl, and she races off, and the convoy lurches into action, and we slowly go over the pontoon bridge spanning the Mohawk River. We take our time, spacing out our vehicles so that there's not much strain on the cables and connections.

On the other side, we maneuver to the right, pass traffic ready to cross over to where we were, and there are two old Schenectady cops, holding the wagons and civilian trucks up. Blank, tired and dirty faces look up at us as we cruise on by, and I turn and look ahead. The Mohawk River is on our right, and we're now on State Highway 29, and through the trees and brush out there, I can make out a flat area that looks like airstrips.

Finally. The base we're going to is an Air National Guard base, which is just fine, since most active duty military bases were blasted during week one of the war. Most of the military action now takes place from Reserve or National Guard bases, or forts like my home back in New Hampshire, taken over from a prep school. Whatever. We do what we can, and right now, I don't care much about weaponry or military bases. My thoughts are pretty basic: Hot showers, hot food, and a soft bed.

The road gets rougher as it rises up. There are railroad tracks to the left, and beyond that, a chain-link fence. All right, lukewarm showers, food at any temperature, and a relatively comfortable bed, that'll do. Honest. Dusk is approaching and there's shadows stretching out on the road.

"Not long now, it looks like," Sully says, leaning over the side. "Hey, who found this place?"

I say, "My dad. Colonel Knox. He's in Intelligence."

"Unh-hunh."

There's a Y intersection, and we bear left. Up on the right is a gate sign made of cement that says:

STRATTON

AIR NATIONAL GUARD BASE

109TH AIRLIFT WING

Behind the sign is another chain-link fence, and a static display of a four-engine C-130 Hercules aircraft.

The gate sign is pockmarked with bullet holes and disfigured with splashed black paint. The C-130's wings are torn off on the grass, the grass about knee-high. To the left of this display is a guard shack, burned out. The gate is open. We slowly pass through, with hangars and buildings on either side.

The windows are broken, the roofs are collapsed. Our convoy slows down. There's a huge hangar to the right, and over the wide doors is another sign:

STRATTON

AIR NATIONAL GUARD BASE

ELEVATION: 376 FEET

That hangar has been blasted as well. Stretching out in front of us is a cracked runway, serving as some sort of parking area for aircraft. I count eleven C-130s stretching out, their tail structures and wing edges painted orange, and each four-engine aircraft is destroyed, the center fuselage burnt and crumpled. The convoy grumbles to a halt. The sky is growing dark. The runway is cracked, buckled, and small trees and brush are growing in the cracks as far as one can see.

A dog trots across. There's not a sign of life, nor a single light, or anything.

Sully says, "Your dad should have chosen better."

An Excerpt From the Journal of Randall Knox

Civilians, God love 'em. Sometimes they love us, more often than not they ignore us, and sometimes, well, sometimes it can get nasty.

About two months after I was assigned Thor as my K-9 companion, I was on a training mission with five other soldiers, four of them a year or two around my age, the last one a woman in her early twenties—a sergeant—who was wearing a Special Forces flash on the side of her BDUs. She was quiet and kept to herself. We others either had German Shepherds or Belgian Malinois to train with, but she had a black and white English Springer Spaniel named Spencer, who seemed friendly enough, unless you got too close to the sergeant and he gave a heavy growl.

We trained with a tall, skinny soldier with no visible rank, an eyepatch over one eye, and plenty of burn tissue on his face and hands. His name was Wood and he worked with a three-legged German Shepherd named Duke, and right at the beginning of our training he gave the following little speech: "You gents and ladies fortunate enough to train with these brave warriors better remember one thing. These dogs are smarter than you are, braver than you are, and have abilities of sight and smell you can't even dream about. You soldiers can be easily replaced. Not these K-9s. They have the intelligence, temperament and ability to help us contain and defeat the Creepers."

A deep breath. "You will care for your warriors, you will look out for their welfare, and you will treat them with respect. In return, they will gladly sacrifice their lives for yours, even though for the

157

most part, you're just worthless men and women not deserving of the love and dedication these fine animals will give you."

One last pause. "You will train with them, you will work with them on the battlefield, and by God, you will not leave them behind, and if you need to ensure that they pass without too much pain and suffering, you will perform that last duty. If you can't meet those requirements, leave now."

None of us left, then or later.

After a training session which involved Wood hiding bits of Creeper arthropod in woods, abandoned homes, and fields, then seeing which dogs could hunt them down—I'm pleased that Thor only missed one—we traveled back to the K-9 training facility outside of Portland, Maine, and stopped at a roadhouse for a rest break.

We were all traveling on an old transport truck powered by steam, and the only real bump was when we got there and Wood noticed a soldier called Crandall leaving the roadhouse with a cup of cold cranberry juice, and Wood came up to him and said, "Where's your dog?"

"She's tied up over by that fence."

"She been watered yet?"

"Uh, no," Crandall said and Wood slapped the cup out of his hand and said, "You get over there right now and take care of your dog. She comes first. Always. And only then can you get a drink."

Crandall bit his lower lip. "But I can't afford to buy another drink."

"Too bad," Wood said. "I'm sure the water is free."

Eventually our dogs were rested and watered, and I came out of the roadhouse with a watery glass of lemonade, sat next to Thor. We were still getting used to each other and I was happy to see that he didn't try to push things with me. He was learning his commands, he was learning how to come back when called, and I thought then we were going to make a good team.

We were about to leave when the trouble started. Three guys came out of the roadhouse, the center one stumbling and laughing, and it was easy to see they were drunk on something, homemade beer or wine or hard cider. The center guy had a glass bottle in his hand with a red and black label. He stared at us and his two buddies wandered off and sat at a picnic table, and the guy, who had a thick beard, patched jeans and a filthy gray sweatshirt, spat on the ground and said, "Lookie here, who's fighting on our behalf. Dogs, kids and a cripple."

One of his buddies said, "Oh, Christ, give it a rest, Brian."

"The hell I will!" He stumbled closer and stared at each and every one of us. "Kids. Dogs. To fight freaking aliens. That's our mighty, mighty armed forces now. Used to be the greatest in the world. Took up almost half of our freaking budget. I paid taxes, year after year, for protection . . . and for what?"

None of us said anything, although Wood was definitely paying attention, sitting on a boulder near the gravel parking lot full of wagons, a few hitched horses, some locked bicycles and two trucks with coveted C ration stickers on the windshield.

The man called Brian said, "I used to be a loan manager, for Citizen's Bank. Great job, great bennies . . . and now what? I slop shit at my stupid brother-in-law's farm."

Wood said, "Maybe you finally found your true calling."

His two buddies smiled but Brian wouldn't have any of it. "We spent billions and billions of dollars with gold-plated weapons, and what happened? Damn cowards didn't even lift a finger when the Creepers revealed themselves. Ran away. Hid their precious tanks, missiles, ships and aircraft. Bastards."

That was one very one-sided statement, and I wished I was brave enough to correct the drunk. The truth was, no government or military was prepared for when the aliens attacked. Who would be? Can you imagine prewar any politician trying to secure funding to defend against . . . what? Little Green Men? Please. And during their months-long journey to Earth, when telescopes first spotted them, the Creepers appeared to be a strange collection of comets traveling in formation.

But once the attack began, what passed for civilization on the third planet got squirted back into the nineteenth century. The United States, China, Russia, Israel and Japan—from what's been pieced together after the Creepers invaded—had highly secret antisatellite weapons that launched in the first hours of the conflict, with every one of them being burned out of the sky. Nuclear-tipped ICBMs that were hastily reconfigured to reach orbit and explode near the Creeper orbital base were either destroyed in air, or on the ground, or in silos, or in submarines. This one-sided battle raged for a few days, while the Creepers upped everything by dropping asteroids into oceans and large lakes, creating tsunamis that took out most major cities, since the most populous cities on Earth were built near large bodies of water.

The drunk went on and on, spittle drooling down his lips, calling us losers, cowards, incompetent. And I think, sure, after the Creepers landed, the slaughter continued. Most first-line military units were dispatched overseas, and hiding aircraft, tanks and other assets from the overhead killer stealth satellites only made sense while reserve, National Guard and other units scrambled like hell to fight the invaders.

We had to learn to fight differently, fight smart, and sure, it took time, but it also took a lot of blood and burned and crisped bodies.

There was a pause. Wood said, "You done?"

"Maybe I am, and maybe I'm not," he said. He held up the bottle he had been drinking, rotated the label. It showed a human hand in red, crushing a Creeper painted black. The name of the drink was RED VENGEANCE.

"See?" he said. "This cider maker...they know what we need... some kind of Red Vengeance to save us. Is that you?"

Wood quietly said, "Come along, squad. Let's saddle up."

We gathered up our packs, called our dogs to our sides, and went back to our truck, the drunk man's laughter and insults following us all the way.

Chapter Seventeen

First Sergeant Hesketh trots down the line of vehicles and shouts, "Disperse, everybody disperse! Get your vehicles undercover, slide into any open building or hangar." As he goes by he slaps the door of our truck. "Move!"

So we move. We roll out and we follow the lead Stryker and Wallace's Humvee, and we and another truck—carrying the Second Platoon—go into the darkness of the first and largest hangar. We park and get out, and the place is a mess. Holes in the roof, water on the floor, broken pieces of equipment scattered around and shoved into the corner. There's a smell of diesel and I look around, Thor next to me. Wallace talks to my dad, and I wander over. The Captain says, "This is your base? This is where you wanted us to go? Where is everyone? Damn it, Colonel, I told you this place had been marked as abandoned. Who's right? You or me?"

Dad looks pissed. "Hold on, hold on, let me check something out."

"Colonel, if you please, that would be one hell of an idea."

"Stand by, Captain, stand by," he says, and he stalks off to the far end of the hangar. I know why we've been dispersed. This place has been the recipient of Creeper attention, and I'm sure any killer stealth satellite up there seeing a military convoy roll in just might decide to attack once again.

Thor is near me, and he sniffs, sniffs some more. He paws at the concrete floor, whines some. I scratch his head, try to look into the darkness.

"What the hell is going on?" Balatnic asks me, and I shrug.

"Beats the hell out of me," I say, which isn't very inspiring but does have the point of being the truth.

Along the far walls are smashed shelves, desks, and cabinets that were probably used to keep tools or equipment. I make sure the First Platoon sticks around—"No wandering outside until we figure out what's going on," I say—and then I violate my own orders when I poke my head out for a quick look-see. Rain is starting to come down, and I wonder how Dad could have been so wrong. This place is dead.

I walk to the other side of the hangar, where I locate Wallace's Humvee. The driver is sitting on the hood, smoking a cigarette, and Wallace and the first sergeant are standing next to a smashed trophy case, talking about something, and Buddy and Serena are sitting still in the rear of the Humvee. The door is open and I lean in.

"Hey."

Buddy doesn't move, until he sees Thor, and he smiles. Serena turns and her face is red, eyes are swollen. "Randy."

"How are you doing?"

She says, "You know what the corporal said, our driver? He said if I'm a deserter, I could be shot. Shot!"

"Not gonna happen."

"Why?"

"Because whoever wants to do the shooting, will have to get through me and Thor. Me, I'm not that tough, but Thor, well, you've seen him work."

I'm hoping for a smile or an expression, but her face is still worn, tired, and filled with grief.

I think of what else I can say to brighten her mood when the hangar lights up with the blaze of a thousand lamps.

Thor starts barking, I reach for my pistol, wondering why in hell I left my M-10 back at the truck, and there's an amplified voice overhead that starts chanting, "Stand down, stand down, stand down."

The lights dim some and I put a hand on my forehead, gaze up at the ceiling, see how carefully the overhead lights and the sound system have been hidden. Then there's the sound of many boots hitting the ground, and the overhead voice starts up again: "Keep your weapons lowered, keep your weapons lowered, keep your weapons lowered."

Armed soldiers are now coming out from an open door, bearing M-4s and shotguns, and there seem to be dozens of them. Once I get done checking out their weapons, I check out their BDUs, which have a different type of pattern from what we wear. And then there are their cloth berets, which are blue.

Then it strikes me.

They are Air Force personnel, and they don't look happy.

An argument is underway from the door, and it comes out into this part of the hangar. Dad is talking loudly with an Air Force officer, and on the officer's BDU is an eagle. His nametag says LAUGHTON. He has broad shoulders, strong-looking hands, and thick black hair cut short, flecked with some white. He's a colonel, just like Dad, but boy, he's giving it right to my father.

"Colonel Knox, this is highly inappropriate," he says, walking out into the main hangar. "This unit of yours has to depart immediately, and only by one or two vehicles at a time. We don't want the Creepers' attention."

"Phil, look—"

"Colonel Knox, you can't stay, and that's that."

Wallace steps forward and says, "Captain Wallace, K Company, 153rd Regiment, Colonel Laughton. I intend to leave as soon as we can. If you can spare fuel and rations, we'll be out of here in an hour."

Laughton says, "Just how in hell did you end up here?"

"Colonel Knox directed us."

"He directed you wrong," he says.

"No doubt," she says. "But I'm ready to take my Company out, if we can refuel and get fed."

Laughton looks over our company and says, "Not your fault, I suppose. All right, that sounds reasonable."

Wallace steps closer to the Air Force colonel, lowers her voice, but for some reason—how close I am or the acoustics—she says, "Since we're being reasonable, I'd like you to tell your airmen to stop pointing their weapons at my company. One shot gets fired, even by accident, and I swear to Christ, I'll kill 'em all."

The colonel's face is impassive, but in a loud voice, he says, "Master Sergeant! Lower your weapons, return to quarters. And let's get some food and fuel to these troops."

A slight flurry of conversations, and Dad comes over to Serena and Buddy and says, "Would you come with me, please? I need to talk to Colonel Laughton."

Serena catches my eye and I feel like she's asking for permission, and I give the slightest nod, just as Dad says, "Specialist, please don't make me issue an order."

"No, I won't do that," she says. "Buddy, come along."

She gets out of the Humvee and with Buddy in hand, follows my dad to the entrance where the airmen had first appeared. Thor stays with me and whines again, scratching at the hangar floor. Rain is coming down heavier and puddles are starting to form under the holes in the wide roof. Pigeons fly off, and I think about the poor aircrews that had kept this hangar and so many others spotless and ready for any kind of military action years ago.

Dad, Colonel Laughton, Serena and Buddy, are clustered around the doorway, and then another Air Force officer emerges, wearing a white coat that makes him look like a doctor. He's in his thirties, short blond hair, with captain's bars on the collars of the coat, wearing BDU trousers.

"Kara!" he calls out. "Hey, Kara, is that you?"

Wallace flips around at somebody calling her name, and I can't believe the smile that comes across her face. "Mark! Damn it!" She runs across the pavement and Mark races right back, and there's a collision and laughter and even a quick kiss on the cheeks, and Mark steps back. "Damn, you look fine. How the hell are you?"

Wallace wipes at her eyes. "What do you think? Look at me."

Mark laughs and his eyes are watering, too. "You? Look at me, hon. I used to be the dopey computer designer and neighborhood nerd before our visitors came. Lots of changes." He looks past her for a moment and says, hesitantly, "David?"

Wallace shakes her head. "Kabul, last I heard. And that was... that was a long time ago."

Mark puts an arm around her, says, "Come along. I hear your folks are getting some food sent their way. I want to show you around some."

Wallace hesitates and Mark says, "No worries, Kara. Swear

to God. No worries. I'll make sure your troops are looked after. Just for a while."

She says, "First Sergeant!"

"Ma'am," he says, and I'm surprised to see him grinning. Maybe he's just happy to see his C.O. with a smile on her face.

"See to the troops while I'm gone, all right? And if some-thing...untoward happens, work with Sergeant Knox."

"Yes, ma'am."

By now the little crowd of Dad, Colonel Laughton, Serena and Buddy have gone into the rear of the hangar, and Captain Wallace and her old friend Mark walk through, and like some damn miracle, I can't believe what starts coming out.

First up are a number of BDU-clad airmen, about my age or younger, carrying folding tables and chairs. They set them up in a clear area of the hangar that isn't being dripped on, and De Los Santos, standing next to me, says, "I see it but I don't god-damn believe it."

"Me neither."

Some more airmen show up, and they're carrying tablecloths. White tablecloths. Carefully washed and folded, and they're spread over the tables, and then almost as one, my platoon and others turn at the scents coming our way, and there's a murmur as more airmen come out, carrying large covered serving dishes, potholders in hands. After a few minutes of putting stuff down and setting up other provisions, an Air Force sergeant approaches First Sergeant Hesketh and says, "We're ready if you are, Sergeant."

Hesketh shakes his head in wonderment. "We're always ready. Troops, line up!"

They only have to be told once, and I take the rear of the line, along with Hesketh. I briefly worry that the food and drink will be gone by the time I get there, but no worries.

There are deep rectangular dishes of chicken cutlets, meatloaf, sliced ham. Two types of gravy. Mashed potatoes and scalloped potatoes. Peas. Carrots. String beans. Lots and lots of fruit juice and water. Squares of chocolate. I sit down at a crowded table, just touching the tablecloth for a moment, and I eat. Thor is with me, and I feed him as I feed myself. I don't think I've ever been in a position to feed him so much food. When I'm finished I see my fellow soldiers are back in line, going for seconds, or thirds. I join them, eat some more, and then Corporal Cellucci, the company's quartermaster, talks quietly to the Air Force sergeant that seems to be in charge, and he nods and says some words to his mess crew, and the leftovers are packaged up and carefully given to Corporal Cellucci.

Then a fuel truck grumbles into the hangar, as rain continues to pour from outside, and Hesketh gets up and goes to the Air Force crew manning the vehicle, and soon enough, one by one, our vehicles are fueled up.

I just sit with members of my platoon, who are leaning back in their chairs, smiling and talking, some just touching their bellies, like they're trying to make sure it isn't all an illusion.

Balatnic shakes her head. "I've never seen the Air Force before."

De Los Santos grunts. "Who has? They can't fly, so they hide. They're experts at hiding."

Sully says, "Yeah, they've been hiding well for ten years. Almost as good as the Navy. And we're the ones out there getting crisped and lased, while they eat all this good food and don't do shit."

Even though I'm warm, comfortable, and about the best fed I've been in a very long time, I can't let this pass. "Sullivan, that's not true."

"The hell it isn't, Sergeant Knox."

"More than a month ago, when the Creepers' Orbital Battle Station got blasted, who do you think did that? Peru? No, it was the Air Force."

Balatnic says, "So what. They were able to toss a few missiles up there and caught them napping. That doesn't mean anything."

I look to all of their satisfied yet defiant faces, and say, "Wait. You don't know the details of the attack? You really don't?"

De Los Santos adjusts his eye patch. "What details? In case you haven't noticed, Sarge, we're sort of a mobile unit."

"You just think it was missiles that went up and destroyed the station?"

A voice up the table. "That's what we heard."

I say, "You heard wrong, then."

By now everyone's looking at me, as the mess crew gather up the serving platters and plates. I say, "Right after the invasion, the Air Force got orders to destroy that station, any way they could. Standard missiles and Earth-to-orbit satellite killers didn't work. They were too complicated, had too many electronics. Anything shot up there got burnt out of the sky."

Sully says, "They figure out a way to shield them, then?"

"No," I say. "They figured out a way to make the missiles simpler. They recovered some old solid-fuel rocket boosters, dragged them by horses to an abandoned base, somewhere in Utah, I think. Worked for years to design them and make them work, because they were sure they only had one chance. And they were right. And nearly two months ago, they launched."

Sully says, "Yeah? So?"

I rub the top of Thor's head. "You didn't hear how they made them simpler then, less complex."

Nobody says anything.

"They were manned," I say. "Each rocket had a warhead, and each rocket was piloted by a volunteer from the Air Force. Eight rockets were launched. One blew up after taking off, and there were no parachutes or escape rockets. Our military got word via telegraph to other countries, to shoot off diversionary ICBMs at the time the Air Force launched. They did that. Six of the rockets found their target, destroyed it."

"What happened to the seventh one?" Balatnic asks. "Did that one make it into orbit?"

"Yes, it did," I say. "It was the squadron commander. A Colonel Victor Minh. His job was to escort them to the orbital battle station, see their attack, and return to Earth. His rocket didn't have a warhead. It had a heat shield, so he could get back safely. The other six pilots, the other six volunteers...it was a one-way mission, and they knew it."

Another Humvee moves toward the hangar entrance, to fuel up. Sully says, "Bullshit. How the hell do you know that, Sergeant?"

"I just know."

"And I still call bullshit," Sully persists. "How the hell would you know something like that, all those details, you being a Nat Guard soldier from New Hampshire?"

I still have my platoon's attention, but the attention is a bit hostile. With reluctance I say, "Because I was there, at the Red House, when the President awarded him the Medal of Honor. That's why."

"Wait," De Los Santos says. "You were there in Albany, before it got smoked?"

"That's right," I say. "I heard him tell the story, right there. From his own mouth."

I shift my gaze around the table, make sure everyone sees my look. "So knock off the chatter about the Air Force being cowards, not eager to fight, all of that crap. The first year or two of the war, their pilots and crews knew that every mission they flew was most likely going to be a suicide mission. Remember that."

There's quiet for a bit, and Sully says, "Hold on, hold on. I read a bit about that in the *Daily Gazette*, just a paragraph or two. Yeah. Air Force guy got the Medal of Honor, something to do with knocking off the orbital battle station. But it also said some sergeant got the Silver Star. A sergeant in the National Guard."

I don't like the attention I'm getting, but before I can say anything, Balatnic says, "Was that you, Sergeant Knox?"

"Yeah, I guess it was."

"What did you get it for?" she asks.

"For getting in the way of things."

"Shit, no," Sully says, leaning back in his chair, his eyes widening. "There was something about that in the story, too. The sergeant who got the Silver Star, it said he got it for killing a Creeper. By himself. With a goddamn knife."

The back of my head is warm and there's a bunch of questions coming at me, and I'm saved by a young airman who comes up to our table and says, "Anybody know where I can find a Sergeant Knox?"

"Right here," I say, standing up.

"Very well," he says. "I got a message from a Colonel Knox, requiring your presence. Will you please come with me?"

I don't like being dragged away like this, but Dad must have something going on. "I guess so."

He nods. His cheeks are scarred with acne. "Also, Colonel Knox requested that your K-9 unit be left behind."

"Really?"

"Yes, Sergeant."

"You know why?"

"No, Sergeant."

I just gather up my belongings, and say, "Sergeant Bronson?"

"Yes?"

"Keep an eye on things while I'm away. Thor, stay."

"Sure," he says, and adds with a smart-ass smile. "Mind asking the Air Force if they have any ice cream they can spare?"

Laughter, and I say, "I'll see what I can do," and I follow the young airman.

Chapter Eighteen

I follow the airman through the door at the rear of the hangar. We enter a large room with a scuffed tiled floor, and a segmented door with a sign overhead saying 173RD AIRLIFT WING, ANY WEATHER, ANY TIME. Unlike the signage outside and in the hangar, it's hung correctly and is in good shape.

The airman inserts a key into a panel by the segmented door, and turns it. The doors separate and open up, and I recognize what it is: an elevator, like the one I rode back at the V.A. hospital outside of Albany. I confidently step in and say, "This is my second ride in an elevator."

"Good for you, Sergeant," he wrinkles his nose, and I know why. I must smell pretty ripe from my own exertions, plus the sweat and blood on my Firebiter vest. Too bad, I think, them's the smelly fortunes of war. Inside the car there's a little square box with numerals on it adjacent to the open doors. He stands in front of it to block my view and quickly punches in a number sequence, and an old memory comes back to me:

Keypad.

The doors slide shut, there's a lurch as we descend, and then the doors open up to reveal—

Paradise.

Right in front of us is a pad to—get this—wipe our feet, and there's dark green carpeting extending in all directions. Overhead lights are burning brightly and the air feels crisp and clean. Sitting in a desk just outside the pad is an older, tough-looking Air Force NCO in BDUs, white hair cut high and tight, suspicious eyes squinting at me. The Air Force has its own set of chevrons, shaped like blue and white wings, and I can't quite get which kind of sergeant is sitting in front of us, but sergeants are sergeants all over the world, especially this one, with a clipboard before him next to an unholstered Model 1911 Colt .45 pistol.

"Identification, please, Sergeant Knox."

I take in the luxurious atmosphere of the place. There are three corridors, running to the left, right, and middle, and there are closed doors, plenty of bright lights, and other Air Force personnel walking along, none of them looking particularly tired, burned, scared or hungry.

"You want my ID?" I ask.

"That's right," he says. "Now, if you please."

I get the feeling it would make his day to pick up the pistol and blow my head off, but I dig through my pockets in my worn and muddy BDUs, in my jacket underneath my vest—finding the dog biscuit that's reserved for Thor one of these days—and then I locate my thin leather wallet, from which I pull my official Armed Services Identification.

The Air Force sergeant snorts, takes it from my hand, writes something down on the clipboard, and says, "Perkins, you know where to take our guest?"

"Yes, Master Sergeant."

"Then run him along, then."

"Yes, Master Sergeant." Perkins points to the center corridor, and we walk briskly along, and the cleanliness of everything just stuns me. Who knew all of this luxury was buried underneath the destroyed base overhead?

Dad, I think. Dad knew.

"Right here," he says, stopping at a door marked CONF 112. He knocks twice on the door, opens it up, and in I go.

There are four people in the conference room, sitting in leather chairs around a brightly polished wooden table, and three of them don't look happy at all. Along the walls are old framed photos of Air Force aircraft in the air, back in the day when Air Force aircraft could actually fly.

The fourth person is Buddy Coulson, who looks as impassive as ever. Next to him is his sister, and then Dad, and sitting at the head of the table is Colonel Laughton. Not a smile or relaxed look among the three of them.

Dad says, "Sergeant Knox, take a seat."

"Yes, sir," and I do so. Damn, the chair feels nice.

The colonel glares at Dad. "Go on, Colonel, say what you want to say."

Dad clears his throat. "We have a situation, Sergeant Knox. I'm working with Colonel Laughton on a matter, and have asked Specialist Coulson and her brother to assist. Specialist Coulson says she won't cooperate unless you join her."

Serena looks to me, eyes nervous, her usually fine blonde hair still a mess, smudges of dirt on her face and hands. I say, "Is that right?"

"Yes," she says.

Colonel Laughton interrupts. "It's a threat, and I don't like threats."

Serena says, "It's no threat, Colonel. It's the truth. Sergeant Knox will be with my brother and me, or I'll tell Buddy not to cooperate."

Laughton says to Dad, "Don't you have any influence over this boy?"

Dad says, "I do. In part."

Laughton says, "Then I refuse—"

Serena says, "Maybe I didn't make myself clear. Either Randy comes with me, remains at my side, or I'll tell Buddy a coded message that will stop him. Block him. Everything he's learned about Creeper language and everything else will be gone. Wiped. Forgotten. Do you want that on your record, Colonel? Or your conscience?"

The only sound now is the hum from the overhead lights. Even that little noise brings back memories of being with Mom, in a supermarket filled with everything. The lights overhead glowing so bright and so soft.

Laughton's face is like stone but he says, "I guess not."

Dad says, "Sergeant Knox, are you all right with this arrangement?"

Serena's face is still troubled. I say, "Absolutely. I'll do as Specialist Coulson requests, and as Colonel Knox requests. But in exchange, I want hot showers and clean clothes for all of Company K. Including the specialist and her brother."

Laughton says, "Damn it, Colonel Knox, what kind of god-damn outfit is this? We don't have the time!"

"Make the time, Colonel," I suggest.

"Shut up," Laughton snaps at me. "Colonel Knox, I've had quite enough from these...kids. Kids making demands, ordering me around, being royal pains in—"

Serena takes Buddy's hand. "Buddy, it's me. Can you hear me? Buddy, Authorization—"

"Stop that!" Dad yells. "Colonel Laughton, are you out of your mind? You're going to threaten all we've learned, all we can manage, because of your damn Air Force pride?"

Laughton's face is bright red and his fists are clenched, but he nods. "All right...We'll set up showers, laundry facilities, do what we can."

I say, "Specialist Coulson and her brother. They go first."

"And you?" Laughton says. "You want to be next?"

"Nope," I say. "I'm a platoon leader. I can wait."

So wait I do, and I try to ask Dad what the hell is going on, but he scurries away with Laughton, and I'm escorted to a waiting area. Some area. It's a small room, two chairs, and a round little table in the center. A little concrete cube, with framed photos again of aircraft that haven't successfully flown in a decade.

On the table is an old prewar magazine called *Time*. On the cover is a photo of a young woman accused of killing her two children in some sort on inheritance scheme. I flip through the bright photos and pages, past lots of pages about sports and movie stars I've never heard of, and I note a couple of news stories about troubles in the Mideast—I'm sure that any tribes still alive in the Mideast are still causing trouble with each other—and in the back is a small story about the oddly shaped Comet Yoko Imai making an approach to Earth. The story quotes a cult leader stating that the comet was a sign from aliens, and a scientist is quoted saying that the comet's arrival would be spectacular.

Funny how they both turned out to be right.

I put the magazine down, see there's a bunch of brochures, all the same. I pick one up. Very slick and bright, showing a jet aircraft shooting up into the sky.

AIR FORCE: AIM HIGH.

I gently put the folder back down.

Aim high.

I take one more glance around the bunker. Some aiming high. Poor guys haven't been doing that for years, save that suicide mission last month.

The floor here is carpeted. I push the chairs aside, stretch out on the floor, and almost instantly go to sleep.

The door opening wakes me right up, and my hand is on my holstered 9 mm before I'm even off the floor. The same airman from before is there, sniffing again at what he smells—me—and says, "Colonel Laughton and Colonel Knox want to see you now, Sergeant. I'll take you to them."

"Thanks," I say, get up, stretch some, think I could really go for a cup of coffee, knowing the Air Force probably has some very fine coffee, but I try to be a good soldier and I walk with the airman as we go down one corridor, then another, and we go to another set of doors. An elevator. Once more, a key is used, we step in, and the airman punches the numbers.

"You ever forget the numbers?"

"Never," he says.

"You sure?"

"I'm sure," he says. "You screw something like that, you get transferred to a unit topside. Nobody wants that."

"Gee," I say. "Nice to have a choice."

The airman says nothing. The doors open up.

Here the floor is bare concrete. The lights are dimmer. It's also cooler.

"There you go," he says.

"You're not escorting me?"

Terror seems to lift right out of his voice. "You got that friggin' right. Sergeant. Go down this hallway, you'll be greeted."

I step out and the airman pushes buttons so hard I think he's trying to break a finger.

The doors slide shut with a heavy thud.

I wait. And then I stroll down the corridor. It's wide and the concrete is scuffed, like heavy equipment has been dragged back and forth. The corridor then makes a sharp left, and there's a cluster of military personnel there, and all look at me as I approach. Dad. Colonel Laughton. Serena. Buddy. And an Air Force officer—a major?—in BDU pants and a white coat. All are standing in front of a metal door that looks like it belongs to a vault.

Laughton says, "Nice of you to join us, Sergeant Knox."

"Got here as quick as I could," I say.

Dad says, "This is Major Paternoster. Once we get beyond this door, he will be in charge of everyone, including me. Do you understand, Sergeant Knox?"

No, I didn't, but I wasn't going to say that. "Yes, sir, I do."

"Good. Major?"

The major has black bushy eyebrows, a sharp hawk-like nose, and his hair is a gray-black flattop. He looks nervous. "Colonel, really, to access this area, it requires a thorough background check of the visitor. This is highly irregular."

"I take responsibility," Laughton says.

"Good," Paternoster says. "Someone should."

Serena turns and offers a slight smile. Her skin is freshly washed, as is her hair. Buddy looks good, too. Their clothes are either freshly issued or washed. Serena says, "Randy?"

"Yes?"

"Stand with us, won't you?"

"Absolutely."

Paternoster says, "Everybody move back, please."

Then I notice a painted area on the floor, black and yellow stripes, and there's another access box or keypad, and Paternoster punches in the numbers, and there's a loud hissing noise, and a *thunk/click*, and the door slowly starts to open up, swinging to the left. It moves slowly and I'm stunned at how thick the door is, almost a third of a meter thick. It moves slowly and then halts.

There's a rectangle shape of darkness before us.

"Is this where we're going?" I ask.

Dad says, "That's right."

I take Serena's hand. "All right, let's do it."

I walk to the darkness.

But there's light, dim as it is. We're in a large room, from what I can tell. A bell rings somewhere and the door starts to move back. I sense other people in the room, and I see they're sitting in opposite corners. Soldiers, it seems like, sitting down.

The door gently slaps shut, there's another *thunk/click*.

I'm smelling something.

God help me, I'm smelling something.

Paternoster quietly says, "Lights, please."

The lights gently brighten. The floor is still concrete. There's a quiet armed man at either corner, and they're not soldiers, they look like Air Force Special Ops, and they're wearing body armor, armed with modified Colt M-10s, and neither one of them is looking at us.

They're looking at the other end of the room.

I'm smelling cinnamon.

Strong.

The other end of the room has thick glass, waist high, going up to the concrete and steel ceiling, and behind the glass, a shape is moving, unwinding, stretching, now turning and looking at us—

I think Serena screams.

I know I do.

I want to run, I want to hide in the corner, I want those two Air Force men to start shooting—now!—for behind the thick glass is a Creeper, out of its exoskeleton, alive in all of its horrible shape and colors, and the twin eyestalks seem to be staring right at me.

An Excerpt from the Journal of Randall Knox

Funny story, I know, but it's true that it took a number of years before I saw a live Creeper out in the open, on the move. In fact, most civilians have never seen a Creeper, unless they're in an area where they operate, or happen to have the bad luck to be in a place that gets a Creeper's attention, like a wheat field, or some group trying to start up an unshielded electrical generator, or flying in a restored civilian aircraft.

But millions had died because of what the Creepers had done in the first weeks of the war, and they became the Fifth Horsemen of the Apocalypse, skittering along the landscape, burning or lasing anything in their path or that caught their attention. For me as a young boy, the first few years after the war started, I thought of them as some terrible species of monster that had killed my mom and sister, made everything cold and wet, kept me hungry most of the time, and also made Dad cry (and only when he thought I didn't see him).

A year after the war I joined the Cub Scouts. When I was ten, I joined the Boy Scouts, and left them at twelve to join the Army, or the N.H. National Guard, which was of course attached to the regular Army. Basic was at an old Boy Scout camp near the White Mountains, and the truth was, I loved it. We were relatively well-fed, our instructors were tough but fair, and it was like an extended Boy Scout Jamboree, except for the classes on military science, weaponry, and the Creepers. There were lots of photos of Creepers, and about then is when the classification of the aliens was becoming known. All of them were armed but they had some differences. Battle Creepers were always the shock troops that led an assault. The Research Creeper was one that spent time examining the battlefield, our weapons, our housing, and humans, both dead and alive. (Rumors of what happened to prisoners were popular stories in the barracks at night, like ghost stories of old around the campfire). And there were the Transport Creepers, which had a large bin-like structure in which they'd dump stuff for later examination, like old computers, books, bones, and whatever.

There were plenty of photos of Creepers in action, as well as some old motion pictures in black and white of them in battle, mostly winning.

When I was done with Basic, I was sent to the First Battalion of the N.H. National Guard, "Bulldog" Company, which was a mix of regular Army, reserve Army and the National Guard. At the time we were still losing, and losing badly, but we were still fighting. The M-10 and its deadly gas cartridge were still a couple of years from being developed and reaching the battlefield.

After some more training, I was assigned to the First Platoon, and was coupled with a Corporal Belinda Garcia, a chubby woman in her forties who had rejoined the Army after that October 10th—10/10, NEVER AGAIN was painted on walls and vehicles everywhere—and she helped guide me through the training and use of the M-4, still the standard infantry rifle.

But the training would eventually end, and one early Sunday morning, it did. We were woken up by bells ringing, were dumped into the backs of horse-drawn wagons, and taken out to a rural town to the west called Warner, which was near the practically abandoned Interstate 89. A Research Creeper had been spotted coming down the highway, and we were going to do our best to stop it.

We were set up in foxholes, stretching from one side of the highway to the other, and the Captain swore and got our wagons to work, dragging off abandoned cars and trucks still in the middle of the road, stopped dead in their tracks six years earlier when the NUDETs had struck, wanting to open up clear fields of fire.

Then I was with Corporal Garcia, both of us breathing hard, M-4s in our hands. We looked to the northwest, where the Creeper was supposedly coming from. A blue flare rocketed up into the cloudy sky, beyond the trees and low hills.

"Here it comes," Garcia whispered.

"Okay."

And as she did a lot during our time together, she gently slapped the top of my helmet. "Hang in there, sport. You'll do fine. Just follow my lead, all right?"

"Yes, Corporal," I said.

The Captain, keeping low, ran from foxhole to foxhole, checking us out, and then a white flare came up.

"Real close now!" the Captain yelled. "Fire on my command, and not a moment earlier!"

The Captain went back to where two pickup trucks—a Ford and a Chevy—had been overturned, and which he was using as his CP.

A slap to the head.

"Eyes forward, sport. Not to the CP."

"Yes, Corporal."

My mouth was dry and my hands were shaking, but I felt good, being next to Corporal Garcia. She was from Lowell in Massachusetts and I said, "Corporal?"

"Yeah?"

"What did you do in the Army . . . I mean, before you reupped?"

She smiled. "Oh, I was real important, sport. Real important. I was in the Finance Corps, making sure everybody got paid on time. Army wouldn't run except for me and my buds."

A shout from the other side of the empty highway. "Here it comes!"

A bright red flare shot up, so close I could see the sparks flying out, and then the Creeper appeared from behind a stalled tractor trailer truck. Some brave soul tossed a smoke grenade in its direction, and there was a billowing cloud of orange, a flare of laser fire from the Creeper's right segmented arm—probably torching the soldier who had tossed the grenade—and another yell, "Incoming!"

Garcia tugged me down and I curled up in the bottom of the foxhole, as the sound of incoming rounds whistled overhead. There were three quick explosions—81 mm mortar fire from a squad up on one of the near hills, firing at the orange smoke—and then we came back up.

A bullhorn up to the mouth of the Captain, and "Fire, fire, fire!"

Our M-4s fired, single shots, all aiming as best as we could to the approaching Creeper, which had emerged from the haze and smoke from the mortar rounds. Three mortar rounds were all that we could spare, and there was no expectation that it was going to kill or hurt the Creeper. Our only hope was to slow it down, and slow it down we did.

The Creeper fired back, using flames from its two arms, lighting some of the cars and trucks.

I should have been scared, terrified, or frozen in fear as the Creeper approached, but I felt powerful, energized.

Pow.

Pow.

Pow.

Each shot from my M-4 echoed out, the recoil jolting my shoulder some, and I knew I was aiming right at the center arthropod, and I knew each round was bouncing off its armor, but I felt great.

I was fighting back.

I was avenging my dead mother, my dead sister, the millions of others, the drowned cities, the dead power lines, dead computers, and everything else.

I emptied my magazine, popped it out, inserted a new one, snapped the action back, kept up the fire. So did Garcia. So did everyone else in our depleted company.

But the Creeper kept on moving, right towards our line of foxholes.

I clenched my teeth, recalled my training, and kept on firing, even though my legs were shaking and part of me felt like dropping my M-4 and running into the woods.

The Creeper got larger in my view. The stench of cinnamon was strong, and the air was hot where the fire poured out of its claws.

Click-click, click-click, click-click noises became louder as the Creeper got closer and closer.

A heavier, deeper POW!

Followed by another shot.

And another shot.

The Creeper halted, paused.

Our outgoing fire dribbled off, even though no one had ordered us to do so.

We waited.

The Creeper was stock-still, not moving.

The wind shifted, and an incredible stench came our way, and there were hoots, hollers and some applause. From a near foxhole a two-person sniper crew emerged, a brother and sister team, the brother being the spotter, the sister being the shooter. She had

*long blonde hair, and waved, and made an exaggerated bow, her
bolt-action rifle with telescopic sight in one hand. More cheers.
She was an accomplished youth shooter training for an upcoming
(and of course cancelled) Olympic games, and was using the only
offensive weapon we had at the time: shooters with perfect aim,
rock-steady nerves, and firing a depleted uranium round that could
penetrate the segmented armor and kill the Creeper inside.*

I took a deep breath. Garcia tapped the top of my helmet.

"Your first engagement, sport," she said. "What do you think?"

I waited, and then said, "I loved it. I want to kill them all."

Garcia's smile got even wider. "Welcome to the war, Private."

I would be thirteen in four months.

Chapter Nineteen

With the Creeper full in my view, I fall back against the closed armored door, my hand going to my holstered Beretta, and part of me thinks, that won't work against a Creeper, and another part of me thinks louder, the damn thing is unarmored. It's out in the open! It should be easy to kill!

Dad's voice cuts through the chatter. "Randy! Stand down! Randy! Stand down! It's all under control."

I shudder, take a breath, feel like throwing up. Serena's twisted to the right, and she's not feeling like puking, she's actually doing it. Buddy stands and stares at the thick glass, looking fascinated.

"Randy!"

I take a deep breath, not wanting to smell cinnamon, not wanting to smell what's just come out of Serena, who's shaking next to me. I put my arm around her, pull her in tight. "Right here, Colonel."

Dad says, "There's nothing to worry about. Nothing. That Creeper is out of its exoskeleton, it's behind this armored glass, and it can't hurt you, or anyone else here."

Serena coughs. "Bullshit. It's evil. It . . . Randy, kill it. Can you kill it?"

Laughton says, "Shut up. Do you know how few prisoners we have, after ten years of this goddamn war?"

It sounds childish but having Dad standing nearby, not panicking, looking calm and collected, well, it helps. I squeeze Serena's shoulder again. "It's all right. I'm right here. It's all right."

Paternoster mutters and goes to a metal cabinet, comes out with a bucket and rags, and cleans up Serena's mess. The Special Forces guys don't pay any attention to us. They keep their eyes forward, on the Creeper. They're sitting in comfortable chairs, with small desk and a Thermos jug in front of them, and their own modified Colt M-10s.

It looks like comfortable duty, being out of the rain and wind and snow, their sole job being to kill this Creeper if something goes wrong, and despite all that I wouldn't be them for anything, for they have to spend a shift, being in the close company of... this thing.

I've seen plenty of after-action photos, drawings, and a couple of jerky movie films that show the Creepers once they've been dragged out of a damaged exoskeleton. After they die, they usually decompose quickly in a stomach-churning process that leaves a puddle of slime behind. It's rare to capture a Creeper. So very rare.

And here's one, right in front of me.

Paternoster is still cleaning and I clench my teeth, take a step forward. Dad is talking to Laughton, and I catch parts of their conversation as I force myself to stare at the imprisoned Creeper.

"...this one looks bigger than Harriet..."

"...that's because she is. This one is Margaret..."

Dad says, "What the hell happened to Harriet?"

"...died. Don't know why..."

"...where did Margaret come from?"

Laughton says, "...up near Churchill, around Hudson Bay. Canadian Special Operations Regiment grabbed her and transported her to us..."

I stand there and stare, even though somewhere in the reptile part of my brain, I so want to look away, or take my pistol out and start firing, or try to get the hell out of this room.

Even out of its exoskeleton, the Creeper maintains the same kind of shape, with an articulated body, six limbs, and a main head that has two eyestalks, and it looks like the eyes can move about, giving it a 360-degree field of vision. The four lower limbs serve as legs—which I've learned both in my regular classroom and the Army's classroom—and its two upper limbs have a complex arrangement of claws.

It's resting on some sort of plant growth, mixed in with blankets or something similar. The blankets and pillows in one area have been shredded, to make some sort of nest.

The eyes rotate, blink, seem to stare at me.

"Can...can it see me?" I ask.

Paternoster gets up from his cleaning. "Barely. The armor glass is mostly one way. It can make out shapes, and that's about it."

I step closer. The eyes have wide dilation, and the light behind the glass is dim. Something happens and a wet mist descends upon the scene, and then it's gone. The Creeper stretches and moves, like it needed that little burst of moisture.

"What does it eat?"

Paternoster is next to me. "Good question, kid. We've removed what we think are ration packages from destroyed exoskeletons and pass it through an airlock. But we try to be careful. About four years ago, when we first captured a couple of Creepers, we gave one of them something we thought was a food package. Turned out to be a hand weapon. Destroyed half the base before it got killed."

"Major?" I ask.

"Yes?" he replies.

I step closer again. "I'm no goddamn kid. I'm a sergeant in the United States Army. Please remember that."

He steps away and now my vision is full of the Creeper, and while my heart is thumping along and my palms are sweaty, and sometimes I take a quick look to make sure the Air Force Special Ops guys are still looking this way, I'm so very proud that I can stand here, so close, without losing it.

The Creeper moves again, like it's adjusting itself for comfort.

And I blurt out, "Why are you here?"

Nobody and nothing answers, of course, and I step even closer, raise my voice. "Why are you here?"

Then, ashamed, I do lose it.

I'm pounding on the glass with my right first, thinking of Mom, my sister Melissa, all the dead from all the years, all the drowned cities, all of my buddies burned, crippled or killed, and even my own close calls.

"Why are you here? Hunh? Answer me, damn it, why the goddamn hell are you here!"

Dad is by me, murmuring something, and I shrug him off, keep at it, hitting the glass with a fist with each shouted sentence. "You assholes! You fuckers! Why the hell are you here? What did we ever do to you? Why do you torture us, year after year? You've got the technology, why the hell didn't you kill us all, right from the start?"

Dad grabs me with his two hands, pulls me back. "She can't

hear you, Randy, honest. She can't. And we've tried talking to them before, with those very same questions, and we've never been able to understand what they're saying. It's like they're answering in puzzles...in poems."

I whirl around, point to Buddy. "Then let's use him! That's why you brought us here, right? None of this crap about feeding or fueling up Kara's Killers. You wanted us here so you could use Buddy to talk to the Creeper."

Dad doesn't hesitate. "That's right. After the raid on the barn, after that PsyOps Humvee broadcasted the wrong message, I wanted to see if...if we could still talk to the Creepers." He points to the thick glass. "But...this isn't the one we've spoken to in the past. This one is different."

"So what?"

Dad says, "We don't know why...it may be because of their class, or caste system, or something else we can't figure out, but sometimes when we communicate with a Creeper, we think we're talking to a representative from the entire invasion force. And sometimes, it's just a foot soldier."

I walk back and grab Buddy's hand. "Then let's do it. Right now. Let's find out what Margaret is all about."

Buddy walks back with me and Serena joins in, and there's a babble of conversation among Dad, Laughton, and Paternoster, about what the hell I'm doing, this is not following the protocol, this isn't the way things should be done.

I stop before the glass, let out a whistle, and say, "Not following protocol? Really? Where is it in your precious protocol that says this war should have happened, that guys and girls my age are in the front lines, getting scorched and barbecued, and for what?"

Laughton says, "Sergeant, you are way out of line, and I'm getting you out of here, now."

I put my hand on my holster. "Sorry, I kind of like it here. I'm not going anywhere."

Paternoster says, "Don't be dumb, kid. There are two airmen in here that'll tear you to pieces if they have to. Get the hell out."

I put my arm around Buddy. Not fair, but I don't care. "Go ahead. Try it. And tell me if you're going to risk injuring your only chance to talk to the Creepers in the process. How's that for protocol? And if you call me kid one more time, I swear to God I'll shoot you. Just try me."

Laughton turns to Dad. "Colonel Knox! Get your son under control. We can't have a circus here. We have to proceed in a logical, scientific and measured response so that we can—"

"So that we can do what?" Dad says, going to a corner of the room, near one of the Airman Special Ops desks. There's a cabinet there with a combination lock and Dad starts spinning the dial. "Putter around here and try to build up a grammar that makes sense, while waiting until the Creeper we're communicating with eventually dies?"

Laughton says, "Get away from that cabinet, Henry."

Dad says, "Or what, Phil? Do I need to remind you that I outrank you when it comes to Creeper intelligence activities? You have physical control of this Creeper, ensuring it's kept alive, protected, and is not allowed to escape. You can also work to learn what you can about its language and other activities. But it's the post-war National Intelligence Cooperative that has overall control of this thing, and that means me."

Dad flips open the small door to the cabinet. "And if you don't want to get all paperwork and procedure on me, I'll remind you that above me is a company of very experienced and very pissed-off combat soldiers, who believe an intelligence failure crisped some of their fellow soldiers a couple of days ago. Bear that in mind, Phil, will you? Before doing something you'll regret."

Laughton looks like if he had the capability—because I'm sure he has the desire—he'd open up that closed-off room next door and toss us all in with the Creeper and see what happens. But as red as his face is, and as clenched as his jaw is as well, he says, "Very well."

Paternoster says, "Colonel, please, this is—"

"Enough, Major," he says, letting out a resigned breath. "Colonel Knox has the lead here. Let's see what hole he marches into."

"Phil, you're an officer and gentleman...still." Dad reaches into the cabinet, flips a couple of switches, and there's a burst of static from speakers in the ceiling. Dad says, "You folks recording?"

"The minute you got in here," Laughton says. "Everything's been recorded."

"All right," Dad says. To me he says, "Sergeant, go ahead."

I turn to Serena and say, "Can you...do you have the codes to get Buddy to translate?"

"Yes, I do," she says.

"Will you do it?"

She says, "Are you asking, Randy? Is that it?"

I'm confused. "Yes, I'm asking. That's what I'm doing."

She wipes at her eyes. "Good. Because if it was anyone else, anyone that I think might have a connection with Hoyt Cranston"—and she stares at Laughton—"I would tell Buddy the codes that would freeze him out, and to hell with the people who helped kill my dad."

I slip my hand into hers. It's soft and warm. I give it a tug. "This is for me, Serena. And for your dad. And for you and Buddy."

She says, "Then I'm ready."

Now we're standing in a line in front of the Creeper, and my legs start shaking. Earlier it was okay, knowing the bug behind there could barely see me, and couldn't hear me, but now . . . now I'm going to start talking to it. There have been stories and tales about Creepers being able to hypnotize or otherwise command military units to surrender through their voices, and I think those stories are horseshit, but still, my legs keep on quivering.

"Ready?" I ask.

Serena takes Buddy's hand and moves around, so he can see her. "Buddy? Hon? Listen up, please. Buddy, Authorization Pappa Hotel Pappa. Pappa Hotel Pappa. Randy"—she reaches out and tugs me to stand next to her. "Randy . . . Buddy, Authorization Delta. Authorization Delta."

Buddy slowly turns his head and looks at me. I say, "What did you just mean with those code phrases?"

Serena says, "I told Buddy that he's to translate, and that you would be the one talking to him."

"But Serena . . . you just heard. We're being recorded."

"Big deal. Unless the codes come from me . . . or my dad . . ." She pauses, swallows, goes on. "If the codes don't come from me, and if they aren't said in the right pattern, then Buddy freezes. Won't talk. But Randy . . . don't waste time. Sometimes my brother, sometimes he talks . . . and then just stops. Please. Start."

I nod. "Buddy?"

"Yeah?" and my arms start quivering now, for the voice coming out of that twelve-year-old boy is like that of a tired old man.

"Buddy, ask the Creeper his name. Or her name."

He turns and raises his voice, and what comes out are the

clicks, sputters, and whirling sounds, and the Creeper on the other side stops moving. Its eyestalks lean forward, like it's trying to see what's what behind the glass.

Buddy stops talking.

Serena has his hand, and without saying anything, I take his left hand. No one else in the room is saying anything.

I wait. Is this going to be a waste of time?

The Creeper speech comes out loud and crisp through the speakers, making me jump, and the crackling noises go on, and then just as suddenly stops.

In a clear voice, Buddy says, "Who are you to...*blank*...ask?"

I say, "Serena, what does *blank* mean?"

"It means that Buddy's hearing a word he can't understand."

I squeeze Buddy's rough hand. "We are the ones who have captured you."

Crackle, sputter, cough, crackle.

The Creeper replies.

Buddy: "I am ready to give up...*blank*...to perform my...*blank*...Are you?"

Despite the gaps, I know exactly what the bug is saying. I answer, "Every hour, every day, sweetie."

An exchange of conversation, and Buddy says: "*Blank*...*blank*." And I practically gasp when he says to me, "Sorry, Randy. I didn't understand the last bit. But based on the pitch of her voice, I think whatever she said was meant to be a joke, something humorous. Or something dismissive. Perhaps arrogant."

"Uh...thanks, Buddy."

But he turns to look at the thick glass, like he hadn't just talked to me. I shake my head. This isn't going where I want. I say, "Ask her, why are they here? Why?"

More moments pass as I wait for the answer to the question that has bedeviled humanity for a decade. Buddy says, "Because my...*blank* failed me...and I was removed...and taken to this...*blank*...this space."

"No," I say. "Why are the Creepers here? Why did they come to this planet? Why did they make war on us?"

Laughton, Dad and Paternoster are now standing behind us. I'm hot, sweating, feeling constricted by my Firebiter vest and the jacket I'm wearing.

Buddy says, "We did not make war...we...*blank*. You are...

arrogant. You needed to be... *blank*. For you are to be humbled... this is not war... this is... *blank*. In this... we have failed..."

I say, "Buddy, have her explain that. What does it mean, that they've failed?"

More to and fro in the clicks and clatters, and I have the dark feeling that these noises will inhabit my nightmares for the rest of my life.

Buddy says, "We have failed... for we have not... *blank*... you. No other species have done what you have done... you... you keep resisting... you keep fighting us... even though... *blank blank*. That is our failure... our shame... our... *blank*..."

"You didn't expect us to fight?" I demand.

A few seconds later, Buddy says simply, "No."

And I yell back, "Then get ready, for we're never going to surrender! Not ever! We'll keep on fighting you, and fighting you, and we may be starving, we may die of cold and disease, but so long as we can pick up a rock or a stick, you will never find peace here! Never!"

I'm finally so goddamn hot and sweaty that I release Buddy's hand, step back, and strip off my Firebiter vest and BDU jacket, throwing them to the floor. I return to my post and the Creeper is saying something very fast, very loud, so very loud and rising in pitch that we all cover our ears.

Then the Creeper turns away, rolls itself so that all we can see is its armored back, and even its eyestalks have retreated. The only thing we hear is the constant hiss of static.

Dad says, "Sweet Jesus..." and Laughton adds, "I don't believe this..."

I take Buddy's hand. "Buddy, what the hell just happened?"

Buddy waits and waits, and I wonder what he's thinking, what he's processing, and he says, "Randy, I don't know. There are levels of their language, from one caste to another, one group to another. She started speaking rapidly, very fast in a different form. I couldn't make out a phrase, or a single word. But I got a sense of what she was feeling."

I ask, "What's that?"

"Fear," he says. "She was fearful."

I try to puzzle that out, and say, "Afraid of what?"

Buddy pulls his hand away. "I'm sorry. I'm... so, so very tired."

And then he sits down on the concrete.

Chapter Twenty

I'm in a conference room with Dad, Laughton, Serena and Buddy. This room is better tricked out than the one I was in earlier, with softer chairs, a shiny table, and a big glass jug with water and ice. Buddy is sitting in the corner, hands folded, staring at his hands. The rest of us are in chairs, and I say, "Dad, what the hell is going on? What the hell could that Creeper be afraid of?"

Dad says, "I wish I knew. Really, I wish I knew."

By now I'm chilled again and my jacket is back on, as well as my Firebiter vest, though I don't bother fastening it. I now feel restricted, confined, and I want to get out of this maze of underground rooms and corridors as soon as I can. Every now and then a quiver ripples through me as I remember how close I had been to that damn bug.

I say, "What now? You said you wanted to bring Buddy here to talk to a Creeper, but the one you were looking for is dead. And this one just talked a bit before stopping."

Dad runs both hands through his hair and Laughton says, "Your boy asks a good question, Henry. You got your way into my facility, you got your... youngster there to talk to the Creeper. Now the boy can't—or won't—talk to her. What's going to happen? You came here with an Army company. You think they're going to wait up top for you to continue an interrogation, or are you going to send them on their way? From what I've seen from their captain, that's exactly what she wants to do."

"A good point, Phil. I might just do that. We need to reopen our lines of communication with them, find out what worked last week when we got a Creeper Dome to surrender."

Laughton says, "I've heard rumors about that, but nothing official. True?"

"Yes," Dad says. "Buddy and my son, they advanced on the Dome, got them to open it up, got the Creepers inside to surrender."

Laughton slowly shakes his head. "Jesus H. Christ. That sounds incredible. Henry, you stay here as long as you want. The girl and her brother. The unit above . . . they should get back to their battalion. We're a pretty quiet installation and I'd like to keep it that way."

I jump in and say, "Works for me. No offense, Colonel, I'm attached to K Company and if they leave, I'm leaving with them. And with Serena and Buddy staying behind, I'll work on a way to get back to New Hampshire."

Serena says, "I go with Randy. If he leaves with K Company, then my brother and I are going with him. I'm not staying without him."

Laughton says, "Specialist, you're in the Army, and you'll follow your superior officer's orders. If you're told to stay here with your brother, that's what you're going to do. You don't have any authority to request Sergeant Knox's detachment here."

Serena's eyes narrow. "With all due respect, Colonel, go to hell. I go where I want to, and if you don't like it, then with a few words on my part, I can tell Buddy to shut up. Forever."

Laughton looks ready to explode once more and I say, "Dad, er, Colonel Knox."

"Yes?"

"What the Creeper said about war, how they weren't making war against us. That they were doing something else. They were trying to humble us. Not kill us, not destroy us, but to humble us. Doesn't that hook up with what you said earlier, that they're here to convert us, to their . . . religion or belief system? And that Buddy might be their first true convert, their first prophet to humanity?"

Laughton looks like we're in the midst of discussing how many Creepers can dance on the head of a pin, but Dad says, "Yes, that's a pretty good analysis."

"Do you think you can make progress with this Creeper?"

"I don't know. The way it responded there, at the end. Rolling up, turning its back on us. We've never seen anything like it."

"Who's 'we'?" Serena asks.

Dad says, "Those of us in Intelligence. Including Colonel Laughton. We've been working for years to talk to the Creepers, to find out why they're here, why they're fighting us."

"No offense, Dad," I say, "but let me repeat what Serena just said. What do you mean 'we'? Back at the surrendered Dome, we were visited by the man from Langley, Hoyt Cranston, and General Scopes, also from Intelligence. We were debriefed, Serena and Buddy left with them, and then we left to approach another Creeper Dome, with a PsyOps Humvee, outfitted with a recorded message that was supposedly from Buddy."

Laughton is paying real strict attention now, and I think maybe Dad hadn't told him the full story. But Dad doesn't stop me and I say, "The PsyOps Humvee had a recording of an insult to Creepers. Instead of surrendering, they attacked K Company. The Creepers have been following us, ambushing us, and even destroyed a bridge to prevent us from getting to Battalion. Like they're doing their very best to get revenge for the insult."

Laughton says, "Henry?"

"Let the sergeant go on," he says.

I do just that. "Serena and her brother find us, having left the base where they were taken. They were getting ready to torture Buddy, to find out how he learned the Creeper language, how he came up with the wording that made the Creepers surrender. He wouldn't talk. Cranston was getting ready to torture Buddy when Serena and he escaped."

Laughton says, "Specialist, is this true?"

"Every damn word."

"Henry?"

"Afraid so," Dad says.

"Hey," I say. "Anybody want to answer the original question? Who is 'we'? If all of this communication effort was part of Intelligence, then why did Cranston and Scopes feel it necessary to torture Buddy? And why did they sabotage K Company with the wrong message on the PsyOps Humvee? Aren't you guys all on the same team?"

Dad quietly says, "Once we were. But then Major Coulson and I were charged with treason, because we were having unauthorized diplomatic discussions with the enemy. We were barely talking with the Creepers and we were supposed to let the Administration take the lead. But they were delaying, and delaying."

Laughton says, "Presidential election coming up this fall."

"That's right," Dad says. "And . . . Serena's dad, and me, and others, we weren't going to wait. No. We weren't going to wait. But others thought differently. We were arrested, placed in a military base, and were sent west on a military police bus. Then it was attacked by two Creepers who tried to take us to a local Dome until my son showed up."

"Where's Major Coulson?" Laughton asks.

"Dead," Serena says, voice flat. "He was shot helping Buddy and me escape."

At that Buddy lifts his head, eyes full of intelligence, and I think he's going to say something, but no, his head goes back down.

"Colonel Laughton?" I ask.

"Er, yes?"

We all saw Buddy move, and I still think we're all in awe of his ability, to talk and to communicate with the Creepers. I slide my hand down to my holstered 9 mm Beretta, slowly take it out so that it's on my lap. "You've now heard what's going on with Serena, her brother, the man from Langley and General Scopes. Do you know where they're located?"

"No, I don't."

I say, "You just heard my dad say he was arrested for treason. Obviously, he's now an escaped prisoner. Mind telling us what you're going to do with that information?"

Two possible answers from Colonel Laughton, and I'm fully prepared to respond to either one. Let's call the answers A and B. If he responds with Answer A, his brains and blood are going to be splattered on the very nice framed photo of a B-52 Stratofortress about a half meter behind his head.

Laughton says, "I haven't heard anything official about Colonel Knox's status. In the meantime, I'm prepared to offer him full cooperation in interrogating the Creeper we have on base. That's what I plan to do, Sergeant Knox."

I slowly return my Beretta back to my holster. Nice to see Answer B suddenly appear out of nowhere.

✧   ✧   ✧

Some sandwiches are brought in and the conference room door remains open, and Dad and Colonel Laughton go across to another office, and I can see them talking to each other, sitting around a small round table. For an outfit that is supposedly geared to jets and rockets, they sure as hell have a lot of tables.

Serena helps feed Buddy and says, "I wasn't joking back there."

"I didn't sense you joking anywhere."

"Cut it out," she says, wiping Buddy's chin with a cloth napkin—cloth!—that had a smear of mustard on it. The sandwiches are ham, cheese, tomato and lettuce, and are moist and delicious. I wonder if the Air Force smarties here grow their vegetables underground, in hydroponic tanks. She says, "I don't trust anyone except for you. That's it. And if you're not here to have my back, then either I'm going with you and K Company, or we're staying here and we're shutting it down."

I take another healthy bite. "Nope, that's not what you're going to do. I'm no fan of Colonel Laughton, but he was right. You're going to follow orders, and so am I."

"Then stay here, damn it," she says. "Stay with me and Buddy, and your dad, and you'll be safe."

She picks up her own sandwich, takes a healthy bite for a girl her size. "And the food... God, the food."

"Very compelling," I say, "but if Captain Wallace needs me, that's where I'm going to be, and you're not coming with us. You and Buddy... for God's sake, it's like it's World War II, and you have the only means of decoding German military messages, and you want to go on a bombing raid to Berlin. Not going to happen. If you're with me topside, you both could be smeared in ten minutes if a killer stealth satellite keys on your transport."

"You'll keep us safe."

"I'd do my best, Specialist, but appearances to the contrary, I'm a sixteen-year-old sergeant in the New Hampshire National Guard, attached to the Army's 26th Division. I ain't Superman, and Thor certainly isn't Superdog."

"Then why not stay here?"

I finish off my sandwich, knowing I'm not that hungry, but believing food should never be taken for granted. It's one of my mottoes, and I wrap up a sandwich and shove it in my pocket. "Because Captain Wallace needs me. I'm a platoon leader. They're pretty thinned out as it is. If I leave with Thor, I'm putting them at risk...I can't do it. I can't."

Serena says, "I don't care about the platoon, or those soldiers, or the Air Force. Right now I don't care much about people and this country, if people like Hoyt Cranston and General Scopes are running things. My mom is somewhere out West, doing work for the Department of Agriculture. I haven't heard from her in months. She doesn't know Dad is dead. She doesn't know anything."

"Serena, look—"

She rolls right over me without hesitation. "Dad found out what was happening. He helped us escape from the base. We were at a dirt access road of some kind, at a gate. Lights came on as we went through the gate. Me and Buddy ran and ran... there was shooting...Dad crumpled up."

Tears are silently running down her cheeks. "I won't help them. I won't."

I wipe my fingers on the cloth napkin—cloth!—and say, "Then help me. Help anyone else you know. And help your mom, wherever she is, by doing the very best to end this war."

"Randy..."

"Specialist, follow your orders."

She turns away, wipes again at Buddy's chin, although there's nothing there to see. There are voices out in the hallway, and I get up to see what's what. Captain Wallace is there, along with her friend from the Air Force, Mark, the one with the white coat and captain's bars, who used to work with computers before the war. Wallace goes into the office with Dad and Colonel Laughton, and Mark says something I can't make out to Wallace, and turns to leave and goes down the corridor.

I follow him and call out, "Captain! Sir! Captain!"

He turns, smiling, and tilts his head. "Sorry, Sergeant, do I know you?"

"No, sir, you don't," I say. "But you know my C.O., Captain Wallace."

"Kara...yes, Captain Wallace. We were neighbors once, back...back then."

I press on, not wanting to have Wallace come out and see what I'm up to. "I just wanted to check on something, if I may, Captain."

He glances at his watch. "If you make it quick, go ahead."

"Captain Wallace. You were neighbors. Was she in the Army?"

He laughs. "Oh, hell, no. Her husband, David. He was the soldier in the family."

I recall what I had overheard earlier. "Kabul, right?"

"Yes, that's right," he says. "So sad. Things were falling apart in Afghanistan and his brigade was dispatched that August. Two months later the Creepers struck. And nobody's heard a word from them since."

"But Captain Wallace...If she wasn't in the Army then, what did she do?"

"You don't know?"

"No, I don't."

He looks at his watch. "Damn, look at the time. Gotta run."

The captain resumes his quick pace down the hallway and turns back. "Oh, yes. You asked what she did before the Creepers got here. She was a kindergarten teacher."

I go back up the hallway, and Serena's still in with Buddy, talking low to him, and the door to the other office is still open, with Dad, Wallace and Laughton. An airman comes out of the office, pushing by me, and his face is troubled. I hang out by the doorway. Laughton is reading a dispatch, and then tosses it on the small table before him.

"That's that," he says. "We got Creepers on the move, heading down Route 50, and coming along west on I-90 and Route 5." He gets up from his chair and lets his finger slide along a wall map. "Never had them move in unison like this, but what's clear, is they're heading this way."

Dad gets up, looks at the map as well. "Either they're coming to Schenectady, or they're coming for you, Phil."

Laughton says, "I don't think the Creepers mind trains. But they do mind us...if they know we're here." He turns to Wallace. "No offense, Captain, but you and your soldiers have tipped them off."

"No offense taken," she says. "We'll saddle up and get the hell out, as quick as we can. Thanks for the grub and the fuel."

"Where will you go?" Laughton asks.

She steps around him and peers at the map. "If your intelligence is right, then we still can't get back to Battalion. We'll have to go east, maybe loop around, head up to the Adirondack parks, maybe go to ground until the Creepers get bored."

I say, "They're not bored. They're after the company, Captain Wallace."

"Maybe so," she says, stepping back from the map, picking up her helmet. "But we're going to give them a run. Unless you want us to stay, put up a fight here."

Laughton shakes his head. "Captain, this installation. We have a lot going on. A lot of important work."

"I know," she says.

"We can't afford to resist. We've survived so far because the Creepers don't know we exist. But if you stay and fight, that will all change. The bugs are used to fighting underground. They'll break in and scorch us all."

"I heard you twice, Colonel Laughton. We'll be going."

"Captain Wallace, if I may," I ask.

"What is it, Knox?"

"With all due respect to Colonel Laughton, this base may already have been compromised. We should take Specialist Coulson and her brother with us, bring them to someplace more safe, even if it's the Adirondacks, or Battalion headquarters."

Dad says, "Phil?"

He slowly nods. "I don't like it. I really don't like it. I'd love to keep you, Serena and her brother here. We could make a lot of progress over the next few months, all of us . . . but not if this base gets scorched, inside and out."

A knock on the side of the door, and another airman steps in, passes along a light yellow message flimsy. Laughton gives it a glance, barks out a short laugh. "Well, Henry, I think this settles it. A message from the Acting Secretary of Defense, to units in this military district, to place you, your son, and the Coulson sister and brother immediately under arrest."

A long cold pause in the office. Laughton crumples up the message flimsy, tosses it in a wastebasket, where it bounces off the rim and drops right in.

Laughton says, "Get the hell out, all of you."

Dad steps forward, shakes his hand, grabs a shoulder. "You be safe."

Laughton smiles. "Damn aliens think they've had the Air Force beat for ten years. Time for them to get ready for a nice big fucking surprise."

✧   ✧   ✧

By the time we ride up in the elevator and step out, there's the grumble of diesel engines in the damaged hangar, and the stench of exhaust. Serena and Buddy follow Wallace and Dad to the command Humvee, and she gives me a look and I quickly take her into my arms, give her a kiss, and then run across the concrete. Probably broke about a half-dozen regulations and I don't give a shit.

My platoon is in the truck, and Thor puts his front paws on the side, starts barking. Now I know why he had been scraping at the concrete floor earlier. Damn fine boy, he knew there was a Creeper in the vicinity. He just knew. I'm helped up on the rear of the truck and meet up with my guys and girls. They have fresh uniforms, bright and freshly washed faces, and Balatnic says, "No offense, Sergeant, you stink."

I grab my M-10, make sure my battlepack is under my feet. "Glad you guys had a chance to shower up. Guess I ran out of time."

Bronson says, "Looks like you had time for something else," and there's some laughter with that, and I don't care.

The truck starts to back up. De Los Santos comes back to me, holding something wrapped in paper. "We heard you got us showers, Sergeant. A couple of guys did some snooping in this base and got this for you."

I tear at the paper, revealing a translucent plastic bag. I carefully tear open the bag and bring the object out.

A brand new Firebiter vest, still in its original packaging from the surviving DuPont plant in Cooper River, South Carolina. My platoon is grinning at me, including the normally sour-looking Sergeant Bronson. I undo the Velcro straps and buckles, take off the old and worn protective vest, slide it on. The old vest I dump on the floor of the truck, and I plan to give it back to the Quartermaster as soon as I can.

The vest feels good, but more importantly, it smells good.

"Thanks guys," I say. "I hope it stays nice and clean for a long time to come."

A couple of hoots about that, and our truck grumbles out onto the shattered remains of this air base, where a steady rain is falling, and just as quick as that, we're back in the war.

Chapter Twenty-One

We exit the air base in small, manageable groups, trying to puzzle whatever killer stealth satellites might be going overhead. Two groups of Humvees and a lead Stryker race down the cracked and disused runway, and our platoon truck—joined by an up-armored Humvee—goes back the way we came, through the main gate, and we circle around. The rain is coming down harder and most civilians have gone under shelter. As we roll, to the south is Schenectady and its smokestacks, belching out thick black clouds of smoke as the city goes back to its roots of building railroad engines and cars. There's a heavy jolt and Sully, the older soldier, bumps into me and says, "Sorry about that, Sarge."

"No worries."

He peers through the rain, notes the city back there, and says, "When I was younger, I belonged to all those fancy environmental groups, you know? Greenpeace. The Nature Conservancy. World Wildlife Fund."

I truly don't know those names but I just grunt in acknowledgment, and Sully says, "Back in the day, those smokestacks would have drawn thousands of protesters, to stop the pollution, stop destroying the planet. Now, there are thousands hoping to get a job in those stinking, polluting and dangerous factories, so they can make money to feed their families. Funny thing about those damn bugs, once they got here, they put a lot of things into focus."

"They sure did."

I don't know where we're going—just a general idea of getting ahead of the maneuvering Creepers and heading up to the mountains and forests of the Adirondacks—but it's rough traveling. States like New York and others, barely recovering ten years into the war, only have funds, equipment and personnel to do some maintenance work on the major federal and state highways. Since we know there are three sets of Creepers coming this way along those highways, it means we're on city or state roads, which by now have broken up into jagged chunks of asphalt, or stretches of dirt and gravel, with lots and lots of bridges.

It's rough, muddy, and slow, and the rain is heavier as we proceed to the northwest, going along two-lane roads where the trees brush by the side. Having gone ten years without being trimmed, they whip and snap against the side of our truck. Without canvas overhead, it's wet indeed, but all of us know there are Creepers out there, and having a canvas roof might keep us dry, dry enough for us to quickly burst into flames if we're ambushed.

Not a good trade.

After an hour of heavy and muddy traveling, we take a break at an old Walmart Supercenter on Route 30, just north of Amsterdam. The store had been looted and emptied years ago, but the roof is still in pretty good shape, and we maneuver through the shattered store entrance, bringing our vehicles under cover, passing a fluttering strand of yellow tape. Two other trucks and a Stryker are parked in the store as well. It's good to get out of the rain and meet up with other soldiers of the company, and stoves are lit off. I get down off the truck with Thor, M-10 over my shoulder. It's dark and gloomy in the store, with empty spaces stretching out in every direction, wires and cables dangling from the crumbling ceiling tiles.

I walk across broken glass to the wide entrance, note the yellow tape that had just been broken by our entrance. It's bright yellow with black letters: NO TRESPASSING.

There are also two signs hanging from the tape, and I pick one up, and in the gloom, manage to puzzle out the lettering:

THIS PROPERTY STILL UNDER THE OWNERSHIP OF

THE WALMART CORPORATION BENTONVILLE AR.

NO TRESPASSING. POLICE TAKE NOTICE.

I drop the sign to the dirty tile floor. If and when the police do show up, I'm sure Captain Wallace will apologize.

Fortified by a cup of coffee, I see Wallace at the other end of the store, and First Sergeant Hesketh catches my attention. I go over, past some destroyed cash registers, followed by Thor, and Wallace goes into an open door, followed by Hesketh and the other two platoon leaders. It's a narrow corridor with a dead electrical sign overhead that says EMPLOYEES ONLY. It's clammy and cool inside, and then there's a concrete and metal staircase, going up. I follow the clanging noises of everyone's footfall, and a door opens up and we're on the roof of the building.

It's still raining, but the clouds are high enough to give us a good 360-degree view. All around us are the dead stores of a past life, a past world. Hannaford and Price Chopper supermarkets. Home Depot and Lowe's. Target and Panera. All just empty shells now, looted and burned and ransacked. Nine or ten years ago, places like this weren't calm anywhere in the country, not at all. I imagine what it must have been like here. The power's been out for days. What radio stations that are on the air are talking about...aliens? For real? Tidal waves and nuclear bombs in the upper atmosphere? Familiar roads are filled with refugees from cities hundreds of miles away, talking about the terrible things they've seen, but they're stripping local stores of gasoline, food, bottled water, medicine.

The stores, running on generators, are crowded. There are fistfights. Shouts. A gunshot or two.

Then these stores and this way of life instantly get kicked back to the life of hundreds of years ago, when the strong and well-armed took what they wanted.

I get the oddest feeling that has struck me in the past, of despair of today's world, and a melancholy sadness about the world left behind. A funny thought comes to mind. If anybody was still out there giving symbolic names—Baby Boomers, Generation X, Generation Y, the Millenials—I guess me and everyone else about my age would be called the Straddlers, straddling two ways of life, two battered civilizations.

I rub Thor's head. "Some things are still constant, right?" and my boy licks my hand, and I walk over to join Wallace, Hesketh, and Lieutenants Morneau and Jackson.

✧　　✧　　✧

Everyone's looking to the south, and Wallace has a pair of binoculars up to her face. I huddle up and look at the roads below us. A few horses, a number of bicycles, three horse-drawn wagons, and two pickup trucks and a red four-door car, all with precomputer engines.

A flicker of light catches my eye. There. Off to the south again. Flickers of light, illuminating and reflecting the bottom of the rainclouds.

"First Sergeant," Wallace says. "Compass and map, if you please."

He silently hands the items over. She works the compass and map, and I note she's trying to determine where the flashes of light are coming from. They seem to grow in intensity, and then she looks up and says quietly, "Well, that tears it. The Creepers have changed their approach since we left the air base. It looks like they're coming up Route 30, right there...and it looks like they've reversed direction on Route 5."

"The chase is on," Lieutenant Morneau murmurs.

She brings up her binoculars again and once more says, "What is it with you bugs? All these years fighting you and now you're pissed off and dogging me? What, you didn't like that eat shit insult back there? Still holding a grudge?"

The chase, I think. There's more than just a chase going on out there. With every flash of light we see, it means the Creepers are burning and lasing whatever's in their way. People are being scorched, buildings are being destroyed, all while the Creepers continue their hunt for Kara's Killers.

Lieutenant Jackson says one simple yet very heavy word: "Reinforcements?"

"Dispatch riders have been sent out," Wallace says, binoculars still up to her eyes. "If they can get to Battalion, if they can avoid being barbecued, a lot of ifs, then maybe we'll get some help. Lots of ifs there, don't you think?"

With his gravelly voice, Hesketh says, "Beggin' the Captain's pardon, I'd give my left nut for two operable SINCGARS systems right now, one for us, one for Battalion, so we can instantly talk to each other."

She lowers the binoculars, and with a wry smile says, "Considering how many times you've said that, First Sergeant, I'm amazed you have any nuts left to sacrifice."

Some tight smiles but no laughs. The rain is steady and so are the flickering lights down there to the south. Until I hooked up with this company, most of my experiences with Creepers were going out on raids to kill them or track them, but when those missions were done, I always had the luxury of going back to the relative safety of Fort St. Paul to rest, regroup, and just unwind, and to get ready for the next mission.

No relaxation time here, that's for damn sure.

"Captain Wallace?" I ask.

"Go ahead Knox."

"Ma'am, I'm sure you know the importance of my . . . er, Colonel Knox, along with Specialist Coulson and her brother."

"Yes, the brother who sometimes can speak bug. The crew, including you, that I should arrest and turn over to the nearest provost marshal, if I could ever find one."

I say, "True enough, ma'am. But their value . . . for the war effort, I mean. I request permission to remove them and get them out of here, to a place of safety."

Wallace says, "Look around, Sergeant Knox. Not many places of safety out there. And it won't do for you to be out there without protection. And if I send troops along to guard you, I'm hollowing out my already pretty damn thin company. Nope. Everyone stays along for the ride."

I bite my tongue. A young soldier bursts out of the stairwell, runs over to Wallace, offers her a sloppy salute and a small leather dispatch bag. She reads what's in there, scribbles something on the end and says to the soldier, "What's it like out there?"

"Panic city, ma'am," he says. "Refugees on the move, rumors that the Creepers are coming down here to scorch everything in sight. Pretty tough. Some of the back roads . . . pretty damn crowded. Almost had my motorcycle knocked over and stolen from me."

Wallace nods, puts the message back into the bag, hands it over. "Sorry, Zeke. I need you to go back. But take a few minutes to rest up. There's some coffee brewing downstairs."

Zeke snaps off another flabby salute. "Thanks for the offer, ma'am, but I'm gonna get out there and get my job done. I'll catch up to you when I can."

"All right," she says. "Go."

He runs back and I look to the south once more. The lights are brighter, meaning the Creepers are coming closer.

"Captain Wallace," I say.

"What is it?"

"Ma'am—" I start, and then freeze. Except for Thor, every sentient being on this old rooftop is looking straight at me. "Ma'am, this isn't right. We're being chased, and I understand that, but the civilians...they're paying the price. The longer we"—and I was going to say "retreat" before I caught myself—"remain mobile like this, the more casualties the civilians are going to suffer."

Lips pursed, she says, "I'm very well aware of that. Sergeant. What do you suggest?"

"We find a redoubt, someplace secure. Set up defensive positions. Wait for the Creepers to arrive, take them on while reinforcements come. That way, we cut down on any collateral damage hitting the local population."

The two lieutenants suddenly have a lot of interest in their feet, for that's where they're looking. The first sergeant looks away as well. I have a feeling that once again, I Have Stepped In It, and I don't care.

More flashes of light. Definitely coming closer. Between what I've just said and seeing the approaching Creeper sign, I'm feeling very alone and exposed. Wallace purses her lips, checks out the map and says, "They teach you a lot back there, at Fort St. Paul?"

I don't know what she's getting at, so I decide to take the safe approach and just answer: "They try."

"Mostly military related?"

"Mostly," I reply, "although with my age, there's other stuff as well. English. Math. Geometry. Old geography, since we still don't have a clear picture of what the current geography is. But unless Dad gets word back to school, I'll probably flunk this semester and have to go to summer school."

Hesketh is smiling widely, so I add, "That depends, of course, on whether I ever get back to Fort St. Paul. Or get picked up by the provost marshal."

Wallace slides her clipboard and map under her right arm. "As long as you're with me, leading First Platoon, don't worry about the provost marshal. And about your schooling...They must be doing something right."

"Ma'am?" I ask.

"Maybe you are officer material, Knox, because that's exactly what we're going to do," she says, now slightly smiling. "Hunker down, fight the Creepers, protect the local population, and wait for reinforcements."

We make a wide and fast-moving loop north on Route 30, and then head west to Route 127, going through a sparsely populated and rural area of what's now Fulton County, passing through the mostly abandoned village of Gloversville. We travel in groups, stopping and starting, going underneath tree cover when we can, moving in spurts and traveling side by side, all in an attempt to dodge any incoming fire from the killer stealth satellites. The drivers for K Company—including the poor young guy I stuck a pistol into the other day—are practiced at this, and we reach our destination in just under an hour.

The rain has finally stopped as we reach the Peck Hill State Forest, and through some slow going and backtracking, the lead Stryker finds an overgrown dirt road that leads up an incline. We're all back as one unit now, and I keep my seat as our truck belches and maneuvers its way along with the other vehicles. Branches whip at our faces and I'm envious of Thor, who's lying down on the floorboards, dodging the slapping branches and leaves.

The vegetation starts to thin out, and then the narrow dirt road swings to the right, and we're going up a hill now, mostly bare rock and gravel.

The road goes up and up, and then widens out onto a parking lot, still populated by low brush and grass. The convoy's vehicles split off, and right above the parking lot is a small building that looks like it's a log cabin, and behind that, a fire tower, reaching up into the soggy sky.

The truck shudders to a halt, and we all get out, into the afternoon sky and underneath the clouds. I take a gander at what's what, and it seems like we're on top of a hill, with clear fields of fire all around, and with a good view that means we'll have a sweet chance of seeing any approaching Creeper come our way.

I pick up my battle pack and M-10, know I have to check in with Wallace to see what she wants. Balatnic stops me and says, "What do you think, Sergeant?"

"I think this is a good, defensible place to wait for reinforcements," I say. "And I'm tired of being chased."

She looks like she still needs to be convinced. "I hope we don't have to stay here long."

"Me neither," I say, heading off to meet Wallace, and I'm pretty sure none of us expect what will happen next, what future military historians—if such a thing would still exist—would call the famed last stand of K Company, First Battalion, 14th Army Regiment, also known as "Kara's Killers."

Chapter Twenty-Two

Wallace is issuing orders when I reach her, standing outside of her command Humvee. I step up, Thor following, as she says, "Knox, I want you and First to set up defensive lines about ten meters down the slope starting from that tree"—she points "—to that rock shaped like an apple. Morneau, you take the Second, move in an arc from that rock, over to...let's say right off to the right edge of that little cabin. Jackson, you and you Third Platoon take the rest."

We all acknowledge and she says, "First Sergeant, that little cabin is going to be our C.P. and first aid station. Grab a detail and have them start piling up dirt and rocks along the side. Wouldn't be nice for the Creepers to torch it once they get here. Lieutenant Jackson."

"Ma'am."

"That fire tower."

He looks over at it. "Yes, ma'am."

"Drop it."

A heartbeat. "Ma'am?"

"You heard me," she says. "Drop it. Demolish it. Remove it from my sight. But make sure you don't hit the cabin."

Morneau says, "Captain, it could be useful as an OP."

She turns. "Really? You want to put someone up there, exposed? A perfect target? Nope. Lieutenant Jackson, once you drop it, take one of the six by sixes, see if you can drag it down one of the slopes. It'd make a nice barrier. First Sergeant."

"Ma'am."

She moves her head around and checks out the small, flat and rocky plateau we're on. "Too exposed for our vehicles. Offload equipment, stores and everything else we need, and then tell the drivers to scram. Make sure Vee's kid and Hernandez are evacuated as well. Have them set up a hidden rally point where they can see us signal. Set up a flare system for a recall, once reinforcements arrive and we can redeploy."

Hesketh doesn't like it. "Even the Strykers?"

"Especially the Strykers," she says. "There's no place up here to conceal them. And they can shepherd the trucks and the Humvees. Got it?"

"Yes, ma'am."

"Good. Morneau and Knox, get to work. Jackson, get that fire tower down."

So we all get to work.

With my platoon following, we go down the slope as ordered, and lucky for us, the soil here isn't that rocky, so we can start digging foxholes. I'd rather dig a trenchline, but we don't have the personnel and we definitely don't have the time. I pace off where we would be hooking up on either side to Second and Third Platoon, and I have them dig holes about three meters apart. I join in to help one of the youngest soldiers, a twelve-year-old boy called Meerson, whose face is pale and who keeps on looking down the hillside, like he expects the Creepers to pop out at any second.

"Hey," I say.

"Sergeant?"

"I've been in this here Army for about four years," I say. "Captain Wallace knows what she's doing. Just do your job, that's all."

"But Sergeant..."

I dump another load of dirt in front of us. Thor is on his side, panting gently, just watching these silly humans dig holes.

"Go ahead."

He leans over, whispers. "Back at that old horse farm, by the two Creeper Domes, when they attacked...I pissed myself. When we got out, I fell in a stream on purpose, so no one would know. I'm scared I'm gonna do it again, and there's no stream up here."

I dig down deep again. "Don't worry. Ninety percent of the

people on the line will admit they've pissed themselves at one time or another, and the other ten percent are lying."

When I'm happy with the depth and width of the hole that we're in, I get out and start checking the other foxholes as well. I'm standing next to De Los Santos when there's a shout, "Fire in the hole! Fire in the hole! Heads down!"

I drop to the ground, curve my arms around my helmet, and De Los Santos is right next to me, and there's a rapid fire sound of explosions—*blam-blam-blam-blam*—and a creaking sound. I lift up my head. The fire tower is canting to one side, and then picks up speed, and it hits the ground with a nice loud metallic bang, the upper wooden platform collapsing in a pile of broken lumber and asphalt shingles.

De Los Santos says, "One hell of a ride."

He picks up his entrenching tool, goes back to his foxhole. Vehicles up here on the gravel parking lot start to head down the slope, except for one 6x6 truck that backs up to where the fire tower has hit the ground.

A sergeant from Second Platoon comes by and says, "Captain Wallace's orders, make sure you set up firing stakes at ten meters, twenty-five meters, and fifty meters."

I dispatch Meerson and another private to do just that, and I watch them as they pace off the distances, and then push lengths of wood into the dirt, tying off bright orange tape at the top to give us a reference when the Creepers attack.

Yeah. Not if.

When.

Lieutenant Jackson is busy with the crumpled fire tower, but I meet up with Lieutenant Morneau, and she nods. "Good job snuggling up to my platoon. Don't want to leave any gaps in the line."

"Neither do I," I say.

The last truck is now heading out, and I watch with a little tremor of fear, seeing the dust cloud roll up as it disappears from view.

Stuck. Abandoned. No transport.

"Part of being 'Kara's Killers' is about being mobile, hitting the Creepers and then zipping out," Morneau says. "Here . . . we're trapped."

"Captain says reinforcements are coming."

"Officers always say help is coming. It's in their nature. Still, nice to know we'll be taking the heat off the civvies in this area...Look over there, Sergeant."

She points to the southwest, where mostly there's tree cover, but up in the lower banks of the clouds there are more insistent flashes of light, representing Creeper fire.

"There's a shitstorm coming this way," she says. "I respect and trust Captain Wallace to the moon and back, but we're in for one hell of a fight."

Thor is bouncing around some, sniffing and getting attention from other soldiers. I go up to the top of the plateau, to the log cabin. Dirt and rocks are being shoveled up along the sides, and I pitch in for a few minutes, until Wallace steps out and sees me, and says, "Morneau and Jackson?"

"With their platoons, ma'am."

"Your foxholes set up?"

"Yes, ma'am."

"Let's go take a look."

She moves with me down the slope and checks each foxhole, nodding with satisfaction in seeing that I've paired a soldier with an M-10 with a soldier with an M-4.

We move to the right, where we're butting up against Second Platoon, and there's a stretch of the hill here where the rock drops off at a sheer cliff. Wallace carefully peers over and says, "Nice break for a change. Doubt the Creepers will be able to climb up here. Still, make sure there's someone nearby, keeping watch."

"Yes, ma'am."

At the Second Platoon line, she nods in satisfaction again at seeing how Lieutenant Morneau and her platoon have used the wreckage of the fire tower to build barriers lower down the slope, heading off to the right.

"Nicely done," she says. "I like it. With the cliff to the left and that trash to the right, you've set up a nice killing zone, make the damn bugs bunch up and come through here. You've got enough M-10s and rounds?"

"For now, ma'am, we do," she says, nodding, strong arms folded. "They try to climb up here, we'll pile up those bugs five or six deep, just you watch."

She slaps her on the shoulder. "Don't be so greedy, Amy. We want to share and share alike, right?"

A kindergarten teacher, I suddenly remember. Before the war, Kara Wallace had been a kindergarten teacher . . .

"Come along with us," she says. "I want to see how Third is doing."

We circle around the plateau's slope, over to the dirt access road, and she shakes her head when Jackson approaches and says, "Too much growth down there. Get a detail with axes and saws, see if we can't widen the approach."

"Yes, ma'am."

She glances at her watch. "All right, let's get to the CP for a briefing."

Jackson takes a moment or two to get a squad down his side of the slope to cut back the overgrowth, and the three of us— me, Morneau and Jackson—follow Wallace as she goes up to the cabin, now isolated since the fire tower has been dropped. I'm still confused over why Wallace ordered the tower's destruction and removal. If she had left it standing, it could have served as a nice decoy for the approaching Creepers, who would probably lase and flame the shit out of it as they attack, injuring or killing no one. But maybe Wallace was concerned that if it was the focus of an attack, it might fall onto the converted command post, or collapse on the Second Platoon's lines, causing one hell of a dangerous distraction with Creepers coming up the slopes.

Maybe.

Inside the CP I spot Dad, Serena and Buddy gathered in one corner. Serena and Buddy sit on the floor, Dad on an overturned plastic bucket. There's a square wooden table in the center where maps have been spread out, and Wallace takes position, next to the first sergeant, who nods at something she says and then ducks out. A gas lantern has been lit, giving flickering light to the dirty interior of the small building. I take a minute to check in on Serena.

"You okay?" I ask.

She says, "All right, I guess. What's going on out there?"

"We're getting ready for some visitors," I say. "If we're lucky, they'll have two legs. If not, they'll have six."

Her arm goes around Buddy. "I'm trusting you to protect us."

"I'm going to do my best, I promise you that."

Dad rubs his hands. "Anything sighted yet?"

"Nope, not yet."

Dr. Pulaski comes in with two soldiers with Red Cross arm-bands, carrying boxes and other gear. She eyes the place, and starts setting up bedding and trays of bandages, medical instruments and IV bottles. Wallace says to Jackson, "Your area cleared up?"

"Yes, ma'am."

"Good."

We three platoon leaders look down at the old topo map of where we're located, and Wallace crisply goes over our positions, our interlocking fields of fire, the bell signaling that will alert us to when the Creepers come.

"One other thing," she says. "I want two soldiers from each of your platoons, M-4 and M-10, up here. They're going to be a ready reserve to plug any holes that might come up."

Such polite and bland language covering what she really means: Creepers breaking through our lines, burning troops in their foxholes, coming up to the command post and overrunning it.

Wallace runs a dirty finger around the top of the craggy peak on the map. "We've got three combat dispatch riders out now, trying to link up with Battalion or any other force out there that can provide us with reinforcements. In the meantime, we're in a good, defensible position. Make sure your folks keep their heads down, your M-10 shooters only fire if they have clear targets and are confident they're zeroed in. Any questions?"

None at the moment, but then the first sergeant comes in and says something that instantly leads to lots of questions.

"Captain Wallace," he says, voice even more gravelly than before. "We got problems. The supply truck left with the main bulk of our rations. We're gonna get hungry pretty soon."

Wallace's face flushes but she keeps it under control. "Lieutenant Morneau."

Morneau looks like she'd rather be out in the field with a dull spoon, going face-to-arthropod with a Battle Creeper, than be in this little cabin with her angry C.O. right across from her. "Ma'am."

"The supply vehicle with our rations, that was under your control."

"Yes, ma'am."

"Apparently not all of it," she says. "Care to add anything to what the first sergeant has reported?"

Her voice is small. "No, ma'am."

"Care to explain how it may have happened?"

"No excuse, ma'am," she says.

"You didn't quite hear me," Wallace points out. "I'm looking for a possible explanation. I'm not assigning blame."

Morneau says, "The driver for that truck...Private Clinton. He has driving experience but he was a recent transfer. This was his first deployment to a front-line unit. I believe he may have panicked, ma'am. He may have seen the other vehicles leaving, and decided to join them before unloading the supplies."

Wallace taps a finger on the map. "Then I suppose when this is over, he'll be reassigned, am I right?"

"Yes, ma'am," Morneau says, relief in her voice.

"All right," Wallace says, picking up her helmet. "Let's go outside."

We all troop out of the cabin into the approaching dusk and line up, looking down at the parking lot, and then the near slope, where my platoon is still working on their foxholes. Wallace says, "First Sergeant, where do we stand on the field telephone setup?"

"About fifteen minutes, Captain."

"Good. I want a line from each platoon leader, right back to the command post. Platoon Leaders, I want test calls as soon as the lines are in place."

We three murmur our acknowledgments, and Wallace says, "Okay, First Sergeant, light up the sky. Let the world know where we are...and then run up the colors."

Hesketh goes to a supply trailer that's been placed near the cabin, works around in the rear for a few seconds, and comes out with a flare pistol in hand, and something folded under his other arm. Working quickly, three flares are fired up into the cloudy sky: red, red, and blue. He holsters the flare gun and looks up at the cabin's roof, where a rusty radio antenna sticks up from a corner.

"Corporal Turcotte," he calls out.

A middle-aged man in a tight and dirty uniform comes from around the cabin, wiping his hands on a rag, helmet bouncing on his MOLLE vest. "First Sergeant?"

He hands the folded package to him. "Take this, secure it up on that antenna. And when you're done, put that helmet back on that bony thing you call a head."

"Yes, First Sergeant."

He takes the fabric, moves over to the parked trailer, and with a quickness of movement that surprises me, he climbs up the trailer and makes a half-meter leap or so to the shingled roof. In a few minutes an American flag is flapping from the antenna. As one, we all salute. The flag is torn, scorched, and ragged at one edge, but it still flies.

Chapter Twenty-Three

Morneau and Jackson go back to their people, and then Captain Pulaski ambles out, and I'm surprised to see her smoking a cigarette. A doc—okay, a veterinarian—smoking? Then it strikes me that, what the hell, if it gives her some pleasure or relaxation in this mess, why not.

Pulaski takes a deep drag from her cigarette, comes over, scratches Thor's head, checks his bandages and the cast on his front leg.

"How's your boy doing?" she asks.

"Finest kind," I say. "He's really bounced back pretty well."

Pulaski's head is still lowered when she says, "You've got a voice command for your dog, to send him back to base if things go to shit, right?"

I don't like her tone of voice, don't like her question. "Just like every other K-9 unit, yes, I do."

"What's the word?"

I say, "Sorry, Captain, I'm not going to tell you."

She continues working Thor's head, and he leans in, knowing he's in the grasp of someone experienced in the care of animals. "I see. Afraid I might use it?"

"I don't like saying it in front of him. I don't want to... confuse things."

She says, "Amazing how these dogs can find their way back. Where's your base again?"

"Fort St. Paul, in Concord. New Hampshire."

Pulaski ponders that, and says, "Read a story in *Stars & Stripes* last year. A dog survived an ambush outside of the old NORAD base in Colorado Springs, and managed to trot its way back to base, at a former Boy Scout camp in New Mexico, place called Fort Philmont. About two hundred miles, and he got there. Starved, dehydrated, and sore paws. He made it."

She looks up and her cold eyes lock with mine. "How far are we from your base in Concord?"

"Not sure," I say. "Probably under two hundred miles. Maybe a hundred and fifty."

"Good," she says. "Then it's possible. Now Sergeant, this is what you're going to promise me, and no arguments. When the Creepers overrun us and we're burning and dying, you send your boy home. Got it?"

My voice is bleak. "We're not going to get overrun. We've got good defensive positions."

She takes a deep drag from her cigarette and does something I've never seen: she lets the smoke dribble out of her nose. "You ever hear of a company-sized unit holding their ground against a Creeper attack? No? That's because it's never happened. Units this size only survive by doing hit-and-run attacks, not by staying in place."

Hard to say anything in reply when she's making sense. She says, "The Creepers are out there now, rounding up reinforcements, and when they come at us, they're going to steamroller over us like a goddamn road project."

"Then why are you here?"

"Me? It's my job, and my duty."

"But . . . Thor. You seem more concerned about my dog."

"Hah," she says. "Of course. I'm a vet. I love God's creatures. They're lively, full of love, and most of all, they're innocent. Got that? The Creepers didn't come here to kill dogs, cats, or horses. They came to kill us. Fair enough. Humanity's sins could fill a thousand-page book, and maybe we deserve what we're getting. But not the creatures. And if I can save even just one, well, I can get lased into pieces and be one happy doc."

After that cheery message, I go back to the foxholes, check on my platoon. The foxholes are nicely dug in, mounds of dirt and rocks have been placed in front, and I find that if I keep hunched over, I can go from spot to spot without exposing too much of my carcass to whatever Creeper presence is out there. But even though there are still the occasional flares of light in the distance marking their advance, Thor remains calm, meaning not yet, not yet. I locate two soldiers—an older guy named Morris and a young soldier named Crotty—and send them back to the CP, as ordered by the Captain. Both silently pick up their gear and go up the slope, across the parking lot, and to the cabin.

In the last foxhole before the one belonging to Second Platoon, I say, "Sergeant Bronson? Platoon huddle-up in five minutes, back at my foxhole. Pass the word."

He grunts and climbs out, and I go back to my pit, which I plan to share with the young and frightened Private Tanner. I sit up on the hole's dirt lip, wait for the platoon to straggle in. And straggle they do, but I don't blame them. This isn't their kind of war, not their kind of fight.

I clear my throat, think about what to say. When the war started there wasn't much need for those chest-pounding, verb-abusing, inspirational speeches. Everyone could see that we were in the fight for our lives, and one of these days, someone should write a book about the thousands of civilians who turned out on their own to fight the Creepers once they landed. They didn't have much success, and often got in the way of the regular military, but I'm sure they fought in the way other civilians in other nations didn't.

But once the war started dragging on, those speeches of inspiration came back, but they could only do so much. Rumor has it that some U.S. Army reserve general, up in Washington state, would often come out and make those kinds of speeches, borrowing from Patton and Shakespeare's *Henry V*, and when the battles started, he'd climb back into his armored Humvee and watch the battle from a distance. That went on for a while, until after one battle, when his body was found in a ditch, head missing, apparently from a sharp blade.

Who knew Creepers used metal cutting instruments for close-in combat, hunh?

So I keep it simple. "We're in for a long night, no doubt about it. I'll be right here, and we're going to have a field telephone hooked up to Captain Wallace. Guys, take turns sleeping, but make sure both of you aren't sleeping at the same time. Keep your eyes and ears open, but especially your noses. We're fortunate that we have Thor, but still, anybody smells cinnamon, come over and tell me soonest."

I pause, look at the tired, burnt, and worn faces, all the way from twelve years old to fifty years old. What an Army. What a platoon. I say, "Captain Wallace has sent out couriers, contacting Battalion and any other forces out there. Relief is on its way. In the meantime, keep your heads down, eyes open." In my next sentence, I almost start off by saying "If" but I don't intend to insult these veterans.

"When the Creepers attack, you M-4 troops keep up a nice, harassing fire, three-round bursts. M-10s...you guys know what to do. Keep watch on the aiming stakes out there on the slope, and adjust your rounds accordingly. Everybody got antiflash cream?"

A few nods. "All right, everybody goop up, and help out anyone who's low on the cream. Any questions?"

Corporal Balatnic says, "Sergeant, I heard a rumor our food truck left without unloading. True?"

I don't fuss around. "Very true, I'm sorry to say. But the Captain is trying to scrounge something together, so we at least we get something to eat before nightfall. Anything else?"

No more questions, and I say, "One more thing. Except for Thor, I want everyone to use the latrine. Third Platoon is digging one as we speak. Got it?"

From the rear someone says, "How come that damn dog gets special treatment?"

I say, "Because he never talks back to his sergeant."

That gains me some smiles and a couple of laughs, and I take that as a victory.

After First Platoon heads out, I climb into my pit and I'm happy to see Tanner has enlarged the place to make room for Thor. I dig out a container of antiflash cream and we each goop up our faces, necks and other exposed skin. It makes us look slightly ridiculous, like we're putting on white-faced makeup for some kind of minstrel show, but I'll take the ridiculous along with the slight protection it offers us.

By the rear of the pit is a canvas-covered field telephone. I lift up the cover, take out the receiver and give the side crank a few whirls.

The phone's quickly answered by the first sergeant. "CP."

"First Platoon up."

"Hear you five by five," he says. "Captain wants hourly updates, beginning at eighteen hundred."

"Got it, First Sergeant."

"CP, out."

I hang up the field phone, grab my M-10, check my bandolier. Seven rounds. The sun is starting to set. The sky is still overcast, and there's a flickering light in the east, where another chunk of space debris has come home to Mother Earth.

To the south there are brighter flashes of light, reflecting off the bottom of the clouds. Creepers on the move, burning as they go, heading this way.

Tanner stands next to me, M-4 in his hands. He wipes at his eyes, and then takes a deep breath.

It's going to be a long night.

At eighteen hundred I check in, and about ten minutes later, a detail comes by with our rations for the evening: clear chicken broth, water, and two stale rolls apiece that can only be eaten by dipping them into the broth until they get soft. I soften up one such roll and pass it on to Thor, and Tanner does the same thing.

"You don't have to do that," I say. "He's my responsibility."

"No offense, Sergeant Knox, but I hope if I feed him, he's happy. And if he's happy, he'll hunt Creepers better."

I can't argue with that, and I put my metal bowl on the ground for Thor to lick the broth I've left behind. So does Tanner. A good kid, I think.

Our messware is picked up a little while later, and we settle in, and I tell Tanner, "I got first watch. You try to get some sleep."

His laugh is a bit high-pitched. "Yeah. Try. Good word, Sergeant Knox."

"No worries, Tanner. Think of it this way. The other foxholes only have one soldier to cover the guy sleeping. You've got two."

It looks like that little bit of confidence building works, for he rolls himself up in a blanket, curls up in a ball, and in a while, he starts snoring. Thor gives me a look and I say, "Oh, lighten up. Let the kid sleep."

I feel wired up, tense, my eyes and ears working hard, even the one missing twenty percent of its hearing. It's a lead-pipe cinch—whatever the hell that means—that we're going to be hit at some moment, and I might screw up and get some of the people in my platoon, trusting in my experience and leadership, smeared as hot ashes across this New York landscape.

"Damn," I whisper. "Wish I was back home."

Home. Fort St. Paul. Heavily guarded, with comfortable beds and a real dining facility, which was usually able to feed us well. Schoolwork and Army training, the occasional raid or support of a larger offensive by a regular Army unit. But...routine. Hard to believe, but routine. I knew my place, knew my buddies and their places, and...

Abby.

Abby Monroe. I feel guilty about not having thought about her for some time. She's a combat courier in my platoon—one of the best—tough and fearless, with pretty long legs scarred with old burns and shrapnel hits. We've been dating for months, have enjoyed some great times. The last time I saw her was when she was standing on a train platform in Concord, waving to me as I left for a supposedly safe trip to Albany, accompanying Serena and her brother and a man from the governor's office, who was later killed in an ambush.

Abby.

I had gotten one letter from her in my travels, a short one, but it ended in the phrase, "Love, Abby." Something she had never written before. I had sent her a letter as well, but God knows if it got to her. But Abby...Unless she's out on a nighttime drill with her modified Trek mountain bike, or doing shooting practice at the fort's range, or just doing homework, I hope she's safe. And that she's thinking of me.

And that she doesn't suspect anything about me and Serena.

I let Tanner sleep an extra hour, and then I wake him, and I'm pleased to see him jump up, startled, M-4 in hand. "It's okay," I say. "Your turn."

He checks his watch and says, "Hey, Sergeant. You're an hour late getting me up."

I take a blanket out of my pack. "Thought you could use the sleep. Nothing's going on. Do me a favor, contact the CP, tell them nothing to report."

"How do I do that?"

So I demonstrate how a field telephone works, and he whirls the hand crank with obvious enthusiasm, and as coached, he says in a loud whisper, "First Platoon up. Nothing to report."

He nods and hangs up. I say, "Anything from their end?"

"Nope. I think it was the first sergeant grunting at me."

"Sounds good."

I sleep and I think Tanner wants to pay me back the same courtesy, but my internal clock wakes me up in exactly one hour. He says, "Nothing going on, Sergeant. Except the flashing lights out there . . . they've stopped."

"Really? For how long?"

"About thirty minutes."

"Did you tell the CP?"

With pride in his twelve-year-old voice, he says, "Yes, Sergeant. I did."

"Good job," I say back, though I'm slightly embarrassed that I hadn't heard him work the telephone crank. I must have been sleeping on my good ear, with my bum ear up. I look at the time, see I have a few minutes before checking in with the CP, and I say, "I'm going to walk the line. You stay put, all right?"

"Will . . . will you leave Thor behind?"

I squeeze his thin shoulder. "No, he's going with me. No worries, Private, you've got everything well in hand."

I can almost make out his smile in the darkness. "Thanks, Sergeant."

"Yeah, well, you can thank me by not falling asleep. Thor, come."

He's at my side as I roll out of the foxhole and then head to the left, down where the access road is located. Somewhere out there is Third Platoon, and I want to make sure we're watching each other. I rustle my way and in the dim light, see a rise of dirt, and in a whisper, call out, "Hey, Third?"

"Right here," comes a woman's voice. "Who's approaching?"

"Sergeant Knox, First Platoon, coming in. Got my dog with me."

"Okay."

I crouch down, make my move, and then lower myself into the foxhole. "Thanks," I say. "Just checking in."

"Specialist Carr, Specialist Holmes," comes the woman's voice. There's a younger woman with her, and I say, "Both awake?"

"Shit, you think we can sleep, knowing the Creepers are coming?"

"Well, the light flashes have stopped. Could be a good sign."

"If it's a good sign for this Company, it'll be the first in a long time."

We talk for a few minutes more, each of them taking a couple of minutes to rub Thor's head, and then I'm back outside in the darkness. I can make out the cabin up on top of the flat peak, and there's a faint haze of light. Must be warm and comfortable in there.

Right, I think. And Serena's in there, too.

I go back up the line.

It goes fairly quickly, and I'm very pleased to see that no one's slacking off, that in each foxhole, one of my troopers is wide awake. It's confirmed that no Creeper sign has been seen in nearly an hour, and at my last foxhole, a Corporal Melendez says, "Things okay, Sergeant Knox?"

"All quiet," I say. "How's Sergeant Bronson?"

There's a long pause, and Melendez says, "He's sleeping."

"All right. And how are you?"

Another pause. "Glad he's sleeping."

Then I leave with Thor, hook up with Second Platoon—one of the two soldiers in their foxhole has an ancient, and I mean *old*, Thermos bottle—and I get to take a few mouthfuls of hot sweet coffee, and then after I thank them, I go back to my platoon and my foxhole, and that's when things start to slide into the shits.

Tanner says, "Everything okay?"

"Yes, things are fine," I say, but I'm overdue to report to the CP. I crank and crank the side of the field telephone, receiver up to my ear, and . . .

Nothing.

"Private, have you touched the field phone?"

"No, Sergeant."

"Has it rung since I've been out?"

"No, Sergeant."

I try again, and again.

No joy.

"What's wrong?" Tanner asks.

"Field phone's dead," I say, telling myself all the different ways this could be nothing at all. "Stay put. I'm going to take a stroll up to the CP, see if there's a break in the line, or if it got unplugged at the other end."

"Sergeant..."

I take pity on the kid. "Thor, stay."

"Thank you."

I flop myself out of the foxhole, find the telephone line, and keep it loosely in my hand as I walk, hunched over, with M-10 bouncing heavily and awkwardly on my back, heading across the parking lot. I keep a low profile, not knowing if there's anything out there watching me. More often than not, the Creepers like to roll in and start attacking, without much stealth or sneaky maneuvering, but there's been tales—and I've seen it twice before—where a hidden Creeper will fire off a laser that will kill a soldier from hundreds of meters away. Once you see a guy cut in half while walking casually across a supposedly safe field full of knee-high hay, with no danger in sight or Creeper scent in the air, that tends to stay with you.

The wire is secure and all in one piece as I get up to the CP, and I'm thinking of banging on the door before going in, but I don't want to wake the people whose turn it is to sleep. So I let the wire drop, softly open the door, and peer in.

To the right, Captain Pulaski and two of her medics are asleep on the cots they've got set up for the wounded. Serena is on the floor, sleeping, cuddled up around Buddy, two blankets covering them. In the center is the table with a gas lantern, set on low, with the field phone setup in the center, and a dozing first sergeant, head on his arms, splayed out on the table. I instantly see what had happened: a movement of his left arm had disconnected the phone line for the First Platoon from the communications apparatus. I step forward to snap it back in and—

Look to the left. A padded bench. Dad is there, with Captain Wallace, and his arms are around her, and they're...they're kissing.

Kissing.

I take a deep breath, move forward, snap the line in place, and turn to get the hell out.

I make it about three steps before Dad catches up to me, hand on my shoulder.

"Hey," he says, voice low.

I shrug off his touch and keep on walking, and he grabs me harder, pulls me around to look at him. "Randy."

"Dad."

He seems to be struggling to say something, or do something, and right then and there, I don't particularly care. The door to the cabin is closed, only some thin rays of light coming out from the cracks, and I don't want to think what Captain Wallace is doing right now.

"Randy, look, Kara and I—"

I can't believe I get the words out but I do. "But Mom... what about Mom..."

His voice is thick. "Son, it's been ten years, and—"

"Damn it, I know it's been ten years! I was there! And I still don't know what happened to Mom or Melissa!"

Dad's mood changes, he steps back, no longer the humiliated father, but now the angry widower. "Is that it? Is that it? You want to know? All right, I'll tell you. I'll tell you every grim detail, if you think you're so big you can handle it."

My eyes are brimming with tears. Oh, Mom. Oh, Melissa. Is this how it comes? Is this how I finally find out? In the middle of a fight in the middle of a battlefield?

I step back. "Colonel, I need to get back to my platoon."

"Randy..."

"Colonel, I'm going back to my unit."

I turn and I can't even wipe at my eyes when the world around me lights up so bright that shadows fall upon the dirt parking lot, and a strangled voice screams:

"CREEPERS!"

Chapter Twenty-Four

I guess it's a tribute to my training or leadership or just plain being scared out of my mind, but I don't run to the site of the attack, which is on the reverse side of the hill. I run across the parking lot, down the slope and into my foxhole, and things get very chaotic, bright and loud all at once.

Hand-held warning bells are ringing, there's the thundering *BLAM!* of M-10s being fired back there, and I slap Tanner on the shoulder, tell him, "Eyes front! Watch your area!" His face is pale but he's a good kid, and he turns away from the action behind us, grabs his M-4 and looks down slope from our foxholes. Thor's growling and I say, "Tanner, I'll be right back. Stay in position!"

I roll out and keep my head down, run along the foxholes, checking in on my squads, saying again and again, "Eyes front, eyes front. That could be a diversion. Second Platoon's got it. Eyes front." Everyone's in position and I make it to our end of the foxholes, where the cliff face is located, and at the end pit Bronson says, "What the hell's going on, Randy?"

I ignore him using my first name and look up at the hill, in time to see a long tongue of flame rise up, along with the flash of lasers from the attacking Creepers. "Second Platoon is taking it. Be on the ball. We might be next."

He mutters something but I don't have time, and I scurry back to my foxhole, and after rolling in, crank up the phone.

It's Hesketh. "CP, go."

227

"First Platoon up," I say. "Our sector's quiet."

"Good for you. CP, out."

I slam the phone back into the receiver, peer over the dirt pile and check out our slope. Quiet all right, and with the Creeper attack back there, it's dimly lit, but a moment later, there's a hissing noise as a parachute flare is sent up, and when it pops open, its slow descent gives us a better view.

Another *BLAM!*, and one more report from an M-10 back there, and it seems to quiet down. The parachute flare stays up for a number of long, long seconds, illuminating everything in a harsh and unforgiving light, and it eventually drifts off to the south, and Tanner says, "Shit, hope it doesn't start a fire."

I can't help myself, and I laugh, and Tanner laughs, too. I say, "All right, I want you looking up at the parking lot. You tell me what you see, all right?"

He turns around and says, "What am I looking for, Sergeant?"

"You're looking for a line of Creepers going over that cabin and coming at us."

"Oh . . ."

I shift some, remove two 50 mm cartridges from my bandolier, click one unsafe, and spin the base so it's locked in to fire at fifty meters. I slide the cartridge in, slam the bolt shut, and wait.

I pat Thor on the head and he growls again, and I say, "Yeah, pal. We ride again . . . except this time, we're stuck in one place."

I stroke his head again, remembering the command that will send him out of here and back to Fort St. Paul if we're overrun. "Lucky you, if we've got to run, you got two extra legs."

Tanner cries out when our field phone rings and I nearly jump out of the foxhole. I pick up the receiver and say, "First Platoon, go."

Hesketh gets right to it. "Command Post. Two Battle Creepers destroyed. Two from Second Platoon injured. Report any movement."

"Hoo-ah, First Sergeant," and I replace the receiver.

"What's going on, Sergeant?" Tanner asks.

"It's—"

I can't believe I don't respond faster, but there you go. A Battle Creeper emerges from the woods below us and that damn thing skitters up at us like its friends are chasing it. I scream, "First Platoon, fire fire fire!" and the M-4s rip off their rounds, and there's an M-10 shot from two foxholes down, but it overshoots the fast moving Creeper, and I'm in the same spot, damn it. I've set my round to explode at fifty meters and the Creeper's raced past that point, and Christ, those six legs are moving faster than I've ever seen before. Its weapon arms are extended, moving, spinning, firing off burst after burst of laser fire.

I yell out, "Check your down range, check your down range!" but I'm not sure if I can be heard over the fire of the M-4s, setting down harassing fire, but I move quickly, ejecting the live round, letting it drop to the dirt—thereby violating a few rules and regs about how to treat live rounds—and I grab another round, twist off the safe, twirl it to ten meters, and I slam it into the breech, ram the bolt home, all without looking, just as another parachute flare is sent up from the CP behind us.

The light bathes everything again in its sharp relief, and as I bring my M-10 to my shoulder, I see a beautiful sight indeed, which is the Creeper, getting about fifteen meters or so from our line of foxholes, and an M-10 round explodes right in front of the fast-moving bastard.

Perfect.

But the damn thing keeps on moving, keeps on moving, and I fire a shot—*BLAM!*—the recoil knocking me back, but my shot misses and explodes at the rear of the Creeper, and then the damn thing noses down, its center arthropod digging into the soft dirt, and by God, it looks dead all right, as its center section and six legs rise up from the ground, and go up, and it looks like the bug is going to somersault onto our line.

It goes up, up, pauses, and then falls back down, twisting, until it collapses on its left side, crushing the three legs on that side. A cheer rises up from my platoon, and I join right in. A hell of a thing. The flare continues to light up the landscape from up there, swinging, and maybe there's an updraft or something, but it hangs for a long time. I take a good long look across our front, and it looks clear. The stench of cinnamon and a dead Creeper comes our way, and Thor barks in excitement. I drop down and ring the CP, and a soldier I don't recognize answers, and I say, "First Platoon, one Battle Creeper, dead."

"Casualties?"

"Unknown, out to check."

I hang up the field phone, roll out, and keep down as I work my way up the line, checking in, and I come to the third foxhole and ask, "Who killed that Creeper? Anybody here?"

De Los Santos is in the hole with Winn, a female PFC, and he says, "Not here, Sarge. Next one up."

"Thanks."

I move onto the next foxhole and it's Balatnic and Lancaster, a corporal. He's holding an M-10 and Balatnic has an M-4. In the fading light of the overhead flare, their faces are drawn and pale underneath their helmets.

"Corporal, you the one who killed the Creeper?"

"Uh..."

"Corporal, did you kill the Creeper? I hear the killing shot came from here."

Lancaster looks miserable and says, "Sergeant...it wasn't me. It was Balatnic."

She looks equally miserable and I say, "But you're not qualified on the M-10."

"That's right, Sergeant."

I give them both a stern look and say, "Then what the hell happened?"

Lancaster says, "Well...it's like this..."

"Make it snappy."

"Sergeant, I had to take a dump," he says, eyes downcast. "I was up at the latrine when the Creeper attacked."

"You left your M-10 behind?"

"Yes, Sergeant."

"For real?"

"Sergeant...I know I shouldn't have done that, but I was in a hurry, and I didn't think anything would happen, and..."

"Balatnic?"

"Sergeant, when the Creeper started up the slope, I grabbed Tony's M-10, switched the cartridge off safe, loaded it up, and shot. It was just...I just reacted."

"You reacted well," I say. "Why did you set the round to ten meters?"

"I...panicked. I thought I had set it to fifty."

"Good job panicking," I say. "Well done. Lancaster?"

"Sergeant?"

"Make sure that M-10 stays with you. And if you get torched...
Balatnic, you're qualified. You get his weapon."

Lancaster doesn't look particularly pleased at what I've just
said, but Balatnic shyly smiles because among other things, being
qualified means a raise of ten new dollars a month.

I check in with the rest of the platoon—no injuries, thank
God—and when I start back down the line, it's Third Platoon's
turn to get hit.

It doesn't last long, as I later learn, for the Battle Creeper just
raced up the dirt access road and got croaked in a crossfire of
at least three M-10 rounds, with no human casualties.

Back in my foxhole with Tanner, he says, "Wow...three dead
Creepers in a row. Not bad, hunh?"

I grab a canteen, take a swig of water, and then pour some
in a metal bowl for my boy Thor, who laps and slurps with
contentment. "It's not over."

"Sergeant?"

"A probing attack, that's all. The Creepers wanted to see how
we're organized. For them, mission accomplished."

Tanner just nods, gulps. "What next?"

"Up to the Creepers, I guess."

I lean back against the dirt side of the foxhole, and to the
east comes a line of pink and light red as the sun starts to make
itself known.

I shiver just thinking of what is waiting for us later in the day.

There are three more probing attacks, each one beaten back
with success, and breakfast comes by, with lukewarm coffee, lukewarm oatmeal, and cold toast. Tanner and I share ours with Thor,
and we both take turns at the latrine, and when we're squared
away, there's the sound of a high-pitched engine. I raise myself
up to take a peek and right next to the dead Battle Creeper that
took on the Second Platoon, a motorcycle roars up, the driver
in blue jeans and leathers, a torn and battered American flag
flying from a whip antenna at the rear of the motorcycle. The
sight warms me right up.

"What's that, Sarge?" Tanner asks.

"Dispatch rider, which is the best news of the day."

"Why's that?"

"Because it means we're not totally isolated. Other units out there know we're on this little peak, which means a relief should be coming soon. Or a well-defended redeployment."

"You mean, retreat?"

The motorcycle parks outside of the cabin, the door flings open. "Private?"

"Yeah?"

"How long you've been with 'Kara's Killers'?"

"Not too long," he says. "A month, maybe."

"You want to stay another month, I wouldn't say the word retreat, ever again."

Some minutes pass and I jump again when the field telephone rings. Tanner answers and then hangs up and says to me, "Captain wants to see you, right away."

"Got it," I say.

I tell Thor to stay and he's about half asleep anyway, and doesn't give me any fuss. I roll my way out and then move up to the gravel parking lot, and then up to the cabin. As I get closer to the door with the sandbags and rocks piled nearby, Lieutenant Morneau and Lieutenant Jackson come in from their respective sides of the hilltop. All are carrying their M-10s, and while one's a white woman, and the other's a black man, their faces are the same, tired and worn.

"Some night, eh?" I ask.

Morneau grunts and Jackson says, "Just living the dream, Knox. Living the dream."

On the right side of the cabin, a tarp has been stretched out and hammered down with stakes and rope. The shelter's for the response force that's been assembled from the three platoons. All of the soldiers are rolled up in blankets or shelter halves, sleeping, and I don't envy them. Right now I'm content to be with First Platoon, assigned to one spot. Moving around in the open during fierce combat is just a sweet invitation to get your head blown off, or to get scorched from head to toe.

Inside the CP the air is stuffy and warm. The gas lantern is still on because the windows have been blocked with dirt and rock. The motorcycle dispatcher has his—oops, her—jacket off, and she's sitting on a stool, drinking a cup of coffee. Her face is tanned, worn, and her dark brown hair—freed from its helmet with an American flag painted on the rear—is streaked with gray.

Wallace gestures to one corner of the room and there's a stove, and we three platoon leaders grab our own cups of coffee, although it tastes pretty watered down.

Serena and Buddy are in a corner, on a mattress, blanket held up against their chests. Serena gives me a quick smile and I feel light on my feet and happy, and Dad is talking low to First Sergeant Hesketh, and I do my best to ignore them both, no longer feeling so light or happy.

Wallace says, "If we can get this little *kaffeeklatsch* moving along, this is the situation. Sergeant Nicholas here has come with news that a relief column is on its way."

I think all of us let out a deep breath at that. Finally, thank God. Wallace says, "It's a QRF from the Third Mobile Combat Team. They're heading in our direction and should be here in..."

The dispatch rider speaks up. "Less than an hour, Captain."

"Outstanding," Wallace says. Her finger moves along the dirty map like some proverbial hand of God...or Goddess. "They'll pick up our vehicles and two Strykers, and convoy their way here, punching through any Creepers that might set up a resistance line."

Lieutenant Morneau asks, "What kind of unit is the Third Mobile Combat Team?"

"Pretty damn new, but pretty damn tough," Nicholas says. "We've been operating up near the Canadian border. We were coming south for rest and refit when we got the word."

"We got a shitload of Creepers closing in on us," Morneau continues. "They might be tough, but how are they going to be able to get past the Creepers and up this hill?"

Nicholas offers a sly grin. "The Third Mobile's got a pair of M1-A2s coming up here," she said. "They're be on tank transporters until they get about three klicks out, and then they'll deploy once they've linked up with your vehicles. The two tanks are supported by two Strykers and up-armored Humvees. The Abrams will hammer through and then provide covering fire as your Company bails out."

I can't quite believe what I'm hearing and I say, "M1-A2 tanks? For real? I haven't seen any of those in years." I didn't mention that the ones I'd seen had been wrecks, smashed by the stealth satellites. "Thought they couldn't move in the open anymore."

"Yeah," she says. "Because of the onboard electronics. But these guys have been retrofitted. All of the electronics, anything high tech, all that stuff's been stripped out. Just a battle tank with a diesel and bare-eyed targeting, that's it. Even more primitive than the tanks we used to fight against the Krauts last century."

Jackson says, "But... They can't kill the Creepers, can they?"

Nicholas smiles once more, swirls around her cup of coffee. "Damn thing fires a 120 millimeter shell. Used to be able to fire a variety of rounds, from antiarmor to antipersonnel, but now it fires a solid chunk of tungsten."

I ask, "Does it penetrate the arthropod?"

"Hell, no," she says, still smiling. "But kinetic energy is our friend. It hits the Creeper in the right place, it sends it sailing right into the next county. Nope, you haven't seen anything 'til you've seen one of these new tanks go up against a Creeper. Prettiest damn thing you'll ever see."

Wallace says, "What are your recognition signals?"

Nicholas says, "Three orange flares, three klicks out. Two orange flares, two klicks out. One orange flare, we're knocking at your front door."

Wallace taps her fingers on the map. "Sounds too good to be true."

Nicholas finishes her coffee. "Every day walking and breathing is too good to be true. With your permission, ma'am, I'm gonna go hook up with the Third Mobile, tell 'em message delivered." She hesitates and then speaks up again. "If I may, ma'am..."

"Go ahead, Sergeant."

She puts her coffee cup on the crowded table. "I've heard from other dispatch riders that something's stirred up those bugs something awful. I suggest... I suggest you be ready to move once we get here. Ain't gonna be enough time to dick around."

Wallace says, "Understood, Sergeant. You can rest assured we won't be dicking around."

Once she leaves and there's only the muttered roar of her motorcycle heading off, Wallace says, "All right, go back to your people, get them ready. We'll do the same here for the CP. Remember the flare signals. The last orange one means they'll be coming up that access road, and then we're gonna have to move fast as hell. Any questions?"

There were none.

"Good. One more thing, though. Spread the word. If anybody

spots a blue flare, in any direction, at any time, they're to get me at once. Understood? At once. I don't care if I'm sleeping, or dreaming about a cheeseburger, or my ass is hanging over the latrine pit. I want to know if a blue flare gets sighted."

The two lieutenants and yours truly acknowledge that, and Dad starts to get up and work his way around the table, but by the time he gets to the door, I'm already halfway down the slope to the gravel parking lot, ignoring his calls.

First Platoon had been resting or slumbering when I left, but the news I bring jolts them all awake, and there's a lot of laughter and high fives exchanged as I go up and down the line of foxholes, making sure everything is policed, picked up and squared away.

Now my guys and girls in the First Platoon are relaxed but a bit tense, knowing that relief is just minutes away. I know what they're thinking: big guns are riding to them, hot showers and food and a comfortable bunk are going to be there at the end of the day, and finally, no more running.

"Look over there!" comes a shout, and we look over to "there" and see a damn pleasing sight indeed, one-two-three orange flares are flying up into the overcast, leaden sky, trailing sparks and little bright twinkles of light.

"Hoo-ah!"

"There you go!"

"Come on, Third Mobile, we're waiting!"

More laughs and canteens are drunk, and without any orders, one and then two and then all platoon members are out of their foxholes, weapons in one hand, packs in the other. They really should be under cover, but it's been a long day and night, so I don't say anything. They stretch out on the dry and brown grass, or a few sit on the edges of their foxholes, letting their feet dangle over. Someone has a rolled up sock and tosses it to Thor, who races back and forth in delight, sometimes not giving up the sock, growling and tugging back at whoever's playing with him at the moment, who happens to be De Los Santos, grinning and teasing Thor, his black eye patch in place.

"Hey, number two's up!" comes another shout, and sure enough, two orange flares race up in the sky, and even I cheer and clap. Members of Second Platoon start wandering away from their foxholes, up to the gravel parking lot, and First Platoon looks to me and I say, "Sure, go ahead. Just get ready to haul your ass on the first empty truck that gets close to you. We've got to make some heavy time."

I join the soldiers as we go up the slight incline, and Thor runs over to me, panting, very happy indeed to be playing as a dog and not a K-9 hunter, and I stroke his back as we get to the lot.

We're bunching up.

A big no-no.

You never bunch up, allowing the Creepers to kill or maim lots of you with a laser beam or flaring torch, but we also have to be ready to get onto the transports and out as fast as we can.

The door opens up to the CP and Wallace comes out, and yells, "Hey, you clowns! Scatter! Spread out...this ain't no bus station."

There's just the slightest movement and I sense Wallace doesn't want to press the point, and like the viewers at an outdoor movie show or concert, we're all staring to the east, where the two previous flares had fired off.

We wait.

The sky remains overcast.

Nothing in view save the dead Creeper, the dirt access road, and lots and lots of trees.

Wait.

A murmur, "Where in hell is that third signal?"

"Yeah."

"Maybe they got hung up."

"Bridge out."

"River flooded."

A stronger voice, "Maybe some peacers decided to block the convoy. You know, sacrificing us for the cause of peace and accommodation."

A couple of obscenities are tossed out in response to that. I peer around the other soldiers.

Still quiet.

Thor is by me, sitting quietly on the gravel parking lot. He's not making a sound, not doing anything, but his intelligent eyes are flickering back and forth, back and forth, like there's something out there, just beyond his senses, something there that has caught his attention.

I don't like it.

"First Platoon!" I call out. "Back to the line. Now!"

Boy, do they grumble, but they pick up their weapons and gear, and I wonder if the two lieutenants are going to follow my lead, and then—

The sky lights up, a thundering noise slapping at our chests and ears.

I drop and roll, covering my eyes, opening my mouth, just in case a nearby concussion rips through me and tears out my eardrums. More thundering explosions, rapid, like someone firing a pump-action shotgun, one shell after another, and I keep my eyes closed tight until it seems the light has faded.

I open my eyes. All around me soldiers are getting up from the dirt, grabbing their weapons and packs, running back to the line. I run too, even though there's nothing going on at the sloping hill before our empty foxholes.

No.

Everything is going on to the west.

I spare a glance as I tumble into my foxhole, Tanner panting and joining me, Thor gracefully jumping in. To the west are rising plumes of smoke, and then, more distant explosions, as bright white lines shoot from the cloud cover, striking targets on the ground.

Killer stealth satellites, still at work.

More explosions.

Tanner is next to me, breathing hard. "Sergeant?"

Out beyond the rising plumes of smoke, a flare rises up, sputtering, and then going off at an angle, like the soldier firing it was using his or her last strength to do so.

It's the color of the sun, yellow, and it's a sign of distress.

"Sergeant?"

I rub at my chin, still looking at the smoke out there, and I say, "Unpack your gear. We're not going anywhere today, or tonight."

Chapter Twenty-Five

Once the sun sets the Creepers come back again, with quick, probing hits to our lines, like they were seeking out weaknesses or a gap. They attack at random, with no rhyme or reason, sometimes sending two at a time at one segment of the line, followed again by another two somewhere else, and then resting, and then sending one by itself at a completely different spot.

And then they flee back to the tree lines, all but one making it back safely. Off to the right, Second Platoon nails one, and while that's usually call for hoots and cheers, it's quiet over there, like they're too tired too care.

But why attack and skitter back without pressing on?

Why? Because they're aliens, that's why.

Dinner is cold chicken broth and another stale roll, and I sip half of the broth, soften the roll in the broth, and then feed it to Thor. He laps my bowl clean. Tanner sees what's left in his own bowl, and he nearly cries. "I'm sorry, Sarge. I'm so damn hungry."

"Go ahead, finish it off."

He finishes it off, turning his back to me like he's ashamed of his hunger and weakness, and so we prepare for the long night.

I let Tanner sleep for as long as he wants, and then when he wakes up, looking like he might be in trouble, I say, "It's okay. I'm going to check the line. Stay alert, stay tight."

"Yes, Sergeant."

I roll out and keep my head down, and check in with my troopers, and I'm startled when I see a soldier named Tyson alone in her foxhole.

"Hey," I whisper. "What's going on? Sully is supposed to be with you, right?"

"Yes, Sergeant," she says, her M-10 in a good firing position through a gap of piled dirt in front of her foxhole, looking down the bare slope.

"Where is he?"

"Sleeping," she says. "I've got the watch."

I peer in, seeing just darkness and a knapsack. "Is he sleeping back at the CP?"

A grumble. "No, damn it, I'm trying to sleep here."

From beneath and to the side of the hole, Sully appears, like a woodchuck slowly emerging. He had dug further into a wall of the foxhole, making a shelter within the shelter. He drags his M-4 out and coughs.

"Sullivan?"

Another cough. "Look, Sarge. You saw those satellites scorch Third Mobile. I heard they weren't using any high-tech stuff in their trucks and tanks. So why the hell did they get scorched?"

That had been troubling me as well. "Don't know, Sully."

"Yeah, well, I know I'm too old for this shit. If those satellites wanted to, they could melt this entire mountain top, and Mrs. Sullivan's only son is gonna keep his head and body covered."

Not much to reply to that, and he says, "Tyson. How much time do I have left?"

"Another hour."

"See ya."

He crawls back in, and I check out the rest of the line, and when I'm back and safe in my foxhole with Tanner, they attack again.

It turns out to be a long night, probing here and there, and we nail two of the bugs, and we hear that Second and Third have done better than us. We lose one trooper to a laser burst, Gould, who loses his right arm just below his shoulder. I spare two troopers to haul him up to Dr. Pulaski at the CP, and they come back a few minutes later, out of breath, saying two had been killed from Second Platoon, and one from Third Platoon.

I move the line some so Tanner and I are covering a wider area, so that the gap from losing Gould can be covered. Over to the east the sky is lightening up, a nice thin red line and a spreading patch of pink and red, meaning another day is approaching. I take in a deep breath, wondering what the day is going to bring, and more importantly, if we might get something to eat anytime soon.

Below us on the slope there are lines of mist, long flowing tendrils rising up from the grass and low brush, only disturbed by the site of three dead Creepers, in various stages of collapse, arthropod legs canted at odd angles, and some churned-up earth from their legs. The sun starts to make its appearance. Thor scrambles up from the foxhole and does his business over by Third, which is okay by me. He sits, sniffs the air, and then trots back, licks my hand and face, and climbs back into the foxhole.

It's quiet.

Tanner yawns and says, "Sarge...okay if I take a snooze 'fore breakfast comes around?"

Brave young lad, thinking that we might actually get breakfast. The sun rises higher and the mists start to move around, almost like there are ghostly phantoms on the move, rising in the air.

"Sure," I say. "I'll wake you up...when breakfast comes."

He smiles and rolls himself in a ball, and in seconds, he goes to sleep.

It's still quiet.

Movement along the line, and De Los Santos comes to me, weapon in hand, keeping himself low, and when he gets to our foxhole, he lifts his head and says, "Sergeant," and then there's a quick flicker of light to my left and he drops into the dirt.

"Corporal?"

He's down, falling in a fetal position, the M-10 falling out of his hand.

No movement.

"Corporal?"

Tanner wakes up. "What's up, Sarge?"

"Hold fast," I say. "Keep watch down the slope."

I move out and Thor joins me. I crawl on my belly and reach the corporal, push his shoulder. "Hey. De Los Santos. What's up? Did you trip? Are you okay?"

The faintest whiff of burnt flesh.

Thor moves around, whines, and pushes a paw against his back. I move closer, look at the rear of his torso, along the Fire-biter vest, down to his buttocks and legs. All clear.

But something's wrong when I get up to his collar.

There's a scorch mark at the base of his neck. Burnt and flaking dark flesh.

"God damn them all," I whisper.

That little flicker of light...from a laser beam shot from a hidden Creeper down there in the woods, a sniper shot, catching De Los Santos right at the base of his head, burning out his spine and lower brain.

God damn them all.

Tanner's still in our foxhole and I say, "My pack. There's a spare poncho. Take it out. Bring it over here."

Thor's still whining, pushing at the body of De Los Santos. I turn him over and thankfully his good eye is closed, the eye patch still in place. Thor digs at a pocket, takes out a rolled-up sock that he had played with earlier with the corporal. Thor's a smart pup; he knows De Los Santos is dead, but with the sock in his mouth, he stretches out and lies down next to the body. There's a sudden stench as the muscles in De Los Santos's trunk let go.

"You poor guy," I ask. "What the hell did you need so badly?"

I close his mouth. His dark skin is smooth. Tanner crawls up next to me, poncho in his hands. Both hands are shaking and his face is white.

"Unfold it, will you?"

Tanner nods, starts working the old green poncho, flattening it out on the dirt and dead grass. Other members of the platoon are staring at us, and I shout back, "First Platoon, eyes front! And keep your heads down!"

Tears spring up in my eyes. I blink at them. A dead trooper? I've seen plenty over the years. Thor's reaction? Maybe. My boy is slow to make friends, but he sure as hell had a bond with De Los Santos. So what's going on?

I reach to his head, start unbuckling his helmet. De Los Santos was mine, that's why. My platoon. My responsibility.

"Tanner."

"Yes, Sergeant."

"What was his first name?"

"It...it was Pepe, Sergeant."

I take the helmet off, put it aside. Pepe's hair is dark black, full and thick. "Where was he from?"

"Puerto Rico."

Puerto Rico... "The hell he was."

"Nope, he was, Sergeant. He was up in Queens, visiting his grandparents when the bugs attacked. All three got out in time... Now they're livin' in a refugee camp in Vermont. He used to send his pay to them every month. Now what?"

"I don't know."

I started undoing his Firebiter vest. On the other side of the hill, it sounds like another Creeper attack. I smell cinnamon and hear the clicking noise, shouts, and the heavy sounds of M-10s being fired.

Moving the Firebiter vest off of him, something tickles at my mind. I don't know what it is, but something is there.

I work some more, gather up his Firebiter vest, helmet, M-10, bandolier of rounds, and a .38 Police Special revolver with a cardboard box full of spare rounds. The box is old, soggy cardboard, the colorful labeling worn away.

Around his neck are his dog tags. I tug one tag off, keep it in my hand. There's a rosary around his neck, and a chain with a crucifix.

I leave them be.

I slip the dog tag into a coat pocket. "Tanner, give me a hand."

"Sure, Sergeant."

The M-10 firing from across the way has stopped. With Tanner's help, we drag Corporal De Los Santos's body onto the poncho, and in a few minutes, we have him wrapped up. It's good now, not seeing his face.

"Tanner, you take his shoulders, I'll take the legs."

"Yes, Sergeant."

"And keep your head and ass as low as possible."

"Yes, Sergeant."

Tanner moves forward, his helmet bouncing on his small head, and I say, "Thor, cover," and my boy whines again, and then crawls back into the foxhole. We pick up the corporal's body and move up to the CP, going way damn slow, with Tanner swearing as he drops De Los Santos twice on the way up the slope. But when we get to the gravel parking lot, we're moving better, right up to the CP. The supply trailer on the left hasn't moved, and the flag is still flapping some on the old radio antenna.

To the right, underneath the tarp, the response force soldiers are huddled up against the log wall, waiting, their M-10s and M-4s across their laps. There seems to be about half of them left, the rest no doubt having been deployed out to the Second or Third Platoon, but this half looks unsettled and spooked.

And I see why.

They're sharing the space with a pile of poncho-wrapped bodies, and Tanner and I gently put the remains of De Los Santos next to them. Tanner stands up, rubs at his lower back. "Head back to the line," I say. "I'll be along in a couple of minutes."

"Sure, Sergeant. Hey, do you think breakfast will be coming anytime soon?"

Hell, no, I think, but I say, "We'll see. Get moving."

I go around to the front of the CP, and there are moans and screams coming from inside, and in there...

It's chaos.

There's an overwhelming stench of burnt hair, burnt flesh—a smell like roast pork suddenly flamed that's hard to describe and which sticks to the roof of your mouth—and there are low moans and sobbing coming from the right. Captain Pulaski is in her white coat, working desperately over a trembling burnt body that's been stripped of its clothes, skin falling off in white flaps, aided by her two medics, illuminated by hissing gas lanterns. Two other soldiers are sitting, eyes wide, holding up arms that are missing hands. Bandages cover their stumps and both are breathing in long, shuddering breaths.

Serena and Buddy are in the corner, looking away from the horrible medical work going on, and Hesketh, Wallace and Dad are huddled over the map, voices low. Wallace spots me.

"Sergeant?" Her voice is strained, high-pitched, and I want to get the hell out of here as soon as possible.

"Captain," I say, passing over the dog tag from Corporal De Los Santos. "Corporal De Los Santos was just killed in action."

She nods. "Put it in the pile. Anything else?"

There's a dented white plastic bowl, the bottom covered with dog tags. With the scent of burning flesh and this ghastly sight, I feel like throwing up, so I say, "No, ma'am. We're just short now."

"Can you still hold the line?"

"Yes, ma'am."

"Then go."

"Yes, ma'am."

I spin out of there without looking back and get out into the supposedly fresh air on top of this hunk of rock, which smells of burnt things, cinnamon and smoke.

A brief thought comes to me. Buddy is in there, who knows the Bug lingo. Maybe... maybe he could come out here, with Serena's encouragement, and call out to the Creepers. Tell them to surrender. Tell them to go away. Tell them anything to save us up here on this lonely hill.

And then I look to the pile of poncho-clad bodies, including De Los Santos, still warm.

And what if Buddy were to come out and get a laser burst to the forehead before speaking a word of Creeper?

No.

He needs to remain as safe as possible.

I lower myself down and run back to the line, moving in a zigzag, trying to avoid De Los Santos's fate. I slide down and roll into the rear of my foxhole, and Tanner and Thor lift their heads, and I say, "Just one sec."

I grab De Los Santos's M-10 and move up the line, and stop at the foxhole occupied by Balatnic and Lancaster. "Lancaster, out you go. Head over to De Los Santos's foxhole. You're replacing him."

Lancaster says, "Is he wounded?"

"He's dead," I say. "Move along, and keep low. He was killed by a sniper shot from a Creeper."

"Yes, Sergeant," he says. Grabbing his gear and M-10, he climbs out of the foxhole, and moves down the line, and then drops into De Los Santos's foxhole. Balatnic looks up at me, face smudged, looking scared indeed. I pass over the M-10 and bandolier. "Congratulations, now your promotion takes effect."

She takes the M-10 and spare rounds. "Will I get someone here to help me out?"

"I'll see what I can do."

Balatnic moves the bulky weapon around and drapes the bandolier over her slim shoulders. "Sergeant?"

"Yes?"

"Sergeant... I'm starving."

I don't feel like lying to her about breakfast coming, so I don't, and she says, "When we got our broth last night, damn him, Lancaster spilled mine. He said he'd share, but he didn't give me half. He just gave me a mouthful. He said he was a man, taller and bigger, and that he deserved more of the food. Asshole."

"Yeah," I say, and her face is so young and strained, and almost automatically, my hands go into my pockets, wishing I still had that sandwich I had scrounged from the air base, eaten a long time ago. I know I don't have anything there, because I never leave any food item in my jacket because it can crumble up too easily, or get dunked in water, and then my left hand grasps something, deep in the pocket, almost hidden by a fold of fabric.

I pull it out. It's the old dog biscuit Captain Pulaski had given to me a number of days ago, to pass onto Thor at some special time.

I hope Thor will understand.

"Here," I say. "Have this."

"What is it?" she asks, taking the dog treat into her small hand.

Now it's time to lie.

"A special food bar, prepared for us Recon Rangers back in New Hampshire."

She sniffs it. "How come we haven't gotten it in our unit?"

"It's experimental."

She takes a bite, chews it with enthusiasm. "Not bad. Pretty dry but it has a good meaty taste." Balatnic holds it out to me. "Want a bite?"

"I'm good," I say. "You finish it up and get back to work, all right?"

Balatnic takes another healthy bite.

"Thanks, Sarge. God, I was starving."

I offer her a smile and then check the rest of the line, and Bronson looks up me with irritation and says, "What's going on?"

"What's going on is the war," I say. "You just worry about your field of fire, all right?"

He mutters something and I say to his companion, M-4 in hand, "Corporal Melendez, how are you doing?"

Melendez keeps his dark brown face looking forward. "Never finer, Sergeant. Never finer."

"You sure?"

"Oh yeah, very sure."

Going up the line means running into Second Platoon, and I note two helmeted heads positioned in their foxhole, and since this is Lieutenant Morneau's responsibility and not mine, I let it be.

But still, I scramble over some, across a rocky ledge, and on my belly, peer over. There's a steep rock cliff that drops about forty meters or so, and it's a sheer drop down, ending at a collection of boulders, and I push myself back.

I hate heights.

I go back down the line, see everybody's nice and ready, looking down the slope at the dead remains of three Creepers, the churned up dirt and grass, and the orange-topped stakes, marking the firing positions, and then the wood line.

As I approach my foxhole, Thor stands up, resting his two front paws on the edge of the dirt, panting, and I roll in, pat his head, and as someone calls out "Creeper!" down the line, I swear to God, the only thing I'm thinking about is how damn hungry I am.

An Excerpt From the Journal of Randall Knox

Since I was six years old when the war started, most of my memories are jumbles here and there, some jumbles still giving me nightmares, and what I remember the most is being cold and being hungry.

Among the many things gone was the cheapness and availability of food. No more restaurants, grocery stores, corner gas stations, Walmarts, drug stores with shelves of edibles, diners, mom & pop stores, bodegas, supermarkets or any other name you'd want to call a place where you could easily go in and get food when you were hungry. Or weren't hungry. It still amazes me that I lived for six years at a time when even a private home could have up to a month's worth of food being stored on shelves, refrigerators and freezers.

A month!

It sounds grim to make note of it, but's historical fact—for those few historians out there—that the initial food shortages and local famines occurred not because of lack of food, but because of lack of easy transportation and refrigeration. Hard to believe as well, but there was actually a time when critics—as Dad would say, people who couldn't do anything reliable, but could always point out the perceived flaws in others—felt that it was "more real" or "more green" to eat only locally grown food, not stuff flown in or trucked in.

Yeah. Well, when the trucks stopped running and the refrigerators and freezers turned warm, those survivors from the first weeks of war instantly turned to local sources, and found the sources wanting.

Because with all the water vapor kicked up into the atmosphere from the tsunami strikes, and with most farming and harvesting

*equipment remaining idle, that meant long years of stunted farm-
ing, which led to food shortages, which led to . . . lots of bad things.*

*Luckily for me, I did have lots of hungry days, but not anything
that threatened me, because Dad was in the Army Reserve and
reupped, and we did okay with his limited rations, plus whatever
black market groceries he could get for whatever the market bore.
But I knew there were problems all around us, and there were
stories and rumors of food riots, or raids on Department of Agriculture relief convoys, and sometimes, you saw it right up front.*

*One late summer day I was doing a training session with Thor,
about six months after we were assigned together as a K-9 unit
for the Second Recon Rangers. We were in a stretch of the White
Mountain National Forest, and we were doing simple hunt and
release. Earlier the testers had gone through the wooded trails,
and at certain points, they'd leave a chunk of Creeper exoskeleton
behind a rock or a tree, to see if the newbie dog could sniff it out.
So far it had been a great day, with Thor finding the initial three
cache spots, and with just one left to go before we could go back
to the trailhead for the truck ride back home to Fort St. Paul.*

*The trail was part of a system that stretched from Georgia to
Maine, where I guess thousands of people each year decided to
hike to get back to nature or something like that. With a constantly growling belly and sore feet, I thought being in the Army
was enough getting back to nature for me for the rest of my life.*

*Thor was up ahead of me, sniffing and scrambling, and some-
times he'd disappear, which was fine. We had bonded pretty
quickly and I had learned that when he would reappear, I'd call
out, "Good boy, good check in!" and then he'd wag his tail, and
disappear again.*

*I was resting near a trail juncture, wondering how much further
it would be in these dark woods before he found that last chunk
of Creeper metal, when I thought I heard a yelp.*

I got right up from the boulder I was sitting on. "Thor?"

*The trail went to the left and to the right. My left ear wasn't
as good as it should have been, but I was pretty sure that's where
the yelp came from.*

"Thor!"

*I started up the trail at a quick trot, wondering if he had fallen,
or if he had gotten a paw caught in a rock crack, or if he had
encountered a porcupine or something. I moved along, climbing*

*up a rise, the trail pretty wide and worn from all those tromping
boots passing through over the decades.*

I stopped, tried to catch my breath.

"Thor!"

*The way ahead was dark, and I checked the sun's position.
Maybe another hour or so of daylight left.*

Damn.

*I picked up the pace, practically running now, and then I
caught a whiff of something, and I froze.*

*Cinnamon? Could a real-life Creeper be here, deep in these
empty woods?*

A slight shift of wind, and I caught the smell again.

Wood smoke.

Somewhere nearby there was a fire.

*I moved along some more, sniffing, turning my head, and the
smell of smoke got thicker. Off to the right. I got off the trail and
heard voices, and the wood smoke was really thick. I moved slowly,
reached down to my side and unbuttoned my holster, where I had
my 9 mm Beretta pistol. I was qualified for the M-4 and should
have been carrying that, but since this was just a routine mission,
none of had been issued one.*

*I stepped closer to the smell and the sound of voices, the Beretta
now in my hands, the safety off, hammer pulled back. There was
a round in the chamber. Always.*

*I moved around a large pine tree that had fallen years back,
dirt hanging down from its root systems, and then I squatted
down, now smelling old clothes, dirty skin, greasy hair.*

*There were three of them. I stared ahead. An older man and
two younger men, maybe in their twenties. Hard to tell. Torn,
tattered clothes. Long beards, long stringy hair, baseball caps so
filthy I couldn't tell what they once advertised. Gaunt faces, deep-
set eyes. On the ground were knapsacks held together with duct
tape. Their boots repaired with twine and duct tape as well.*

Something whining.

*Thor on his side, legs bound, thin rope wrapped around his
muzzle.*

The fire crackled and grew higher.

*The older man said, "Remember, Tom, we gotta drain the blood
real thorough 'fore we start butchering. Otherwise . . . a goddamn
mess . . . "*

One of the younger men said, "You got it, Pop."

The other guy complained. "I should get a bigger portion, right Pop? I caught 'em... I should get rewarded..."

I stepped into view, holding the Beretta tight with both hands, knowing with humiliation that my hands were shaking.

"Hey! You three! Let my dog go."

The older man stared at me with dead, cold eyes, and said, "Billy, shut your mouth and find that damn frying pan..."

"Okay."

I stepped closer. Thor whimpered some more. "Hey! Cut my dog loose... or else."

The two younger men kept on ignoring me, filthy hands going through their packs, and their father said, "Go 'way. Leave us alone. We'll leave you a leg... but leave us alone... it's ours... we found it..."

"That's my dog," I said. "And I'm with the National Guard, and I'm telling you to cut him loose. Now."

The older man said, "National Guard? Like the Army, son? The Army that couldn't protect us, couldn't feed us, couldn't evacuate us?"

"Found it!" Billy said, holding up a small frying pan. His brother said, "Give me a hand haulin' that dog up the tree, okay? Hind legs first, so the blood runs out once I slice his throat."

Tom drew a knife from a scabbard at his side and he went to Thor.

I shot him.

He gasped and spun around, fell to his knees, grabbing at his shoulder.

It was a lousy shot.

I tried better the second time and got him in the throat. Blood sprayed and he fell back, gasping and wheezing, and his father stared at me and said, "Don't mean you'll get his portion," as he headed over to Thor, a large knife in hand.

My third shot nailed his hip, and he collapsed, one hand still on the knife, the other going to his hip, and he gasped and said, "Damn, that don't hurt so bad... how about another one?"

My breathing was harsh, my mouth was dry, my legs were shaking and so were my hands, and I walked two paces and fired once more, into his forehead. I quickly turned and the second son—Billy—was again ignoring me. He was frantically digging through his father's knapsack and then let out a yelp of joy. He held up something raw and bloody wrapped in a Shop & Save plastic grocery bag and said, "Damn him, I knew he was holding out on me and my bro. Damn him!"

His dirty fingers tore at the plastic, and whatever raw bloody chunk of something in there was chewed at and swallowed in seconds. He then gathered up all three knapsacks and laughing with a high-pitched tone, ran into the woods.

It took me three tries to reholster my pistol.

I then knelt down and cut Thor loose with my Army-issued blade, and checked him over, and I bawled for a couple of minutes, and then we went back to the trail, to wrap up our training.

I was proud that I wasn't crying over the two men I had killed.

Chapter Twenty-Six

There's a brief firefight down the line and a Creeper in front of the Second Platoon skitters back to the woodline, and the rest of the day just drags and drags and drags, until the sun finally sets, with no more food, no relief, not much of anything.

Tanner wakes me up during the night, when he's on watch. I snap to and grab my M-10, and whisper, "What's up?"

Tanner says, "It's Corporal Melendez. From the end of the line."

"What about him?"

"He's here," he says. "The corporal says there's something going on near his foxhole."

I stretch some and in the dim light, make out the form of Melendez, lying on his stomach. "Sergeant."

I yawn. "Why the hell are you here? What's up with Sergeant Bronson?"

"He told me to let him sleep, or he'd kick me in the balls in the morning."

Joyful. "All right, what's up?"

Melendez pauses, and says, "I'm hearing something. I don't know what it is, but I'm hearing something. Don't make sense. I tell you, there's something going on."

I turn and say, "Good job, waking me up. Thor, stay. Melendez, show me what's what."

With M-4 in hand, Melendez half-crawls, half-trots his way back down the line, and I follow him, M-10 and bandolier over

255

one shoulder. We're getting pretty damn low on M-10 rounds, pretty damn low on food and bandages, and if we were any lower, we'd be in the water and would have to transfer to the Navy.

We pass the last foxhole, where I hear Bronson snoring. Melendez lowers himself down and whispers to me, "It's . . . a snapping sound. Damndest thing. I've heard it three times, and I don't see a thing."

"Did Bronson hear it?"

"He only heard me, and told me to go back to watch."

"Okay."

We're near Second Platoon at the patch of bare rock, and Melendez flattens out, and I do the same. Some of the cloud cover is gone and there's a crescent moon, lighting up some of the landscape. When a piece of debris burns its way through the atmosphere, it lights everything up and makes the shadows look like they're moving. Part of the trick of being on watch is knowing the difference.

A nice big chunk burns through and the shadows move along with its descent. Melendez keeps quiet. He knows the difference.

The rock is damn cold against my belly and chest, and I hope we have something hot for breakfast. Even hot, weak coffee. Or hot, weak tea. Or hot water with a couple of spoonfuls of honey in it.

Anything hot.

Melendez whispers, "I swear to God, Sergeant, I heard it."

"Relax. Besides, gives me a chance to stretch my legs."

The night slides along. Another piece of debris really lights up the joint, and I can easily make out the wood line, the churned-up ground, and the dead Creepers scattered in front of us, looking almost like those post-battle Civil War photos, showing the dead stretched out, sometimes in a formal-looking line.

My legs are cold.

So are my hands.

I turn to see if Melendez is still awake, and he is, and—

Snap.

"That's it, that's it, did you hear it?" he whispers fiercely.

"Shhh," I say. "Yeah, I did."

Now what?

The sound didn't come from the slope, and didn't come from Second Platoon.

It came from the rock cliff.

Oh, how I hate heights.

"Corporal, I'm crawling over to take a look. Stay right here. If I...fall or disappear, raise hell, okay?"

"Hoo-ah, Sergeant," he whispers back.

My M-10 is too large and bulky for me to crawl silently across this flat rock, so I shrug it off and slowly move forward, away from the line of foxholes, away from Melendez. Alone again. I'm beginning to think it's a habit I need to break.

The flat rock angles down. My breathing gets harder and faster. I'm thinking of a small spring suddenly opening up, wetting everything and causing me to slide and fall...

I bite my lower lip, the snap of pain putting everything into focus. I keep on crawling, my hands in front of me, and damned if I don't hear something else, something...whispering? Voices?

I find the edge of the cliff with my left hand, and then the right. I take a break, no longer cold, now warm and sweating. My heart is thudding so hard I think it could actually crack the rock I'm pressed up against.

One more deep breath, and I slide forward about a half meter or so, and then I peer over the edge of the cliff and look down.

Right into the center arthropod of a Battle Creeper, looking right up at me, its weaponized arms at its side, so close not only can I smell the cinnamon, but I can also hear the gentle whir of machinery from inside the bug's exoskeleton.

I pull back, wait wait wait, and then I grit my teeth and slide forward again, trying not to panic at what I see, and what I see is more than one Creeper. It's a whole line of Creepers, in a formation I've never seen before. Four of them are up against the base of the cliff, holding up three more, and in turn...holding up the Creeper I've just spotted. Other Creepers are milling about. They're making a goddamn pyramid, they are, trying to sneak through, working to get one of their Creepers over the edge.

And now they're damn close.

I slide back to Melendez, grab his shoulder, and whisper in his ear, "Haul ass to the CP. Tell Wallace or Hesketh we've got a half-dozen Creepers coming up the cliff. I need a satchel charge, a couple of hand grenades, anything that can make an explosion. And two more soldiers with M-10s...and go!"

He went.

I back up some, retrieving my M-10. Everything that's me is shaking. I think of that damn bug coming over the cliff edge, followed by other bugs, and right now it's just me. In the darkness I retrieve a round, unsafe it, and click it to ten meters, not your usual optimal range, because if you miss after ten meters, what's left of you can be scraped together and bundled in a small canvas bag.

I could alert First and Second Platoon, but to what point? They're in a lousy firing position, and if I get them stirred up, the damn bugs might just charge, right past me, right up to the CP.

I adjust myself in the approved firing position, and wait.

And wait.

The whisper of booted feet on gravel. Two soldiers I don't recognize drop themselves next to me, and then there's Melendez and First Sergeant Hesketh.

"Situation?" Hesketh whispers.

I tell him what's what and I spot the square canvas bag he has next to him, which is an M183 demolition charge, basically sixteen M112 demolition blocks of C4 explosive—twenty pounds worth—packed in a carrying case.

"First Sergeant, if you want, I can slip over there and drop the charge. It should disrupt the hell out of them."

Hesketh whispers back in his gravelly voice, "You mind it here, Knox. When I was in the Corps I was using these babies in Fallujah before your parents ever met. I'll take care of it. When I duck it means I've dropped it, and when it blows, you fellas come over and let them have it. Savvy?"

"Yes, First Sergeant."

Hesketh fiddles with the fuse on the side, slides forward, and then with a gentle movement, tosses it over the side, and I swear, I think I hear a *click-click* before a teeth-rattling *BOOM!* shakes the cliff top and nearly liquefies my guts. A cloud of dust and smoke rises up and like it was planned, an illumination flare is fired up from the CP, back up there on the hill.

"Go!" Hesketh yells, and me and the other two M-10 soldiers move forward, lean over, and start firing rounds down at the mess, and God, what a glorious mess it is, the harsh light of the illumination flare highlighting everything below us. Of course the satchel charge didn't kill them or crack open their exoskeletons, but it caused the pyramid to collapse, and there are five or so

Creepers in a tangled mess, and we fire off round after round, ten meters to twenty-five meters, and the clouds of gas drift down to the trapped Creepers, killing them all, and before the survivors can open up on us, Hesketh orders us back and says under his breath, "Think ya used enough dynamite there, Butch?"

I don't know who he's referring to—maybe one of those two soldiers is named Butch—and I go up to Melendez, slap him on the shoulder and say, "When this is wrapped up and done, Melendez, I'm going to recommend you to Captain Wallace for a field promotion. Good work back there."

"Thanks, Sergeant Knox."

I lead him back to his foxhole and Bronson is there, M-10 at the ready, and I suppose I should stick around and chew out his ample ass, but I'm too tired, so I just say, "Sorry we disturbed your beauty sleep, Bronson, and sorry to say, it doesn't look like it took."

I get back to my foxhole, rub Thor on his belly, slap the top of Tanner's helmet, and he says, "What happened over there?"

"Creepers tried to sneak up on us. We beat them to it. Anything happen over here?"

Tanner says, "CP called about a minute ago. Says there are couriers infiltrating through the woods and such. Warned us not to shoot them."

"Good," I say, lying down, finding my poncho, ready to wrap myself in it and go back to sleep. "And Private?"

"Sergeant?"

"The day you shoot at a two-legged human and think it's a six-legged alien, I'll shoot you. Got it?"

"Yes, Sergeant."

"Good. You keep your watch going, then."

And I sleep for exactly seventeen minutes, and I'm woken by voices, and I don't mind at all when I'm disturbed.

For it's a young woman's voice, out there by the foxhole, and she whispers and wakes me up. "Hey," she calls out. "Is this the First Platoon?"

Tanner whisper back, "Sure is."

"I'm looking for a Knox. Sergeant Randy Knox."

I cough, toss off my poncho. "He's here. Sleeping."

"Oh." The young woman laughs. "Maybe I should come back later."

Mother of God. Could it be?

"Don't do that," I say, standing up. "Don't."

She laughs, lowers herself in my foxhole, and in the dim light from the moon, I see who it is, right away.

Corporal Abby Monroe, 2nd Recon Rangers, the best combat courier I know, from my unit in New Hampshire and—

"Tanner."

"Sergeant."

"Go inspect the latrine."

"Sergeant?"

"Don't make me say it twice. Go ... and be careful."

He goes, and I bring Abby into me, and we kiss, and we kiss, and we kiss, and she tastes of old food and maybe a forbidden cigarette, and she tastes wonderful.

"Abby ..."

"Shhh," she says. "Not much time. Make it quick."

"How the hell did you end up here?"

She gives me a good hug and I hug her back. She says, "Are you kidding me? What's going on here has been in all the newspapers and across the telegraph wires. 'The brave stand of Kara's Killers.' The Creepers are all in an uproar in this part of New York, and there's a shortage of combat couriers. I heard that you got detached to K Company and I volunteered to come out on a special troop train and see what kind of fun you're having, silly boy."

I bend forward to kiss her once more and our helmets strike each other. Laughing now, we both take our helmets off and kiss and fall to the ground, and Thor is yelping with joy at seeing his old friend come back, and he sticks his big nose between us, laps at her chin and face, and she giggles, and oh God, does that sound good, and all this fun and pleasure is stabbed with the knowledge of Serena up there in the CP. What should I do? What should I say?

"Off, you big smelly lump of fur," she says, laughing and sitting up, and Thor is burrowing his snout into her side, and Abby moves a hand and comes out with a fistful of dried venison strips. She tosses one, two, and three in the air, and Thor expertly snaps and devours each one before it hits the ground.

Abby says, "Something for you, too, sport," and she passes

over two Hershey bars in their dark green wrapping and two MRE packages.

"How did you know?" I ask.

"How did we not know?" she says. "You guys...you're famous, you're cut off, making a stand against overwhelming odds. We know you're running low...all us couriers are doing our best to hump in some supplies with our messages. I dropped off two bandoliers of M-10 rounds up at the CP."

Someone on the other side of the hilltop fires off a few M-4 rounds. I sure as hell hope they haven't just taken out a courier. Abby says, "Upper New York Military District is trying to get a couple of relief columns your way, but the Creepers are knocking down bridges, cutting up roads, doing everything to delay them." Thor settles down and Abby rubs at a special place behind his ear, and Thor starts moaning and thumping his right rear leg. His sweet spot.

She says, "The news reporters...they're calling this another famous battle, like that one in South Africa, back in the 1890s. 'Battle of Rorke's Drift.'"

"Oh, great," I say. "Abby, about a hundred and fifty British troops were facing three or four thousand Zulu warriors during that fight. If there's even thirty or forty Creepers out there, getting ready for a mass attack, this place will be scorched to bedrock."

"Then it won't happen."

My heart is flipping right along with love, affection and happiness, and I go forward and we kiss some more, deep, soul-satisfying kisses, and my hands move under her jacket and her Firebiter vest and she sighs, "Randy, come run away with me."

"Would if I could."

She giggles again and it's only been a couple of weeks since I've last seen and held her, and it seems like forever, and then a man's voice up near the CP yells out, "Monroe! Get a move on! Now!"

Abby says, "Shit," and breaks away, gets on her hands and knees, retrieves her helmet. "Gotta run. That's my new best friend, Sergeant Fong from the 14th Calvary, and he doesn't like any of his couriers being out of sight."

I feel fuzzy and out of sorts, not too sure what to say or do, and I blurt out, "I got your letter, about me getting my Silver Star. Did you get mine?"

"No, I didn't," she says, strapping on her helmet. "When did you send it?"

"A few days back, when Albany got hit."

Abby shakes her head. "Nope. Probably waiting for me when I get back to Fort St. Paul. Did it say anything important?"

I think of what I had written back then, up on the side of a hill, watching the capitol city burn, remembering...

Abby, Off to see the elephant again, big time. Not sure if I'll be back to Fort St. Paul. Being with you this past year has been the best of my life. All my love, always, Randy.

I wimp out. "It'll wait."

She's done. I kiss her one more time and she says, "But I can't wait. Now I gotta get out of here and Randy?"

I'm holding her hand. "Yes?"

"Don't take this the wrong way, but you stink. Even Thor smells better than you. I bet I'll be able to smell you all the way back to the CP."

I squeeze her hand. "Always the romantic one, Corporal."

"Don't get scorched, Sergeant," she says, and I grab her slim hips, help her up over the foxhole, and Thor barks his displeasure at seeing her leave, and then she's gone.

And in about ten minutes, so am I.

Chapter Twenty-Seven

Private Tanner comes back, all smirking and full of questions, and I shut him up by passing over a Hershey's bar, which does the trick, and he says something about how the reserve force is now digging a trench line around the CP. I tune him out and remember what Abby had just said, and I remember being back at the Air Force base, seeing that Creeper, and then I remember our night bivouac, that little squad after we had ambushed the three Creepers advancing on that dirt road, killing...

Peterson?

Petrov?

No. Picard. That had been her name.

For just a brief moment I'm happy I've recalled her name, and then I keep on remembering, and then I make the decision.

"Tanner."

"Sergeant."

I hand him the two MRE packages and he whistles in appreciation. "When dawn comes, bring these up to whoever's doing mess duties up at the CP."

"All right, Sergeant."

"In the meantime..." I sling my M-10 over my shoulder, pick up my battlepack, and say, "I'm going up to the CP. You stay put...and whatever you do, keep your damn head down."

"Yes, Sergeant," he says, and I climb out of the foxhole, say, "Thor, come," and my boy comes right with me.

There's a lightening to the east that marks another day coming. Tanner says, "Sergeant?"

"Make it quick."

"Don't... don't be long, okay?"

"I'll do my best," I say, hating myself, for this is the last time I'll ever speak to Tanner.

I make a crouched walk up to the CP, see the digging going on up there, and then I suddenly veer right, making my way down the access road, doing my best to carefully slip through the Third Platoon's lines. I take my time, moving slow, using whatever cover I can—a boulder, a tossed-over tree trunk, even a Creeper exoskeleton—and then I'm free.

Thor stays with me. I pause for just a moment, take off my Firebiter vest and shove it into my battle pack, and I slowly walk down the road, officially and without a doubt, a deserter from the armed forces of the United States.

My good boy doesn't ask any questions, which is sweet, for I'm not sure what kind of answers I can provide.

About ten minutes later, a voice from the left of the access road loudly whispers, "Freeze, or I'll drop you right there."

Shit.

A ten-minute desertion. How pathetic. No matter, though, if it was ten minutes, ten hours or ten days, the Army won't like it, and if I'm very, very lucky, I'll get sentenced to life at hard labor at the remaining sections of Leavenworth.

"I'm standing still," I say.

"Okay," the voice says. "You stay, and your mutt stays, too. I don't want to shoot either you or the dog, but I will."

"Got it."

The soldier emerges from some low saplings and brush, and he has a crystal night-viewing device over one eye. Very pricey, very expensive, and not as good as the prewar stuff, but it's not run by electronics, so there you go. And as crude as it might be, it was good enough for this trooper to spot me.

"I.D. yourself," he says.

"Knox, First Platoon."

"You're the guy that came from New Hampshire, right?"

"Yeah."

"You heading back to New Hampshire tonight?"

I'm not about to explain my motivations to this picket line soldier, so I say, "It was a thought."

"You thought wrong, bud. I'm here to watch for couriers coming up and soldiers slipping out. You're the first one heading out...coward."

Unlikely, I know, but I'm not in a mood to argue the point.

He says, "Somebody told me that you got the Silver Star, for killing a Creeper with a knife."

"That's right."

"Sounds like a bullshit story."

"You're half-right," I say. "Getting the Silver Star was bullshit. But everything else is true."

"Fine, whatever," he says. "You turn around, you head back up that trail, keep your hands out in the open. We're going to see Captain Wallace. You do what I tell you...or I'll have to eliminate a threat. And that threat is your pooch, okay?"

"Understood," I say.

Then his voice quickly changes, almost a pleading, and he says, "Knox, I lost my dog Harry back when the war started. Had to leave him behind when our house got flooded back in Connecticut. Don't make me have to shoot your dog."

I find the words. "I won't."

The walk back to the CP is quicker than the walk out, and now dawn is starting to break. There are five wounded soldiers sitting up or on stretchers outside the small building, and a medic is checking on their bandages and giving them sips of water. Some heavy shovel and pick work is still being done around the CP by another half-dozen soldiers, but it doesn't look like the number of heavy and sagging poncho-clad bodies under the tarp has increased.

I go up to the open front door of the CP and take in what's there. To the right Captain Pulaski is on one of the cots, snoring, and her other medic is sitting up against the wall, slumped, also sleeping. Dad is on the other bed, wrapped up in a blanket. Serena is also sleeping but her brother Buddy is sitting on a chair, calmly taking everything in. The gas lanterns seem empty, for it's nothing but lit candles inside.

First Sergeant Hesketh and Captain Wallace both look up as I shadow the door, and Hesketh says, "Knox, what are you doing here?"

"Ask him," I reply, stepping aside so the corporal who had stopped me—BUDLONG—steps forward and says, "First Sergeant, caught Sergeant Knox trying to desert. He was walking out the access road with his K-9 unit."

Even though I'm in the doorway, the smell of burnt hair and flesh is pretty thick, and I see the high windows have been broken to allow fresh air in. Hesketh gets up, face red, and Wallace says, "I'll handle it."

She looks beaten, tired, worn, and I flash back to the time I saw her alone at the stream, hugging herself and crying, and then to what her Air Force friend had told me, that before joining up after the war started, Kara Wallace had been a kindergarten teacher.

"Knox?"

"Captain..." and now I feel stupid, like I've been called up in class back at Fort St. Paul to write out an algebra problem from homework that I had skipped. "Ma'am...Begging the Captain's permission, could I have a moment?"

She wearily stands up, her face stained with soot, scratches on her chin and cheeks. She picks up her helmet and says to Hesketh, "I'll be right outside."

"Yes, ma'am," and he sits back, and she says, "Besides, I could use some fresh air."

Outside the eastern sky is now tinged pink and red as the sun comes up, and she says to a soldier nearby standing watch, "Roberts, any signal flares?"

"None, ma'am," she says.

"Damn. All right," and she turns to me. "Knox. Desertion. Really?"

"No, ma'am."

"Then what were you doing? Chasing after your courier friend, looking to get back to New Hampshire?"

I'm surprised that she knows about Abby Monroe, but I guess I shouldn't, because good officers know everything about their personnel. "No, ma'am."

"Sergeant, spit it out right now, or I'll have you sort through those wrapped ponchos and have you start digging out personal effects from our KIAs. Got it?"

Thor flops down on the dirt and starts to snooze, and I envy him. "Ma'am, I wasn't deserting, and I wasn't running back to New Hampshire. I was leaving here to save all of you."

Her helmet is held against her waist, and she rubs the back of her neck and says, "Mind repeating that, Sergeant? What do you mean, save us? We've got about a half-dozen combat couriers out there, trying to find routes to allow a relief force to come in. What do you know that they don't?"

"Why the Creepers are letting us live."

She turns in fury and grabs my shoulder. "Live? Like those seven over there? Is that what you mean?"

"No, ma'am, I don't mean that," I say. "But the Creepers...if they wanted us dead, they'd blast off the top meter of this hilltop. You saw what they did to the relief force with their killer stealth satellites. If they wanted everyone dead up here, they could have done it days ago. Why haven't they done that?"

She lets go of my shoulder. I say, "We've been followed and stalked by the Creepers, ever since we left that destroyed horse farm and the two Domes. They've chased us and chased us, something the Creepers have never done before. They've cut us off, and sure, they've attacked us...but never with an overwhelming attack. It's like...Ma'am, it's like they're trying to overrun us, and make a capture. Not a clean kill."

"That boy and her sister," she says. "All right. You think the Creepers are after them?"

"No, ma'am," I say. "The way the Creepers reacted oddly happened before Serena and Buddy showed up."

"And?"

"Ma'am, they're after me."

That really gets her attention and she slowly says, "Sergeant Knox..."

"Ma'am, they know who I am. They saw me at the Dome where that Creeper squad surrendered. And they know I was at the horse farm...and I told you, when I was leading that squad back to you, I spotted a Research Creeper examining clothing and torn bandages. Sounds crazy, but I think...I think they can smell me. And they were tracking me."

"Smell?"

"Captain, since I've been with your company, I haven't used my own Firebiter vest. I was issued one that had been used by a previous soldier. It had his smell on it, the smell of sweat and blood. I think that masked most of my scent. And back at the

Air Force base, I was with a group, interrogating a captured Creeper. I took my vest off, and...something happened. The Creeper responded, and soon afterwards, they were coming after the Company. They can smell me."

"And you were walking away because...?"

I say simply, "I was going to draw them away from your position, ma'am. A single soldier...I was going to lead them away."

"Until what? Until you were surrounded by Creepers, somewhere out there on a road or field?"

"I guess so," I say. "I hadn't thought that far."

"Apparently not," she says, now putting her helmet back on. "Why do you think they're after you?"

"No idea, ma'am. But they know I killed a Creeper with a knife...and that I was present when that Dome surrendered... maybe they're just pissed at me."

"Join the club," she says, pulling her chinstrap tight. "All right, Knox. Get along."

I feel a hell of a lot better, though I still don't know what's facing me. "Go on back down that road?"

She shakes her head. "No. Get back to First Platoon, get back to your foxhole."

"But Captain..."

"That's an order, Sergeant." She takes a deep breath, looks back at the open door leading into the CP, like she would do or say anything to avoid going back in. "You're with Company K, and under my command, until I say otherwise. And if that means defending you along with everyone else, that's what we're going to do. So get back to your position, you and your dog."

"Yes, ma'am," I say, and I call out, "Thor! Come!" and head back down to where I had earlier left, feeling hungry, tired, and a little bit awestruck that the Captain is sticking with me.

I say, "Knox, coming in," and there's no answer as I roll back into my foxhole. Tanner is standing looking down at the now-deserted slope, his M-4 pointing up at an awkward angle, and when I put my M-10 and gear down, I say, "Private, what, are you bird hunting this morning?"

No answer.

I smell cooked meat.

"Tanner?"

I go over and touch him and his M-4 falls to the ground, and his head lolls to the left, and below the rim of his helmet and above his small nose is a round, puckered burned hole, right through the front of his head.

"Oh, Tanner, damn it," I say.

I slowly lower him to the ground and check his dog tags, and take one of the two medallions, slip it into my pocket. I rub his shoulder for a moment. I close his eyes and say, "Kid, I told you to keep your head down. Ah, shit."

I drag him into the far corner of the hole, and Thor watches me impassively, not whining, not panting, not doing much of anything. I pull out a poncho from Tanner's battlepack and a folded stiff piece of paper drops out, and in the dim morning light I unfold it, see it's an old color photograph of what looks to be a mom and dad, sitting in their best clothes in a photo studio, a very young boy sitting on Mom's lap, laughing and holding a brightly colored toy in his chubby hands. I stare at it for longer than necessary, and then I fold the photograph back up, slide it down the front of his coat—I should strip him of his gear and Firebiter vest but not now—and then drape and tug the poncho around him.

Damn.

Left alone, he was probably scared out of his twelve-year-old mind, wondering when his sergeant was coming back, wondering why he was alone, and maybe he panicked or heard a noise, but whatever happened, he was killed, and it's my fault.

All mine.

I go to the field telephone, crank the handle a few times. Hesketh answers it with a brusque, "CP, go."

"First Platoon, Knox," I say. "Private Tanner is dead."

Hesketh says, "We'll send you a replacement. CP, out."

I put the phone back down and I should stand watch, but all I do now is sit down in the dirt, back up against the foxhole side, and I stare at the kid's body. Thor sees I'm upset and gets up and flops his head down on my lap, but I refuse to rub his head. That would just make me feel better, and right now, I don't want to do that.

Dirt trickles down and a soldier thumps his way into the foxhole, stumbling, and more dirt showers down, getting into the back of my neck, and I stand up and say, "Jesus Christ, didn't anybody train you on how to enter a foxhole?"

The soldier stands up, adjusts his black-rimmed glasses. "Sorry, Sergeant. It's been a while."

It's Dad.

"Dad...what the hell are you doing here?"

"What do you think?" He spots Tanner's M-4, picks it up and says, "The CP needed someone to replace your dead soldier. They're short-handed, and they need to get that trench system finished. So I volunteered."

"Dad..."

He checks the M-4, manages not to shoot himself in the foot, and says, "Randy, my background is Intelligence. Captain Wallace and the rest of the company don't need those skills right now. What they need is a rifleman, and I'm your man."

"Dad..."

He snaps, "Sergeant, I'm on the line here, with you, M-4 at the ready. Do you mind telling me what the situation is, and what we might expect? Or do you expect me to find out for myself?"

I settle down and say, "Colonel, we're on the far left side of First Platoon. Second Platoon is off to the right, and Third Platoon is over there, to the left. Keep your head down, as best as you can. You need to hit the latrine, let me know, but keep down on the way out and the way back."

I point through one of the aiming holes. "The Creepers have occupied those woods. That's where they come up when they strike. It might be hard to make out, but there's aiming stakes pounded in the ground at fifty meters, twenty-five meters and ten meters. You're job is to provide harassing and suppressing fire."

Dad peers through his slit. "Does it do any good?"

"In hurting or killing the Creepers? No. But hearing and seeing gunfire helps morale, and also gives those soldiers who aren't qualified for the M-10 the feeling they're doing something."

Dad glances over to the poncho-covered form. "What happened to your man there?"

"That man was twelve years old," I say. "He died because he poked his head up over the edge of the foxhole, and because I wasn't here to tell him otherwise. He's dead because of me."

"No, Sergeant," he says. "He's dead because of the Creepers. Not you. Did he have any spare magazines for his M-4?"

"Check his battlepack."

Dad squats down, moves over and says, "Hey, Thor, sorry to bother you," and he gets two spare magazines in his hands, and when he comes back, there's a shout from down the line.

"Here they come!"

And in a few minutes, we're fighting once again.

Some long, long minutes later, this latest skirmish is over, and I share some water with Dad, who has done some pretty good shooting, much to my amazement. I was concerned that he'd "pray and spray"—lifting his M-4 up over the dirt and fire at full auto without proper aiming—but he showed good fire discipline, sending off two- or three-shot bursts as the Creepers rolled toward us.

He says, "Randy..."

"Yes?" My shoulder hurts, I'm down to three rounds for my M-10, and there are four more dead Creepers out on the slope, but we've taken some hits as well. The frantic cries of, "Medic! Medic! Medic!" seem to be all over the hill, from Third Platoon and my own.

"Randy, you—"

"Hold on, Dad, okay?"

I gingerly look up and about, seeing two medics down the line hauling a soldier up to the CP, and then I look down at the slope. The wood line seems busy, with Creepers moving in and out, and Christ, if I don't get any more ammo, this next attack might be the last, at least from where I'm standing.

"Randy, I heard part of what you said back there, about the Creepers hunting you. I think you might be right. We still don't know much but I do know—"

I say, "Dad, that's great. Really. But I've got to check the rest of the line, okay? Keep your head down, keep watch, all right?"

"Sure," he says. Then he says, almost shyly, "That boy's body... sorry, it's starting to smell, Randy. When can it get moved?"

"You and I will move him when it's time," I say. "Hold tight. Thor, stay."

I'm out and go up the line, checking on the tired, frightened and exhausted members of my much-reduced platoon, and I learn that the wounded trooper was a quiet teen girl named Lileks, who was scorched on the side of her face. Not fatal, so that's a bit—a tiny bit—of good news. But I don't make any friends when

I inventory the remaining M-10 rounds and try to even them out. It pisses off the troops who've been carefully hoarding their ammo, but at least it gives everyone the same number of rounds.

Back to the foxhole, and Dad says, "The CP called a couple of minutes ago. When we see a white flare, we're to pull back to the ditch line."

"All right," I say.

He looks around, rubs his chin, and says, "Two more things, okay, Randy?"

"Sure, Dad," I say. My feet are hurting and my stomach is grumbling loud.

He says, "I . . . I've always known you were sharp, that you were tough, that you were good. But I've never seen you in the field. You were amazing. You were . . . you were incredible."

I guess I should feel all warm and tingly and like the good son, but I chamber a round into my M-10, and I put my two spare rounds on top of the dirt lip to my foxhole. There's more movement down at the edge of the woods. Damn bugs are starting to form up again.

"Thanks, Dad. You better saddle up, it looks like the bugs are getting ready to do something."

"And the other thing. It's time you know what happened to your mom. And your sister Melissa. Back when the war started. After I've seen you in action . . . You deserve to know. Right now."

That nails me and I start to ask him, when the shouts of "Creepers on the move!" comes up, and I'm quickly very, very busy. One Creeper is moving right along, and then he's leading right up to the fifty-meter line, and *BLAM!* and my shot arcs out, and the damn bug jogs to the right and my exploding round sets up a cloud that misses.

I eject the round, grab another one from the dirt and—

And I knock the third one over, which flies off the dirt and hits the slope and rolls.

Damn it!

And damn it again, Dad sees it and starts going out of the hole, and I yell, "Dad, don't!"

He doesn't listen to me.

He's outside the foxhole, standing for shit's sake, and he takes three quick steps, triumphantly holds up the cartridge, and as he turns to come back to the foxhole, a Creeper laser cuts him down.

Chapter Twenty-Eight

"Dad!" I scream, and he flops right over, and I see the Creeper that nailed him is still skittering up the slope, and I fire off a round—*BLAM!*—that stops the Creeper dead in its six tracks, and I climb up the foxhole, roll over, and crawl down the slope, and there's Dad, flattened right out.

And I hate myself but the first thing I do, I grab the spare round and shove it into my pocket, and I say, "Dad? Dad?"

I grab his coat collar, start trying to drag him back, and Christ, he's heavy, and I'm dragging, trying to get some traction, but it's tough, so goddamn tough.

"Dad!" I yell. "Are you awake? Can you move?"

Nothing.

I try to drag him some more, back to my foxhole, and there's gunfire all around me, M-4s being fired off, M-10s booming, and the smell of cinnamon, the *click-click* sound of the Creepers, smoke drifting across, and I focus on Dad, trying to drag him, and shit, I'm just not doing it.

"Dad!"

For Christ's sake, I can't believe how heavy he is, and—

Somebody's helping me.

Somebody's next to me.

I turn.

It's Thor, splayed out but with his strong jaws clamped around the loose jacket cloth above Dad's shoulder, and he growls and pulls back—like he's playing with one damn large chew toy—and the two of us manage to keep down, working Dad back, and then Thor leaps into the safety of the foxhole, and I get Dad's upper torso over as I go first, and then I pull him in.

His body flattens me right out.

I smell burnt flesh.

I crawl out from underneath him, check him out.

His left leg is gone below the knee.

I stand up. "Medic! Medic!"

Nothing's moving along the line.

Nothing.

And nobody's coming out from the CP.

The Creepers are close now, three of them in front of our line, and from the sounds coming from other parts of the hill, it's clear we're being attacked on all sides.

I leave Dad for a moment, sight in the best I can, and one more blasting shot, and one more dead Creeper, and the other two Creepers flip around and race back to the safety of the tree line.

From the CP I see movement, and a white flare flies up, and there are yells of, "Move it, move it, move it!"

I grab my battlepack, shoulder my M-10 and the M-4, and grab Dad and with a deep lunge and burst of energy that I didn't know was there, I get him out of the foxhole.

Balatnic races over, sees what's going on, and without a word, puts her arm under Dad's shoulder. We drag him up to the CP and at the edge of the trenchline, two medics grab him and bring him into the CP, and the overworked and swearing Dr. Pulaski.

I collapse into the freshly dug trench, exhausted and weeping.

Thor joins me, his legs and head across my lap, and this time, I rub his head and ears, and I lean back against the dirt and start crying, and everyone on either side just leaves me alone.

Balatnic comes across to me, with a cup of hot water that is barely tinged with the taste of coffee, and I take a heavy sip and she says, "I checked on your dad."

"Yeah?"

"He's alive. Unconscious but alive."

I pass the cup over to her. "Finish it off, okay?"

"Sure, Sergeant," she says.

I slowly get up, tell Thor to stay put, and then I get out of the trench and head into the CP.

Inside Hesketh and Wallace are looking over the map, setting up positions. Buddy is sitting, face impassive, quietly aware, taking everything in. I think again of anyway to bring out Buddy to help us, and I see my dad's form and push that thought away. Dad is on a portable bed, while Dr. Pulaski works on him. His BDU trousers have been cut away and there's an IV running into an arm, and he's unconscious. Pulaski is spreading a salve over his cauterized stump and Serena is at the other end of the bed, wiping Dad's forehead with a wet cloth.

"How is he?" I ask.

Dr. Pulaski ignores me and Serena says, "Still alive. The IV is putting in fluids and antishock medicine, as well as a sedative."

"Okay."

Serena says, "I'm so sorry, Randy. But still . . . his heartbeat is strong, his blood pressure's coming back up."

Of course, I think. Dad was about to tell me all, about Mom and Melissa, and what really happened, and Pulaski glances back and says, "Knox?"

"Yes, ma'am."

"Just remember what I said," she says. "When it gets to a point, send that dog away. Save him."

"I'll think about it, but—"

"Soon," she says, turning back to my dad. "It's gonna be soon."

Wallace speaks up without lifting her head. "Stick to your job, Doc. Please. Stick to your job. Knox, I know you're worried about your dad but he's getting the best treatment possible, and I need you out with your platoon."

"Yes, Captain," I say, and I duck out of the CP and I'm ashamed to say, I'd rather be back with my platoon than inside, with the smell of burnt flesh, burnt hair, sweat, fear, and the scent of an approaching defeat.

The air outside isn't much better. Sweat, smoke, piss, and the ever-present stench of cinnamon. I move up the trench line, checking in on my folks, until I run into Second Platoon, and then I reverse course, head back to Third Platoon. A Sergeant Miller looks to be running the show, and I ask, "Where's Lieutenant Jackson?"

Miller, older guy in his thirties, says, "Scorched. You need something?"

"No."

"Then leave me the hell alone, okay? Got a shitload of work to do."

I just nod and work my way back to my platoon, check on their weapons, see I'm down to one cartridge for my M-10, and that nobody else has more than two. For those carrying the M-4, the news isn't much better, the most being three spare magazines in reserve.

I walk back along the line, and Balatnic says, "Sergeant? We getting any help?"

"Captain's working on it, Specialist, you know it," I say.

She bites her lower lip, looks back down the slope. I don't think she believes me, and I don't blame her. There's movement in the woods, and the *click-click* sound gets louder and louder. I stand next to Thor and think of what Pulaski had said. Get ready to say that word, the word that would send Thor back to New Hampshire and save him.

Asgard, I think. Asgard.

Say that one word aloud and Thor would go home, and I'd save him.

I rub his head.

Should I?

Thor rubs his head against my hand. What should I do?

He's been with me for a long time, in too many battles and skirmishes, always at my side, always there.

Is it right for him to be here when we get overrun?

Click-click.

Click-click.

Click-click.

Hesketh comes out of the CP, joined by Wallace. She looks down at the wood line with binoculars, scans from side to side. She looks so tired I can imagine her just sliding to the ground and collapsing.

A kindergarten teacher.

She says something to Hesketh and he nods, yells out, "Platoon leaders, up here!"

I climb out of the trench, and I'm joined by Lieutenant Morneau and Sergeant Miller, and we go up to the doorway of the CP. Wallace says to me, "Your dad's doing as well as can be expected. The rest of us...Well, who knows."

She asks us questions about where we stand, and yes, the Second and Third Platoons are as depleted as the First, and she takes that all in and looks up at the sky.

Click-click.

Click-click.

Click-click.

Louder and louder. I don't think I've ever heard them so loud.

Wallace says, "Looks like they're massing for another attack, First Sergeant."

"Yes, ma'am."

"Damn."

She looks through her binoculars again. "Also looks like they're gathering to come up right this slope, no fooling around, no flanking moves, just straight on."

"Yes, ma'am."

Wallace lowers her binoculars and I can make out trees whipping back and forth, as a lot of Creepers are on the move in the woods. Damn. I'm cold now, thinking that yeah, the thought of running away when we're overrun is a nice thought, but there are so many damn Creepers down there, I probably wouldn't last more than five minutes.

Asgard, I think to myself. Asgard.

She says, "You know what Wellington once said?"

By now I think we platoon leaders and even the first sergeant are getting more and more terrified with each passing minute, and none of us say anything, until I cough and say, "Boy, this Waterloo place sucks?"

Some laughter, which is good, because it breaks up the mood, and with a smile on her face, Wallace says, "No. He said, 'They came on in the same old way and we defeated them in the same old way.' No worries, guys and gals. That's what we're going to do."

I swallow and there's nothing there. No spit, no saliva. My tongue is sticking to the roof of my mouth. Lots and lots of Creepers down there. How the hell are we going to defeat them with such low ammo? Maybe two or so volleys from our M-10s, and then that's it.

That's it.

"First Sergeant?"

"Yes, ma'am."

"Get Specialist MacRae, will you?"

"Yes, ma'am."

He leaps down into the trench, calls out, "MacRae! MacRae! Front and center!"

Motion and bodies moving around, and then MacRae comes back with Hesketh, carrying a black canvas bag in one hand. He's plump, red-faced, with a scraggly red moustache and beard.

"Ma'am?" he says, in a young and squeaky voice.

"Corporal, so glad of you to join us," she says. "You hear those bugs down there?"

He nods in their direction. "Hard not to."

"You think its music, or some sort of talking?"

"Hard to tell. Lots of theories, you know. Communication, something going on with their limbs, a warning or a joyful noise. But it sure is loud."

"Distracting, too," Wallace says.

"You know it, ma'am," he says.

"Think a dedicated piper could drown them out?"

MacRae puts the bag down, zips it open. "Let's give it a shot, Captain."

"Good. Give us *Cock o' the North*, if you please."

I watch, fascinated, even being in the middle of a war zone, for I've never seen a piper at work before. A bundle of thick sticks connected to a brown leather bag emerges from the carrying case, and MacRae quickly and expertly slides the bag under his right arm. Three long black sticks fall against his left shoulder, and he places a thin pipe into his mouth, starts inflating the bag with deep puffs. Below the bag is a holed pipe that he manipulates with his two hands.

There's an ear-splitting screech, and then the sticks on his shoulder—one long and two shorter—emit a steady drone, and then MacRae kicks into a loud tune that I swear to God sweeps across our battered hilltop and travels down the slope to the woods where the Creepers have gathered. The tune goes on and on, damn near making my hair stand on its end and my arms and neck tingle, and now I know why the Scots have marched into wars—all the way through history and up to today's Creepers—with bagpipes leading them on.

MacRae keeps time by gently pumping his right leg up and down, and Wallace wipes at her eyes, nods to me and Lieutenant

Morneau and Sergeant Miller, and we go back to the trench and our respective platoons, and the piping grows and grows, wailing and sighing and most of all fighting, and the music stirs our blood and I see nothing but firm and determined faces to the left and right of me, my soldiers, my platoon, my boys and girls and men and women, we Americans and humans, and we steady on as the Creepers come up at us on the line, the loud and stirring sound of the bagpipes behind us thankfully drowning out that damn clicking sound.

They move quickly, and just as quickly, a barrage of M-10 rounds fly out and take down a good portion, and the rest keep on approaching. I keep mine in reserve, the cartridge spun out to ten meters, because I want to make mine count and I want to kill one more, right in front of me, one for Dad and Tanner and De Los Santos, and Mom and my sister Melissa, and hell, even for Major Coulson, the father of Buddy and Serena.

Thor is whining and barking, and even after I say, "Thor, settle!" he won't listen to me this time, and he paces in a circle, still needlessly warning all of us about the approaching danger.

Up near the CP I hear a *boom/whoosh* sound, and mortar rounds fly out, landing in the tree branches in the wood line, causing large limbs and trunks to shatter and fall, upsetting and trapping some of the Creepers, and then there's a heavier *BOOM/WHOOSH* sound, and it's the Company's closely kept antitank missiles, being fired in one more last desperate attempt. Two of the missiles strike home, causing two of the advancing Creepers to fly up, like some large hand of God or invisible Big Child has flipped them over like beetles, their articulated legs frantically moving and getting no traction. The Creepers are now down to four, and their weaponized arms are firing out quick flashes of lasers, and long tongues of fire, and a couple of soldiers down the line, in the Second Platoon, are scorched and they run out of their trenches, engulfed in flames, running up the hill, like mechanized dolls caught on fire, and they run and run until they stumble and burn and die.

Three Creepers now. The M-4 fire is rattling off, and the near Creeper is close enough to me for a good firing solution, and it starts to approach the painted stake marking ten meters. I fire and I kill the buggy bastard.

That's it.

I'm out of M-10 rounds.

I drop my M-10, pick up the M-4 that was Tanner's, that briefly belonged to Dad, and that's now mine, and I aim and fire carefully at the exoskeletons of the two remaining Creepers. I can hardly feel the gentle recoil of the M-4, as I ration my shots, firing two or three round bursts. I aim as best I can but it's hard work, with the dust and smoke rising up, making my swollen eyes water.

Two are marching right up to the center of the trench line, and in my mind's eye, I can see what's going to happen next: the Creepers will overrun the trench line and one will pivot left, and the other will pivot right, and in less than a minute, K Company, "Kara's Killers," will be a smoldering mess of flesh, boots, and scraps of uniform.

MacRae is still there, outside of the CP, piping away. Hesketh and Wallace are by him, near piles of dirt and sandbags, both now with pistols in their hands, carefully shooting with both hands.

The piping is loud, and so are the yells and screams and cries of "Medic! Medic!"

Another *BLAM!* of an M-10 being fired, and the near Creeper is engulfed in the gas cloud and it dies spectacularly, so close that when it collapses and rolls, it nearly tangles up the last advancing Creeper, and Wallace stops shooting and puts her hands together by her mouth and yells, "K Company, hold the line! Hold the line! Hose that bitch! Hose that bitch!"

And hose her we do, firing and firing our M-4s, bullets racing in, bouncing off, ricocheting, and I glance down at Thor, and I think of the word, *Asgard,* and in a few seconds, I know I will, for when that Creeper reaches the trench, it's over.

And I won't let my boy die next to me.

I look up.

The Creeper is almost upon us, ugly as sin, the dark blue-gray exoskeleton marked up and dented, which means it's a vet of the war, and there's probably one smart and wiley buggy bastard inside. The weaponized arms fire one more time and the roof of the CP bursts into flames, and now it's coming to the trench, I could practically throw a stone at it, and—

"Thor!"

My boy sits at attention and I start to form the words, and I stop.

The Creeper has halted.

It's not moving.

The firing is continuing, until the first sergeant screams out, "Cease fire, cease fire, cease fire!"

I lower my M-4, my hands shaking.

MacRae pipes one more flourish and then stops.

Smoke and dust and everything else kicked up drifts by.

A bloody miracle it is, for it seems like a golden BB, a magic bullet, some spectral round from one of us has penetrated between the armor plating in this Creeper's exoskeleton, and has killed it.

The Creeper exoskeleton slowly collapses, its legs losing power, and the front end of the arthropod collapses across the trench.

I scratch Thor's head.

"Not today, bud, not today," I whisper, and then something from one of my military history classes comes back to me, and I remember another Wellington quote, from right after the battle of Waterloo: *It has been a damned nice thing—the nearest run thing you ever saw in your life . . .*

I can't say anything better than that.

We platoon leaders straggle up back to the CP—where the fire on the roof has been extinguished—and an exhausted Wallace says, "First Sergeant . . . smoke rounds and flares, if you please," and that simple phrase nearly makes me halt in my tracks though damn it, it does make sense. We have exhausted our M-10 rounds and what was left of our mortars and antitank weapons, and we can't stay up here anymore. The concentrated and close-up M-4 fire of this depleted Company was lucky enough to kill one Creeper. We won't have that luck again, especially if the Creepers form up for another mass attack. Hell, one Creeper coming at us from the north and another from the south would be enough to do the job.

Which means a dispersion is our only option, with the Company melting away, each soldier going on his or own path, with those damn Creepers on the run, and clouds of smoke to help us just a bit in camouflage as we make our escape, the flares sending out heat to mess up whatever thermal sensors the Creepers might have.

Damn it.

There have been whispered stories from the first bloody and desperate years of the war, when the regular Army, Reserve units and the National Guard bravely mobilized and deployed to fight the Domes and Creepers and were simply massacred. When they broke and some ran and others dispersed, Creepers would chase them down, almost as sport, killing and burning them, chasing them like they were Englishmen on horses, running down foxes. It makes me want to throw up to think we're getting ready to face that.

"Captain," I say.

"Knox."

"Ma'am, I still say the Creepers are here after me." I can't believe what I'm thinking so I blurt it right out. "I think if I surrender, the Creepers will leave the rest of the Company alone."

"No," she says, violently shaking her head. "You're part of Company K, and I won't allow anyone here to voluntarily give themselves up."

I hate to admit it, but my bravery evaporated when I said what I said, and I'm relieved—though still scared out of my wits—to hear her turn down my offer. She says, "Pulaski?"

The exhausted doc is sitting on a chair, looking down at Dad, and she turns and Wallace says, "How many of the wounded can travel?"

"About half."

"Get them ready, if you can."

She says, "All right, but I stay with the non-mobile wounded."

"No," Wallace says.

"Captain, I—"

"Out of the question," she says, voice quivering. "The Army needs your skills. You help get the mobile wounded together but when the time comes, you get."

I say, "Doctor, my dad, can he move?"

"No," she says. "He'd die within minutes."

"Captain," I say, trying to choke out the words, "I—"

"Damn it," she yells, "We all follow orders, got it? You platoon leaders, sixty seconds after the smoke rounds are fired off, you get your people moving. No more than two in a group. Make sure all M-10s are picked up and taken with us. Try to head on foot back to—"

A private whose uniform and face are blackened with dirt and soot bursts into the room and shouts, "Cap'n Wallace, Cap'n Wallace, I saw it! I saw a blue flare! Just like you said!"

Wallace leaps up from her stool, pushes by us and goes outside, and we all follow, and the excited soldier points to the west, and I see something dribbling down from the darkening sky, and maybe it's a flare, maybe it's blue, or maybe it's just space debris. Just below us the smoke grenades have been lit off, and gray-white smoke is clouding up the churned-up battlefield, and then flares sputter their hot yellow-white flames.

She says, "Are you sure? Are you sure it was a blue flare?"

"Yes, Cap'n," the soldier says, and now I realize he's a she, but I don't have time to process that, for Wallace pulls a flare gun from her MOLLE vest and holds it up and pulls the trigger. A soft *plop!* and the flare shoots up, and it's a blue one as well, and by God, a blue flare answers the Captain's shot not more than five seconds later.

She whirls and says, "Platoon leaders, get your people ready to move. Now!"

I don't know what the hell she means by that, or what the blue flares indicate, but I start toward the trenchline where First Platoon is located, and then a sudden roaring noise and bright lights overwhelm me.

I turn back to the CP. Something has risen up in the distance and is approaching. I bring up my M-4, don't fire, because I don't know what I see. A base part of my mind thinks it's a huge Creeper, jumping up or flying in the air, and then the object and its accompanying noise grows bigger and louder, and dirt is flying off in clouds, and it swoops and whirls and in the dim light of the setting sun, I see an Air Force insignia stenciled on... what?

Then it snaps into view, and I lower my M-4.

It's a V-22 Boeing Osprey, a twin-engine troop transport aircraft that can fly or hover, and it's safely hovering down near the CP, its rear lamp lowering down, and there's a shout, "Wounded! Get the wounded on board! Third Platoon, prepare for departure!"

My M-4 is at my side.

I still can't believe what I see.

We've been saved.

Chapter Twenty-Nine

Third Platoon races up to the CP, and there's a lot of confused and hurried movement, but the walking wounded are being led to the V-22, and the stretchers with the other wounded are being hustled over as well, and then the survivors from Third Platoon. I start bawling, not crying out or anything, but I'm positive that one of those stretchers was carrying Dad.

Then the ramp swings up and the V-22 takes off and dips off to the right, without once being fired upon, and now it strikes me—Stratton Air Force Base, where that Creeper is prisoner, is also a research facility—and now we're seeing the fruits of their labor.

V-22s that are shielded from the Creepers' sensors.

Another V-22 comes up and rotates and lowers itself down to the cleared hilltop, and through my tears I whisper, "I'll be damned."

Now I know why Captain Wallace had the fire tower destroyed when we got here. She was preparing an LZ for us, just in case, with the blue flare telling her a rescue mission was nearby if she needed it.

Damn.

Maybe grown-ups aren't so dumb after all.

The V-22 lands and its ramp lowers down, and the first sergeant yells, "Second Platoon, move!"

And he doesn't have to yell that blessed order twice, and Second Platoon and more walking wounded get on board, and in a minute or two, the V-22 takes off, the ramp closing down as it lifts and speeds off the hill.

Quick silence. I clear my throat. "First Platoon! Hustle up! Prepare for departure!"

I lead them out of our trench and Thor comes right with me, and there's the roar of another Osprey coming at us, and I glance back, and through the widening smoke clouds I hear something.

Click-click.

Click-click.

Click-click.

They're coming up the hill.

I have my M-10 over one shoulder, M-4 on the other, my battlepack in hand, and Thor's whimpering, afraid, I'm sure, of these giant flying machines, but I'm not about to let him go. I grab his collar and make sure he keeps up with me as we race with the others to the left side of the CP. There, Hesketh is arguing something awful with Captain Wallace, and he turns his back on her—what the hell?—and then he—

—goes to the broken antenna complex at the CP's side, scrambles up it, and then pulls down the flag. He starts down and there's a laser line—easy to see in the growing darkness and the smoke—that almost takes his head off, but he jumps to the ground and stuffs the colors into the front of his Firebiter vest, and damned if Wallace doesn't kiss him on the cheek.

The Osprey rotates and lands like its two brethren, and the ramp whines down, and Wallace and Hesketh are there, shoving and pushing the soldiers in, and they move pretty damn quick. I stay at the rear of my guys and girls, making sure no one's behind me—doubtful, I know—and I move up and there's Hesketh, Wallace, Serena and Buddy, and Serena goes in and turns around, to help Buddy, and—

Buddy screams something awful, loud and bloodcurdling, and he won't go into the Osprey.

He freezes!

Serena yells, "Buddy, it's okay, it's okay!" but Buddy breaks away from her, runs away in terror from the Osprey, and barrels down the slope, into the darkness and smoke clouds.

I swear and get to the lip of the ramp, toss my weapons and battlepack into the crowded rear of the aircraft, and God help me, it takes every bit of energy and effort to turn my back on that rescue aircraft, ready to bring me and the others away from this barbecue pit and off to safety.

But turn I do, and I yell, "Buddy! Get back here!" and run into the darkness as well, and Thor's by my side, and I skitter to a halt, make sure he has my attention, and I say, "Thor, hunt Buddy. Got it? Find Buddy!"

He races past me into the darkness, and I try to follow him, best as I can, and I trip and fall into the trench we were just defending a few minutes ago, and I scream because I've fallen on a poncho-wrapped body of some dead Third Platoon member, and I scramble out, and—

The world lights up. Criss-crossing laser beams, bursts of flame illuminating the smoke clouds. The Creepers seem to be firing blind into the twilight and smoke, and it'd just take one lucky shot to destroy the V-22.

It should be taking off.

It should.

So why isn't it?

Growling and barking up ahead. I push on, yelling something nasty, because I've twisted my ankle, and a bright burst of flame overhead warms my face and hands and also lights up the ground.

Thor has his teeth around Buddy's pants leg, trying to pull him back.

Buddy screams again.

I get to him, grab his shoulders, "Buddy, c'mon, we've got to get moving!"

And the kid turns around and slugs me.

I fall down.

Thor is growling, still working, and Buddy screams again, and I get up, grab his waist, but sweet Jesus, for a kid he's putting up one hell of a fight, one hell of a struggle, and I'm aware that precious seconds are burning away, that I'm still hearing the V-22's twin engines and I'm expecting to hear them grow louder as it finally takes off, and somebody crashes into me, and I fall down again.

Shit!

I get up and there's another soldier there, and I'm thinking it's Serena, or Balatnic, or even First Sergeant Hesketh, but no, it's none of them.

It's Sergeant Bronson.

He has one of Buddy's arms and I grab the other, and with Thor tugging at his leg, we start back up the hillside. Bronson yells, "This kid, he can talk to the Creepers, right?"

"Yeah," I yell back.

Bronson shouts something and says, "Those damn bugs killed near everyone I've ever known, every friend, every family member. If this kid can end this friggin' war . . ."

More laser flashes overhead. The CP is burning. The lights from the open hull of the Osprey come into view. Wallace and Hesketh are at the end of the ramp, Serena next to them, all of them gesturing and screaming and yelling. Bronson and I push Buddy in front of us and Hesketh practically tackles him, and with Serena's help, drags him forward into the well-lit interior, First Platoon members sitting upright on folded-down seats.

It's me, Wallace, and Bronson, and we move forward, and I'm blinded by a laser flash. There's a scream.

We start taking off.

Wallace is behind me, dragging me into the Osprey, and I flip over and there's Bronson, on his face, dangling out of the lowered ramp. I push forward—working against the Captain's attempts to drag me in—and I grab his jacket collar, drag him in, wondering why I'm doing it so easily, and as I drag him in, I quickly realize why.

That last Creeper laser beam had cut him in half, right below his belly.

The ramp rises up and I let go, and Sergeant Bronson's body slips off into the darkness.

Thor comes to me, licking my face and hands as I sit up, the ramp finally closing. There are whoops and hollers from the other First Platoon members, and Wallace pats the top of my helmet, Serena bustles through and hugs and kisses me, and I close my eyes and open them up, and then everything just clears up, and I'll be damned.

I'm flying.

I'm really flying.

A grinding thumping noise rattles through the interior, and I guess it's the wheels underneath us—landing gear?—have finally come up and closed inside. I get to my knees and take in my surroundings. Two rows of folded seats stretching up forward, and I can make out the cockpit, as the pilot and copilot fly the machine. Two gals in Air Force BDUs move up and down the crowded hull, trying to get us to buckle in. Overhead there's a massive tangle of cables and wiring. Near me is a very small window and I peer out. Hard to say but it looks like there are two little sets of lights out there, heading away from us, and then the lights blink off.

Heading away from us.

Wallace is up forward, wearing a headset, talking to the pilots. Hesketh joins in, and whatever they're discussing is quickly decided. I step forward, over rucksacks and battlepacks, and poor Thor is huddled along the side, a puddle of urine near him. I pat his head and Wallace spots me, and I raise my hand, and she moves to me, cocks her head, and I yell in her ear, "Where are we going?"

Wallace moves her head to my mine, luckily picking my good ear. "What?"

Another movement, and I yell, "The other two Ospreys are going away from us. So where are we going?"

She moves her head around, "One last debt to settle."

Wallace moves back, a grim look on her face, and I know "Kara's Killers" have one more mission to complete tonight.

The travel time is only a few minutes, and I find myself enjoying those few minutes. I've always been terrified of heights, but this is my first true flight—although Dad told me that I had been on a couple of flights when I was much younger, before the war began—and it doesn't scare me at all. If anything, I find it exhilarating.

Who knew?

The pilots keep us close to the ground, sweeping and diving, and I hold onto the overhead cables to keep myself upright, and then there's a pitch change in the engines, as the two propellers begin to swivel to bring us into a hovering movement, and then there are thumping noises as the wheels or undercarriage or whatever is lowered from the hull, and with a gentle thump, we land.

The rear ramp whines itself down, and Hesketh is the first off, yelling, "Follow me!"

We do just that, Thor very glad to be on solid ground, and

we're at some military base, with fencing in the distance and no lights, and Wallace goes by, and she sees me and says, "Welcome to Naval Support Activity Saratoga Springs."

The name means nothing to me, but it sure as hell means something to Serena, who's near me, holding Buddy's hand. "Randy...this is the place...this is where we were kept prisoner." She sobs. "This is where they killed Dad."

I unlimber my M-4, check to make sure I have a spare magazine, and I run with the rest of my platoon, as the Osprey takes off and leaves us be, far away from the Creepers, and right in the middle of another battle.

Wallace knows where to go, where to send the troops, and maybe I should be upset that she's taken control of First Platoon but I'm not. The burden lifts off my shoulders and flies away, leaving me free to concentrate on the weapon in my hands and the dog at my side.

We barrel through a double-glass door, knocking over two men in Navy uniforms who start to yell and then shut up when they feel the business ends of our M-4s. Wallace continues to move down a hallway, followed by Hesketh, me, Balatnic, and Melendez. We smash straight into a small office, and then, a door connecting to the office swings open, and there's Hoyt Cranston, in black jumpsuit, Kevlar vest, and slippers—honest to Christ—coming out of a small bedroom. His white hair is as unruly as I remember, but there's no cheery smile or look on his face. He has a holstered pistol at his side, and he lowers a hand and just as quickly, I lift up my M-4 and point it right at his shiny forehead. His hand pulls away from his pistol.

"Captain...Wallace," he says. "What the hell are you doing here?"

Wallace steps forward so quickly I think she's going to punch him out, but in a clipped voice, says, "Surprising you, no doubt. Since you sent my company and some good soldiers into an ambush. You son of a bitch."

We all turn as another man enters the office, and I see it's General Brad Scopes of Intelligence, who was also back at the initial surrender site. He has BDUs on and he's yawning, rubbing at his eyes, and even with thick gray hair parted on one side, he looks like he's just woken up.

"Captain Wallace," he says.

"General," she replies, and says, "With all due respect, this is not your concern." She turns to the man from Langley and says, "You knew there were two Creeper Domes there, not one. And you knew that PsyOps Humvee didn't have any recording of that young Coulson boy. It had an insult, a Creeper insult, and resulted in lots of good soldiers getting scorched or lased. We weren't sent there to have them surrender to us. We were sacrificed...and for what?"

Even with me pointing my M-4 at Cranston, he manages to keep his cool and says, "You troops in the field, you had one success, and you think you know everything? Do you? This is a war that's been going on for years, including every nation in the world. It has killed billions, and you think you can end it in a few days?"

I speak up. "Why not? Somebody had to do it."

Cranston looks like I've just done on his shoes what Thor had done on the Osprey. With a dismissive tone he says, "Don't you know your history, kid? 'War is too important to be left to the generals.'"

I keep my M-4 rock steady. "With all due respect, sir, that's not right. Clemenceau said, 'War is too serious a matter to entrust to military men.' If you're going to toss quotes at us, at least make them accurate."

Cranston laughs. "Shut up, kid. There are other negotiations going on, other parties involved. You think the Chinese and Russians are going to let us talk alone with the Creepers to end this war? Do you?"

Wallace says, "That's neither here nor there, Mr. Cranston."

No more laughing from the man from Langley, and his voice lowers. "We have choices, and we have to make the right one. Maybe we should end the war on our terms, and not bother the rest of the world. Maybe we should do what we can to benefit the United States, and the hell with the rest of the world. And do you think the Creepers, they all speak as one? Even as interstellar creatures, don't you think they have factions, tribes, alliances? Shouldn't we get this all settled before you...kids go out to play diplomats?"

Wallace steps closer, and I really think she's about to slug him. "And by sabotaging our efforts here, that's in the best interest of our country and the world?"

"Above your pay grade, Captain," Cranston says. "Did you really think something as important as ending the Creeper War would be left to children and a few grown-ups playing soldier? You had to be...ignored. Removed. So the big picture wouldn't be upset."

Before Wallace says anything, Cranston goes on. "You're going to leave this base, and go back to your war. Oh, I believe that Coulson and his sister are with you? True?"

Wallace doesn't say anything, but the expression on her face says it all. How the hell did this creep know the whereabouts of Serena and Buddy?

Because, I think, he's a Langley man, that's why.

"Very well," Cranston says. "Now. You're going to leave, and you're going to leave the Coulson boy and his sister behind. Understand? You're going away and we're going to use that freak to our best advantage. I've served this nation in Iraq, Afghanistan, Yemen and Nigeria. It's going to be up to the experts, it's going to be up to *me*. I have had too much invested in this to let you...dirty grunts take it away from me."

My turn, my M-4 still pointing at him. "No offense, but that really isn't an impressive honor roll. For decades you adults knew we were being watched, evaluated, targeted...and you did nothing. And even though we outnumber you in the field, doing the fighting and bleeding and scarring, you think you know it all. You don't!"

Cranston shakes his head. "I'm not going to stand around and listen to this nonsense. I'm leaving."

Wallace snaps. "No, you're not leaving. There has to be a reckoning, a resolution, for what happened to our troops and the civilians who were killed because of what you did, because of your thickheadedness and narcissism."

Cranston nods in the direction of Scopes. "General? Could you explain to Wallace the true circumstances?"

General Scopes says, with reluctance in his voice, "Stand down, Captain. Deputy Director Cranston has had operational control of your unit from the very start."

There's a lot of shouting, arguing, finger-pointing, and when there's a slight pause in the action, I say, "General Scopes?"

He seems surprised I'm reaching out to him. "Er, Sergeant?"

"General Scopes, is Mr. Cranston the senior CIA official on base?"

Scopes says, "Yes, he is."

"And you, Captain Wallace, and all of her troops, are all under his command. Correct?"

With a smirk on his face, Cranston says, "That's right, kiddo. You want me to draw you a picture?"

I keep my M-4 aimed right at Cranston but turn to Wallace. "Captain, do you remember what you told me up on that hilltop? When I wanted to leave? You said I was under your command, until you released me. Correct?"

Wallace has a huge grin on her face. "I do."

"I thought so."

She says in a firm voice, "Sergeant Knox, you are hereby released from my unit. You are no longer under my command."

I turn to Cranston. "I'm New Hampshire National Guard, so I'm not under your orders, jerk. I'm leaving, and I'm taking Buddy and Serena with me."

Cranston's hand moves to the holster, grabbing his pistol, but it's not even a fair fight.

So what.

I shoot him right in the chest, and he falls right back into his bedroom. Everyone jerks at the sound, and I turn to General Scopes. My M-4 is lowered but still pointed in his direction.

The whole room seems to wait, all of us with ears ringing from the gunshot, smelling the burnt gunpowder.

"General?" I ask.

No hesitation. "I saw what happened. Hoyt Cranston was going to shoot you. Sergeant, you responded appropriately."

Somehow, I'm not surprised. "Thank you, General."

Scopes's shoulders sag and he looks at us all with a bleak expression. "Ah, the hell with it... I'm no real general. I'm an insurance adjuster from Billingham. And I'm tired of it all."

Wallace nods. "Aren't we all."

An Excerpt From the Journal of Randall Knox

Maybe there are other soldiers out there like me, frustrated writers who are in the military, and who have no other outlet but a private journal. We've all been warned, over and over again, about not keeping diaries or even letters, for the purpose of OpSec—Operational Security—but with a global war going on for years and years, I never thought a Creeper would be interested in what I had to write, no matter how many lectures I had gotten from Intelligence officers, including Dad.

Maybe that's arrogance, maybe that's smugness on my part for being a teenager who thinks he knows it all, but I've always been glad I've put pen to paper, though sometimes the pen has been replaced by a dull pencil when the pen has run out of ink. My English teachers at Fort St. Paul have always complimented me on my writing, and maybe those good words went to my head, but so the writing as gone on.

One time I was caught by a drill sergeant, and his response, if anything, encouraged me more.

I was barely twelve, having transferred from the Boy Scouts to the Army, and at a training center at an old Scout camp in the White Mountains, a very heavyset sergeant named Piper—he must have been seventy or so, for he'd sometimes tell us stories about fighting in Vietnam—and he caught me slipping my journal into my battlepack just before lights out.

He sat down heavily on my bunk, held out his hand, and I passed it over to him. Piper said, "This is illegal, you know."

"I know, Sergeant."

"Then why keep it?"

"Because...It's hard to explain."

"Then explain it, Knox, or I'll seize it and you'll never see it again."

I was glad this portion of the barracks—an old camp building that had been divided up—was quiet, and I said, "Sergeant, I just want to write it all down. To record what happens. So I'll never forget it, no matter what."

"You think you might forget?"

"I might."

He rubbed the leather cover of my journal. "Then...well, you keep at it, Knox, okay? Someday this will be over, or someday, you and your kids will be starving and fighting in the ruins, trying to kill those buggy bastards with sticks and stones, and you should keep it straight. So they know their history, know why they're fighting."

He gave the journal back to me. "But for Christ's sake, do a better job keeping it under wraps, all right?"

"Yes, Sergeant."

Chapter Thirty

There's a flurry of activity as Navy corpsmen come in and take Cranston away—he's unconscious; my 5.56 mm round apparently broke his sternum and some ribs—and with Captain Wallace's encouragement, General Scopes takes control of the base. I'm sure it won't last long, but it will last long enough.

After a quick meal and shower—my first in I can't remember when—Captain Wallace assembles us in a small open hangar. She takes me aside and tells me that she received a telegraph message from Battalion saying Dad is still alive and being treated at a military hospital. I just nod, not able to say a word. I'm no longer in her command, but I'll be damned if I'll leave her side.

The survivors of Company K are lined up and some curious Navy personnel watch as prayers are said for the dead and wounded of Company K—boots marking them lined up in a depressingly long line—and Captain Wallace's voice breaks a few times as she reads out the list, and I bite my lip, as she mentions the last name, Sergeant Bronson, who had sacrificed himself to get me and Buddy out on that last Osprey.

I'm standing next to Balatnic, who gently nudges me in the side and passes over a hand-written scrap of paper. She whispers, "We're going to be singing a hymn shortly, called *Sergeant Mackenzie*. I don't want you to be left out."

"Thanks," I say, and then MacRae, the piper, steps forward, and starts playing a tune, and as one, the Company starts to sing, and I join them, later learning that this particular lament was a century and a half old, written somewhere in the muddy trenches of France, though it's been adapted to this time.

> *Lay me down in the cold cold ground*
> *Where before many more have gone*
> *Lay me down in the cold cold ground*
> *Where before many more have gone*
>
> *When Creepers come I will stand my ground*
> *Stand my ground I'll not be afraid*
>
> *Thoughts of home take away my fear*
> *Sweat and blood hide my veil of tears*
>
> *Once a year say a prayer for me*
> *Close your eyes and remember me*
>
> *Never more shall I see the sun*
> *For I fell to a Creeper's arm*
>
> *Lay me down in the cold cold ground*
> *Where before many more have gone*
> *Lay me down in the cold cold ground*
> *Where before many more have gone*
>
> *Where before many more have gone*

When the tune is done, I turn and leave and bring Thor with me, my eyes so swollen I can barely see.

Outside is an overcast, cool night, though the clouds look like they're breaking apart. Serena is talking to three soldiers from K Company, and she comes up to me, and we hug, and I take her hand and lead her to a park bench, set next to a tangled lawn that must have looked spectacular back in the day, when there was fuel and time enough to waste to mow the lawn. She has a bottle in her hand and offers it to me, and I take a swig. Cold, hard cider, and I shouldn't be drinking it, but what the hell. I take one more swallow and give it back to her.

"How are you?" I ask.

"I'm . . . I'm all right," she says, bringing the bottle up for a quick sip. "It's hard to be back here but since Captain Wallace has taken over, a couple of Cranston's fellow Langley men have disappeared. Someday... someday I'll find out who killed Father, and I'll do something about it."

I put my arm around her. "I'll be there to help. Where's Buddy?"

"In the canteen, eating ice cream. Thor is with him."

"No surprise there."

We cuddle there for a moment, and she says, "Randy, who's Abby? Was she the girl that waved at you on the train, back in Concord?"

I feel splayed out and embarrassed, like I've been caught doing something against regs, dressed only in my underwear. "Yes," I said. "She was the girl back in Concord. I guess you could say... she was my girlfriend."

Serena says, "All right, but what do *you* say? Back at the hilltop, she came into the CP, looking for you. Had a quick chat with your dad. And I thought I recognized her."

What the heck. "Yes, Abby's my girlfriend."

Serena shifts around so her pretty face is so close to me, and she says, "So what."

And we kiss and touch and kiss some more, and she tastes so different from Abby, and I guess I should feel guilty, but I'm just confused.

That's all.

For a moment we break away, and I say, "But... You're okay with that? With me and Abby?"

Serena sighs and moves in with me, even closer. "Fool. I haven't told you about Brian, back in Maine, have I?"

I feel even more foolish. "No, you haven't."

"He's in Bar Harbor. Your Abby is out there somewhere. For all we know, they're dead. For all they know, we're dead. But I know we're safe and we're here, and that's all I care about."

I'm not about to argue, though I do feel a twinge of guilt, thinking of Abby, how she made her way from Concord to New York and—

Serena reaches down and takes the bottle of cider, and in the dim light, I spot the label.

RED VENGEANCE.

She notices the label too, and says, "What's it mean, 'Red Vengeance'?"

"Cider's made in Vermont. Named after a kick-ass Marine who grew up there, returned to Vermont after World War II, ran the State Police for a while. Guy's nickname was 'Red Mike.' Got the Medal of Honor and Navy Cross. Fought on Guadalcanal. There's no Domes in Vermont, and the rumor is, the ghost of Red Mike is scaring them off."

"What do you think?" she asks.

"If it works, it works," I say.

I stroke Serena's shoulder, and she puts the bottle on the ground and sits up suddenly. "Did you mean what you said back there?"

"You're going to have to do better than that," I say.

She's looking up at the sky. "Back at that Air Force base, underground, facing that ... thing. That damn bug. You challenged her. You told her that we would never give up, that we'd always fight. Even with sticks and stones. Did you mean that?"

"I certainly did," I say.

"Oh ... Randy. For God's sake. Look up, will you?"

I do and the clouds have broken away, and about half the sky is clear, and there are a few little streams of orbital debris coming back to Earth, and there's a small bright disc, and for one quick moment, I think, the Moon looks odd tonight.

Then I'm frozen in place, right next to a terrified Serena. Out on the base there are shouts, and the ringing of a bell, as others notice what's above us.

"I see it."

Holy God.

"It's ... it's another orbital base. Replacing the one that got destroyed last month."

"That's right."

"Randy ... where do you think it came from?" she asks.

I pull her closer to me, feel her shivering, either from cold or fear, I can't tell, and really, does it make a difference?

"From the dark side of the moon? In orbit somewhere around the Sun? Who knows?"

"Oh Randy ... What the hell are we going to do?"

I pull her even tighter. "We're going to keep on fighting. And we're going to win, no matter what."

She doesn't say anything, and to make it clear, I say it again.

"We're going to win, no matter what."

There's a rustling noise, and Buddy emerges through some

waist-high brush and grass, being followed by dependable Thor. He has a dish and a spoon, and seems to be eating ice cream. Buddy comes to us and then stands still, looking up at the bright and deadly orb in the sky.

"Oh," he says, and I whirl and stare right at him.

He keeps on looking up.

"Sister," he says, in his young boy/old man voice.

"Yes, Buddy, right here."

A heavy sigh comes from him, like a walker bearing an impossibly heavy pack and realizing he has many more miles to march.

"Sister...Please don't let them take me back up there again. Please."